Red Shadows On Liberty's Soil

Stephen Knight

Contact
+1-201-335-4765
marketing@amzpublishingplus.com
Mailing Address: 101 Hudson Street, 21st Floor, Jersey City, NJ, USA 07302

Dedication

To my grandfather Cyril Knight whose 1947 oil painting, Atomic Man, was the inspiration for this book.

February 1982

Many beers had been drunk that night at the Thunderbird Motel across the road from the entrance to the local snow-covered fairgrounds. Mike and Larry Fuller staggered out of the motel's restaurant into the frigidly cold morning air. Almost at the same time, Wolford Byford's pickup truck screeched to a halt in front of them, its headlights momentarily blinding them. Larry opened the passenger door and the brothers scrambled up into the big pickup's cab. Wolf, as Byford was known, gunned the truck out of the icy motel parking lot, spitting up snow and gravel. On the radio, Bruce Springsteen was belting out his latest hit Hungry Heart. About a mile up the highway, Wolf turned north onto Foxhollow Road, screeching the tires as he took the bend too fast. The community of Foxhollow where they lived, was about ten miles north of where they were. Mike, the younger and drunker of the Fuller brothers, had passed out, resting his head on his brother's shoulder.

The snow banks along the side of the dark highway were unusually high. More snow than normal had fallen in the area since the beginning of the year. It must have been at least twenty below outside. Wolf could see his breath and his hands were getting cold. He was rubbing them together to try to warm them. Wolf asked Larry if he wanted a smoke and when he declined, lit one up himself, filling the cab with white drifting smoke. As they sped north, they were the only vehicle on the road on that bitterly cold night.

The flying saucer could easily be seen with the naked eye, although it took Wolf awhile to notice it. Even after seeing it, he didn't believe it. He figured it must be a reflection on the windshield and turned the pickup's headlights off, but the object could still be clearly seen. He pulled off the highway alongside a high snow bank, turned the radio off and said to Larry, "Look over there," pointing to the top of the windshield.

Larry tilted his head slightly and looking under the rear-view mirror, focused as best he could on what looked like a flying saucer, moving across the night sky.

"I see it!" he yelled excitedly and nudged his brother Mike until he came awake.

"What is it?" Mike asked. "Are we home?"

"Can you see it?" Larry asked. "Look over there."

Mike leaned forward and looked where Larry was pointing. Yawning, he said, "Yeah I see it, what is it, but now I can't see it no more."

They had all lost sight of the object behind the snow-covered trees along the side of the highway. Wolf pulled back onto the highway and it came back into view again. He was trying to figure out what it could be. It could be a plane coming into land at the nearby Air Force base; then again it might have just taken off, but it seemed to be heading towards the base rather than away from it. He lost sight of it again.

The trip home had passed very quickly thanks to the strange object; they were already passing an old abandoned farmhouse on the outskirts of

Foxhollow. Another few minutes and Wolf would be dropping the Fullers off. As he turned into the street where they lived, the object came into view again, but a moment later disappeared behind one of the huge elms that had originally given the street its name. Wolf stopped in front of the Fullers' house, and shouted "You're home."

Larry struggled with the passenger door, pushed his brother out and followed after him, landing on top of him on the snow-covered boulevard. Wolf could see the brothers pushing each other as he stretched across and pulled the passenger door shut. He drove off and in his rear-view mirror could still see the Fullers lying in a heap in front of their house.

Wolf was of two minds what to do. He could go home and put the incident down to a case of being disoriented due to having drunk too much, or he could try to find if the mysterious object was for real. He thought that since the Fullers had seen it too, it must be real. He checked his watch; it was twenty-five minutes after three. He sped through the back roads between Foxhollow and the local Air Force base, driving as fast as he could, the back end of his truck fishtailing from side to side as he flew around tight bends leaving clouds of swirling snow behind him. He just hoped he didn't run into a base security patrol, because it would be difficult to explain what he was doing out here, at that time in the morning. As he came out of the trees into a clearing, he could see the object high in the sky, circling above the northern base perimeter road. He was beginning to have second thoughts about finding out what it was, when he saw two parachutes open up against the night sky.

Soviet Union - February 1981

Deep in the bowels of a building within the walls of the Kremlin, a Soviet general was sitting in a deserted meeting room. He was wearing a blue Air Force general's tunic, with embroidered gold leaves on the collar and stars on the shoulder boards. To impress he was wearing his considerable collection of service ribbons and medals, including the Hero of *the* Soviet Union and the Order of the Red Star, which were pinned to his chest. Like most older Soviets, the general looked older than he actually was - in his case, the result of a combination of too much stress and vodka over the years. He was bald, with a pencil-thin moustache, his bloodshot weasel eyes framed within a deeply lined face.

He had been in the Soviet military since graduating with a PhD in Nuclear Physics from the Technical University of Kiev, in the Soviet Republic of Ukraine, in 1948. His whole career had been devoted to the study of nuclear missiles, both Soviet and American. The general looked towards the open door where he could see an officer accompanied by two civilians, who he already knew to be Americans.

"Good morning gentlemen. I've been looking forward to meeting you. Please come in and take a seat. Thank you, that will be all," he said to the officer standing at the open door.

"Which one of you is Mr. Williams?"

"I am," responded the taller of the two strikingly handsome men.

Red Shadows On Liberty's Soil

Gerry Williams appeared to be in his early thirties. He was lean and powerful looking, with short dark hair, brown eyes and a square jaw. He was wearing an open neck, light blue shirt under a heavy grey suit. He didn't look happy.

The general leaned over the table, shook his hand, handed him a large envelope and said, "Your personal belongings, Mr. Williams. I trust you will find them in order?"

Williams tipped the contents of the envelope out onto the polished veneer table in front of him. He slipped his tiger's eye ring back onto the ring finger on his right hand, secured his watch band on his left wrist and checked the money in his treasured alligator skin wallet. He put the wallet, his keys, comb and cigarette lighter into his various pockets. Then he looked up and said, "I hope you found what you were looking for? I see you didn't return my passport."

"Mr. Williams, I know you haven't been treated very well since your arrival here in Moscow," responded the general. "Please accept my apologies but for the time being, we will be keeping your passport. You must be Mr. Shelby," he continued, leaning over the table to shake the other man's hand.

Peter Shelby appeared to be in his mid-thirties, with short blonde hair and an ashen complexion. He looked to be in excellent shape also. He had taken off his overcoat and was wearing a navy blue crew neck sweater and matching navy pants. He looked to be somewhat unsure of his surroundings and was fixated on the general sitting in front of him.

The general passed a large envelope to him saying, "Your personal belongings, Mr. Shelby."

Shelby opened the envelope, looked inside and checked the contents. He told the general that everything seemed to be there, except for his passport and placed the envelope down on the chair beside him.

"Gentlemen, please get comfortable," said the general, mainly for Shelby's sake.

The general began to talk in a low, drowsy monotone voice; his English was excellent. "Unfortunately, I have some bad news for you both. Our meeting here this morning is one of those situations where, when I have told you what I have to tell you, I will have to kill you 'unless'. You will find out what the 'unless' is by the end of our discussions. The good news is that you are the chosen ones. Do you have any idea how many westerners visit the Soviet Union every year? Literally thousands, a significant number of them never seeing the light of day again. Anyway, I am digressing. I take it the two of you have met, if only briefly, so I will introduce myself. I am General Vladimir Ulanov of the Soviet Strategic Rocket Forces Division of the Soviet Department of Defence. My prime responsibility for many years now has been to supply the Defence Council of the Supreme Soviet with information on the latest developments in the nuclear arsenals of both the Soviet Union and the United States. As you might know, the arms race has been extremely close over the last three decades; our two countries have been racing neck and neck to see who could gain a strategic advantage. Both nations have built up a more-than-adequate nuclear deterrent, to the point where a stalemate position has essentially been reached and de-escalation has become most desirable. The one big difference between our two countries has been that the United States has managed to support a significant number of conventional and nuclear defence programs, while at the same time sustain a relatively buoyant economy and high standard of living for its people. The Soviet Union on the other hand, although defensively debatably perhaps slightly superior, continues to face economic decline. I have been asked to look into ways to minimize spending on our nuclear arsenal, in order to use any savings to prop up the spluttering economy. My ultimate goal for a long time has been the complete elimination of nuclear weapons. As you can probably imagine, it is extremely expensive to sustain a fully operational nuclear capability. If any savings can be realized and channelled back into the economy, it could help raise the standard of living of every Soviet."

"General, I'm not sure what you're getting at," said Shelby with a sigh.

"It will soon become clear," snapped the general. "Let me tell you, much work has gone into trying to slow down and even halt the production of nuclear weapons in both countries. You may know that Strategic Arms Limitation

Talks have taken place over the last decade. They became known as SALT I and II and were thought to be a step forward in trying to halt the production of Inter-Continental Ballistic Missiles. SALT I was an agreement to essentially freeze production of new launching systems. These talks concluded when the President and General Secretary signed the treaty in Moscow, in May 1972. The SALT II agreement was signed seven years later in Vienna and was intended to further limit the production of nuclear arms. To help you better understand, as you put it Mr. Shelby, what I am getting at, I have some slides which should give you a better idea of what this is all about." The general moved to the back of the room, turned on a projector and dimmed the lights. A photo appeared showing what looked like the entrance to a military base.

"That is Minot Air Force base in North Dakota, one of the largest nuclear missile sites in the United States. It is home to six Strategic Air Command missile squadrons, with a total of three hundred ready-to-launch missiles, with a combined payload of well over one thousand nuclear warheads," the general continued, flipping to the next slide, which showed an impressive-looking rocket.

"That, gentlemen, is a Minuteman missile, capable of carrying a payload of three, one hundred kiloton nuclear warheads." He flipped to the next slide which showed another rocket. "That is the so called Peacekeeper missile, capable of carrying a much bigger payload of ten, five hundred kiloton nuclear warheads," he said, bringing up the room lights.

"As you can see, gentlemen, these are awesome and frightening weapons, capable of causing mass destruction and lasting misery. If a quote, accident, unquote, ever occurred on a base involving one of these weapons; it would create a national dilemma and cast their future into doubt. Over the years, my department has been putting proposals forward on how to cause such a quote, accident, unquote, but to date, none of them has been accepted by the Supreme Soviet. Now, with your coincidental arrival in Moscow, I think I may have a chance of getting one of my proposals approved."

The general went back to where the projector was, dimmed the room lights and clicked to another slide which seemed to be an aerial photograph which, as far as Williams and Shelby could tell, was a close-up of the dark side of the moon. He continued, "This is a computer-enhanced spy satellite photograph of the northern part of the base. To try and minimize the losses due to retaliatory missile strikes, the underground missile silos are five miles apart."

The general pointed to a barren-looking area on the photograph. "Here, below ground, is a launch control facility; there is one of these for every flight or ten silos. The unmanned missile silos, eighty feet deep, are constructed of concrete and are adjacent to a three-level maintenance room containing environmental control equipment. The missiles are actually fired from these remote underground launch control facilities, which are manned twenty-four hours a day. The health of each missile and its support systems is continually monitored. Any of the missiles can also be fired from airborne command posts during a conflict."

The general turned the room lights up, switched the projector off and walked back to where the Americans were sitting somewhat wide-eyed.

"Gentlemen, you have an opportunity to help ensure that the world will be rid of the threat of these menacing weapons before the end of the twentieth century. We must do all we can to tame the atomic demon for the benefit, rather than the destruction, of mankind."

Shelby spoke up. "Is this stuff for real, General?"

The general, looking somewhat annoyed, said with a snarl, "Mr. Shelby, I can assure you that everything I have just presented to you is factual."

Shelby asked why such a mission was still being contemplated when the Strategic Arms Limitation Talks agreements seemed to be working. The general explained that although SALT I and II were a step in the right direction, what was needed right now was to make a giant step forward to bring about rapid nuclear disarmament. Reluctantly, he told the men that the Soviet Union could not continue to keep spending as much as the United States on its nuclear defence program for very much longer in a climate of discontent and unrest in most of its Republics.

Williams chipped in, "What makes you think that one nuclear explosion in a sparsely populated region of the United States will cause the Administration and Congress to abandon their nuclear defence program?"

General Ulanov, who had calmed down somewhat, began to speak more softly. "Mr. Williams, as I am sure you are aware, in life there are no guarantees; however there is currently a public outcry over the condition of many federally-owned nuclear fuel production factories and their associated waste sites. In fact, in certain states, whole communities are beginning to link nuclear waste to unusually high rates of leukemia, Downs Syndrome and cancer-related deaths. Without a doubt, the public will be profoundly disturbed by a nuclear explosion in the heartland of their nation. Even the Canadians will be affected. This will also undoubtedly be a most unpleasant development for the new president. This could potentially result in him having to consider taking all of the nuclear missiles in the United States out of operational service."

Shelby spoke up again. "If this plan is for real, how do we know that the Soviet Union's motive is speedy disarmament and world peace, and that this is not part of a larger plan to strengthen its power in the world?"

Just as Shelby finished speaking, an officer appeared in the doorway to the meeting room.

"Let's take a break and resume again this afternoon. Please let me introduce Major Alexei Khotov; he will take you for lunch. Major, this is Mr. Williams and Mr. Shelby."

"This way gentlemen," said the major.

Before leaving the room, Shelby removed his personal belongings from the large envelope General Ulanov had given him earlier and stashed them into his various pockets. Outside the room, they saw two heavily armed guards, talking in the hallway.

Unlike the general, Major Khotov looked young, with bright eyes and a handsome face. He was wearing an immaculately cut Soviet Air Force uniform. As he led the Americans along a hallway, he asked them if they had any questions he could try and answer. His English was very good and he seemed to have more of an American accent than an eastern European one.

"You bet!" responded Shelby. He and Williams were more relaxed now that they were out of the presence of the seemingly authoritarian general. As they moved along the long dimly lit hallway, Shelby continued, "What will I tell my friends and work associates about my extended stay in Moscow, of all places?"

"Mr. Shelby, please be assured that we will provide you with a very plausible explanation. Perhaps a prolonged illness or a serious accident of some kind," said the major.

"What about my flat in London, my job, my car and everything?"

"I emphasize that everything, no matter how trivial, will be taken care of. The things you are mentioning are minor details in the general's overall plan."

As they turned into another long hallway, Williams asked if they would be well compensated.

The major laughed. "Believe me, if you are successful, neither of you will lack for anything for the rest of your lives, if that's what you mean."

The questions continued and after traveling what seemed like miles through the maze of hallways, they came to an open area. This area was a hive of activity; some people were sitting eating and others standing in line, most wearing Soviet Air Force uniforms. There were many tables and chairs and a self-service food area. Williams and Shelby each accepted a large bowl of what looked like beef stew, helped themselves to bread rolls and were given a small carafe of what they thought was water, but later turned out to be vodka. The major also got a bowl of stew, a bread roll, and two small carafes. At the checkout, he gave the cashier a chit for all three of their meals. The major grabbed some small drinking glasses as he led Williams and Shelby to an empty table. Although initially somewhat reluctant to eat the stew, once they had their first taste, Williams and Shelby quickly ate the rest along with the bread. Neither of them quite knew what to do with the vodka.

Williams eyed the two carafes the major had and jokingly said, "How does any work get done around here in the afternoon or are you guys really immune to this stuff like they say?"

The major looked up. "You mean the vodka? Well for one thing, we need something to keep our blood warm through the long cold winters and it also makes working here a lot easier," he said laughing.

Williams had to admit he liked the major already; he had never realized how honest Soviets could be and if Major Khotov was an example, he thought he was probably going to enjoy his time here.

Although Williams and Shelby were smokers, they were taken aback by the amount of smoking that was going on in the food area. Smoke filled the air and everyone was smoking strong smelling cigarettes. The major offered them black filter tipped cigarettes from a pack featuring a woman dressed in a flowing white dress. They each took one and the major offered them a light with an impressive-looking silver lighter.

"I get these cigarettes sent to me by my parents back in the Soviet Republic of Armenia. They are called Akhtamars. I am originally from

Yerevan, the capital of Armenia. It's close to the borders of Turkey and Iran. I acquired a taste for them a number of years ago," said the major.

Williams and Shelby smoked the strong Armenian cigarettes, which neither of them particularly cared for, but didn't show it. Williams commented to the major that they were certainly different from American cigarettes.

"Funny you should say that," he replied, getting the cigarette packet out of his pocket and showing it to them.

"Look, they are made by the Grand Tobacco Company and are labelled 'American Blend'."

"Are we actually in the Kremlin?" asked Shelby, unintentionally changing the subject.

"Yes. The Kremlin was originally a fortress or citadel, built on a hill at the confluence; I think you call it, of the Moskva and Neglinka rivers."

Williams said, "If you mean it is where two rivers flow together, you are correct and I am amazed you know such an English word. It's a credit to your knowledge of the language. I would venture to speculate that only one in ten thousand Americans would know the meaning of that word."

The major continued. "Within the Kremlin walls are a number of ancient cathedrals, palaces and government offices. I could give you more information if you are interested, but all you really need to know is that this is the cultural and power centre of the Soviet Union."

Williams, trying to lighten up the conversation, said, "I guess one day we can tell our grandchildren we were within the walls of the Kremlin."

After they had finished their cigarettes and vodka, the major led them back through the maze of hallways to the meeting room.

Once they were back in the meeting room, the major said, "Please get comfortable. The general has asked me to provide you with some further information about the mission."

"I guess there's no turning back for us?" enquired Williams. "Are the things the general described to us this morning top secret?"

"You are correct. There is no turning back for you and Mr. Shelby and there is only one way out, which I am sure the general will discuss with you in due course," the major replied. He turned the projector on, dimmed the lights and flipped to a slide saying, "The map you see shows the northern part of the state of North Dakota and the southern portions of the Canadian provinces of Manitoba and Saskatchewan. This is an area you will become familiar with during your training."

Pointing to the map he said, "During the mission, you will be based in this area on a farm near the Manitoba-North Dakota border. The farm is about seventy miles due north of the military base and very well situated for your purposes. You will be supported by local Soviet agents in the area. You would be surprised how many agents we have in the United States and Canada. The general's key agent in North America, Major Trsenkov, will take care of all your needs during the mission."

The major flipped to the next slide saying, "This is an approximation of the actual mission timeframe, which begins with your take-off from the farm. You will fly close to the base in an aircraft disguised as a flying saucer and one of you will parachute out from several thousand feet. The aircraft will then return to the farm. The paratrooper will enter onto the base, ski to the designated silo, set the missile warhead detonation process in motion, then ski to a nearby ski resort, where you will meet up and begin your return journey. Surrounding the actual mission, it is planned that you will fly from here to Havana, then onto Winnipeg via Montreal. Your return trip will be the exact opposite of your outbound trip. The complete mission, including travel time, is planned to be accomplished within three days."

The major flipped to the next slide. It showed a table of training activities under the headings, "Pilot and Paratrooper".

"As you can see, these are very specialized training activities. The pilot will be certified to the level required to accomplish the mission."

The major exhaled quite loudly; he wasn't used to talking this much and was definitely not immune to the vodka he had consumed at lunchtime. He could already feel a hangover coming on. He continued, "This same person will also be trained to cross-country ski. The paratrooper will be given extensive rocketry training, including the environments that the missiles are housed in. In addition, he will be trained how to trigger the nuclear detonation process and will also be trained to parachute from a low flying aircraft."

The major turned up the lights, turned the projector off and was about to ask Williams and Shelby if they had any questions, when General Ulanov entered the room saying, "Thank you, Major Khotov. I will take over from here."

The major said his good-byes and left the room.

The general told them that wherever their training took them, they were to tell no one about the mission. "People in the Soviet Union have very little and information can be turned into money," he warned. "There are people whose very existence relies on providing information to others and you would be surprised at how many foreign agents are operating in the Soviet Union. The Americans and British almost know as much about what is going on in this country as our Communist leaders.

Well, gentlemen, I am sure you must have many questions, but I would ask that you to hold them until tomorrow, when I would like you to come back to further discuss the mission."

"It's been like being back at college," Shelby muttered.

Just then, the same officer who had escorted them to the meeting room earlier in the day appeared at the open doorway.

"Please take Mr. Williams and Mr. Shelby to the KGB headquarters complex. I will see you both tomorrow," said the general as they left the meeting room.

General Ulanov followed after them, going down the hall to his dimly lit office. He slumped down into his desk chair feeling very tired. On his desk were framed photographs of his late wife and famous Soviet leaders, including Nikita Khrushchev and Leonid Brezhnev. Hanging on the wall were old paintings of Lenin and Stalin. Today had been one of the most exciting days of his career. He was pleased that he had found the Americans and felt sure they could pull off the mission; their training would confirm this. The majority of the Soviet agents in North America were unsophisticated, even though most of them were very well educated. None of them were anywhere near as worldly and well rounded as the Americans nor could they communicate anywhere near as well. In fact they were all quite rough around the edges, with very little class and none of them spoke English without an accent. Even the head of the operatives in North America was considered to be somewhat uncouth, but had proven to be very effective at carrying out orders without asking too many questions. The general didn't really trust any of his people in North America and provided them with as little information as he could to ensure that, in the event that any of them were ever apprehended, they wouldn't know anything of any consequence. They were always told what to do, without being given the big picture. This was the Soviet way. If they became too inquisitive, an unfortunate accident would be arranged - hunting accidents and poisoning were the most common methods of elimination. His superiors, the Americans, Majors Khotov and Trsenkov and himself would be the only ones who would know the full mission plan. That is how he wanted it.

He began shuffling through the folders and papers piled high on his ancient looking desk and for some reason, began to think about his late wife. She had passed away several years before after a long battle with cancer. They had never had children due to the passion he had for his work. His wife had led a very lonely life, but had been very comfortable compared to most of the other women in the Soviet Union. She could have had anything she wanted, the very best champagne and caviar if she wished, but she never took advantage of it. She spent the summers in comfortable accommodations in Yalta, directly south of Moscow on the Crimean peninsula, in the Soviet Republic of Ukraine. Located on the northern shore of the Black Sea, the area is famous for its warm dry summers and magnificent natural landscape. Surrounded by mountains with lush, Mediterranean-like vegetation growing on the lower slopes, temperatures in the months of July and August were between seventy and eighty degrees, the sea was warm and the air dry. The weeks in the summer when her husband had joined her had been the happiest of her life. He was such a passionate man, versed in the history of Alexander the Great, the Tsars and the World Wars. When he was with her, they spent their evenings walking up and down the majestic promenade along the seafront. She knew she was blessed to have such a wonderful man for a husband and respected how important his work was to him. She also accepted that he was an alcoholic. She knew that although he was involved with perhaps the most deadly weapons ever invented, he was a good man and was always full of good intentions. She knew her husband was very different in that whenever he had any spare time, he would read books and papers written by famous scientists like Einstein. Her husband had very few friends, preferring instead to work many hours a day, seven days a week, for the Soviet military. Although they hadn't seen much of each other over the years, they were really good friends in that whenever they did see each other, it was as if they had never been apart. The general had fond memories of those summer weeks he had spent with his wife. Although wholly and completely dedicated to his work, he had loved the summer sun, which always breathed new life into his aching body, but he had not been back to Yalta since his wife had died.

The general opened the bottom drawer of his desk and took out a small glass and a half-full bottle of vodka; it was time for his nightly indulgence.

By the time Williams and Shelby got to their rooms, it was already getting dark. Williams invited Shelby into his room and checked to see if any beer or liquor had been provided. He found some in the kitchen and filled a glass with what smelled like Scotch. He dropped some ice cubes into his glass and as he came out of the kitchen, handed Shelby the beer he had asked for.

Shelby went over to the window, looked out and saw an awesome sight. The multi-colored onion shaped domes of St Basil's Cathedral and the towers along the wall of the Kremlin looked spectacular in the gathering twilight. Williams meanwhile slumped down into an armchair saying, "I think we should get to know each other, given we may be depending on each other to stay alive in the not too distant future. You start."

Shelby turned, looked over to where Williams was sitting and began. "Let me see, I'm an only child; I was married once for a short time, until my wife, or more likely her parents, decided she'd made a mistake. There were no kids in the marriage. My parents still live in North Dakota, where I am originally from. I went to college up in Minnesota and I work for an international advertising agency and have been working in their London office for just over a year. About a month ago, I came here to Moscow on a whim. I had just broken up with a lady friend and needed to get away for awhile. I was only planning on being here for two weeks. Moscow in winter really appealed to me for some strange reason. I booked a flight without much trouble and the woman at passport control at Heathrow airport checked my ticket and passport and let me through without a word. I don't think she even looked at my ticket, I guess she probably figured I was flying to the States. I arrived here and all hell broke loose. You'd have thought the Abominable Snowman had arrived. I was shuffled from one interrogation room to the next. Why had I come to the Soviet Union? Was I in the United States military? Why didn't I have a visitor's visa or entry papers of any kind? They wouldn't believe I'd just come here on two weeks vacation. I was told I would be taking the next flight out of the Soviet Bloc. That was about a month ago and I've been kept secluded in some broken-down hovel ever since. Talk about being in the wrong place at the wrong time! And now I seem to be involved in a situation where there is no way out. What do you think? Do you think there is any way out of this for us?"

"It seems to me that you and I are in too deep already, after what we were told today and did you see the number of barrel-chested, Goldfinger-look-a-likes, standing around on every floor of this building? Anyway why don't you speak to the general about it tomorrow?" Williams suggested.

"What about you?" asked Shelby.

Williams began, "About three weeks ago, I arrived here, but unlike you, I did have the appropriate papers for a visiting westerner. However, I didn't come here just to be a tourist. I was working in sales for IBM in New York City and was their number one salesman globally last year. You know, something happens to you when you become number one at something. You feel as if there is nothing left to achieve; it's weird.

I'm originally from Albany, New York, had a pretty normal upbringing - a public and high school education. I spent several years at Syracuse University where I majored in Business Administration, a totally generalist degree. I played on the varsity football and hockey teams during my first and second years there, but was only a fill-in, not a first stringer on either team. My first job was in sales for a business machine company in Syracuse. After working there for several years I joined IBM. I initially worked out of a regional sales office in Rochester and sold so well, that they moved me to their US sales headquarters in New York City.

My father was a prisoner of war in Vietnam for several years and although he was eventually released, he never recovered and is in an upstate New York mental institution. My mother was killed a few years back in an automobile accident involving a carload of drunken teenagers. My sister recently married an Aussy and moved to Australia. I've never been married. I have an apartment in lower Manhattan and can see the Staten Island Ferry going back and forth all day long. I paid the landlord two years' rent in advance to keep it for me, just in case things don't work out. With my father's condition, my mother's death and my sister's move to Australia, I figured I'd give Communism a try."

"What do you mean, give Communism a try?"

"I thought I could perhaps get a job with IBM or some other computer company in Moscow; you know, the international language of the computer business is English and I have a lot of experience in computer sales and lots of ideas on how to be successful in the computer industry," Williams replied.

"It just seemed funny when you said you would give Communism a try, especially when you were born and grew up in the States."

"I'm sure people all over the world try different things every day," said Williams. "I was looking for a new challenge, and anyway I've pretty much had it with the States and all it stands for. There's got to be something better."

Just then there was a knock on the door and Shelby, being the closest, went over and opened it. Standing in the hallway were two of the most beautiful women he had ever seen. They had blonde hair, were wearing matching white, full-length fur coats and black, backless high heeled stilettos.

"Hello. We have come to visit with you and your friend," said one of the women in a soft sexy voice. "Could we come in?"

"Someone delivering a pizza?" yelled Williams jokingly, from inside the room.

Shelby didn't hear Williams, as he had lapsed into a trance. Quickly coming out of it he said, "Yes, yes, please come in."

The women entered the room and on seeing them, Williams was taken aback, but he managed to jump up, rush over and begin the introductions.

"Well hello there! I'm Gerry and this is Peter. Would you ladies like a drink and could I take your coats?"

The woman who had previously spoken, said, "Yes, two vodkas please, no ice and we'll keep our coats on for now, thank you."

Williams went into the kitchen, found a bottle of what he thought was vodka, quickly poured two drinks, came back into the room and handed the drinks to the two absolutely gorgeous women.

"To what do we owe the pleasure of your company?" asked Williams.

The second woman spoke. "General Ulanov mentioned you might like some company tonight; he told us you gentlemen are very important and wants us to give you a good time."

"Well, wasn't that nice of him? Don't you think so, Pete?"

"Yes, oh yes," said Shelby coming out of another trance.

The woman who had spoken first introduced herself as Natasha and her friend as Anna and said, "Anna is from Moscow and I am from near Saint Petersburg. We are both with the Intelligence Service. Anna is an assistant to a member of the Council of Ministers and I work for several members of the Congress of People's Deputies."

Anna spoke up. "General Ulanov told us you are from America. Please tell us about it; we have seen some Hollywood movies and it seems wonderful."

"What movies have you seen?" asked Williams.

"Let me think; help me Natasha," said Anna.

Natasha said, "*Gone with the Wind* and *Breakfast at Tiffany's* are my favourites."

"Those are classic movies," replied Williams.

"You know, we still only see movies in black and white," said Natasha.

"Things have changed a lot in America since those movies were made; these days things are not as innocent as they were then," said Williams. "Some of the latest movies portray life pretty much as it is."

"What do you mean?" asked Anna.

"Well, there are now movies about how horrible war can be, how hard it can be living in a poor neighbourhood and others about crime and murder," Williams replied.

"This sounds similar to the way things are here in the Soviet Union. We thought things were different in America, but they sound like they are the same," Natasha frowned.

"We thought everyone in America drove big fast cars, had swimming pools and lots of money," said Anna.

"Some people do, but the majority of the people probably live similar lives to the average Soviet. I think you get a particular stereotype of

Americans from watching old Hollywood movies," said Williams.

"Do you and Peter have a good life there?" Anna asked.

Shelby spoke up. "Actually, I've been living and working in London for the past year and it's a great city."

Williams said, "I've been dealing with a lot of personal problems lately, but anyway, let's hear about you. Can I freshen up your drinks?"

"Mine's fine, thank you."

"Mine too, thank you."

"For us there is not much to tell," Anna said. "We are just starting our careers."

"Who's staying in this room?" asked Natasha.

"That would be me little old me," responded Williams.

"Not too little I hope?" giggled Natasha.

Anna turned to Shelby and said, "Would you like to show me your room?" Before Shelby could answer, she was ushering him into the adjoining room. After watching Shelby and Anna leave, Williams turned and saw that Natasha had let her coat fall open and to his great delight, was wearing nothing but a bra, garter belt and nylons, all black. She threw her coat off and moved to where he was sitting, knelt down, unzipped his pants and quickly went to work. She was an expert with her mouth and began to make Williams curse out loud.

After a while, she suggested they find the bedroom. Williams quickly got undressed, pulled back the sheets and slid in. Natasha threw off her high heels and got in beside him. Williams removed her bra and began to kiss her red hot nipples. He felt down between her legs and began to manipulate her like a puppet, making her twitch and cry out in unison with his gentle touches. After several minutes she let out a huge sigh and pushed his hand away.

"Thank you," she said breathlessly. "Now, it's your turn."

Williams easily slipped into her as she moved on top of him and within a few never-to-be-forgotten moments, had erupted inside her.

Next door, Shelby and Anna had found the bed and she was attacking him with her mouth. Shelby had once again relapsed into a trance, thinking this couldn't really be happening. Anna found a working rhythm and quickly took him to paradise, leaving him gasping. Shelby, wanting to satisfy her, buried his head between her nylon-covered legs and busied himself with pleasuring her.

It would be a night of pure ecstasy for both men.

The next morning when they awoke, they were alone, which didn't seem like a big deal as Natasha and Anna had said they were staying in the same complex. They rushed through their room service breakfasts and were escorted back to the meeting room where they had met the general the day before.

General Ulanov greeted them as they came through the door.

"Good morning gentlemen. I trust you slept well," he said with a wink.

"You can be assured of that!" said Williams, returning the wink.

"Please take a seat. Are you both ready to continue?"

Shelby came alive nodding and said, "General, it seems you have chosen me for this mission. Can I ask why?"

"You and Mr. Williams, you are perhaps the most physically fit Americans I have encountered for quite sometime. As you probably know, most of your fellow countrymen are usually overweight and out of shape."

"That aside," said Shelby, "Don't I get a say in this?"

"I'm afraid not. You chose to come here and in the Soviet Union, people are recruited whenever they are needed, for the good of the Motherland."

"This is crazy!" said Shelby angrily. "For the good of the Motherland? I am an American, not a Soviet. I came here on vacation and I obviously wouldn't have come if I knew this was going to happen to me!"

"Would you rather spend the next twenty years as a political prisoner in Siberia? I hear Siberia has wonderful skyscapes at this time of the year. I can easily arrange this, by fabricating sufficient drug smuggling or spying evidence to convict you. You know, you should really have done your homework before coming here. Have you ever heard the famous expression, *When in Rome do as the Romans do*? Well, I think this is applicable to the situation you find yourself in at the moment - only replace Rome with Moscow and Romans with Soviets. You know, you and Mr. Williams should feel honoured that you have been chosen for this mission. Anyway, you did come here and that is all that really matters at this point in time. Why don't you look on the bright side? Once the mission is completed successfully, you will be on vacation for the rest of your life."

Williams broke into the conversation. "While we are on this subject, why do you think I want to join the Soviet Air Force? I had decided to give Communism a try, not the Soviet military."

"As I just told Mr. Shelby, as soon as you arrived on Soviet soil it was our prerogative as to what to do with you. Most people we could care less about, but you and Mr. Shelby are special and ideal for the mission."

"How do you know?" shouted Williams angrily. "Really, how do you know this?"

The general stood up and leaning forward over the table, shouted, "Calm down, Mr. Williams!"

Red Shadows On Liberty's Soil

With the discussion suddenly becoming very loud, there was a knock at the open door, an armed guard stood at the door looking into the room and asked if everything was alright.

"Yes, everything is fine," said the general, walking over to the door, closing and locking it.

Shelby continued, "How can you do this to us? I came here on vacation. I am not a Soviet. I am not a citizen of this country. This is absolutely ridiculous!"

"I understand how you feel, Mr. Shelby, but you must understand when you come to a foreign country, you have to follow that country's rules," the general replied.

"I can understand that, but surely you cannot force someone to join the military. This is insane and you also want us to attack our own country. This situation is truly unreal," said Shelby.

"Mr. Shelby, you came to this country of your own free will. Nobody forced you to come here. You know, we could debate this for days, but the fact is, you are here and we need you to do a job for us," said the general sternly. "As I said earlier, if you want to spend the next twenty years in Siberia, this can be arranged."

"Obviously, I don't want to do that, but why do I have to do anything you want me to?" Shelby replied.

"That is the way it is, unfortunately. I'm sorry but we need your assistance and if we don't get it, your life as you know it will essentially be over."

"Well, I guess I really have no choice, but this whole thing is unbelievable. I can't believe this is really happening to me and I don't understand how you can do this to me! I really don't," said Shelby.

"I take it from what you said earlier you feel the same way Mr. Williams?"

"Well, it wasn't my intention to join the Soviet military upon my arrival here, but I do understand what you are trying to accomplish. I am willing to go on the mission, provided you keep your word about setting us up for life afterwards," Williams replied.

"You can both be assured that I will keep my word. This will be the greatest mission in the history of the Soviet Union. Keeping my word will not be a problem," said the general proudly.

He handed them some papers. "If you gentlemen could sign these, I would be most grateful."

While they were signing the papers, Major Khotov entered the room.

"Gentlemen, Major Khotov will be responsible for your training over the next year and you know, of course, that the Soviet Union will be forever in your debt when you have succeeded in accelerating nuclear disarmament. Our government will ensure that you are comfortable for the rest of your lives, in the place of your choosing, anywhere in the world. This, gentleman, is all I have to tell you, except that I will now do my best to answer any questions you may have." The general sat down.

Williams asked the first question. "One thing that has been puzzling me about your plan is flying to the base in an aircraft disguised as a flying saucer. Why couldn't we just drive there?"

General Ulanov started to smile for the first time in two days, and said excitedly, "Mr. Williams, you have asked an excellent question. I must tell you, I am extremely pleased to see that you have been taking what the major and I have been presenting to you, seriously."

Williams cut in. "Alright General, can you please just answer the question?"

"Please Mr. Williams, I had not really planned on getting into such detail here today, as all aspects of the mission will be presented to you in great detail during your training. However, I see no reason why I shouldn't answer your question at this time. As I mentioned yesterday, we have been planning this mission for many years. One of the things we have discovered during that time is that the guards at the border crossings north of Minot Air Force base are trained to be very observant of unfamiliar persons crossing the border. They normally enter your vehicle license plate number into their system, and unless they already have you on file, search your vehicle, often with the help of sniffer dogs. Therefore, when one of you crosses the border to meet the other at the ski resort, although you will be driving, you will be clean and shouldn't have a problem with having your vehicle searched; all they should find is ski equipment. However, the night of the mission, if they searched your vehicle, they would find some unusual electronic equipment and firearms, as you call them. As for your question regarding disguising the aircraft as a flying saucer the night of the mission, I am sure you both know from browsing through the tabloids, I think they're called, there are always sensational articles about people who say they saw a flying saucer somewhere in a remote part of the United States. Therefore, it is conjectured that even if you are seen by someone - an extremely remote possibility given the bleak frozen terrain you will be flying over in the dead of night - disguised as you will be, they will have the problem of deciding whether or not what they really saw was a flying saucer and who to tell, who would believe them?"

Williams asked, "Don't these bases have sophisticated radar for detecting approaching aircraft?"

"Good point Mr. Williams. Of course they do, but it is planned that you be flying so low on your approach to the base that night, that you will be lost in the ground clutter and filtered out of any screen-displayable data. Even if you do momentarily show up on radar, it will be three in the morning. All the base fighters should be grounded at that time and they will not be expecting a hostile aircraft that close to the base in the interior of the country. Their guard should be down. These are the assumptions we are making, based on our own Soviet system. I hope that answers your question?"

"Yes," said Williams looking at Shelby.

The general continued. "What do you think surveillance and espionage are all about? Obviously, one of the main purposes is to allow organizations to work out almost every angle and detail of a mission before it is undertaken, thus ensuring its success in most cases. However, even the best of planners sometimes neglect one or two minor details during the planning of every mission and that is where you and Mr. Shelby come in."

The general sighed; he looked very tired - too tired. Williams figured he must be dying of some debilitating disease; nobody could look that tired just from a lack of sleep. The general was now breathing heavier and asked if there were any more questions.

Williams asked, "What if we have problems?"

"We will do everything we can to get you back safely." Williams didn't really believe this and had a bad feeling in the pit of his stomach, but figured he could look after himself if it became necessary.

"Do you have any other questions?" asked the general.

"Yes" said Shelby. "I have one. Will Natasha and Anna be coming to visit us again tonight?"

"Mr. Shelby, unfortunately Natasha and Anna are very busy in the service of their country. They are both still undergoing training. However, I am sure before your training is over, they will visit you again. By the way, I hear they enjoyed last night as much as you and Mr. Williams probably did. When they will visit you again, I cannot say. Sorry. Any more questions?"

There was a pause and then the general spoke again, this time, more quietly. "For your information, the Supreme Soviet approved your training last night, so the mission should be approved also. Thank you both and I will see you in approximately one year from now. Oh I nearly forgot the 'unless'. The "unless" is that you fully execute the mission as planned. Now that you know what the 'unless' is, please train well so you will be able to carry out this mission successfully. Please be aware that if you don't complete the mission, we will track you down and kill you. Please have no doubt about this if opportunities to escape present themselves to you."

General Ulanov wished them well, shook their hands and Major Khotov led Williams and Shelby from the meeting room to one of the barracks within the Kremlin garrison. Their training had begun.

Unexpectedly, the first weeks of their training consisted of no training at all, but instead a series of tests and what seemed like every medical examination known to man. Although the mission was planned to last for only a few days, it seemed the general wanted them to be in excellent, if not, perfect physical condition. From the numerous tests and examinations they had undergone, it was determined that Williams was in top physical shape apart from one serious problem - a weak left knee. It seemed he had cartilage damage from an old sports injury which would need to be repaired. As a result of this surgery, he had all his classroom training during the first six months. His field training would follow, when his knee was fully rehabilitated.

Shelby's tests and examinations showed he was also in excellent physical condition, except his eyesight and hearing were not at the required levels to train as a pilot. He had corrective eye surgery and treatments to remove tiny blockages in his ears. This delayed the start of his training for several weeks, during which time he managed to improve his already considerable physique.

William's classroom training took place at the Moscow Institute of Physics and Technology, the Flight Test Centre at Balkinur and the Security Assessment and Training Centre at Sergie Prosad. By far his most intense training was on the computer systems and software within the Minuteman missile. He was amazed that the Soviets had so much detailed information about American missiles. Although he had always been in computer sales, he knew enough about software that he was confident he could make the required modifications when the time came. During his training he successfully performed the software downloading process a number of times. Shelby, whose main function would be to fly Williams to the base the night of the mission, spent many months at Vukovo Airfield training to be a pilot. He passed the written tests with extremely high scores and completed one hundred hours of classroom study. He took his flying lessons in a Soviet Yakolev two-seater trainer aircraft, with a top speed of two hundred kilometers an hour and a range of seven hundred. He received over ninety hours of pilot training with an experienced Soviet squadron leader and over sixty hours of solo flight training. Most of his flight training was at night, like the mission would be. By the end of his flight training, Shelby felt quite at home flying the YAK trainer and enjoyed flying so much he planned to take it up as hobby when the mission was over.

William's missile field training took place at the Uzhur Missile Base in the eastern Soviet Union and although the Soviets were reluctant to show him operational underground missile silos, they were more than willing to explain what was involved in mobile missile launches and he spent several weeks on a missile firing range watching unarmed short range test missiles being fired.

During the last week of his field training he was eventually allowed into an underground silo which is normally used for training newly hired maintenance technicians. It contained an unarmed missile and allowed him to get a hands-on understanding of how to access the missile's nosecone electronics rack and cables.

In November, Williams's training switched to the Vukovo Airfield, southwest of Moscow, where Shelby was still undergoing his flight training. For a number of weeks, he learned about parachute harness packing and jumping. He made jumps from towers from heights up to four hundred and fifty feet and during the final weeks, practiced parachute jumping out of low flying aircraft. By the end of his training, he had overcome the fear of jumping and was able to hit the ground standing upright, in designated landing areas.

Towards the end of their training, Shelby and Williams trained together. Shelby flew the Yakolev flight trainer at very low altitudes and Williams practiced parachute jumping. Williams did four jumps each day, two in the morning, one in the afternoon and one at night, until they became routine.

Once they had completed their flight and parachute training, they returned to the barracks in the Kremlin garrison and began sleep-depravation training. They were trained to be able to perform complex tasks for several days at a time, without sleep. The use of energy enhancing stamina pills was a necessary part of staying alert and they got used to taking them. They learned that this is what gives agents an edge over regular people, who would eventually become tired and fall asleep. On the last day of this training, they were each given cyanide pills and told to use them if they were ever in a situation where they would rather die than live.

A few days later, they spent a day at a small arms firing range outside Moscow, which was perhaps the most fun they had during their whole year of training. They fired off round after round from Russian AK-47 automatic assault weapons and semi-automatic Makorov P-8 pistols. They learned that the AK-47 designed and developed by Mikhail Kalashnikov at the end of the Second World War, is still the most widely used weapon in the world today. Firing at targets, pinned to bales of hay, on the side of a snowy hill was really fun for them. The intent of their weapons training was to ensure they were comfortable using firearms. If they had to do any shooting, they would likely be shooting from the hip, so they didn't need to be sharpshooters or marksman. Williams remembered he'd had an air gun in his teens, which was the only gun he'd ever owned or fired. Shelby had been hunting with his father several times and had been allowed to fire his father's hunting rifle on occasion. He thought it was either a Remington or Winchester. He had never owned a gun himself. Neither of them had certainly ever fired multiple round rapid fire assault weapons before. After the day at the firing range, they both had sore shoulders from firing off so many rounds. The day at the firing range had come just before they were due to leave for their cross-country skiing training.

Their ski training took place in Murmansk, near the Arctic Circle. Every year the Festival of the North, a mini Winter Olympics, is held there. Their cover story was that they had won a trip-of-a-lifetime contest and because they had heard of the Murmansk Festival of the North, thought they would like to experience it for themselves.

William's training was far more intensive than Shelby's because of the skiing he would be doing on the base. For two weeks, he was pushed to the point of exhaustion, skiing for many hours at a time, with different instructors, at different times during the day.

While they were at Murmansk, Williams and Shelby met the local Karelians and people from all over northern Scandinavia. They found out that most of them had never heard of America. They had both learned a number of Russian words during their training, but still had trouble putting sentences together. They had learned greetings, small talk and many other expressions used in daily life. When talking to people it was nice to be able to speak their language, if only just a little bit, especially when very few of them spoke any English.

The days spent skiing and the nights spent socializing were most welcome after the previous year of intense studying and training. The weeks they spent in Murmansk were most memorable and a wonderful finale to their year of training before they had to make the long train ride south, back to Moscow, where they were scheduled to meet with General Ulanov the next day.

Leading up to the meeting with the Americans, as he had begun to call them, General Ulanov had attended a number of high level meetings with the Chairman of the Supreme Soviet. Although the chairman had approved the training for the Americans the year before, he had still not given approval for the mission to go ahead. The general had made a number of detailed presentations and had returned to answer questions on several occasions. He had also prepared a number of mission briefs. The chairman was concerned that Williams would not have the sufficient knowledge and experience to set the warhead detonation process in motion. General Ulanov was concerned that the chairman might not approve the mission because if it went wrong, it may lead to a nuclear confrontation between the superpowers. However, after reviewing the impressive training reports of the Americans and being aware of the thorough planning done by the general, the chairman had given his approval for the mission to proceed. He knew that for the Communist Party to survive, they had to start improving the lives of each and every Soviet. The mission seemed like a perfect vehicle to help bring a speedy end to the nuclear arms race and launch a more prosperous era for the Soviet Union.

Williams and Shelby looked well tanned as they entered the familiar meeting room; the general had thought of everything. They would both be expected to have good tans after a week in Cuba. Pale complexions on such good looking men would most certainly draw attention to them. In front of them were brand new uniforms, large envelopes and small, velvet-covered cases. The general had just presented these to them in an impromptu ceremony. Williams had been given a Soviet Paratrooper uniform, badges for completing rocketry and parachute training and a master skier certificate. Shelby had been given a Soviet Air Force uniform, pilot's wings and an expert skier certificate. They had also been presented with plaques displaying the Soviet Strategic Rocket Forces Division of the Soviet Department of Defense insignia.

General Ulanov congratulated them both once more, wished them luck and asked an officer to escort them over to the KGB headquarters complex, a place with which they were also very familiar.

Back in his office, General Ulanov was in a thoughtful mood that night. Although he knew for sure that Williams had the right stuff, he still wasn't sure about Shelby; he seemed like too much of a dreamer. That is why he had given him the lesser mission responsibilities. He knew it wasn't going to be easy and potentially a multitude of things could go wrong. He chuckled to himself that even in the Soviet Union they were familiar with Murphy's Law.

The general remembered a famous proverb "Everything comes to he who waits" and this was one of the happiest nights of his life. He knew the Soviet Union was taking a huge gamble undertaking this mission, because if the Americans got caught, the incident could lead to World War III.

He opened the bottom drawer of his desk and took out a small glass and an unopened bottle of vodka.

Red Shadows On Liberty's Soil

On the way over to the KGB headquarters complex, Williams wondered if the women would visit them that night. Unbeknownst to Shelby, Williams had been with several women during his year of training. He had romanced a young nurse while he was rehabilitating his knee and had been with a technician's sister while training at the Uzhur missile base. In return, he had told the technician he would do whatever he could to get him and his family to the States when his secret mission was over. He'd also had a one-night stand with a waitress at the resort where they had just been staying in Murmansk. He guessed Shelby hadn't had sex since the last time the women had visited them, but he didn't know for sure and wasn't going to ask.

As they entered William's room, they found Natasha and Anna sitting on the couch clad in skimpy see-through negligees, both looking amazingly sexy. They were both holding glasses, which, if William's memory served him well, would have vodka, no ice in them.

"Wow!" said Williams. "Our prayers have been answered once again, Pete."

Shelby had gone into a predictable trance, fixated on the women.

"Hey Pete, what's your poison?" asked Williams, making his way towards the kitchen.

Shelby came out of his daze and asked for a beer.

Williams grabbed two beers and handed one to Shelby as he came out of the kitchen. "Well ladies," he said, "I'm sure I don't need to tell you how wonderful it is to see you again."

He moved over to the couch and clinked the women's glasses. "Na Zdorovje!"

"Na Zdorovje," said Natasha and Anna, laughing.

Natasha said, "I hope you don't mind, but we asked a cleaner to let us in."

"I certainly don't mind; how about you Pete?" said Williams as he was moving around to the back couch. He leaned forward and put his arms around Natasha and Anna.

"I wish I had a camera; this is definitely one of life's special moments," he laughed, hugging both women around the neck.

Williams and Shelby alternately told the women about Murmansk and the Festival of the

North. Natasha and Anna seemed to be most impressed and while Shelby was still talking, Williams got up and went over to the window overlooking Red Square. He was thinking that although he had been in the Soviet Union for over a year now, he had still not seen any of the sights of Moscow. Natasha noticed him looking out of the window and got up and went over to where he was standing.

"You seem to be in deep thought. What are you thinking about?" she asked.

"Oh, just what a wonderful old city this seems to be and so far I haven't seen any of it."

"I'll tell you what. If I'm allowed, when you get back, I'll personally show you around; how about that?" she said, pecking him on the cheek.

Williams, smiling, said, "You have a deal; that would be wonderful."

Anna shouted to them to come and join her and Shelby, to discuss the plans for the night.

"This sounds exciting," said Williams, coming back over towards the couch with Natasha.

Anna told them that they wanted to swap partners - she with Williams and Natasha with Shelby.

"That is, if you don't mind of course?" she said.

"Sounds good to me," said Williams. "What do think Pete? Any problem with you?"

"No" said Shelby, shaking his head in agreement, transfixed on the women once again.

Natasha took Shelby's hand and led him towards the adjoining room. He was emotionally overcome with Natasha's attractiveness and began to sigh as she embraced and kissed him. Her perfume was overpowering and her nipples were hard and hot. She quickly undressed him, removed her negligee and began to use her mouth to calm him. Shelby had never felt so good in his whole life. Natasha slowly and rhythmically took him to every man's nirvana, after which he returned the favour. They slept for awhile and worked to find their heaven on earth on several more occasions.

In the other room, Williams and Anna were entwined, finding their own paradise. Like

Natasha and Shelby, they slept occasionally, but primarily pleasured each other all night.

Friday February 12, 1982

Williams and Shelby awoke alone, early Friday morning, to the sound of Major Khotov shouting loudly and knocking on the doors to their rooms. It was just after four thirty and although they were very tired, they showered with knowing smiles on their faces.

By five fifteen they were on their way to Sherymetevo airport which they were told had been especially built for the 1980 Summer Olympic Games. It was snowing lightly as they entered the modern looking terminal building. Their seats had been pre-selected, so they went directly to the departure gate. The major spoke to a woman at the gate, who in turn spoke to someone on the phone and they were let through to board the aircraft. They were greeted at the aircraft door by the aircrew and an attractive flight attendant who took their bags and showed them to their seats. Shelby took the window,

Williams the middle and the major the aisle seat. The seat covers showed they were flying Aeroflot Russian Airlines. Williams and Shelby had flown on a number of different airlines over the last several years, but had never had so much room or felt so comfortable. The plane was massive; however, they soon realized this might be the only highlight of the flight. There didn't seem to be any in-flight entertainment and from what they could smell coming from one of the serving areas, the food would probably not be to their liking. None of this would matter soon, as the major would be sedating both of them. General Ulanov knew that neither of the men would have had much sleep the previous night, and wouldn't get much once the mission began, so he had asked Major Khotov to ensure they slept through the flight. The major was really looking forward to his weekend in Havana; this was his first trip outside the Soviet Union and he was most excited. He envisaged himself drinking endless chilled bottles of vodka while sunbathing by the hotel pool.

After the aircraft had been de-iced, it taxied out onto the dark runway. Through the window,

Shelby could see flashing lights all around. As the Russian IIyushin aircraft took off and gained height, he could see many more lights spread out across the city, which disappeared as the aircraft ascended into dark billowing snow clouds. The major medicated them once the aircraft had reached its cruising altitude and took a stamina pill to ensure he would stay alert throughout the flight. The flight attendants had obviously been told that the major was someone special and were constantly asking him if they could get him anything. Although on duty, he had several glasses of champagne, quite a few vodkas and a number of liqueurs with unpronounceable Russian names. The flight attendants, not knowing the major's companions were sedated, were amazed at how soundly they were sleeping and were unable to offer them any food or drinks throughout the whole flight. This agitated them, even though the major kept telling them not to worry about it. The major asked the flight attendants about Havana and in a quiet moment, the most attractive one whispered that she would love to show him around when they got there. Although rather reluctant, he accepted a slip of paper from her with a phone number on it. He was thinking he should be able to get away for a few hours, even though he knew the general would be expecting him to be available at all times of the day and night. He thought he could go back to the hotel and periodically check for messages. Anyway, he would have to play it by ear.

The medication had worked perfectly and Williams and Shelby started to come awake as the huge airliner was into its final approach and golden beaches were coming into view. The airliner was approaching from over the Caribbean Sea, due to an imposed no-fly zone along the northern coast of Cuba and the Straits of Florida. As the airliner approached the airport landing strip, the shadow of the giant mechanical bird swept across the island's sparsely populated landscape. The massive passenger jet glided in over the tops of the palm trees, skirting the runway of Havana's Jose Marti International airport.

It was ten fifteen local time and Gerry Williams and Peter Shelby had arrived back in North America.

Back in Moscow, another cold winter night had set in and General Ulanov was sitting in his office, anxiously awaiting the news that Major Khotov and the Americans had arrived in communist Cuba.

Earlier in the day, he had phoned Major Trsenkov at the farm to make sure everything was ready for the Americans' arrival. The major reported that all the modifications to the mission aircraft had been made and a Ford Bronco had been hired for the Americans to use on the trip to and from the ski resort. The major asked the general if there was anything he should know about the Americans before they arrived later that evening.

"Not really," said General Ulanov, "but you should know that I need you to do everything you can to ensure the mission is successful. Please understand that this is the culmination of my career and if everything goes as planned, I will be retiring a happy man."

"I will certainly do my best. You can count on that," said Major Trsenkov. "I think you would agree, I have never let you down before."

"That is very true. Please call me as soon as the Americans have taken off from the farm. Thank you." The general hung up.

The monster aircraft came to a stop and a short time later, its front and rear doors were opened. Williams was thinking about the temperature swing; it must have been at least twenty below when they left Moscow and now they were in eighty degree heat. The sunshine and heat felt very good and he was sorry that they would be soon making their way back to the northern hemisphere. After bypassing Cuban Immigration and Customs with the major, the men met up with a heavy-set agent who handed them boarding passes. They changed in one of the airport washrooms, putting on colourful summer clothes and stashing their cold weather clothes for later use. They said goodbye to the major, who wished them luck and said he had to go and find a phone to call General Ulanov and they headed off to their departure gate. They noticed the burly agent was trailing behind them and when they got to their gate and found somewhere to sit, he sat several rows behind them. They blended in really well with the other tanned and casually dressed vacationers flying to Montreal. The Air Canada flight was on schedule and due to depart in fifty minutes. Two agents using their names had flown down from Montreal a week earlier.

Cuba had proven to be a most useful base for the Soviets since the revolution. For over two decades, they had moved agents through Cuba to all parts of North and South America. Senior members of the Communist Party had been vacationing with their families in Cuba since the early '70's.

Their plane left the ramp on time and early into the flight, Williams and Shelby noticed that everyone on board, almost without exception, was speaking French. They spoke very infrequently and pretended to be sleeping, which wasn't easy, given they had been asleep for the last nine hours. They were extremely hungry and were glad to eat the complimentary meal offered to them. Upon arrival at Montreal's Dorval airport, just under three and a half hours later, they came through Canadian Immigration and Customs without incident, using their false Canadian passports. They were asked where they were coming from and how long they had been away. Even though they looked nothing like the two Soviet agents who had flown down to Cuba the previous week, the only thing that mattered was that the names and passport numbers were the same. They were met by a nondescript agent who gave them boarding passes and showed them where to get their connecting flight. They found a washroom and changed into their cold weather clothes, packing away the summer clothes for use on the return trip. It was now four-thirty in the afternoon and their flight to Winnipeg was scheduled to leave at six. They waited at the departure gate for about an hour before boarding the plane. They noticed that the agent, who had given them their boarding passes, was standing across from their gate, reading a newspaper while they were waiting to board the aircraft.

Upon arrival at Winnipeg International airport, Williams and Shelby did not have to go through Canadian Immigration and Customs, as it was a domestic flight. In the arrivals area they were met by Major Yuri Trsenkov, a greying, grizzled-looking Russian, old enough to be their father. He was wearing a long black coat and ankle length black boots. There was a younger man with him, whom the major introduced as Sam. Sam took their bags and led the way to the exit.

The major began to make small talk with a heavy eastern European accent. "How was your trip?" he asked.

"So far, so good," said Williams.

"Well the first part of your journey is almost over. It shouldn't take us long to get to where we're going."

After putting their bags in the trunk, Sam got behind the wheel of the new-smelling, dark Lincoln. The Americans got in the back and the major got in the front next to Sam.

"I've heard a lot about you both during the last year. It sounds like you've been very well trained and are ready for the mission," said the major.

"Never been readier," responded Williams.

"That's good. We'll soon have you on your way."

The major told them he had an apartment overlooking Lake Ontario in Toronto and they said they knew where that was.

"Sounds nice," said Shelby.

"You know, I get lonely sometimes, but I enjoy living in Canada, because it has many of the same sports as the Soviet Union; ice hockey, skiing, soccer and I have even learned to enjoy American football."

Williams said, "Actually, it's Canadian Football, not American. They have three downs and we have four."

"Yes, I know that," said the major. "Toronto also has a baseball team called the Blue Jays."

"The Minnesota Twins used to be my team." said Shelby.

Following Shelby's statement, the major didn't speak again until just before they got to the farm, just over an hour later. He and Sam listened to classical music all the way. Shelby dozed off and Williams sat thinking about what he was about to do. The gravity of the situation was beginning to sink in now that it was almost time to carry out the mission.

Red Shadows On Liberty's Soil

As they approached the farm, the major told them that it was representative of those built in the Canadian prairies after the First World War and had been a grain producing farm for many years. He told them that where the farm was located, it was almost inaccessible and several dirt roads had to be navigated to get to it. He said it had been rented from an old retired Russian who had jumped at the offer of a generous monthly income for several months, and it had only been occupied for the last few weeks, since a used turbo fan Cessna had been acquired. The light aircraft had been dismantled in California and transported to the farm. Once reassembled, the major had recruited a local metal worker to fabricate the additions, telling him they were needed for a movie shoot. Four larger-than-normal lights had been attached to either side of the aircraft, creating the typical flying saucer lighted porthole effect. Test flights had shown that the new additions had not affected the aircraft's aerodynamic characteristics or performance in any way.

When Williams and Shelby entered the farmhouse, although it looked primitive, they could see people watching TV, so knew it had electricity. The major told them each agent brought groceries with them and by making use of a large freezer in one of the barns; they had accumulated a more than ample supply of food for their stay. The major told them to follow him and he took them upstairs to a small bedroom. He told them they could leave their belongings in the bedroom during their stay.

"Now, you must be hungry. How about some goulash? There are always a few pots of goulash cooking on the stove."

"That would be great," said Shelby.

"I agree," said Williams. "Airline food is not very filling."

They were both given a bowl of goulash and some fresh bread rolls. While they were eating, the major introduced them to Anton, whom the major said would be going over the flight plan with them and would be showing them the aircraft. Anton shook hands with them and left. The major told them to come and join him and Anton in the dining room when they had finished eating.

When they got to the dining room, the men found it to be a hive of activity, with many agents talking on phones. The major explained to them that the phones they were using had coders/decoders attached to them and similar coders/decoders were being used by General Ulanov and his staff in Moscow. It seemed to Williams and Shelby that the Soviet agents at the farm had formed a brotherhood of sorts, sleeping, eating and working together. Anton drew their attention to a large map laid out on the dining room table. He showed them where the farm was on the map and where they would be flying to. He told them although it would be dark, they should still be able to see rivers and roads because they would be flying so low to the ground. After spending half an hour or so with Anton, the major told them to go and relax for awhile and they went into the room with the TV and watched the local late night news for awhile.

Saturday February 13

Williams and Shelby were relaxing, watching TV, when the major came into the room and said it was time for them to get ready. They went up to the small bedroom and changed into their thermal underwear and new Soviet Air Force and Paratrooper uniforms.

The major said, "You have to wear the uniforms just in case you are captured. You have to be treated in accordance with the Geneva Convention – Rules for the Treatment of Prisoners of War, which you may have heard of?"

"Yes I've heard of it," said Williams. "I always wondered what it was."

The major said, "I am not an expert on it, but my understanding of it is, if you are captured, you must be treated humanely. Some countries adhere to it; others don't. The Americans do."

"Well, things will really have gone wrong if we have to worry about the Geneva Convention," said Williams jokingly.

They were led out to a large barn behind the farmhouse. Inside was a bizarre looking plane, which they were told looked like a flying saucer when being flown at night. Anton told them that the aircraft only had enough fuel to get to the drop-off point and return to the farm. Williams thought to himself, *these people have thought of everything.* Anton showed Shelby the aircraft's cockpit controls and instrument panel, while Williams was checking the parachutes and maneuvering a large supply package closer to the side door. Once Anton was confident Shelby was sufficiently familiar with the controls, he went through the flight plan with him once more and helped him enter some waypoints into the navigation system. Satisfied that Shelby was ready, Anton exited the aircraft. He removed the chocks from under the aircraft's wheels and signaled to Shelby he was clear to proceed.

Shelby eased the aircraft out of the barn, towards the dimly lit, snow-covered runway. There were four or five large drums with flames rising out of them on both sides of the makeshift runway. Shelby told Williams to strap himself in and the aircraft gradually began to accelerate, creating an ever-increasing bumping sensation as it gained speed, before it became airborne. Once the aircraft had gained sufficient altitude, Shelby banked it in a westerly direction, flying west until he came to a river, which he began to follow in a southerly direction.

Back at the farmhouse, the major rang through to Moscow and informed General Ulanov that the Americans had just taken off. The general thanked him for the information and told him to keep him updated as the mission progressed. The major said he would and hung up.

Williams leaned into the cockpit and asked Shelby if he realized this was the first time that someone wasn't watching them since they had arrived in Moscow, over a year ago. Shelby said it was a good feeling.

Once he began to see the outline of the air base, Shelby flew east to the northern perimeter. He maintained as low an altitude as he could, in the hope the base radar would not detect the aircraft. He circled over the northern perimeter fence a number of times to get into the right position for the drop. Once he got positioned where he needed to be, he pulled the plane up into a steep climb, reached the required altitude and leveled off. He waved wildly and shouted to Williams to jump. Williams threw the supply package out of the side door and followed after it. Both chutes opened almost immediately and several minutes later, Williams was standing on the snow-covered, frozen ground. His landing had been precise.

He unfastened the chute's harness, broke free from the parachute and set off to find the supply package. He moved quickly, shining a high powered flashlight up into the trees and within several minutes had located the supply package. With some climbing and tugging, he managed to pull it down. He opened it up and removed the AK-47, a pistol, a sheaved hunting knife, ski equipment, metal cutters, a small axe, electronic devices, cables, garbage bags, work boots, a folded metal frame, some tools, a medical kit and a backpack. The backpack contained twenty thousand dollars and other needed supplies. General Ulanov had figured this amount of money might be of great benefit if the Americans found themselves in a tight spot during the mission but was expecting to get most of it back. The mission would be the crowning point of his career and he wanted to do all he could to make sure it was successful. The amount of money requested had been questioned by the Chairman of the Supreme Soviet, but he had approved it after the general had reasoned with him late one night. The general had told him how crucial it was to do everything possible to ensure the success of the mission, arguing that if it was successful, it could change the nuclear landscape forever.

Williams was not planning to take the medical kit with him; it had been included on a just-in-case-it-might-be-needed basis. He carefully put the electronic devices, work boots and other items into the backpack. He holstered the pistol and strapped the sheaved hunting knife to his leg. He put on his ski equipment, shouldered the automatic weapon and set off across a small clearing.

Unbeknownst to Wolford Byford, who was hiding behind some snow-covered bushes, Williams had seen him while unpacking the supply package. Williams approached the bushes Wolf was hiding behind and administered an almighty blow to the side of his head with the butt of his automatic weapon. The blow stunned Wolf and he fell sideways, lying motionless in the snow. Williams pulled his head up by the hair and wondered what the hell he was doing out here in the middle of nowhere, on a freezing cold night. Williams figured that whoever found him would figure he'd stayed out in the cold too long.

Williams headed for a gap in the trees. Within a short time, he'd reached the base perimeter fence on the opposite side of a snow-covered road. Just along from where he was standing there was a large sign, warning that this was a restricted area patrolled by armed guards and vicious sentry dogs. *Funny*, thought Williams, *the general had neglected to mention this*. He cut a hole in the fence, squeezed through and started to ski across the snowy surface of the base. He thought it was no wonder they had selected this place for a missile base; it wasn't good for much else. He knew from spy satellite photos that there should be a silo several miles south of where he was, and as he skied towards it, he periodically checked a small compass to make sure he was maintaining a southerly course.

Red Shadows On Liberty's Soil

As he skied towards the silo, red shards of light began to pierce the dark sky above the eastern horizon. As the daylight broke through, Williams couldn't see a cloud in the sky. He was now being blinded by a combination of the sun and snow and put on his anti-glare sunglasses. If it were not for the compass he had been given by Major Trsenkov, he would have been completely lost and have no idea which direction to go in. He also began to understand how important the stamina and endurance cross-country ski training that he had done was. Without it, he knew he likely wouldn't have even made it this far and he still had to ski back to the ski lodge when he was finished, a few hours from now. The biggest problem he had was the uneven terrain he was skiing over, which resulted in him having to exert a great deal of energy to even make reasonable progress. There were no groomed trails out here and because of the uneven surface, he had to put a lot of concentration into his skiing and had very little time to think about anything else, including what he was about to do once he got into the silo. He was struck by the vastness of where he found himself and knew that if it wasn't for the fact his clothes, skis and poles were all white, he could easily have been seen from the air. The wind had got up and blowing snow was often obscuring his view. It wasn't until it temporarily subsided that he saw what he knew to be a silo security fence up ahead. Finding this meant he'd found the silo.

When he reached the silo security fence and had stopped skiing, he started to feel very cold. As he struggled to get through the fence, he started to shiver and couldn't stop his teeth from chattering. He knew the silo security fence was actually a seismic shock sensor fence, designed to detect intrusion attempts by either climbing, lifting or cutting. He unfolded and carefully attached the specially-made metal frame he had brought with him, to the fence, ensuring it would maintain its structure, and cut out the fencing inside the frame. He climbed through, confident he wouldn't set off any alarms. He was now close to the silo which, from above, looked like a collection of different sized circular covers. He could see a van parked next to the main silo cover. He swapped his ski shoes for his work boots and stowed them along with the rest of his ski equipment and automatic weapon, into an orange garbage bag, which he buried in the snow. He walked towards the silo and located the concrete stairs that led down to the door leading inside. The door was closed, but unlocked, so he cautiously entered, hoping no one would be on the other side to greet him. Once inside, he could hear voices and crouched down behind a row of storage lockers.

The maintenance crew inside the silo had no idea they had a visitor early on that Saturday morning. They were busy checking the feed pipes attached to the rocket for signs of rodents. So far they had found no damage, even though a fuel line sensor had indicated there was a problem of some kind. They had replaced the faulty sensor and were standing admiring the sleek white projectile, the Stars and Stripes shining brightly in the silo lights. The seemingly awesome power of such a weapon always overwhelmed them and they hoped it would never be launched.

While he was waiting, Williams tried to thaw out his frozen fingers and thought about how his thinking was fully aligned with the general's, in that such an incident on American soil might force the people to rise up and demand an end to nuclear weapons. He was determined to make a difference and bring about change for the better. How ingenious the general's plan was, to make the missile blow itself up.

Once the maintenance crew had finished their checks, they made their way up to the top of the silo and stowed their equipment in one of the storage lockers. Williams heard them talking about going for breakfast and a few moments later, all the lights in the silo went out. He wondered why there was no emergency lighting, but never gave it another thought. He hadn't moved for quite awhile and upon hearing the silo maintenance door being slammed shut, stood up and stretched his legs.

He found his way to the light switches and turned the silo lights back on. The first thing he had to do was bypass the alarm panel, because what he would be doing soon would set off alarms. He carefully removed the duplicate alarm panel from his backpack and installed it next to the existing one. He removed the external connector cover from the existing alarm panel and connected the wires to the signal override generator in the duplicate alarm panel, doubling up the wires in each slot. Once the last wire had been inserted, he powered up the duplicate alarm panel and cut the power to the existing panel.

He made his way down a ladder onto the metal platform surrounding the upper rocket stage of the missile, allowing him to access the nosecone electronics maintenance panel. He searched around in his backpack and found the special screwdriver he had brought with him. Looking at the screwdriver in his hand, he thought to himself, *This is it! Show time - the moment of truth.*

Williams moved close to the nosecone electronics maintenance panel and attempted to remove the screws. His hand was shaking so wildly that he couldn't get the screwdriver locked on any of the screw heads. Sweat began to stream down from his brow, onto his hands, and made them wet and sticky. Until now he hadn't realized how difficult this was going to be; obviously the magnitude of what he was about to do was already overwhelming him. He began to shake uncontrollably and feel nauseous; his legs suddenly gave way and he found himself kneeling on the metal platform. *My god*! he thought, *what is wrong with me?* He had never felt so much anxiety in his life and figured he must be having some kind of panic attack. The only other times he could remember having such feelings of nervousness was before an important exam or presentation, but it had been nowhere near as bad as this. He figured his nervous system must have gone into what is called adrenaline overload, he had many of the classic symptoms of fear. Kneeling on the metal platform, he began to take in his surroundings, reached out and touched the surface of the missile, which felt steely cold. Where he had touched it, he had left a wet fingerprint. Gradually, the multiple symptoms of fear began to subside. He'd stopped sweating and his hands had stopped shaking. Feeling better and more in control, he stood up and reached up to the nosecone electronics maintenance panel again.

Not shaking as much anymore, he managed to remove the screws and had just lifted the panel away from the nosecone, when he heard voices above him. His first reaction was the maintenance crew must have returned. He heard someone saying something about the lights and heard a storage locker being opened. He thought to himself they must have been surprised to find the lights on. He hoped they wouldn't notice the duplicate alarm panel on the far wall. He carefully put the nosecone electronics maintenance panel back in place and fortuitously, it stayed there, without requiring any screws. He quietly put the screwdriver and screws into his backpack and moved out of sight behind the missile. He could hear his heart pounding as he sat there and for some reason felt completely detached from his surroundings. Several minutes later, he was brought back to reality when the silo lights went out, leaving him in total darkness. Upon hearing the silo door being slammed shut, he thought to himself that they must have returned because they had forgotten something. Now he needed to find his way up to the light switches, on the level above, in total darkness. There was not a single solitary beam of light visible anywhere in the silo, which he thought was a credit to those who had built it. He guessed everything would have been built to military specification, which he had heard of, but had never really understood what it meant until now. He was beginning to sweat again and was experiencing a choking sensation in his throat. Despite this, he stood up and felt his way around the missile. He had a rough idea where the ladder should be and started to feel his way around on the metal platform as if he was blindfolded. His heart was pounding again and he felt light headed, which was affecting his balance. He found his way to the bottom of the ladder, climbed up and once up on the next level, felt his way around again, until he found the first row of storage lockers. He knew that the light switches were off to the side of these and with both arms outstretched in front of him, walked towards where he thought they should be. He touched concrete, thinking it was the wall, but when he got closer, found it was a support pillar. He moved around the pillar until he came to the wall, then felt his way along until he located the light switches. He was just about to switch the lights on again, when he had the thought, perhaps they were being monitored and that was the reason the maintenance crew had returned. There were four light switches in total, so he tried each one until he found the lights that lit up the area where he was working and just left those lights on, hoping all the lights had to be on before any kind of an alarm signal would be sent. Anyway, he needed light, so there wasn't much he could do about it. He just hoped the maintenance crew didn't return again.

He ran his fingers through his now soaking wet hair and wiped the beads of sweat from his brow. He had begun to shake again, as he climbed down the ladder to the metal platform. He couldn't believe how this was affecting him! He dragged his backpack from where he'd hidden it behind the missile, and shakily reached up and removed the nosecone electronics maintenance panel again, revealing a large electronics rack and a tangle of cables and wires. Mimicking Strategic Air Command's top secret communications protocol, he would be making the required modifications to arm the missile's warheads and start a prolonged detonation countdown, allowing him and Shelby sufficient time to be back in Moscow before the explosion.

The return of the maintenance crew was all Williams hadn't needed, and he found he couldn't stop shaking once again. Very shakily, he took an odd looking electronics device out of his backpack, connected it to one of the back plane connectors on the electronics rack and powered it up. Just as he was about to enter the command string to start the downloading process, he paused, thinking that he really hoped positive things would come as a result of this. Not second guessing himself for long, he entered the command string to start the downloading process and after a few seconds was prompted to insert the cassette containing the new software. Once he had inserted it, he hit the small Enter key. A tiny yellow light on the top of the electronics device was supposed to start flashing, but it didn't. Williams couldn't believe it wasn't working! He'd performed the same downloading process numerous times during his training and it had worked every single time. Why wasn't it working? He thought perhaps Strategic Air Command, commonly known as SAC had changed the downloading process and the Soviets' information was out of date. Perhaps a password was needed after all, although he had been instructed it wasn't if you were directly connected to the missile's electronics rack and he had not been asked for one.

Puzzled, he ejected the cassette and inspected it. There didn't look to be anything wrong with it. He turned the wheels and the tape rolled and seemed to be working as it should. He re-inserted the cassette and tried the command string again - still nothing. Streams of sweat started to pour from his brow once again. He thought to himself that perhaps this whole thing was too much for him; after all, up until a year ago he had been a computer salesman. He hadn't been trained for years like special assignment specialists normally were. He was essentially just a regular guy. No wonder he was having problems with this! He was quickly brought back to reality when the lights started flashing on and off. He climbed back up the ladder and reset the light switch. He remembered he had once worked in an office where the lights did this at night and on weekends, to indicate to anyone working that they would be automatically turning themselves off soon. This made him a feel a bit better, knowing that the lights probably weren't being monitored. It meant it was most unlikely the maintenance crew would be returning. He made his way back down onto the metal platform and began to focus on the problem again. He had no way of diagnosing what the problem was because he had only been trained to enter the command string and observe the tiny yellow light flashing. He was racking his brain as to what could be wrong. Perhaps the programming device had been damaged during the parachute drop. The cassette seemed to be functioning correctly and had started turning slowly once he'd pressed the Enter key. He was still sweating and shaking but was beginning to feel in control again. He began to focus on the cable with the large connector on the end. He disconnected it from the missile's electronics rack and looked at the connector and it looked fine. He looked as best he could at the pins in the connecting slot in the missile's electronics rack and they looked straight and undamaged. He powered the electronics device down, reconnected the cable, turned the power on and within a few seconds, the command prompt appeared on the small display screen. Shakily he entered the download command string again. The cassette started to turn slowly and the tiny yellow light began to flash. It was working! Williams jumped up, shot his fist into the air and shouted, "Yes!"

The only difference between this time and last time was that the cassette was already loaded in the electronics device when he entered the initial command string. He thought back to his training and remembered the cassette had always been inserted into the device. Not having the cassette already loaded seemed to have been the problem. Even though you were prompted to insert the cassette, if it wasn't already loaded, there must be some kind of software bug. When the tiny yellow light stopped flashing, a tiny green one came on, which meant the software had been successfully downloaded. He entered a command to activate the newly downloaded software and the green light turned off which indicated the new software was being executed. He had done it! From what he knew the detonation countdown should now be underway. It had taken him an hour and a half to successfully download the new software. Now that it was done, he disconnected the electronics device and cable and using a pair of pliers, pulled the majority of the pins off all the electronics rack back plan connector slots, rendering them unusable. He screwed the nosecone electronics maintenance panel back on so that outwardly there was no sign it had been tampered with.

He still had another task to take care of before leaving the silo. He had to damage the main silo cover controls sufficiently to ensure the missile couldn't be launched or extracted. He took the small axe out of his backpack, climbed up to the hydraulic control box above the missile and vigorously smashed at it several times. He broke the cover and badly damaged most of the servo motors and cogs inside. The damage was extensive. *Good job!* he thought; it will take them a while to fix this baby.

Wolf awoke to bright sunshine and found himself lying in the snow on top of a shrub with yellow flowers. He felt colder than he could ever remember and it hurt him to move his fingers, even slightly. He hoped they weren't frostbitten. He noticed frozen blood on the shoulder of his jacket and although he felt dizzy, could clearly recall what had happened only a few hours earlier. He remembered seeing the flying saucer, the parachutes and the paratrooper, who had jumped him. All he could think about right now was getting warm. He struggled to his feet and picked up his hunting rifle. He hooked the strap over his shoulder, and painfully began to make his way towards the road. Every bone in his body ached with every step he took; his toes and fingers were throbbing. As he slowly made his way through the snow-covered trees, he couldn't help thinking that he had been witness to something very sinister. The paratrooper, who had left him for dead, was obviously a professional.

Wolf's sense of direction was excellent and he came out of the woods close to where his truck was parked. With great difficulty he managed to remove the keys from his jacket pocket and unlock the driver's side door. He threw the hunting rifle onto the passenger seat and pulled himself up onto the driver's seat.

Wolf managed to start the engine and as he was reaching to turn the heater fan to maximum, noticed it was fifteen minutes past eleven. Slowly the feeling was beginning to return to his hands and his pounding headache was beginning to subside. Although groggy and thinking he should go home, he really wanted to find out who the mystery man was and where he had gone, and figured it had to have something to do with the base. Having warmed up sufficiently, he made his way back to where he had been left to die. He followed a set of ski tracks out of the woods, across the base perimeter road to the fence and could see where a hole had been cut. He made his way back to his truck and drove to where the fence had been cut and parked, leaving the engine running. His throat was parched and he really needed a drink. He searched around in the truck and found an old used paper cup, which he filled with snow and held next to the heater blower until it melted into ice water. He repeated this process several times until he had quenched his thirst. Wolf thought he would wait a little bit longer and got comfortable, putting his feet up on the bench seat and propping his head up on a rolled-up hunting jacket. Soon he was asleep in the warm cab.

By now, the community of Foxhollow was feverish with the Fuller brothers' story about the flying saucer and Wolf's disappearance. The talk in Morgan's Bar and Grill, just after noon on that Saturday, was that Wolf had been abducted by Aliens. Wolf's girlfriend, Carol, was asking the Fullers what they remembered and not surprisingly they could barely remember anything that had happened after they had left work at the tractor plant yesterday afternoon. Carol had gone to public and high school with the Fuller brothers and knew they were good people, but these days they drank too much. Her father, Gil, had been very good friends with Larry and Mike's father, Greg, up until his untimely death in a snowmobile accident a few years ago. Since then, Gil had been like a father to the boys and often invited them and their mother, Sybil, over to join Carol and his wife, Sarah, for a barbeque during the warm summer months. The Fuller brothers were in their early twenties and had been born less than a year apart. They were both single and still lived at home with their mother. Larry, the older and taller of the two brothers, had long dark hair which was frequently hidden under a Minnesota Twins baseball cap. He had bright eyes and a long thin face and was wearing a thick dark brown leather jacket over a dirty looking suit vest. His brother, Mike, had long dirty blonde hair, blue eyes and a kind of California surfer look. He was wearing multiple layers of shirts under a greasy looking dark blue ski jacket. The Fullers had grown up in Foxhollow and in their later years at school had both excelled at cross-country running. In their last year, they had represented the northern Minot schools region at state track meets in Fargo and Bismarck, but neither of them had finished in the top twenty.

"I'll tell you what I remember "said Larry in a dry raspy voice. "It had been a real late night at the Bird and on the way home, we saw a flying saucer. Wolf stopped his truck for a while and we watched it move across the sky, right Mike?"

"Yea, that's right," said Mike. "I saw it plain as day."

"Do you have any idea what happened to Wolf?" asked Carol, bursting into tears.

"I remember he dropped us off outside our house," said Larry.

Williams now had to get out of the silo. He already knew from his training that the maintenance door was the only way in and out and it would very likely be locked on the outside.

The original plan had been for him to remove the padlock, and enter the silo. But having arrived when the door was unlocked and having nowhere to hide, he felt he had no choice but to enter. He hadn't noticed the padlock at the time. He checked the hinges and they were welded to the door. He banged at the door with the small axe, but it just slipped off the metal. Panic began to set in. He was entombed with a nuclear missile that was going to detonate within less than seventy-two hours. Realizing it would be impossible to leave through the maintenance door, he began to investigate if there was any other way out. He couldn't see any other doors on the level he was on and because the lower levels were further below ground, he figured it was highly unlikely he would find a way out down there either, but checked anyway and as expected, found only solid steel and concrete all around. He knew there was no way to stop the detonation countdown and if he wasn't able to get out before the explosion, at least his death would be instantaneous. However, he still had lots of time ahead of the planned Monday afternoon detonation, so his panic gradually began to subside and he began to focus his attention on the large silo cover above the missile. He thought to himself that if he hadn't damaged it so badly, he may have been able to open it and leave that way. While looking up at the large cover, he noticed a smaller cover, off to one side. He climbed up a wall-mounted ladder and studied it. He figured it would be padlocked on the outside but the hinge attaching it was visible and was attached with very large screws. Williams figured he should be able to remove the screws and unhinge the cover, so he climbed down and using the small axe, sliced into a number of locked storage lockers, until he found some toolboxes. He searched around inside them and found a very large screwdriver, a hammer and vice grips. He climbed back up the ladder and using the screwdriver, tried to remove the screws, but none of them would budge. He fastened the vice grips around the handle of the screwdriver, held it up to one of the screws and hammered at the vice grips. Using this method, he managed to loosen and remove two of the large screws, but the others seemed to be rusted to the hinge. He climbed back down and smashed into some more locked storage lockers until he located a power drill and some assorted drill bits. After linking several extension cords together, he climbed back up and was able to slowly drill out the centers of the other large rusted screws. He then pushed the small, but surprisingly heavy, cover up and out of the way. He climbed back down the ladder one last time, retrieved his backpack, climbed back up and squeezed out through the small hatch into the bright sunshine. It had taken him almost two hours to break out of the silo and it was just before two o'clock in the afternoon; he was several hours behind schedule.

At Morgan's, Biff told Carol that he and some of Wolf's friends and neighbours were going to look for him.

Carol grabbed her coat. "I'm coming too."

About a dozen men and Carol came out of Morgan's and jumped into their cars, trucks and vans.

"Follow me," shouted Biff, leaning out of his truck window. He led the convoy out onto the road that led to the base.

Carol and Larry were riding with Biff.

"You know, it must have something to do with the base. Most things around here do," said Biff.

The convoy soon reached the northern perimeter road.

"Look in the snow banks and ditches," said Biff.

There wasn't much to see apart from snow-covered trees. When they reached the western end of the northern perimeter road, they turned south. About fifty minutes later, they had reached the western entrance to the base. Biff pulled over to the side of the road and jumped out of his truck. Those following in the convoy also got out of their vehicles. They gathered around Biff and he told them he was going to talk to whoever would listen to him on the base, about the Fullers' story and told them to wait here for him. Biff got back into his truck and turned into the base entrance, stopping beside a guardhouse. A young man in an Air Force uniform greeted him and asked if he could help him. Biff said he needed to speak to someone about an incident near the base, earlier that morning.

"Do you have ID?" asked the guard.

"Here," said Biff, handing him his tattered old wallet "Take whatever you want - driver's license, Medicaid card, whatever."

"I mean base ID," said the guard, pushing the wallet back towards Biff.

"No, I don't, but I still need to talk to someone."

The young airman, seeing Biff was becoming visibly agitated, told him to wait while he made a phone call.

He went to the back of the guardhouse and called through to the base headquarters building. He had a short conversation with someone on the other end and came back to the window.

"Someone is on their way to talk with you. Please go back and wait in your truck."

After quite a while, a Jeep pulled up next to where Biff was parked. Biff got out of his truck and a clean cut, uniformed officer asked him if he was the person who had something to report and introduced himself as Major John Lang, of the United States Air Force.

"Yes," said Biff. "Early this morning, three young men from Foxhollow saw a flying saucer moving towards the base and one of them has disappeared. That's it. I just thought someone on the base should know."

"I haven't heard of anything unusual happening today, but I will report this to the base commander. Could I please have your name and phone number?" asked the major.

"They call me Biff and my last name is Morgan. I will write my phone number down for you." said Biff, snatching the notepad out of the major's hand.

"Thank you for the information," said the major, retrieving his notepad from Biff. "I guess we'll keep looking for our friend," said Biff, shaking the major's hand.

Major Lang drove back to the base headquarters building and informed Base Commander William S. Maty about the information he had just been given. After he had finished, Will Maty, chuckling, commented that usually he read about these kinds of things in the local supermarket checkout line.

"Nothing out of the ordinary has been reported, but I'll check with the tower to see if they noticed anything unusual and get them to check their logs. You say this guy seemed believable?"

"Yes. He had a small convoy with him."

"Quite strange," said the base commander. "Leave it with me, Thank you, Major."

After the major had left, Base Commander Maty got up and walked over to look at the Minot Air Force base emblem hanging on the far wall of his office. There was an M, followed by a missile representing I, then an N. Following the N was what looked like the head of an old wild west Cavalry officer representing the O, followed by a T. When he was troubled, he often looked at the base emblem for inspiration. He wondered what this was about.

Biff led the convoy back the way they had come north, then east, along the northern perimeter road, until they came to the road back to Foxhollow. It was starting to get dark. They had found no trace of Wolf or his truck. Little did they know that if they had turned east instead of west on the northern perimeter road, when they had first started out, they would have found Wolf and his truck within a matter of minutes. Larry had slept most of the way home, so Carol hadn't been able to get any new information from him.

Once he was out of the silo, Williams quickly got his bearings and made his way to where he had buried his ski equipment. He found the orange garbage bag, put his work boots in the backpack and put his ski equipment on again. He shouldered the automatic weapon, checked his compass and began to head in a northerly direction, across the barren, snow-covered landscape. After skiing for a while, he remembered as a youngster reading about the native Plains Indians who had roamed these lands during the winter months and began to visualize a train of them far off in the distance. He could see multi-coloured ponies, pulling what he thought were called travois. There were a number of older men, chiefs he guessed, at the head of the train, followed by warriors of all ages and behind them lots of women and children. They were all wearing long colourful fur cloaks and he could hear the children laughing as they played. Still in the moment, he thought about what he had just set in motion and although it wouldn't bring their way of life back, it may make their ancestors think back to the way things used to be a hundred or so years ago.

Williams almost slipped on a rough patch of icy snow and lost the mirage. He was thinking how under circumstances of total isolation, the mind was capable of amazing things. He thought to himself that whenever he reached his Shangri-La, he would try and cultivate this amazing phenomenon. As he was making his way off the base, he was unaware that a local search party was looking for the man he had left for dead, earlier in the day. He was now primarily thinking about meeting up with Shelby at the ski resort and how late he already was. He was finding the skiing quite tough and was doing his best to keep up a steady pace. He kept checking the compass to ensure he was still heading north. One thing he had going for him was that the weather conditions were clear, even though he had a biting wind to contend with.

A number of miles north-east of the military base, Peter Shelby was waiting at the southern border of the Ebdon ski resort. After returning to the farm and letting everyone know that the drop had gone well, he had managed to get a few hours' sleep before starting out for the resort. As General Ulanov or Major Khotov - he couldn't remember which one - had predicted, his vehicle had been thoroughly searched at the border. He had compensated for this eventuality by leaving the farm several hours early. He and his vehicle were now on file with US Immigration and Customs. He had indicated to them that he was going skiing at the Ebdon ski resort, which was true. Once across the border, as he was merging onto Interstate number 83, he realized he'd crossed the border here before. The interstate ran north from Bismarck to the Canadian border. He had been fishing up in Manitoba with his father on several occasions when he was a teenager.

He arrived at the resort just after eleven. He took his overnight bag and ski equipment inside with him, leaving Williams' bag in the Bronco. When he got to reception, he found out that he and Williams had pre-paid rooms for the night. He planned to meet up with Williams around noon.

Wolf came awake just after three-thirty in the afternoon. The truck's engine was not running and he felt quite cold. He figured he must have woken up at some point, turned it off, then dozed off again. He decided he would go home, thinking his girlfriend must be worried sick about him. He took one last glance at the base perimeter fence and noticed something off in the distance. After locating his high powered hunting binoculars, he could see a skier off in the distance coming his way, so he waited until they got closer. He waited until he could see the skier pushing his way through the fence, then grabbed his hunting rifle, jumped out of his truck and ran towards the fence.

As Williams was squeezing through the fence, Wolf recognized him and shouted, "Drop the weapon and put your hands up."

Williams looked up and recognized Wolf, too. With all the problems he'd had in the silo, he'd completely forgotten about the encounter earlier that morning. However, it all came back to him in a hurry now.

"You again? Let me get through the fence first," he said angrily.

"Yep, it's me again," replied Wolf. "Figured you'd left me for dead, did you?"

William's mind was already working a mile a minute.

"Listen," he said, collecting himself. "I'm on a military mission, testing the base security."

"What are you talking about?" said Wolf, looking confused. He moved over to where Williams was standing and hit him square in the face with the butt of his rifle. Because Williams was wearing sunglasses, the blow shattered one of the lenses, cutting him above the left eye. His nose also started to bleed, blood dripping down into the snow.

"There! I owe you that. Maybe I'll leave you to die out here; how would you like that?" said Wolf.

When Wolf hit Williams, he'd been knocked back but he hadn't fallen, and with his back to Wolf, had pulled out his pistol. He swung around and pointed it at Wolf's head.

"Drop the rifle!"

Williams cleared the blood from his face with his jacket sleeve, leaving a red smear across his face. He told Wolf to go and get in his truck. He picked up Wolf's rifle, along with his own automatic weapon, and as he was walking towards Wolf's truck, he asked him what he was doing out here.

"I saw the flying saucer and wanted to know what was going on," said Wolf.

"As I told you," said Williams, "you are interfering with a United States government top secret mission."

Once they got to the truck, Williams ran around and jumped into the passenger seat, pushing the pistol into Wolf's face as he climbed up into the drivers' seat. Williams asked Wolf if he knew how to get to the Ebdon ski resort from here and when he said he did, told him to drive there as quickly as he could. Williams told him he was going up to the resort for a debriefing meeting on what he had found out about the base security. Wolf still didn't know what to think about the situation.

"I'm Gerry," said Williams. "What's your name?"

"They call me Wolf."

On the way to the resort, Williams threw his automatic weapon and a number of items out of his backpack into the snow-covered trees as they sped by. He also threw Wolf's hunting rifle into the trees, much to his dismay.

While they were making their way up to the resort, Williams couldn't believe what a talker this guy, Wolf, was! In the half hour it took them to get to the resort, he had heard his whole life story. He apparently liked to hunt and snowmobile in the winter, fish and camp in the summer, and always went to the Indy 500 on Memorial Day weekend. He was currently living with his girlfriend and her two children, in a rented house, in a town called Foxhollow, west of here. He had grown up in St Cloud, just north of the twin cities of Minneapolis/St Paul and had got into trouble with the law at an early age. He had married young and had always had difficulty holding down a regular job. Several years back, with warrants out for his arrest, his marriage falling apart, he had decided to make a clean break and had headed up the interstate to Fargo. In Fargo, he worked for a number of different courier and delivery companies, and after a year or so of scraping by, living in subsidized housing, had moved further upstate to Grand Forks. He had only stayed there for a few weeks, due to the lack of employment opportunities and a shortage of subsidized housing. Since moving west to Minot, his luck had changed and things had really started to work out for him. On his first day in Minot, he found an assembly line job at an agricultural equipment manufacturing plant, the largest employer in Minot apart from the Air Force base. The company had found him rental accommodation in Foxhollow and he had met Carol and liked her so much that he had willingly accepted her children as part of the package. He had been living happily with her and her kids ever since. The last year had been the best of his life so far and he was seriously thinking about putting down roots.

Williams had forgotten what people who stayed close to home were like. He still knew people he had grown up with in upstate New York who had stayed close to home. He realized it was only when you left home and travelled that you became "worldly", as they say. This guy, Wolf, was the normal one of the two of them, with his simple life. It was him who was now different. He had left home over a decade ago and become very independent, living a life that could in no way be termed simple. He had now become national, if not international, but had never really realized it, up until now. *Yes*, he thought, *this guy Wolf is the normal one, not me. It's true what they say about never being able to go home again.* Just as he was having this thought, they arrived at the resort.

It was getting late into the afternoon and Shelby had already consumed a hip flask of Scotch in an effort to try and keep warm. It was beginning to snow and get dark. He scanned the bleak snow-covered landscape along the northern edge of the base. Williams had obviously been delayed, but he figured they still had plenty of time to get their return flight. Right then, though, he needed to get back to the resort lodge before nightfall.

When Shelby got back to the lodge, he went up to his room, changed and went down to the lobby bar where he couldn't avoid getting into a conversation with the perky young barman. The barman said he had never seen him there before. Shelby's training had not included how to make small talk, which he had never been good at. He thought about it for a second or two, and said he was from Bismarck and hadn't come this far north to ski before and was meeting a friend down from Canada. The barman didn't pursue the fact Shelby was from Bismarck, as he was not from North Dakota himself and didn't know much about the cities in the state. Seeing Shelby was not much of a talker, he didn't bother with him anymore and got busy collecting empty glasses and loading them into the dishwasher.

Most people were still on the floodlit slopes and the resort was very quiet. Shelby could hear the old standard, "Moon River" playing, which took him back to his childhood when he was growing up a hundred miles or so south of here. Although he'd had a fairly normal upbringing, he felt that by living in Bismarck, he had missed out on the pop culture of the sixties. TV and radio had been the only way he could enjoy any of it. He remembered his parents often listened to tunes like this.

He had gone to the local schools, followed by college, up in Minnesota. He had majored in advertising and because he was naturally creative, had done very well. So well in fact, that he had been snapped up by a top advertising agency in New York City after graduation. When, a number of years later, an opportunity to work in their London office had come up, he'd jumped at the opportunity, thinking he could make up for the lost sixties. He remembered the words from a Roger Miller song, "England swings like a pendulum do," but instead, upon his arrival had found the city to be dirty, dingy and lacking in even basic amenities. He had thought to himself at the time. *You obviously had to have been here back then.*

Now as he sat there at the bar on a cold North Dakota winter afternoon, he just hoped that General Ulanov would be true to his word when they got back. His old life hadn't been so bad and if he hadn't decided to go to Moscow, he probably would have returned to the States once his current assignment had been completed. Anyway, now he hoped he would end up somewhere warm and tropical, with lots of toys. Although he knew he had been chosen to play a lesser role in the mission, he felt he had already made a significant contribution, flying and dropping Williams off, returning to the farm without incident and now being at the ski resort to meet up with Williams. He knew that the general had taken an immediate liking to Williams and that he was much more of a take-charge kind of person than himself. Only one of them could set the missile warhead detonation process in motion and it was fine with him that Williams had been chosen. He was now, however, starting to get concerned about Williams' whereabouts and wasn't quite sure what to do. He decided he would have another drink and if Williams hadn't shown up by the time he had finished it, he'd phone Major Trsenkov.

After finishing his drink and paying his bill, he phoned the farm from a public phone in the lobby, using the long distance calling card Major Trsenkov had given him. The major suggested he should go to his room in the resort and wait for Williams to show up. The major figured Williams would likely meet up with him very soon and asked Shelby to call him in an hour if he still hadn't shown up. Otherwise he would see them at the farm tomorrow. Shelby did as the major had suggested, went to his room and took a shower.

Red Shadows On Liberty's Soil

Major Trsenkov thought he would wait and see if Shelby phoned again before informing General Ulanov that Williams had not shown up at the resort yet. He knew that once the general heard there was a problem, he would spend a great deal of time analyzing all the possible scenarios and he wasn't feeling very well at the moment. He also knew from previous experience that he would only end up with more work to do. He had to be careful though, because if Williams didn't show up, the general would want to know why he hadn't been informed earlier. The major checked his watch; it was almost twenty minutes past four. He wondered what could have delayed Williams; surely he couldn't have been caught. Perhaps he'd hurt himself somehow or maybe everything had taken longer than planned. He began to think whether there was anything he could do. Should he send agents out to look for him? But given it was almost dark, it didn't make much sense to do this. He figured the best thing he could do was sit tight and wait and see if Shelby phoned again.

Biff was back behind the bar at Morgan's. His regular customers were all still there, discussing the Fuller brothers' flying saucer story. In a quiet moment, Biff called the local police station to inform them of Wolf's disappearance and ended up completing a missing persons report.

"You know, Mildred," he said to his wife, "Wolf is still out there somewhere. I don't think even the Martians could get the better of him. I'm sure he'll turn up, aren't you?"

Mildred, the ever-agreeing spouse, indicated her concurrence by nodding her head as she moved off to serve some newly arrived customers.

The lodge was quite an impressive structure, built from large logs with white caulking between them. It gave it the luxurious look of other lodges Williams had seen numerous times in travel magazines. It looked as if it could accommodate a significant number of overnight guests. As they made their way towards the entrance, Williams pointed to the large hunting knife strapped to his leg and said to Wolf, "I know you're a nice guy and all that, but cause me any trouble in here and I'll cut you real bad, no kidding. We're going to the bar as soon as we get inside."

They went in through the main entrance and over at the reception desk, they could see someone behind the counter, talking to a group of skiers. Williams looked like a nondescript appliance repairman, having ripped off all the Soviet paratrooper badges from his uniform. Wolf looked like a backwoodsman. The few people they could see were all wearing brightly coloured sweaters and pants. There was a full-sized stuffed bear just inside the door, which Wolf told Williams was a grizzly. To Williams, it was just a big bear; he couldn't tell the difference. Williams was amazed how big it was, at least eight feet high, with large, scary looking claws and teeth.

They manoeuvred their way through a number of wooden lacquered tables and chairs on the way to the bar. There were several moose and deer heads mounted on the wall behind the bar. They sat at the bar, facing the end wall of the lodge, with the lobby reception area at their backs. They were the only ones sitting at the long bar. There was a young barman behind the bar who seemed reluctant to serve them, until Williams smoothed him over, saying they were meeting someone and wouldn't be there long.

"I guessed you boys weren't here for the skiing, but as far as I know, we don't have a dress code," commented the bright-eyed barman. "What can I get you?"

Williams ordered two shots of whiskey and two beers and when they came, quickly downed his whiskey and took a sip of the beer. He reached into his backpack, brought out a hundred dollar bill and handed it to the barman, who didn't show any surprise at being handed such a large bill. Williams grabbed his backpack and when the barman came back with the change, picked it up leaving some small bills. He stood up, moved away from the bar and told Wolf he was going to the washroom. After going to the washroom, he went to the reception desk and asked which room Peter Shelby was staying in. The woman behind the desk said she couldn't give out that information, but if he would like to go over to one of the lobby phones, she could put him through to Mr. Shelby's room. Shelby answered the phone almost immediately.

"Guess who!" said Williams. "What's your room number?"

Williams quickly found the room. Shelby had lots of questions about what had delayed him.

"It took me hours to start the detonation countdown and get out of the silo, but we need to get out of here right away. Get your things and let's go!"

"But I thought we were staying here tonight?" said Shelby with a puzzled look.

"The situation has changed, we need to get out of here as quickly as we can, I'll explain the reason later".

On their way across the resort parking lot, Williams opened the hood of a truck and pulled a handful of wires and cables off their housings. He threw them into the back of the Bronco as he got in.

"That should slow him down."

"Who?" said Shelby.

"I'll tell you about that later too," said Williams laughing.

They left the ski resort driving north.

It seemed like a long time since the paratrooper had gone to the washroom and Wolf, having finished his whisky and beer, was wondering whether he should order another round, the paratrooper's beer was still almost full. He decided instead to go and look for him. He wasn't in the washroom and coming out, Wolf looked over to the bar and he still hadn't returned. He looked around the lobby and couldn't see him anywhere. After looking along each of the hallways leading from the lobby and still not seeing him, he went to the reception desk.

"Have you seen the guy in white coveralls that came in with me, a little while ago?" he asked the receptionist.

"Yes, I just saw him leaving with another man a few minutes ago. You might still be able to catch them," she said.

Wolf rushed out into the parking lot and saw a vehicle turning out into the road. It was dark, but he could tell it didn't have North Dakota license plates. He ran and jumped in his truck, but it wouldn't start. He got out, lifted the hood and saw that the battery cables were missing. He kicked one of the front tires, hurried back into the resort, found a phone and dialed 911. After giving his name, he was surprised when the operator told him he had been reported as a missing person. Wolf began to tell his story and the operator immediately interrupted him and told him someone would be coming out to the resort to speak with him very shortly.

When Williams and Shelby came to the first crossroads, they turned west. Williams reached into his backpack, took out a pill bottle, shook out some stamina pills and swallowed them. He asked Shelby if he wanted any and when he declined, put the bottle back into his backpack. Shelby asked him if they were going back to the farm. Williams said he didn't think it would be a good idea to cross the border right now, with a guy back at the resort who knew he'd been on the base. Shelby was very puzzled by this.

"Let's keep going west for now. I think we should try and find somewhere to stay for the night; we've still got plenty of time."

As Williams was changing into the ski clothes Shelby had brought for him, he was thinking about adding an additional twist to their current situation - picking up some women. They were passing through a small town when he noticed a country bar set back from the road.

"Can you do a U-turn? I think we should get off the road for awhile and the bar back there looks like it might be a good place to kill a few hours."

A few minutes later, they were walking towards the door of a bar that looked about as country as you could get. On the way through the door, Williams was telling Shelby why having women along with them could be of great help.

Not very long after Wolf had called 911, a police car arrived at the resort. Standing out in the parking lot, Wolf told the police officers about the flying saucer, the guy who had jumped him and left him to die, and who had forced him to bring him up here to the resort. He showed them the skis in the back of his truck and the ski shoes inside the truck's cab. Wolf told them that the paratrooper had thrown his automatic weapon and some other things into the trees along the side road on the way up to the resort. He told them that he had also thrown his hunting rifle into the trees and he was planning to go back to look for it when his truck had been repaired. One of the police officers told him if he found any of the things that had been thrown into the trees he should take them to the closest police station. The police officers asked Wolf to come into the resort with them. When they got inside, the officers asked the receptionist if someone had recently left the resort in a hurry, with another man. The receptionist confirmed that a man wearing coveralls had left in a hurry not long ago.

"He looked like some kind of repairman," chipped in the young bartender, who was cleaning off a nearby table.

"Him and that guy came in about an hour ago," he said, pointing at Wolf.

"Thanks; we may need to talk to you again later," said one of the police officers. The officers talked to the receptionist for awhile and then asked Wolf to come back out to the parking lot with them. They told him they were taking him to the local police station to put a description of his abductors together, and asked him to get in the back of their patrol car. Wolf told them he could only give them a description of the guy who had forced him to drive him up here. He said he hadn't seen the other person or their vehicle up close. He had only seen tail lights and an out-of-state license plate, but didn't see the number. The police officers ignored him and as they pulled out of the resort parking lot, one of them was talking into a citizens band radio, requesting a tow truck to come and pick up Wolf's truck.

As they came through the door, Williams and Shelby could see they were in an authentic country and western bar. There were bear, big horn sheep and a multitude of other wild animal heads mounted on the walls and a country and western singer was whaling out a sad tune on the jukebox. Williams rapidly took the place in and was surprised by the number of what seemed like unescorted women - at least five or six. Surely he and Shelby could get lucky in here, even though they seemed to have a problem based on the looks they were getting. It must have been obvious to everyone in the bar, that they were strangers, their bright ski clothes standing out from everyone else's drab jeans and leather jackets. Their clothes would have been fine at the ski resort, but here they looked totally out of place. Williams suggested that they should at least take their ski jackets off. He could see there were some really good things about the bar - no TV's, a loud juke box and a few people already dancing off to the end of the bar.

The bartender leaned over towards them and said, "You boys just passing through?"

"We're down from Canada, doing some skiing and partying," said Williams loudly, hoping that this would explain their inappropriate clothes to anyone within ear shot. Williams had become the spokesman for himself and Shelby, as Shelby normally shied away from interactions with other people. Williams didn't have a problem with this as he was naturally outgoing and enjoyed meeting people.

"Are there any motels close to here?"

"On the other side of town, you'll find the Moonlight," chipped in the sexy bartender's assistant.

"We'll check it out later, thanks," said Williams. "Two Buds please."

The cold beers were quickly passed their way.

"Cheers!" said Williams clinking Shelby's beer. "You know, I was just thinking, I don't remember any discussions with the general on what would happen if things really went wrong."

Shelby asked Williams what had happened to him since he had jumped out of the plane, which now seemed like a long time ago.

"Well, to say things got off to a bad start would be an understatement. The jump went well and I was setting off for the base when some guy hiding in the woods tried to jump me. Can you believe it? Someone was out there in the woods, at four in the morning? What was that all about? Anyway, I'd seen him while I was unpacking the supply package, so before he knew what hit him, I'd knocked him out cold. Later I found out he recovered."

"Surely General Ulanov hadn't arranged this?" said Shelby.

"No. This guy was a just a curious local."

Just then, three women who looked to be in their late twenties, came into the bar. They made their way to a vacant table next to the makeshift dance floor; one of them was extremely attractive.

Williams continued, "I got to the silo just about on schedule; however, that didn't go exactly as planned either. It turned out there was a maintenance crew inside. Because I had nowhere to hide outside, I foolishly entered the silo. In hindsight, I should have waited for them to leave and then gone in. When the crew left, they locked the only door in and out of the silo, on the outside. Setting the detonation process in motion went relatively smoothly, although I was pretty shaky and had a few problems. It was when I came to get out of the silo that I had major problems. I tried, but couldn't break out through the door. After about almost two hours, I finally managed to get out through a small opening at the top of the silo. I skied off the base and as I was squeezing through the perimeter fence, guess who was waiting for me? Yes, the same guy who had tried to jump me earlier in the morning. Eventually I got the better of him for a second time, getting a bloody nose and a nick above my left eye in the process, and forced him to bring me up to the resort."

"Who was this guy?" asked Shelby.

Williams continued "I don't have a clue. He said his name was Wolf. It turned out that he had seen the plane-flying saucer come over and hover, saw the parachutes open and wanted to find out what had landed. Gutsy guy really. Anyway, let's hope that's the last we've seen of him."

Little did Williams know that only a mile up the road from where they currently were, Wolf was on the phone talking to his girlfriend, telling her he was at the Tollesbury police station. While he was talking to her, he saw a tow truck, with his truck in tow, go past the window. Carol was telling him not to worry, Biff and the Fullers would be coming to get him. Once he got off the phone, he was given some forms and asked to write out a statement and provide a description of the paratrooper. As he was completing these, Biff and the Fullers came bursting into the police station and were told that Wolf would be with them soon.

When Wolf came out the interrogation room a few minutes later, he saw Biff and the Fullers. He handed the statement and description to the duty officer and asked if it would be alright if he left his truck overnight and he would come back and get it in the morning. The duty officer agreed and Wolf, Biff and the Fullers left.

Looking around the bar, Williams said, "Let's see if we can find someone to spend the night with." He asked Shelby to move along to end of the bar, closer to the makeshift dance floor. "So who do you fancy?"

"The sexy young girl behind the bar; how about you?" said Shelby laughing.

Williams checked his watch. They had been in the bar for almost an hour now and he figured it was time to make a move. He walked over to the table where the three recent arrivals were sitting and asked the attractive blonde if she would like to dance.

"No thank you, not right now. We're waiting for our drinks to come, but you and your friend are welcome to join us, if you like," she replied.

This friendliness surprised Williams and he waved to Shelby to come and join him while he was asking the people at the next table if he could take one of their chairs. Shelby, carrying their ski jackets, the backpack and beers, joined Williams at the table with the three women.

"Hi, I'm Gerry," said Williams.

"I'm Peter," said Shelby.

The women's drinks arrived and Williams asked the waitress to put them on his bill. He raised his beer saying "Cheers" and they all clinked their glasses and beers together.

The blonde said, "I'm Jill and these are my friends Sylvie and Vi. We rent a house together."

Vi didn't seem to be very tall; she had short black hair and a pale face. She was very well dressed in a black leather skirt and a white fluffy blouse. Sylvie appeared to be quite tall and slender and was wearing a tight-fitting slinky light blue dress. She had a friendly face and was quite animated when she talked. She seemed to be the glue between the women. Jill, a natural blond, was by far the most attractive, with a very pretty face and jaw-dropping cleavage displayed to its best advantage in a pink low cut wool sweater, accented with a short black skirt and a pair of black and white high heels with a fifties look to them.

None of the women looked very country and with Williams and Shelby sitting with them, their group looked out of place in comparison to everyone else in the bar. Williams, with his rugged good looks and five o'clock shadow, looked like one of the models who advertise men's grooming products. Shelby, with his handsome good looks, also stood out from the crowd. Their table looked like an island of chic in the middle of a sea of leather and denim.

Sylvie asked the men where they were from. Williams said they were down from Canada and had been skiing at the Ebdon ski resort and that they were planning to stay the night somewhere close by and head home in the morning. He said they were from Winnipeg, even though neither he nor Shelby knew much about the place. It seemed to be the closest big city up in Canada. This immediately led to some awkward moments when Vi said she had lived there at one time. Williams let Shelby answer the questions about where they lived and did they know so and so. Williams was thinking how clever General Ulanov had been to have sent them on the mission. Soviet agents would have stood out like fish out of water in a place like this.

Williams heard Roberta Flack starting to sing "Stromin' my pain with his fingers, singin' my life with his words" and whispered to Shelby that he should ask Sylvie to dance. He touched Jill's arm and asked her if she would dance because, he said, he really loved this song. She jumped up to dance. Shelby asked Sylvie and once they got on the dance floor found out she was a pretty good dancer.

When they sat back down and started talking again, Sylvie said the girls all worked together in the billing office of a local power company. Williams described himself as an investment advisor and Shelby as being in advertising. Jill said she could use some investment advice and Williams gave her a rudimentary overview of investment options, from savings accounts to speculative penny stocks and everything in between. Jill seemed most impressed with him.

Williams had to admit with her pretty face and voluptuous figure, Jill looked most enticing. Already after only the one dance, he knew she would do whatever he wanted, it seemed like she couldn't get enough of him. Shelby, on the other hand, being nowhere near as smooth as Williams, was struggling to make the right connection with Sylvie. His natural shyness wasn't helping the situation, but when they danced, she felt really good in his arms.

As the evening progressed, the bar filled up and the lights were dimmed. It was so busy now that Williams and Shelby were no longer being noticed. After several beers, Williams was beginning to feel light headed and realized he'd been up since two in the morning and hadn't eaten anything all day. He got the attention of one of the busy waitresses and ordered nachos for the table. Already knowing the chemistry was right between him and Jill, he now wanted to ensure Shelby got paired up with Sylvie. He had taken an immediate dislike to Vi and wondered if her name was short for Viper. Williams danced exclusively with Jill while Shelby danced alternately with Sylvie and Vi, much to William's annoyance. He noticed again how impeccably dressed Vi was and thought maybe she wasn't really that bad. They were sitting back at the table when Vi checked her watch and said she had to leave to meet someone and asked Jill and Sylvie if they would get ready to go.

"Are you girls leaving already?" asked Williams with emphasis, trying his best to act surprised and disappointed.

"Afraid so," said Sylvie. "We came in Vi's car."

"We could give you a ride if you like, right Pete?"

"How long are you guys staying?" enquired Jill.

"As long as you want," said Williams.

"Anyway, I really have to go," said Vi, putting her coat on.

Williams could see that Jill wanted to stay, but Sylvie wasn't sure. Jill, sensing the same thing, asked Vi if she could wait a minute and asked Sylvie to come to the washroom with her. When Jill and Sylvie returned, Jill told Vi that she and Sylvie would get a ride with Gerry and Peter. Vi, looking somewhat hurt, thanked Williams for the drinks, said her goodbyes and left.

Wolf, the Fullers and Biff drove straight to Morgan's, where Wolf's friends and neighbours were still gathered. Wolf told his story to anyone who was interested and although the Fullers and Biff had already heard it on the way back from the police station, they were listening just as intently as everyone else, hearing it for the second time.

"No, I wasn't abducted by Aliens; sorry to disappoint you all. Apparently I got mixed up in a military exercise, testing the base security. I never did find out why they were using an aircraft disguised as a flying saucer - all part of the testing, I guess. I did meet the paratrooper involved in the exercise, who thought I was there to stop him. I don't know if you know, but he knocked me out cold and I didn't come around for a number of hours. Another hour or so more and I could have died from exposure!"

Biff interrupted him. "You know, we went to the base looking for you and they didn't tell us anything about any exercise."

"Apparently, it was top secret," Wolf replied, "so they probably couldn't mention it or maybe they didn't even know about it.

"I waited around for a few hours and then met up with the paratrooper again as he came off the base and then took him up to the Ebdon ski resort. He said he had a de-briefing meeting there but soon after left with another man for some reason.

Biff interrupted him again. "Don't you think it's strange that he would be having a meeting about a top secret exercise at a public ski resort?

You'd think he'd be having the meeting on the base."

"Maybe he didn't want the base to know about it - he was testing the base security after all. Anyway, I'm here with you all now and no harm has come to me."

Carol noticed that Wolf's eyes were beginning to close and asked their next door neighbours if they could get a ride home with them. Biff told Carol that he would take Wolf to get his truck tomorrow morning before he opened the bar. Wolf and Carol left with their neighbours. The Fullers left right after them, saying they were tired too and needed an early night.

Less than a hundred miles from where Williams and Shelby were sitting in the country bar, Captain Bradley Wilcox was driving in through the main gates of Minot Air Force base. As he drove onto the base, he passed a large sign that read, "The Proud Home of the United States Air Force 5th Bomber Wing and 91st Missile Wing." He was working the ten-to-six shift that Saturday night. He always liked to get to work early, so he could have a coffee and a smoke before starting his shift. He was coming off two weeks' vacation and was in an excellent frame of mind. As one of the launch control facility operators, Wilcox had a security pass that allowed him to go anywhere on the base. Tonight he was working Charlie flight of Bravo squadron at the north end of the base. His job was quite mundane and very repetitive - the way you would expect a job to be after you'd been doing it for more than twenty years. He felt like a glorified night watchman, even though he was minding some of the most potent weapons ever invented by mankind. There were continuous checks to be done and frequent launch readiness tests, known to everyone on the base, as LRTs. The technology involved was now rather outdated and although the missiles were automatically monitored, operators were still required to note and report any anomalies. Significant incidents with the missiles had been very few and far between over the years, the most serious having been the first year the missiles were installed. A missile's main engines started up and it was in the process of lifting off before they were shutdown. Obviously, the initial LRTs had been a little too realistic and extensive damage was done to the almost launched missiles silo. There had also been a number of false alarms over the years, mainly due to feed pipes or sensors freezing up, but the almost-launch was the only real major incident. Wilcox, originally from Chicago, really enjoyed the outdoor activities North Dakota offered. During the fishing and hunting seasons he would go off with his friends into the remoter parts of the state for several days at a time. He found these trips to be very challenging and enjoyable. Although his job at the base was not particularly difficult, it was stressful, knowing the awesome power of the weapons for which he was responsible. A number of operators had cracked up over the years, becoming alcoholics or even committing suicide. Minot, North Dakota was a pretty god-forsaken place, especially during the cold winter months. Due to the lack of sun in the winter, it was almost as if night turned into night again. Although the Air Force paid these keepers of the peace very well, it was difficult to attract and keep people for very long at Minot. Wilcox was an exception.

Wilcox, like most operators, rotated through a different flight every week and a different squadron every two months. This allowed him to work each flight within a squadron at least once before taking two weeks off. He worked all five Minutemen squadrons and the new Peacekeeper squadron each year. This kind of schedule was fine with him. Although the launch control facilities were identical, each week tended to be different, depending on the LRTs that were scheduled. This week he and his partner were scheduled to perform a number of LRTs on the Charlie flight missiles. Upon his arrival at the Charlie flight launch control facility that night, he headed for the small lunch room. It had a sink, counter top, table, chairs, coffee making machine, microwave and a full size refrigerator. Hanging over the sink was a rack of coffee mugs, all bearing the insignia of SAC. Wilcox poured himself a cup of coffee, sat down and was just lighting up a cigarette, when his partner, Captain Mike Green, strode through the door.

"Hi Mike, how are you tonight?" asked Wilcox.

"Good, thanks. Did you hear they're having all kinds of problems with the new control system over at the new Peacekeeper squadron? One of the operators told me they almost let one off last week. Some kind of software glitch."

Wilcox said he hadn't heard anything.

Green poured himself a cup of coffee, sat down opposite Wilcox and asked him what was on the agenda tonight.

"LRTs with SAC."

"Great!" said Green sarcastically. "That's all we need, those geeks from SAC breathing down our necks."

"They're only doing their job," replied Wilcox.

Williams and Shelby danced Jill and Sylvie through a marathon of sad country love songs until Sylvie said she wanted to leave to catch one of her favourite sitcoms. Shelby and the two women put their coats on and made their way out to the icy parking lot. Williams stayed behind to pay the bill and then joined them. The others were already in the Bronco when Williams caught up with them. Sylvie was in the front with Shelby, so Williams joined Jill in the back.

"Hey, why don't we get some beer and go over to the Moonlight Motel?" Williams suggested. "I understand it isn't far from here and I'm sure they have TV's in every room."

"Sounds like fun to me," said Jill, squeezing Williams' arm. "It's still quite early."

Sylvie said she still wanted to go home.

Williams nudged Jill.

"Oh come on Sylvie, let's have a little more fun tonight," Jill said.

Sylvie thought about it for a few moments and reluctantly agreed, saying "Can we hurry then, so I don't miss my show?"

"Great!" said Williams and asked Jill if there was a gas station on the way.

Jill said she thought there was one just up the road. Sure enough, it was about a mile up the road, next to a police station. Williams ran in and grabbed two six packs of beer.

When they got to the motel, Williams went into the office and paid in advance for two adjoining rooms for one night. When they got into one of the rooms, Sylvie ran over, turned the TV on and flipped the dial until she found her show. Williams gave Shelby a plastic ice bucket and asked him if he would mind going to get some ice.

"What would you ladies like to drink? A beer or a beer or a beer?" asked Williams jokingly.

"Beer please," they both shouted.

"Two beers coming right up! I think you'll need to drink right out of the can - the plastic glasses in the bathroom are real small."

Both women said the can would be fine and Williams pulled two off the plastic carrying ring, passing one to Jill. He walked over to where Sylvie was sitting and handed her the other one. Just then, Shelby came back with the ice and Williams put the remaining cans into the sink in the bathroom and threw the ice on top of them. He handed Shelby a beer and got one for himself. Shelby went and sat at the end of one of the beds next to Sylvie and Williams bounced onto the bed next to Jill, hitting her can with his saying, "Cheers!"

"You know, if I'd thought about it, I would have bought a pack of cards," said Williams.

Turning around, Sylvie said, "I don't play cards."

"So how about we just talk?"

"You go ahead," said Sylvie. "I'm watching my show, thank you."

Jill asked Williams if he'd ever been skiing around there before and he said he hadn't.

Shelby, being more forward than usual, whispered to Sylvie that when the next commercial came on would she like to watch TV in the other room with him.

A few minutes later, as Shelby and Sylvie were approaching the adjoining room door, Williams said, "We need you ladies to stay with us tonight. I promise we'll take good care of you. Pete obviously can't drive anymore - he's had too much to drink."

"We can get a taxi," responded Sylvie immediately.

"No, you are staying with us tonight, end of discussion," said Williams firmly.

Sylvie burst into tears.

"Look," said Williams, "Don't make this harder than it already is."

Sylvie moved towards the door and said, "Oh no? Just watch me."

Williams jumped up, blocking her way and pulled his pistol out of his backpack. Pointing it at her he shouted, "Move away from the door or I'll shoot you and I'm not kidding!"

Sylvie backed away staring at Williams in horror.

"Now ladies please try and relax. We don't want to hurt you," said Williams.

He reached down, pulled his sheathed hunting knife out and handed it to Shelby, saying, "Here. If she tries anything, cut her."

Shelby and Sylvie, who was still in shock, went into the adjoining room.

Jill is amazing, thought Williams. *She doesn't seem to care at all about what's going on; it seems all she wants is sex!*

When they got into their room, Shelby apologized to Sylvie and asked her if she would stop crying.

"I don't care who you people are; just don't hurt us," said Sylvie, still weeping.

Shelby turned on the TV, found her show and she calmed down. After about half an hour there was a knock on the adjoining room door.

"Can I come in?" asked Williams.

Shelby opened the door.

"Here" said Williams, handing them each a can of beer. "Sylvie, I'm sorry, but you will have to be tied up" he said, ripping long strips from a linen bed sheet.

"Why don't you let me tie her up?" said Shelby.

"Sure, no problem," Williams said, handing the bed sheet and the strips he had already ripped off to Shelby. "You take care of it."

Through the open adjoining room doors, Shelby could see Jill lying on the bed, with her hands and feet tied together. He figured Williams had already had his way with her and he was beginning to really dislike him.

"Goodnight. Sweet dreams," said Williams, leaving the room.

After finishing her beer, Sylvie said, "I'm ready to go to bed."

"Where do you want me to sleep?" asked Shelby.

"With me and will you please make love to me before you tie me up? You seem like such a nice man," she whispered.

"If this is a trick, forget it. I have the knife right here," said Shelby, waving it in the air.

"No, I mean it! I promise I won't try anything," pleaded Sylvie.

They both got undressed, slid into bed and turned off their bedside lights.

It was exactly ten o'clock on Saturday night when Captains Wilcox and Green took over from the two operators at the Charlie flight launch control facility.

At the same time Wilcox and Green were starting their shift over at the base headquarters building, Technical Sergeant Sven Jacobsen was completing his. Jacobsen worked in the scheduling department and was responsible for planning the launch readiness testing rotations. He had made a number of subtle scheduling changes over the last several months to ensure that the missile in one of the northernmost silos, Bravo Charlie missile number four, would not be undergoing LRTs during the time that Major Trsenkov's software modifications were being made. He thought the major would be very pleased with the work he'd done. Jacobsen had been recruited while he was on a fishing trip up in Canada several years earlier. He had met the major at a time in his life when he had been at his lowest. He had been taking the trip to try and take his mind off his serious financial problems. He had even contemplated committing suicide but had been too chicken. He knew that running into the Soviet major had not been a chance encounter and later learned that the Soviets had been trying to find someone on the base to work with them for quite a while.

The launch control facility where Wilcox and Green worked was shaped like a hexagon, with distinctly different compartments. Two of the compartments had identical racks containing rows of switches and small status lights. There were multiple phones on either side of these racks. The controls in these compartments would be used in the event the order was received to launch missiles. Both operators would enter the launch codes simultaneously. There were also test simulators and control equipment in these compartments. The two adjacent compartments were taken up with all kinds of gauges, small and large. These were visually monitored on a continuous basis to ensure any malfunctions with any of the missiles or associated equipment were immediately noted and reported. The remaining two compartments were usually locked and contained the controls that would be used once the missiles had been launched. Each launch control facility had the capability to launch any flight of missiles on the base, to ensure that if a particular launch control facility was taken out by an enemy strike, its missiles could still be launched. During their shift that night, Wilcox and Green would be performing LRTs on Bravo Charlie missile number one. They were early into their shift when the phone rang and Wilcox was informed that a maintenance crew had discovered that Bravo Charlie missile number four's silo had been infiltrated. The head of base security told Wilcox that the maintenance crew would be phoning in again soon with another update. He told him that all LRTs were to be suspended indefinitely. Wilcox informed Green, and the engineers from SAC working with them, about the news.

Sunday February 14

Further examination of Bravo Charlie missile number four's silo in the early hours of Sunday morning revealed that the main silo cover's hydraulics and a small silo service cover had been damaged.

The automatic wake-up message on the phone in Williams' motel room rang and rang just after six o'clock Sunday morning. He eventually answered it and although he felt dog tired, dragged himself out of bed. He walked over and banged on the adjoining room door, shouting that it was time for Shelby and Sylvie to get up. Jill, woken by Williams' shouts, looked over at the clock and asked why they were getting up so early.

"Pete and I have a plane to catch," said Williams moodily.

"What?"

Williams realized he'd goofed and said, "Don't worry about it. I'm going to take a quick shower; then I'll untie you and you can use the bathroom."

Sylvie, woken by the banging and shouting, asked Shelby what time it was. Shelby said he didn't know but felt as if he'd just gotten off to sleep. "Sit tight. I'm sure Gerry will be in here very soon telling us exactly what to do."

"What do you mean? What to do?" asked Sylvie. "I thought you were taking us home today?"

"Just relax" said Shelby.

The shower in William's room stopped and a few minutes later there was a knock on the adjoining door.

"Can I come in?" asked Williams.

"Hold on" said Shelby, as he moved to unlock the door.

Williams burst into the room dripping wet with a towel wrapped around his waist. "Get ready. You've got time to take showers if you like."

"Why are we getting up so early?" asked Sylvie.

"You'll find out soon enough," said Williams, leaving the adjoining room door open as he left the room.

A few minutes later, Williams came back into their room fully dressed and asked Shelby for the keys to the Bronco. Shelby grabbed them off the bedside table and tossed them to him. Sylvie couldn't see Jill, but could hear the shower going in the other room. She saw Williams carrying a pile of folded sheets and blankets across the room and heard the room door open. This puzzled her greatly.

Within an hour they had left the motel. Williams still believed that the authorities would not be looking for two couples. Once they turned out onto the highway, Williams waved his large hunting knife at the women and told them he would use it if they didn't keep quiet if they were stopped by the police.

"Why would we be stopped by the police?" asked Sylvie.

"I heard there are two escaped convicts on the run," said Williams.

Sure enough, within ten minutes they came to a police roadblock. The state trooper could see that their vehicle had province of Manitoba license plates. He approached the driver's side of the Bronco and asked Shelby where he was headed and where he was coming from. Shelby said they were on their way back to Canada and had been visiting some friends in Minot. When asked where they were from in Canada, Shelby said Winnipeg. The trooper put his head in the window and asked Williams and the women if they were also from Winnipeg and they all said they were. This seemed acceptable to the impeccably dressed trooper and he let them pass through the roadblock.

At first light on Sunday morning, two of Base Commander Maty's senior officers went to inspect the damaged silo. They found there were already a number of people inside when they got there. They were shown the damage to the main silo cover hydraulics and could see that a lot of oil had dripped onto the missile's nosecone. They learned that an axe had been used to do the damage and were told the cover couldn't be opened until the hydraulics had been repaired. They were shown the hole where a smaller cover had been removed and were also shown the newly installed alarm override panel, which had obviously been installed to stop alarm alerts from being sent, but nobody knew why yet.

Major Scott Waltham and Lieutenant Colonel Graham Smith left the silo and began to look for any clues the intruders may have left outside. They made their way to the silo security fence and found the metal frame surrounding a hole in the fence. They soon figured out that it had allowed someone to crawl through without setting off any alarms. *Quite ingenious!* thought Waltham. Close by, they found an empty orange garbage bag partially buried in the snow. They put on their ski equipment and began to follow a single set of ski tracks. After following the tracks for miles, they reached the base perimeter fence. They skied along beside it until they found a hole cut in the fence. The tracks they had followed seemed to indicate that there had only been one skier on the base. On the other side of the fence it was a different story. There were numerous footprints and fresh tire tracks in the snow. It seemed the skier had been picked up by an accomplice. Before setting off, Waltham had arranged for a base security patrol vehicle to pick him and Smith up and within fifteen minutes, it had arrived.

Red Shadows On Liberty's Soil

It was now just after seven o'clock in the morning and Williams knew they would be coming to the border soon. He'd already decided the border could be a completely different proposition from a police roadblock. They might be allowed to go through without incident because they were couples but any other scenario could mean big trouble. The women probably had identification, but this would be confusing because they were Americans. Also, who knew what they would say if they were questioned individually? And what would they do with the women once they got across the border? Williams didn't think they could take the gamble and started to look for a trail leading into the forest. They hadn't gone far when they passed one and he asked Shelby to do a U-turn and take the trail into the woods, to his surprise. As they drove down the trail, numerous leafless tree limbs brushed against the Bronco's windows. Once the trail began to narrow, Williams asked Shelby to stop. Using strips of bed sheets, Williams tied the women's hands and feet together. While he was doing this, he asked Shelby to lay blankets out on the ground in front of the Bronco. Jill was her usual calm self and Williams thought he would really have liked to have spent more time with her. Sylvie, on the other hand, was pleading with Shelby not to leave them there. Williams carried them one at a time and laid them down on the blankets and Shelby covered them up as best he could. Williams told the women that once he and Shelby had crossed the border into Canada, they would let the authorities know where they were, so they shouldn't worry too much.

As they backed up along the trail, Williams told Shelby he was dumping the women because he didn't know what they'd do or say at the border. Shelby didn't look happy and knew now that he definitely didn't like Williams. Seeing the unhappy look on Shelby's face, Williams said, "Don't worry. They'll be fine; they're warmly dressed, covered with blankets and it's not supposed to snow until tonight."

They soon reached the border and were informed by the border guard that all vehicles with out-of-state license plates were required to check in with Canadian Immigration and Customs and asked them to drive over to the

Customs building. Williams, knowing they couldn't be detained because the authorities would have a description of him by now, leaned over and quietly whispered to Shelby that they needed to get out of there pronto. Shelby, although reluctant, launched the Bronco into the wooden barrier blocking their way, splintering it into pieces and sped off up the hill leading away from the border crossing. They were definitely on the run now and every cop in the area would soon be looking for them. Now that they were in Canada, Williams wondered if the US authorities could touch them. They had only traveled a few miles when they could see flashing lights up ahead in the distance. Williams figured it was probably a police roadblock and the border police could only be minutes behind them. He asked Shelby to take the next trail into the woods that they came to. They soon reached one and Shelby drove down it, over several large fallen tree branches, crossing a frozen creek. The trail came to an abrupt end, overlooking a spectacular view of massive rocks on the side of a deep gorge. Williams told Shelby to back up and drive along beside the frozen creek. They came to an overhanging weeping willow and Williams told Shelby to drive under it, stop and turn the engine off. Under the willow tree, the Bronco was well hidden from the trail.

Two border police patrol cars had reached the police roadblock and were being informed by Canadian police that no vehicles coming north from the border had been stopped. The Canadian police told them that several minutes earlier they had seen headlights approaching from the south off in the distance, but they had disappeared. While they were talking, another Canadian police car arrived. Officer Gettis, who seemed to be in charge, said he would check the trails between there and the border and suggested the border police, return there in case they were needed. He asked the newly arrived police officers to take over the roadblock.

Williams and Shelby had been parked, talking quietly for almost twenty minutes, and had not seen or heard anything. Shelby was concerned that they were running out of time to get back to the farm.

Officer Gettis was following the fresh tire tracks on the trail Williams and Shelby had recently driven down until he was stopped by a fallen branch. Not being able to get over it in the police car, he backed up the trail and stretched out several lengths of yellow *Police Line Do Not Cross* tape across the entrance. He called dispatch and asked them to arrange to have some heavy moving equipment sent to where he was located as soon as possible.

After waiting another ten minutes or so, Williams and Shelby agreed that if they were going to get to the farm on time, they needed to keep moving. Shelby drove out from under the willow tree in the opposite direction from the trail and almost immediately found his path blocked by a rotting tree trunk.

"Let's start hiking. They'll be looking for the Bronco anyway, not us," said Williams, grabbing his backpack.

They made their way over numerous fallen trees, following the winding creek northward. Williams knew they needed to get to the road and hitch a ride.

At the Tollesbury police station just after nine o'clock on that Sunday morning, Wolf had discovered that so many cables and wires had been ripped from under the hood of his truck, he would need to have it repaired by a mechanic. He told the duty officer he would have to arrange to have it towed to a service station in Foxhollow and asked if he could use the phone.

As they came out of the woods, Shelby mentioned that they needed to call the police about the women. Williams, somewhat agitated, said he hadn't forgotten, but there didn't seem to be telephone out here in the woods. After standing in the trees off to the side of the road for quite a while, they heard a truck approaching from the north. A huge logging truck came barrelling around the bend, heading straight towards them. Although it was heading south, Williams figured it might be the only chance they might have of getting a ride before the police caught up with them.

"Quick, go down like you're hurt!" said Williams. "I'll try to get him to stop."

Williams ran out into the road, in front of the approaching truck, waving his arms wildly. He immediately heard the *pssst* sound as the truck's air brakes were applied and heard the rumbling sound coming from it's chassis as it came to a stop further up the road. Williams sprinted to it, climbed up onto the running board and opened the truck's heavy passenger door. He told the burly tough-looking driver that his friend was hurt and needed medical attention and asked if they could get a ride to the nearest town. The driver told him to hurry up and Williams waved to Shelby to come and join him. Shelby limped as quickly as he could to the truck and Williams pulled him up into the cab beside him.

Waltham and Smith reported their findings to Base Commander Maty. The base commander said he was concerned about the damage to the main silo cover and during their debriefing, phoned the Minot police chief explained the situation to him and told him where to start the search for those responsible for damaging the silo on the base. The base commander informed his officers that while they were gone, there had been an incident at the border crossing directly north of the base which might well be connected to the break-in.

By now Officer Gettis, with the help of a bulldozer, had located the deserted Bronco and phoned in the Manitoba license plate number. He had found what looked like two overnight bags, ski equipment, some white coveralls, some cables and a pair of work boots in the back of the Bronco. The Bronco had been traced to a car rental company in Winnipeg and the records showed that it had been rented several days earlier by a Mr. Davis, whose address in Brandon, Manitoba didn't exist. Gettis arranged for a tow truck to come and take the Bronco in for a forensics examination. He had followed two sets of footprints in the snow out to the forest road and it looked like whoever they belonged to had hitched a ride south. He guessed by now he was several hours behind them, whoever they were.

At the border crossing, Williams and Shelby could see a lot of commotion. Outside one of the buildings there were six or seven police cruisers parked at different angles, all with different emblems and lettering on their sides. There were two covered army trucks parked to one side of the police cars and a number of the soldiers were standing smoking and talking.

The logging truck driver indicated to the border guard that he had a passenger who needed medical attention and was told to go and check over at the US Customs building. The driver checked with Customs and it turned out that the closest emergency facility was ironically in Minot. So that's where they were headed, until Williams spotted a motel up ahead and asked the driver to drop them off there. Williams said he would ice his friend's injury and get a taxi to the hospital in Minot if it didn't get any better. The logging truck driver obliged him even though he felt somewhat put out and dropped them off outside the Elk Motel.

As soon as they got into their room, Williams phoned 911 and told the operator where to find the women. When he was asked for his name, he said, "You need to find them as quickly as possible," and hung up. Shelby hoped the women would be alright and wondered if there might have been any wild animals in the woods. He didn't think Williams had thought about that or likely cared. He remembered there were many wild animal heads mounted on the walls of the country bar they had been in the night before. He was still very unhappy about the way Williams had treated the women. He turned on the TV and could only get two snowy channels, one showing "I Love Lucy" and the other "The Beverly Hillbillies".

"Should we phone the farm?" asked Shelby.

"No. I don't think that would be a good idea. I think the mission plan will have changed by now. They will probably already know that the police authorities are looking for us. I know how people like them think; they will want us dead now. There is no way we can go back to Moscow now. But this might be the best thing that could have happened to us. Do you really think General Ulanov would have set us up for life, in a place of our choosing, anywhere in the world? I've thought about that a great deal and it wouldn't have happened. It is much more likely they would have shot and buried us right where we'd been killed."

"You're probably right. If they could force us to do this, they could do anything to us," agreed Shelby.

Technical Sergeant Sven Jacobsen had arranged to meet with Major Trsenkov on Sunday morning at a family restaurant several miles south-west of the farm. He had crossed the border into Canada, at a different border crossing from Williams and Shelby, without incident and was already in the restaurant when the major came in and sat down opposite him. The major didn't appear to be very happy, which disappointed Jacobsen because he thought he had done a good job.

Major Trsenkov passed Jacobsen an envelope under the table and whispered, "I'm sure you will be very pleased with our generosity, but please don't open the envelope until you get home."

Jacobsen stashed the envelope inside his jacket. They talked about the news and weather for several minutes, after which the major got up and left the restaurant. A few minutes later, Jacobsen was out in the parking lot unlocking his car when he suddenly felt a terrible pain in his side. He had been shot twice from close range with a gun with a silencer. He dropped his car keys, went limp and was caught as he fell by two of Major Trsenkov's agents. They dragged him over to the major's dark sedan and dumped him in the trunk. Before he closed it, the major reached inside Jacobsen's jacket and removed the envelope he had just given him. He knew

Jacobsen was just starting his days off from work and lived alone, so it would be awhile before anyone missed him. His body was going to be taken to the farm and buried. An agent driving Jacobsen's car followed the dark Lincoln sedan out of the restaurant parking lot.

When the Americans failed to show up at the farm, it presented a dilemma for Major Trsenkov because it had been planned that he would be joining them on their return trip to Moscow. General Ulanov apparently wanted the major back in Moscow in the aftermath of the explosion. The major phoned the general with the news. General Ulanov asked him to change his flight to tomorrow and rang off.

Soviet agents monitoring local police transmissions already knew about the incident at the border and figured it had to be Shelby's Bronco as it was too much of a coincidence not to be. Some agents had already been dispatched to find out what they could about where the Americans might be. They were dressed like hunters and when they stopped at the police roadblock just north of the border, were surprised how much information they were able to gain about the ongoing search for the two men who had crashed the border. It seemed they had abandoned the Bronco in the woods, just north of the border and had hitched a ride south. This new information was quickly relayed back to the farm.

In addition to Jacobsen, the Soviets had informants working in the North Dakota highway patrol central dispatching office and the Minot police department. They had already reported that the damaged silo had been discovered. These informants had been singled out as being most vulnerable to threats to their loved ones and were under threat that one or more of their family members would be harmed if they didn't cooperate.

Sunday afternoon, after reading Wolf's statement and speaking with the officers who had brought him in, Tollesbury Police Chief Gordy Wilkins, commented that he wasn't sure about the flying saucer at the beginning but thought the end seemed real enough, as there was no other plausible explanation for this guy to be at the Ebdon ski resort. In addition, some of the resort employees had seen both him and the man in the coveralls. One of his officers phoned the base and informed them about Wolf's statement and was told the information would be passed on to the base commander. As it turned out, it would be several days before Base Commander Maty would get the message and by then he knew all about the problems with Bravo Charlie missile number four.

At the Elk Motel, when the six o'clock news came on, there was no mention of anything going on at the Air Force base. The lead story was about a homicide in a downtown Minot hotel the night before. Some other nondescript news was followed by the local weather forecast.

While Williams and Shelby were watching the news, a state trooper was in the Elk Motel office asking the owner who was staying there. The trooper learned that two men had checked in a few hours earlier and were the only ones currently staying there. He asked the owner to call the police station if the two men showed any signs of leaving.

Upon returning to the station, the trooper reported the information to the duty officer. Knowing the Elk Motel was situated very close to the border crossing where an incident had occurred earlier in the day, the duty officer insisted an arrest warrant be obtained to bring the two men in for questioning. A patrol car was dispatched to get a warrant for the arrest of the two men on suspicion of crashing the border.

At the Elk Motel, Williams and Shelby were discussing their next move.

"We obviously need to get as far away from here as we can, as quickly as we can," said Williams.

"You know," said Shelby, "I'm getting to know this area pretty well. I've been through the same border crossing three times in the last two days. We could go to my parents' place; they only live about a hundred miles south of here."

"Think about it; do you really want to get your parents mixed up in this? I'm pretty sure the general's men are trying to catch us to kill us. Do you want your parents killed too?"

"I thought I could warn them about the explosion," said Shelby.

"Nobody can know about it, not even your parents. Its better they don't know and especially about your involvement in the whole thing!"

"Who are you to decide this?" said Shelby angrily.

"All I'm saying is, this is our problem, nobody else's. Let's keep it that way. Your parents should be fine. Why didn't you mention them before?"

"It only just occurred to me," said Shelby, still angry.

"Check with them after the explosion." said Williams. "So we agree, we don't want to go south towards the base and we don't want to go north through the border crossing again, so it just leaves east or west. I personally think west is our best bet, because it's much less populated. Are you alright with this?"

"I guess so," said Shelby sulkily. "Should we take the interstate?"

"No, I don't think that would be a good idea because it's where the highway patrol is much more likely to be and if we break down for any reason, they're more likely to locate us. I think we're better staying on the local roads and highways."

"What about the weather forecast we just saw? Do you think we should be setting off when there's so much snow forecast?"

"We don't have a choice. If we don't keep moving, either the police or the Soviets will catch up with us. I'm sure of it. If the weather conditions are bad, it will be the same for everyone. I'll go and see if I can find us some wheels," Williams said, leaving to go to the motel office.

Just after seven o'clock on Sunday evening, Williams and Shelby set off on the journey westward. Williams had made the motel owner an offer he couldn't refuse, paying him two thousand dollars for a pickup truck that wasn't worth more than a few hundred. After leaving the motel, they filled up at the first gas station they came to. The motel owner had told Williams the truck was great on gas and he sure hoped so. He had given Williams directions west and they soon reached State Highway 5. It was snowing heavily now and visibility was reduced due to the blowing snow.

Once the truck he had sold to the two strangers had pulled out of the motel parking lot, the owner phoned the number the trooper had left him. Very soon afterwards, two state troopers arrived and were not at all happy when they heard the men had already left the motel. They took descriptions of the two of them and the particulars of the truck. They radioed in the information on the suspects and the vehicle, and an All Points Bulletin was immediately put out to the highway patrol. They were asked to be on the lookout for a dark blue, half ton, GMC Cheyenne pickup, license plate number DGTYH.

At the same time the state police learned that Williams and Shelby had left the Elk Motel, so did Major Trsenkov's agents, monitoring local police communication frequencies.

Shelby was not very impressed with the old pickup truck Williams had purchased. The bench seat's upholstery was ripped and springs were pushing through everywhere. It also sounded like the muffler or tail pipe had a hole in it.

"How far do you think we'll be able to get in this old crate?"

"The guy at the motel said it had been a great runabout truck and had never let him down."

"I hope he's right, because if it breaks down, we could be in big trouble."

"Let's cross that bridge when we get to it and anyway don't you know by now my middle name is Trouble? Why don't you try and get some rest so you'll be able to take over the driving later."

"I'll try, but it's a pretty bumpy ride and look at the foam and springs pushing up through everywhere!"

"Yea, I know," said Williams "but these were the only wheels he was willing to sell me. Try not to let it bother you. Think about something enjoyable, like your old girlfriend."

Shelby did exactly what Williams had suggested and began to think about Christina. He wondered what she was doing. For sure it wouldn't be snowing where she was, but it could well be raining though. That was one thing he really didn't like about London; it always seemed to be raining and often drizzled for days. It really restricted the things you could do outside and it was almost impossible to plan any kind of outdoor event. He thought about the parties he used to go to with Christina. She was always telling interesting stories about when she was growing up in Italy, where, from what he could tell, it rarely rained. He was in the middle of remembering one of her stories about jumping off high cliffs into the sea, when sleep overtook him. Williams was pleased when he heard Shelby starting to snore.

It was snowing really hard and Williams was finding it difficult to see past the large snowflakes hitting the windshield. The wipers weren't clearing the windshield very well and were leaving smears of frozen ice. He tried to tune in the radio, but only got noisy static all the way across the dial. He figured either the antenna or the radio must be broken. Shelby had been right about the seat; he could feel something pushing up into his backside and had to move around to find a more comfortable spot. He thought to himself that, with the weather conditions being so bad, it was unlikely anyone would find them out on the roads tonight. He couldn't get the planned detonation out of his mind, but thought for sure he and Shelby would be forgotten once the mushroom cloud appeared high in the prairie sky.

As they drove west through the raging blizzard, the truck seemed to be holding up well despite Shelby's concerns. It did seem to be good on gas, the temperature gauge was consistently in the normal position and the engine was running smoothly. On the downside, the heater, although working, wasn't keeping the cab very warm. The seat wasn't very comfortable and he couldn't get anything on the radio. Shelby woke up just as they were driving into a gas station at the North Dakota-Montana state border. Williams had been driving for almost four hours and asked Shelby if he'd take over once they had filled up.

As they left the gas station with Shelby driving he could hear Williams snoring softly and realized the driving was up to him now, so he'd have to concentrate. It was still snowing heavily and the visibility was very poor. As he drove on into the night, he occasionally lost control of the back end of the truck and had to slow down until it righted itself. The tires were probably bald and there was no weight over the back axle to help with the traction. If he kept at around fifty-five miles per hour, he found the truck was more stable. They were now in the state of Montana and it seemed to be snowing even heavier, if that was possible. Shelby was also glad that they seemed to be the only vehicle on the road that night.

Just before midnight, information was received at the farm that some agents down from Canada had spotted the beaten-up old truck they had been watching out for at the North Dakota-Montana state border. The Canadian agents had been getting coffee at a gas station, when they noticed an old dark blue Cheyenne pickup truck pull in. Although the license plate was obscured by a build-up of snow and ice, they figured there could only be one of these trucks out on the road tonight. Major Trsenkov told them to just follow it.

Monday February 15

As Sunday turned into Monday, Shelby continued to drive west along State Highway 5, until it ended at a place called Scottly. He turned south and drove through a maze of snow-covered county and unpaved roads until he reached State

Highway 2, near the town of Glastonby. The snow had almost stopped now and he was able to gradually increase his speed.

Early Monday morning, Major Trsenkov phoned General Ulanov to update him about Jacobsen and the Americans; it was just after nine on Monday morning in Moscow. The general was pleased to hear the news about Jacobsen and said he was confident that the Americans would soon also be dealt with. After the major told him the Americans were heading west, the general asked him to change his plans and follow them west and kill them. He told the major to make sure he got far enough west to ensure he wouldn't be affected by the explosion later in the day. The change in plan was most acceptable to Major Trsenkov, as he now had the opportunity to ask all the agents within a wide area of the base to head west to assist him in the search. This would take them all out of harm's way also.

Once he got off the phone with Major Trsenkov, General Ulanov phoned Major Khotov in Havana, even though he knew it was already after midnight there. When the major answered, the general explained the situation to him and told him to take the next available flight back to Moscow. Since arriving in Cuba, Khotov and the attractive flight attendant had seen the sights of Havana and had made a very attractive couple. Major Khotov said he would look into the available flights first thing in the morning. The general wished him a good flight home and hung up.

While Major Trsenkov was discussing the best way to go west with Sam and Anton, General Ulanov phoned him and told him that he had just been given full authority over all of the Soviet agents in North America, so now the major had them all at his disposal. The major thanked him, hung up and went back to planning his trip. He was concerned about crossing the border south of the farm because they would be carrying all kinds of weapons and he was worried their vehicle would be searched as it was not already on file. Sam suggested they stay in Canada and travel west as far as they could before entering the United States. He said this would be faster anyway, because the roads in Canada were better. So it was agreed.

Although the Soviet intelligence agency, the KGB, was aware of General Ulanov's mission, it was not until it started to go wrong that they asked to get directly involved. When they found out that the Americans would not be returning to Moscow, they contacted the general. He updated them on the current situation and suggested they call Major Trsenkov and ask him how they could assist him in tracking the Americans down. The general provided the telephone number at the farm.

Just as Major Trsenkov was about to leave the farm, early Monday morning, a senior KGB officer phoned him and told him the KGB would be assisting him to find the Americans. The officer asked the major to keep him updated on his progress.

The call from the KGB was not a welcome development for the major. His previous dealings with the KGB or the Committee for State Security, the Komitet Gosudarstevannoy Besopasnosty, had not been good. He knew they already had a file on him and this situation could well result in another black mark against his name. That is, unless the nuclear explosion still occurred as planned. Having to keep the KGB updated was an additional chore he didn't need right now. The fact that the Americans were on the run was not as a result of anything he had or had not done, but it wouldn't matter in the end. All he knew was that Williams had been delayed, and for some reason the Americans had crashed the border north of the base.

That the KGB had a file on him was not unusual. They had files on many citizens who had come to their attention when, supposedly, investigating matters of national security. The major's file had been clean up until an incident about ten years ago. Sitting in the back of the Lincoln on his way west, the major recalled the incident that had happened almost a decade ago, like it was only yesterday. He had been working on another assignment for General Ulanov that had gone badly wrong. He was dealing with a senior engineer from a top secret military weapons manufacturing facility in Wisconsin. The engineer had been providing specifications for a new, ship-launched missile called the Tomahawk. The new missile was planned to be used by the United States Navy. It could carry a nuclear warhead and deliver its payload with pinpoint accuracy. The major was meeting with the engineer for the third time, in a downtown Chicago hotel, which, if he remembered, was called the Ambassador. Because this was the engineer's third delivery of top secret information, he was expecting to be paid. So far he had not been paid for any of the information he had provided. At the last meeting, the major had foolishly promised him that he would definitely be paid next time. The major had told the general that he thought the engineer was unstable and that they should at least give him some money. The general had argued that he still needed more detailed information before he would pay out the thousands of dollars the engineer was asking for. When the engineer found out that the major didn't have any money for him this time, he became very angry and screaming obscenities kicked out at a closet door, making a large hole in it at the bottom.

"Calm down!" said the major.

"Why don't you have the money?" demanded the engineer.

"My superiors want more detailed information, before giving you any money. I am very sorry."

"Sorry, is that all you can say? I'm risking my life coming here and all you can say is sorry?" The engineer threw the papers he had brought with him all over the room.

"Calm down! I know you're upset," said the major.

"Upset! You people have tricked me. I have made a huge mistake" he shouted loudly.

"No, no, please, calm down. You will get your money. These things are difficult and always take time."

A woman in the room next door had heard a loud bang and could hear a lot of shouting going on. She had phoned down to the front desk and said she thought the people in the next room were fighting. The hotel manager and a security guard quickly came up to the room, knocked on the room door and asked if everything was alright. The engineer, not able to control himself, had run over and opened the door and said, "No everything's not alright!"

He had pushed by the manager and security guard and run down the hallway towards the elevators. He was quickly caught and subdued by the security guard, while the manager was surveying the damage to the door and asking the major what was going on. With the obvious damage to the door and papers marked "Top Secret" strewn all over the room, the manager had told Major Trsenkov he would have to call the police. While he was on the phone with the police, the major had coolly left the room, taken the stairs down out of the hotel and got into a waiting vehicle, which had sped off. While he had been briefly in the hallway, he had seen the security guard trying to cuff the engineer near the elevators. Several years later, the major had heard that the engineer had been found guilty of divulging military secrets and had been sentenced to fifteen years. Trsenkov knew this would have been portrayed negatively in his file, but really, he hadn't done anything wrong. It was the bureaucracy of the Soviet Union's military that was at fault, not him. He had asked General Ulanov to clear his name with regard the incident, but had never received any confirmation that this had happened.

Early Monday morning the chief engineer on Minot Air Force base was informed that a potentially catastrophic problem had just been discovered with one of the missiles. Engineers had been reviewing alarm message logs from over the weekend and to their surprise, had found that Bravo Charlie missile number four was armed and programmed to detonate later that day. Upon receiving the news, the chief engineer immediately informed Base Commander Maty.

The base commander, still half a sleep and in a state of shock, made his way over to his office in the base headquarters building. Following standard escalation procedures, he notified the SAC commander on duty. He explained that the nuclear warheads in one of his Minuteman missiles were armed and due to detonate in just over twelve hours. This information resulted in red alerts being sent out to all SAC and Air Force senior officers. News of the situation quickly moved up the chain of command to the President himself, in his role as Commander in Chief.

Sitting in his brightly lit office, Base Commander Maty began to make a list of what he needed to focus on. So far he had written: evacuate the base and relocate all bomber and transport aircraft. As he was trying to think of other things that needed to be done, his thoughts began to wander and he began to think about his mercurial rise through the ranks of the United States Air Force since his graduation from the Air Force Academy in 1969. He had been a bomber pilot towards the end of the Vietnam War and had achieved the rank of Captain. Two years later, by being in the right place at the right time, he had been promoted to the rank of Major. At the time, he had just been assigned to Malmstrom Air Force base, in Montana, when a vacancy became available as a result of a sex scandal involving several senior officers on the base. Following this, he had shown himself to be an outstanding leader and had progressed to the rank of Lieutenant Colonel in less than two years. There were many changes in the United States Air Force after the Vietnam War ended, with many senior officers retiring. This created an abundance of opportunities for young, ambitious

Air Force officers. Having further proven he had the skills to assume higher responsibility, he had been promoted to the rank of Colonel, when he was appointed the commanding officer of the two active United States Air Force Wings at Minot Air Force base in North Dakota.

Suddenly realizing his thoughts had been wondering, Maty began to think about the crisis at hand. He really felt he needed more information about what he was dealing with here and decided to phone an old friend. A number of years back, he had spent several months at the Department of Energy's Los Alamos, New Mexico, facility and had become friendly with one of the technical directors there, Dr. Jim Swann. He found his numbers and phoned him at his home. When Jim answered, Base Commander Maty already knew he would be able to learn all he needed to know about what he was dealing with here at the base.

"Hello Jim, its Will Maty. Remember me?"

"How could I forget you? What's up at this hour of the night?"

The base commander asked him to swear he would keep their discussion secret. Swann told him whatever it was about, not to worry and swore no one would ever know about their conversation. The base commander explained the situation to him and Swann told him he would do his best to tell him what he thought he needed to know.

Swann began, "The Minuteman III missile has a yield of hundreds of kilotons and if one explodes, it will very likely directly impact anything within a radius of five miles. Like most conventional bombs, most of the damage tends to be done by the explosive blast, except with a nuclear explosion, a much larger area is eventually impacted. When a nuclear bomb explodes, sudden changes in atmospheric air pressure occur, which results in everything in the immediate vicinity being crushed. Tremendous winds, up to five hundred miles an hour, are created, which will uproot trees and snap utility poles. You may have seen the famous films, taken during early nuclear tests, which provided visual evidence of the crushing effect of the winds generated by the blast. In addition to the immediate blast, there will be radiation contamination. Radiation around the immediate blast area will be extremely intense and is commonly known as direct radiation. Fallout radiation is when the dust particulates from the debris cloud settle back to earth. It is very similar to the ash that settles after a volcano erupts. The radioactive fallout can be over an area of hundreds of miles".

Maty interrupted him. "Where is the best place to be if you are in close proximity to an imminent nuclear explosion?"

"I would say below ground, away from the initial blast and resultant direct radiation. A crater will be created, but it will be limited in size. Radioactive dust will be shot high into the air above the explosion site, creating the familiar mushroom cloud. After the explosion, it will be necessary to move through the zone surrounding the crater, wearing special suits that protect against the effects of radiation." Swann's voice broke a little as he said, "Will, I know what you're like and I know you will be there right up until you know for sure the explosion can't be avoided, but please promise me, you will get yourself into an underground shelter ahead of the blast. You are only human and can only do so much and you should save your own life."

"Thank you Jim. I really appreciate this. The information you have given me will allow me to be better prepared for the decisions that will need to be made during the next twelve hours and I promise you that I will get myself and my family safely underground, if it is determined the explosion cannot be avoided. Thank you again. We'll either stop the detonation or you'll hear about it on the six o'clock evening news tonight."

The situation on the base right now was by far the greatest challenge he had faced in his career to date. He had already decided to be up front with his officers when informing them about the situation. It was going to be most important not to lose focus in any particular area and he began to try and compartmentalize everything that would need to be addressed in the coming hours. He had decided to focus all of his own attention on stopping the detonation and he began to think about who he could assign other responsibilities to. He would ask Major Waltham to be responsible for the base evacuation, Major Lang the relocation of all the large aircraft and

Lieutenant Colonel Smith for all ongoing operational activities. All non-essential personnel in the Bomber Wing could be evacuated and Major Waltham would need to come up with a reason for doing this. He was trying to put the situation into some kind of perspective, but was having difficulty. In approximately twelve hours there could be an unprecedented nuclear explosion a number of miles from where he was sitting. He would have loved to have been able to assemble every man and women on the base and tell them to go home to their families and get them as far away from the base as possible. But he knew the situation couldn't be handled in this way. Firstly, he and everyone else was going to be doing all they could to avoid the explosion, so why create utter panic and mass chaos over something that hopefully wasn't going to happen? Secondly, just the knowledge of what had transpired on the base over the last day would almost have the same affect as if the explosion had happened.

If it became obvious the explosion couldn't be avoided, protocol dictated that although he was expected to continue to oversee all base activities, he was allowed to ensure the safety of himself and his family. He had been involved in fallout shelter drills before and knew that he would have similar facilities in the shelter to those he currently had. It would obviously be a new experience for him and everyone else. No one, to his knowledge, had actually had to live and work in a fallout shelter for any length of time. The one thing he did know for sure was that the United States military would be doing everything possible to ensure that everyone in the shelters got out safely. He assumed the American public would be told it was an accident, to ensure there was minimal panic throughout the country. He didn't have the time or energy right now to try and envisage all the other ramifications of such a nuclear explosion on American soil, but he knew they would be far-reaching.

Shelby had been driving through the night and it was only snowing lightly now. For quite a number of miles now he had noticed headlights in his rear view mirror that always seemed to be about the same distance behind. He thought this was strange, considering the old truck didn't have much power and almost any vehicle on the road could easily overtake it. After going around a long bend, he pulled the truck off to the side of the road. A black, full sized luxury sedan came cruising by and carried on up the road. He waited a few minutes then pulled back onto the road. The agents had seen the truck by the side of the road and continued up the highway until they came to the first intersection. They went about a hundred yards, did a U-turn, turned the car's lights off and waited. Several minutes later, the beaten up old pickup came puttering by. The agents got back on the highway and began to follow the truck again, this time making sure they kept out of sight. Shelby never saw the vehicle again for the rest of the trip, so never gave it another thought.

As Base Commander Maty sat making his list, he was thinking that if a volcano erupts, it is only those living in the immediate vicinity whose lives are impacted. Life goes on normally for everyone else. His mind was rambling and he couldn't stop it. He was thinking that if there is an explosion, it will be interesting to see if life is impacted in the rest of the country. When there was almost a meltdown at Three Mile Island a few years back, life went on in the rest of the country as if nothing had happened. The base commander thought to himself, *Humans are like ants; someone can step on a few of them, but the rest continue to go about their business.*

The President was awoken just after three-thirty on that Monday morning, by his Chief of Staff, informing him about the situation at Minot Air Force base. The President immediately became concerned about all aspects of a potential nuclear explosion. However, he said he didn't want to cause any panic unless it became absolutely necessary and it looked like the explosion couldn't be avoided. He asked to be brought up-to-date on a regular basis and wondered who could be behind this and what could have motivated them to do such a potentially disastrous thing!

Base Commander Maty was contacted by the President's Chief of Staff just after four on Monday morning. He asked the base commander to be available to attend an eight o'clock conference call, being chaired by the Deputy Secretary of Defence. The base commander said he would be available to attend and already feeling a little tired, wondered when he would be able to sleep again.

At five thirty Monday morning, after listening intently to a briefing by Deputy Secretary of Defence, John Craig, on the situation at Minot Air Force base, the President said, "As well as stopping the missile from detonating, we must focus on containment. We must be extremely careful not to create any suspicions among the American people while we are tracking down the perpetrators. We shouldn't mount a large task force. If we bring in helicopters or vehicles with the FBI logo plastered all over them, it will draw too much attention. We must rely on the state and local police authorities, with the FBI supporting them in the background, to find those responsible.

"Ross, I would like you to take charge. I think it's most appropriate for you, in your role as the Chief of Staff for Strategic Air Command." Looking at Deputy Secretary of Defence Craig, the President said, "Are you in agreement with me here John, that Ross should take the lead?

""Yes overall, Mr. President, but I think the base commander needs to be in charge of the hour-by-hour, day-to-day activities. He is the only one who can bring sufficient focus," said Craig.

"Is that alright with you Ross?" asked the President.

"Yes. William Maty, the Base Commander at Minot, is quite capable of taking on such a role," said Strategic Air Command Chief of Staff Ross Callaghan.

"Although I'm very optimistic that collectively we'll find a way to stop the explosion, we must plan for the worst case scenario, so let's start at ground zero. What should we do at the base?" asked the President.

Craig said, "If it is determined that the explosion cannot be avoided, all base personnel should be ordered to seek cover in underground fallout shelters."

"What about those people living in the immediate vicinity of the base?" the President asked.

"Fortunately, it is very sparsely populated around the base; the actual town of Minot has the largest population in the area and most of the people who live there, work at the base. At the same time the base personnel are being ordered to take cover, the state and local police authorities will be notified about the imminent nuclear explosion and asked to invoke area evacuation procedures as quickly as they can. The initial blast should only affect those on the base in the immediate vicinity of the explosion, so there should be time to evacuate people in the surrounding areas."

"I would suggest the Chief of Staff of the Army be responsible for the overall evacuation. The state and local police authorities will need the support of both the regular Army and National Guard" said the President dryly. "By the way, do we have an estimate of how many people could potentially be affected, if the warheads do explode?"

Craig said quietly, "Early estimates from the Department of Energy indicate it could potentially affect in the region of eleven million people. They indicate that the residual radiation or fallout will most likely drift north-east, affecting eastern North Dakota and upstate Minnesota the worst. Some Canadian provinces will also likely be affected."

"So I guess I should alert the Canadian Prime Minister?" said the President.

Craig continued, "The scientists from the Department of Energy have provided a brief, of which you have a copy Mr. President. In essence they are saying the direct radiation will be very intensive, but limited in range. The radiation particles from the debris cloud will affect a much larger area and it could take days or perhaps weeks until all the contaminated radioactive particles have fallen back to earth, some of them being brought back in the form of rain or snow. It is likely that for years afterwards, people may die from the complications of being exposed to the resultant radiation."

The President interrupted him. "Can we go back to the evacuation? I was thinking that evacuating people may result in more of them being exposed to the fallout radiation. Would it not perhaps be better to ask everyone to stay in their homes or wherever they are, at the time of the blast? Keep all the windows and doors closed and then use the Army or National Guard to get uncontaminated food and supplies to them?"

Craig said, "I am told that staying in their homes or offices with everything shut up would initially protect them, but eventually they will have to come out and when they do, they will find the whole area contaminated and will have to be immediately evacuated. It is preferred that everyone be evacuated as soon as possible, before all the contaminated radioactive debris and dust particles settle back down to earth. Following the explosion, many of the particles will be up in the stratosphere, so the much wider fallout area will be only partially contaminated initially.

"I see your point," said the President softly. "So let's get ready to mobilize for a full evacuation of the upper parts of the states you mentioned and the lower parts of the Canadian provinces that may also be affected. As I said earlier Matt, I think you need to take the lead here, given it looks like the Army and National Guard will be handling the evacuation. I'm sure the Air Force will also play their part and be involved in airlifting the evacuees, wherever possible. After having looked at the worst case scenario, we know now that we must do all that is humanly possible to avoid the explosion. Ross, I would like you to ensure the Base Commander gets whatever he needs. Thank you all, and God Bless America."

Shelby had had to stop on several occasions through the night to clear the build-up of snow and ice on the truck's windshield wipers. Although the truck's heater was working, it had been no match for the blizzard-like conditions they had come through and he had felt cold for most of the night. It was now beginning to get light and it was warming up inside the cab. Shelby could see that the local snow removal vehicles had been busy throughout the night. Snow was piled high on both sides of the road. Williams, who was awake now, was taking in the magnificent scenery of the rugged mountains and vast snow-covered plains.

Shelby, seeing Williams was awake, said, "You know the trip has gone pretty well so far considering the snowy weather conditions we've come through. You were right about the truck."

Williams asked if he wanted him to take over the driving and Shelby said he was alright for now. It was six-thirty in the morning and Shelby was fiddling with the radio. "It doesn't look like the radio works," he said.

"I know. I tried it last night," said Williams. "Maybe we can sing some songs ourselves. Who were your favorite groups growing up?"

"I really liked the Motown sound, the Supremes, Four Tops and the Temptations. I always found their songs wonderfully up-lifting. How about you?"

"For me it was the Beach Boys and Creedence," said Williams, "but I didn't listen to much music growing up. I had one of those, 'Turn that jungle music off' fathers. So what do you want to sing?"

Shelby thought for a few seconds and said, "How about 'My Girl'?"

"Who did that?" said Williams.

"The Temptations of course."

"You start and I'll join in, wherever I can."

Following "My Girl", they sang one of Williams' favorites, "Bad Moon Rising". They both really enjoyed singing the old songs and it passed the time.

Just as he was about to join the eight o'clock conference call, Base Commander Will Maty, for some reason, began to think about the local people who had come to the base Saturday afternoon with the story about the flying saucer and their missing friend and wondered if it was somehow connected. He thought it had to be.

On the conference call, chaired by Deputy Secretary of Defence Craig, were the Director of the National Security Agency, Chief of Staff for the Army, Chief of Staff for the Air Force, Chief of Staff for Strategic Air Command, Commander of Strategic Command, the Director of the Ballistic Defence Organization, Commander of Pacific Command, Commander of Central Command, Commander of the Northern Command and Base Commander Maty.

Deputy Secretary of Defence Craig began. "Gentlemen, we have an unprecedented situation unfolding at Minot Air Force base today and your discretion is essential. I will try and bring you all up to date as best I can on the facts as I know them. Base Commander Maty, please feel free to cut in at any time if I am missing something important.

Over the weekend, a maintenance crew at the base found that one of the silos housing a

Minutemen III missile had been damaged. Then early this morning, it was determined that the missile in the damaged silo has been tampered with. Its software has been modified and a prolonged detonation countdown is well underway. If it cannot be stopped by late this afternoon, it will result in the detonation of the missile's three, one hundred kiloton nuclear warheads. I hope I have captured the essence of the situation, Base Commander?"

"Yes, I have nothing to add."

Craig continued, "So let me try and put the situation in perspective. First and foremost, under no circumstances do we want the missile's warheads to explode. Secondly, we need to find those responsible for doing this, as quickly as possible, and just as important as the first two, we must not let any information about this situation get out.

The FBI has already been contacted and will be providing backup support to the state and local police authorities and the President wants Base Commander Maty to remain in charge. He feels he is in the best position to provide the required focus. Base Commander, I think we should open the call up for questions, unless you have anything to add?"

Base Commander Maty said he didn't and the Director of the Ballistic Defence Organization asked the first question. "Do we know if any other silos or missiles on the base have been compromised?"

"Can you take this question, please Base Commander?" said Craig.

"No damage has been reported to any of the other silos and a review of the status of all the other missiles on the base this morning showed no significant issues," said the commander.

"So you are saying that the damage and tampering is isolated to just the one silo and missile?" asked the Director of the Ballistic Defence Organization, for clarification.

"Yes, that is correct."

The Director of the National Security Agency requested clarification of the time the detonation was expected to happen and was told four o'clock local time that afternoon.

"If there are no more questions gentlemen, then I would suggest we let Base Commander Maty focus on the situation at hand. Base

Commander, please feel free to contact any of us, at any time. Thank you everyone," said Deputy Secretary of Defence Craig, and ended the call.

Immediately following the conference call, Base Commander Maty met face-to-face with his senior officers. He told them that what he was about to tell them should be treated as confidential. He explained the situation to them and tongue in cheek, asked if any of them had any ideas on how to stop the detonation. The silence in the room was deafening. They agreed that an impromptu air raid drill would be the best way to get everyone into the fallout shelters. The base commander said he would be focusing all his attention on stopping the detonation and asked Major Lang to find a base outside the fallout area that could temporarily accommodate Minot's B-52 bomber and C5 Galaxy transport aircraft. He asked Lieutenant Colonel Smith to take care of all ongoing operations and asked Major Waltham to ensure that all non-essential base personnel were sent home. He said he knew he could depend on them all and excused himself, saying he had to set up a conference call with SAC.

Base Commander Maty chaired a ten o'clock conference call with engineers from SAC, representatives from the missile manufacturer, engineers from the base and scientists from the Defence and Energy departments. He told everyone on the call that everything they were about to discuss was confidential and then explained the situation. He said he wanted to know what options were available to stop the missile's nuclear warheads from detonating. A technical director from the missile manufacturer told everyone on the call that he had been contacted several hours earlier and said so far the most promising option was resetting the countdown variable to its highest value. He said this would obviously buy time to allow them to find a permanent fix and he hoped to confirm whether this was possible within the next few hours.

The base commander said, "Time is obviously of the essence here. We need to find a solution sooner rather than later, so I will set up another conference call, for noon."

He thanked everyone for attending and ended the call.

Following the call, Base Commander Maty went back to his office where he found Major Lang waiting for him. Lang told him rumours were rampant on the base, with everyone having their own theories on what was going on. Some of the more popular ones were the new President was going after the Iranian Ayatollah, the base was being closed or the United States was going into El Salvador to make sure they didn't become communist, like Cuba. It seemed that readying the B-52's and Galaxies to leave the base had fuelled most of the rumours. The base commander said he wasn't concerned about the rumours because they were so far off-base and asked Lang how the aircraft evacuation was going. Lang told him that unlike the base fighter aircraft, which were always in a state of readiness, the B-52's and Galaxies had to be essentially taken out of mothballs. All but a few of them had a minimal amount of gas in their fuel tanks, having been out of service for several years now, and getting them all fired up simultaneously was proving to be quite a challenge. Extra air and maintenance crews had even had to be brought in on their days off.

Bringing additional manpower onto the base at this time was not really what the base commander wanted to do, but given the circumstances, he figured it couldn't be avoided. He could hear the noise from the monster aircraft as they taxied to the fuelling and de-icing stations and figured he would have to use one of the meeting rooms in the basement of the building for his next conference call.

It was just after ten thirty when Williams and Shelby passed a large sign indicating they were entering the town of Cold Water Falls, Montana. A few minutes later, they passed a monument store, set back from the road.

"Look at the size of some of those monuments!" said Shelby. "Can you see that huge cross with life-size angels on either side?"

"It's hard to see any of them; they're all covered in snow."

"Have you ever considered what you'll have engraved on yours?" asked Shelby.

"No, I've never really thought about it before. I thought that was up to others to decide, after you're gone," said Williams.

"Usually it has some kind of meaning, like a famous quote or something personal about you, but I'm no expert on this either."

"Hopefully we won't need them for awhile, whatever we have engraved on them," said Williams laughing.

It was just before eleven o'clock and snowing lightly when they parked the old truck on the main street of Cold Water Falls, a small town in the foothills of the Rockies. Williams suggested they needed a change of clothes and they headed into a men's clothing store across the street. They bought jeans, long sleeved shirts, underwear, socks and winter jackets and changed into the new clothes in the store, discarding their bright ski suits. They then walked up the street and entered a restaurant called Al's.

The agents who had been trailing them all night watched them park and go into the clothing store. Twenty minutes later, now parked a few cars behind the Americans' old truck, they watched them walk further up the street and enter a restaurant. It had been a long night and as they sat parked there, they hoped the police didn't catch up to the Americans before they had a chance to kill them. But their orders had been to just follow them.

Upon entering the restaurant, Williams thought to himself that this looks like a good place to spend the day, at least up until the explosion. The restaurant was almost empty and looked to be a combined restaurant and bar. It had booths on one side and a bar and a number of tables and chairs on the other and at the back there were several pool tables. They slid into a booth towards the back of the restaurant side and ordered the all-day breakfast special. While they were waiting for the food to come, Shelby began to talk about his ex-girlfriend for some reason. He said she was originally from Italy, Milan, he thought, but she had been working in London for a number of years. She was the manager of a shoe store, located close to Piccadilly Circus, which he likened to the Times Square of London. He said she was very attractive and spoke broken English, with a fabulous accent. He said although he'd been ready to make a long-term commitment, she hadn't. "She'd said she was happy with her life the way it was and marrying an 'Americano', as she called me, would only complicate it. I had only known her for six months, but she was anyone's dream girl. She had it all - looks, brains and a real zest for life. I really miss her a lot."

"Why are you telling me this? I thought it was over?" said Williams, just as their food was arriving.

"I don't know. It's just that I do truly love her," replied Shelby.

"You never know - maybe she feels the same way about you, now you're apart."

"I really hope you're right."

"What's her name?" asked Williams, with his mouth full.

"Christina. I truly hope you meet her one day," said Shelby.

"I can't say I've ever met anyone like her from the way you describe her. Has she got a sister?" said Williams while wiping some egg off his face with his napkin.

"She does, actually," said Shelby. "However, she still lives in Italy and I've never met her."

"You know, I had a foreign girlfriend once," said Williams. "In my final year at Syracuse I dated an exchange student from Egypt and she had a sexy accent too. It would never have worked out between us though, because she said she found America lacking in class compared to Egypt, if you can believe that? Maybe her father was a Sheik or something. Anyway, I honestly think she only dated me to improve her English. She was never comfortable with the American way of life because I think she was already too set in her ways. She was like a celebrity wherever we went, so I know exactly what you mean about women with fabulous, foreign accents."

Al thought it was very unusual for anyone to stay in his restaurant after eating breakfast and figured the two strangers must be killing time or lying low for some reason. He could see them playing pool at the back of the bar and walked back to where they were and asked them if he could get them anything.

Williams checked his watch. It was almost noon and he said, "Well it's almost afternoon; I think I'll have a beer, how about you, Pete?"

"Sounds good to me."

Al came back with the beers and asked them if they were just passing through or staying in town.

Williams replied, "We're passing through, on our way to see some of my relatives, out on the west coast. This was all he could think of on the spur of the moment. We've been driving all night and need a little down time. Us being here isn't a problem, is it?"

"No, no problem, not at all," said Al. "Stay as long as you like and if you need anything, just holler. I'm Al by the way."

"The Al of Al's restaurant?" asked Williams.

"Yes, that's me, in living color."

"Pleased to meet you, I'm Gerry and this is my friend Pete," said Williams shaking the restaurant owner's hand.

"Nice to meet you too and as I said if you need anything just holler." Al said starting to make his way back to the bar.

Shelby whispered, "Good, I'm glad we cleared the air with him."

"Yes, I know what you mean," Williams agreed.

Al was still wary of the two men playing pool in his restaurant. Something wasn't right. These guys were both strikingly good looking, in tremendous shape and seemed to be very personable. Al wondered who they could be, but was coming up blank.

A short while after, two young men came striding into the restaurant and headed straight to the back where Williams and Shelby were playing pool. One of them asked if they wanted to have a game of doubles, for ten dollars a game and before they could answer, had inserted some coins into one of the other tables and was racking the balls. Williams and Shelby got into some small talk with the young men and found out they were from a small town to the south of there and were seasonal workers. One of them said they hadn't seen Williams and Shelby there before. Williams replied that they were passing through on their way to visit some of his relatives in Seattle. This seemed to be a good reason to explain what they were doing there.

The young men accepted this, one of them saying, "I guess you're not in any big hurry to get there?"

"Well, we are and we aren't," muttered Williams. "It will be nice to see relatives I haven't seen for quite awhile but we don't want to impose on them for very long."

Not fully understanding what Williams meant, the young men began to talk about how close the games had been. They were obviously pool sharks and after having beaten Williams and Shelby three times in a row, said they had to go. Williams paid them their winnings and they left.

At the noon conference call, chaired by Base Commander Maty, the technical director from the missile manufacturing plant told everyone on the call that they had successfully simulated the reset of the detonation counter to its maximum value, without causing the warheads to detonate and engineers had already been dispatched to reset the counter in the missile. Base Commander Maty asked him what time they would be arriving and was told around three o'clock. The base commander was concerned that this would only give them an hour to work on the missile once they arrived, but was reassured that the change wouldn't take long. The commander reluctantly accepted this and ended the call.

Following the call, Base Commander Maty met with his officers and was extremely pleased to hear about the cooperation they were getting from the base commander at Edwards Air Force base, in California. He had agreed to accommodate all their B-52's and C-5's and most of them were already in the air on their way. He thought to himself this was the United States military at its finest. It always upset him when he heard the military being criticized. If people could only realize it was because of them that the United States was the most powerful country in the world.

Just after noon on Monday afternoon, Major Trsenkov arrived in Cold Water Falls and met up with the agents who had been trailing the Americans all night. The trip west had gone very well for him because there had apparently been blizzard-like conditions south of the border, but the weather in Canada had been clear. Sam had driven along the trans-Canada highway at speeds over one hundred miles an hour and had made excellent time. At a British Columbia-Montana border crossing, an hour or so earlier, nobody had paid any attention to the dark Lincoln with Ontario plates as they entered into the United States.

At a very brief conference call Monday afternoon, Base Commander Maty told Deputy

Secretary of Defence Craig and senior officials from the Pentagon that a way had been found to postpone the detonation of the warheads. They were obviously all very pleased to hear this news, but like the base commander, concerned that the engineers doing the resetting wouldn't be arriving at the base for another hour.

Around two-thirty Monday afternoon, the Soviet informant in the Minot police department phoned the farm to let them know there was a rumour that the Americans had found a way to stop the missile from exploding. The agents at the farm said they would pass the information along and immediately communicated the information to Major Trsenkov.

Just before three o'clock, Base Commander Maty drove out to the main airstrip and waited for the missile manufacturer's engineers to arrive. They touched down in an old Huron turboprop and taxied over to the hangar area where the base commander was waiting. Once the aircraft came to a stop, he drove and parked below its cargo door and waited for the passenger stairs to be lowered. Although the majority of his officers knew about the crisis, by picking up the engineers himself he was avoiding having to explain their mission to anyone else. He greeted them as they stepped down off the plane and asked them to get into his Jeep. It was only just big enough for the four of them and all their equipment. Luckily, three of them had slight builds which allowed them to squeeze into the back. The base commander told them he realized the Jeep wasn't very comfortable, but said it wouldn't take them long to get to the damaged silo. He said he hoped that whatever they had to do wouldn't take long. The engineer sitting in the front said that as long as the damaged electronics rack back plane connectors had been replaced, which he said he understood to be the case, it would only take a few minutes to make the change. Each of the engineers was carrying a large metal case and the base commander asked them what was in them. One of the engineers sitting in the back said they had each brought a complete air data computer unit and diagnostics equipment with them, in case a complete unit or any replacement parts were needed.

"Good" said the base commander. "I like people who plan ahead, especially in a situation like this, where we could all be blown to kingdom come in less than an hour from now."

As soon as they reached the silo, the base commander asked everyone inside to leave, regardless of what they were doing. He told them engineers were there to make modifications to the missile's electronics systems. As the base commander was leaving the silo, he gave one of the engineers a phone number and asked him to call him the instant the counter had been successfully reset.

Base Commander Maty drove to the nearest launch control facility, where the operators were most surprised to see him. He told them he was conducting a routine check. They found this to be most unusual because normally his senior officers accompanied him when he conducted inspections. Although feeling distracted by the real issue, he listened briefly to their comments about the day-to-day operation of the facility. Their comments were all fairly benign, from they were still waiting for some small warning light bulbs to be replaced, to the need for a new coffee maker. It was three twenty-two when he sat down at the console closest to an air raid siren activation button and waited for the phone to ring. As he sat there, drinking a coffee from a vending machine, he watched the second hand ticking on the large clock on the wall.

While the base commander waited, he conjectured about what would happen if he did actually have to sound the air raid siren. He knew the main concentrations of personnel were either in the headquarters buildings or around the hangers, next to the main airstrip and that there were underground fallout shelters under each of the areas. Operational personnel in the underground launch control facilities should be safe and knew not to leave their stations. It was the personnel in transit at the time of the explosion that would be most vulnerable. Impromptu air raid drills were conducted twice a year, so everyone on the base should know exactly where to go when the siren sounded. It was planned that he would be meeting his wife and boys in the fallout shelter under the base headquarters building, where he had an office and accommodations for him and his family. He was confident that if there was an explosion, it would only be a matter of time until everyone below ground would be rescued safely. He had total faith in the United States military's commitment to those in its employment. He knew that military personnel would always come first in the time of conflict. After all, they were the defenders of all the people and without them, the people and country would perish.

Once everyone had left the silo, the engineers from the missile manufacturer set up their equipment. The now-nervous engineers saw that the electronics rack back plane connectors had already been replaced. They attached a small programming device to one of the connectors. After monitoring instruction execution for several minutes, one of the engineers, his hands shaking, entered the command string to reset the detonation countdown variable. No ill effects to the missile's electronic systems were observed and the engineers congratulated each other. The modification had gained them three more days to try and come up with a permanent fix. If they got close to the next detonation countdown deadline, the counter could be reset again. One of the engineers climbed up to the top level of the silo and phoned the base commander with the good news. It was three twenty-eight.

"Great news!" said the base commander. "Great job."

Following the call, the base commander, much perkier now the immediate crisis had been averted, said his goodbyes to the launch control operators and left the facility.

Al could see the two strangers watching TV at the back of the bar, as his happy hour regulars started to come in. He walked back to where the strangers were sitting and asked if he could get them anything.

"I could use something to eat; it seems like hours since I ate," said Shelby.

"How about a burger and fries?" asked Al.

"Yes, me too," said Williams.

"Two burgers and fries coming right up," said Al, carrying some empty beer bottles back to the bar.

It was just after four and another afternoon talk show had just begun, there were no breaking news bulletins yet. Williams and Shelby ate the burgers and fries and decided they would wait for the six o'clock evening news. They played some more pool and watched a sports talk show to pass the time.

Major Trsenkov, parked on the main street of Cold Water Falls, was tuned to an all-news radio station. It was now four-thirty and there was no news about an explosion, so it seemed the rumour about them finding a way to stop the detonation had been true. He walked down the street until he found a payphone and phoned General Ulanov using an international calling card. When he got through to the general, he just said, "Explosion stopped," and hung up. He hated speaking with the general like this, but it wasn't a secure phone line.

In Al's restaurant, six o'clock arrived and at the top of the news there was no mention of an explosion.

"They must have found a way to stop it," whispered Shelby.

"But how?" whispered Williams. "Stopping the detonation countdown should have caused the warheads to immediately explode."

While Williams and Shelby were watching the news, Alan Ascot, the owner of Al's, was in his office behind the bar, whispering into the phone.

"Could I speak to Dick please?" he said quietly.

Al was told that Dick Farley, the Cold Water Falls police chief, had already left for the day.

Al asked for the Chief's home number and was told it couldn't be given out.

"Who am I speaking to?" asked Al.

He was told it was the evening shift supervisor.

"I just wanted to let him know that two strangers have been in my restaurant all day. They haven't caused any trouble, but I just heard on the radio that two escaped convicts are on the run," said Al quietly.

After providing his name and phone number, he was thanked for the information. The shift supervisor didn't really want to bother the chief at his home, although it seemed as though this guy knew him. He decided he would let him know about the call in the morning, because he hadn't heard anything about two escaped convicts.

Red Shadows On Liberty's Soil

As soon as the news finished, Williams paid the bill and he and Shelby left the restaurant.

Major Trsenkov and his agents saw the Americans come out of the restaurant. After taking a few minutes to warm up their old truck, they drove off in a westerly direction, unaware that they were being followed as they left Cold Water Falls early on that Monday evening. After about an hour or so, they came to a small town called Liberty and Williams suggested to Shelby that they find a place to stay so they could get some sleep. Sure enough, it wasn't too long until they found a motel.

They put the TV on as soon as they got into their room at the Spruce Motel; there were still no breaking news bulletins, just the usual nightly sitcoms. The explosion obviously hadn't happened there was no way to cover it up.

"They must have found a way to stop it, but how?" said Williams.

"Let's talk about it in the morning," said Shelby, yawning.

"Anyway, I'm still confident we can escape," yawned Williams.

Shelby was already snoring and Williams soon joined him.

Tuesday February 16

Shelby was woken out of a deep sleep by bright lights shining on the wall of the motel room. He peeked out from behind the curtains and saw a police car.

He woke Williams saying, "You need to get up! It looks like the cops might be on to us. They're outside, checking license plates."

"What time is it?" Williams asked, yawning.

Shelby checked his watch. "Three fifteen."

"We'd better get out of here!" said Williams, quickly getting dressed.

Not seeing anything moving outside, they got into their snow-covered truck and headed out of the motel parking lot, driving past a police car parked outside the motel office. They could see two police officers in conversation with someone behind the counter. Once they got out on the highway, Williams checked the rear view mirror and saw that no one was following them.

"Do you think they're on to us?" asked Shelby.

"Who knows?" Williams reached back, opened his backpack, took out the stamina pills bottle and offered it to Shelby. Shelby took two pills, swallowed them and handed the bottle back to Williams who took three pills out of the bottle, swallowed them and put the bottle back in his backpack.

"These things are great; I don't think we'd have got this far without them."

This was the first time Williams and Shelby had come anywhere close to getting caught by the police - as far as they knew.

Major Trsenkov and his agents, after following the Americans to the motel, had spent the night in a diner along the highway close to the motel. After seeing the Americans leave the motel, they began to follow them again.

As they travelled west, Williams apologized to Shelby for not being able, in General Ulanov's words, "…fully execute the mission as planned." They had traveled for about twenty miles, Williams continuing to rehash the events of the last few days, when bright headlights appeared right behind them and they heard what sounded like gunfire. The truck's rear window shattered just as Shelby was turning to see what was happening behind them. Automatic gunfire lit up the morning darkness.

"I guess the general's men have caught up with us too!" said Williams.

"Looks like it," said Shelby.

"I told you not to open fire!" shouted Major Trsenkov, trying to grab an automatic weapon. "Now they know we've found them."

Williams told Shelby to get the pistol out of his backpack. Williams could see that the dark vehicle behind them no longer had its headlights on and thought, *Two can play at this game* and turned his lights off. It was now difficult for both drivers to see ahead of them. There were no tail lights for Sam to follow and it was difficult for Williams to see the road ahead, but gradually their eyes adjusted.

"Sam, pull up beside the truck. We need to kill them now! This is the perfect time and place," said the major.

Sam accelerated and moved up alongside the old truck, but almost immediately had to brake and pull in behind it again when he saw approaching headlights.

"What are you doing?" asked the major somewhat agitated.

"There was a car coming towards us," said Sam nervously.

The car passed and Sam came up alongside the truck again. Looking out of the driver's side window, Williams could see what looked like an automatic weapon beginning to protrude out of the passenger side front window of the car, now alongside him. He fired off a round of bullets at the car and they ricocheted off its hood and roof, making loud metallic popping sounds. The car braked and disappeared out of sight.

The major told Ivan , sitting next to him in the backseat, to try and shoot them from behind and automatic gunfire lit up the darkness once again.

Williams shouted, "Here!" giving the pistol to Shelby "Return fire. There are more ammunition clips in the backpack."

Shelby quickly reloaded the pistol and shot at the dark car behind, through the truck's smashed back window.

The major told Anton to start shooting as well and Anton readied his automatic weapon as Sam came right up behind the truck. Both automatic weapons started firing into the back of truck's cab. Both Ivan and Anton were firing out of the front passenger side window. Shelby exchanged fire as best he could while ducking behind the bench seat, while bullets were thudding into the back of it. A bullet smashed into the dashboard, just missing Williams and he pressed down as hard as he could on the accelerator pedal, but the truck wouldn't go any faster. Shots continued to ricochet around inside the truck's cab.

Williams said, "This truck won't go any faster, so let's see how good its brakes are. Brace yourself."

Shelby held onto the dashboard with both hands, as Williams put both feet down on the brake pedal. Almost instantly, there was a loud metal-on-metal crunching sound and a strong smell of burning rubber.

Upon impact, Anton had dropped his automatic weapon out of the passenger side window and banged his head on the windshield. Next to him, Sam's chest had been crushed by the steering wheel and both of their heads were drooping forward. Through the rear view mirror, Williams could see that the vehicle behind them was engulfed in billowing steam, its hazard lights flashing.

Neither Williams nor Shelby had been hurt on impact. Williams managed to untangle the truck from the wreckage and turning the headlights back on, slowly drove off into the pitch black night.

Shelby let out a sigh. "Can you believe this? Less than forty eight hours ago these people were our friends, doing all they could for us and now they're trying to kill us?"

"Things change quickly in this business, especially when things go wrong. Life is cheap to these people, particularly the lives of Americans, we've been their enemies for decades," said Williams.

"You would think they'd cut us some slack after what we've done for them!"

"They don't care. As we discussed, if we'd gone back to Moscow, they would have likely killed us. At least now we're in control of our own destiny."

"Yes, I guess you're right. You know, this whole thing has been totally crazy. I go on vacation and end up in the Soviet Air Force and a key member of one of the most important missions in their history. It's been like a bad dream," Shelby said.

Williams asked him if he could hear a scraping noise and still smell burning rubber. Shelby said he could.

Sam and Anton appeared to be dead. Major Trsenkov had banged his head on the seat in front and was bleeding slightly from his forehead. Ivan, sitting in the back seat beside the major, was rubbing his neck and cursing loudly. They could feel the heat from the scalding hot steam from the cracked radiator coming in through the shattered windshield. The major tried to open his door but it wouldn't budge. He asked Ivan if he could open his and Ivan said he couldn't. They could see lights outside and someone was banging on Ivan's window. Ivan tried to lower it, but it wouldn't move. Someone shouted in through the windshield that they were going to smash the back window, so they should cover their faces. Ivan's window shattered just as he was putting his hands up to protect his face. Someone peered in and enquired how badly they were hurt.

The major said, "Check those in the front first. They are hurt far worse than us and may even be dead."

The major and Ivan were told to get out the car as quickly as they could because it could catch fire at any moment. Ivan said that all the glass needed to be removed from the smashed window before they could get out and asked for the tire jack that had been used to smash it. With great difficulty, Ivan and the major squeezed out through the shattered back window. By then there were a number of vehicles and people surrounding the wrecked Lincoln, most of them asking what had happened. The major collected himself and calmly said he thought they had hit an animal and it must have run off. Some people were holding shell casings and others were pointing at an automatic weapon lying by the side of the road. Without explanation, the major picked up the weapon and asked those with shell casings to give them to him. He then asked if someone could give them a ride to the nearest town so they could call the police. Although reluctant to allow them to leave the scene of the accident, the person who had smashed the window agreed to give them a ride.

When they came to a gas station on the outskirts of Liberty, Major Trsenkov asked the driver to stop next to a payphone. He called the farm, told them what had happened and asked them to arrange for local agents to pick him and Ivan up. He did his best to tell them where they were currently located. He went back to the vehicle and told the driver that the police were on their way. He asked the driver how he took his coffee and motioned to Ivan to get out of the car. The two of them headed towards the gas station building. As they were walking, the major told Ivan that they were not going back to the scene of the accident, but would be staying there until they were picked up.

They entered the gas station office and the major told the mechanic, the only person there that someone was coming to pick them up and asked if it was alright if they waited there. The mechanic, somewhat confused, said that it was not a problem and asked what the guy in the car was waiting for. The major said he didn't know and the mechanic went out to the car. He came back and said the person in the car was waiting for them to bring him a coffee. The major waved the automatic weapon, which had been concealed under his coat, at the mechanic and told him to stand facing the wall of the office. He told Ivan to go and tell the driver to come and get his own coffee. The driver came into the gas station office complaining about why he had to get his own coffee and the major pointed the automatic weapon at him. He told him to shut up and go and stand next to the mechanic, facing the wall.

Once Williams could see that they weren't being followed, he pulled over to the side of the road, jumped out and went to look at the back of the truck. One of the tail lights was smashed and he could see that the truck's box had shifted off its frame and was sloping down to one side. The underside of the box was touching on one of the back tires. He called to Shelby to come and help him. They pushed the box back up onto the truck's frame as best they could, so it was no longer touching the tire.

"I think that should do it," said Williams.

"Let's get out of here then," said Shelby. "We just came very close to getting killed back there!"

"You know," said Williams, "I don't think the police are on to us yet, but it seems the major and his men definitely are."

"You're not kidding!" said Shelby. "I saw my life flash right before my eyes, just now."

It was almost five in the morning and still very dark as they drove off.

"I think we should head for Spokane," said Williams. "It will be much harder for anyone to find us in a big city."

Driving west they hadn't seen an open gas station and the truck was almost out of gas. Williams had decided that whenever he did find one open, he would buy some gas cans, so that at least they would have a reserve from now on.

Major Trsenkov was sitting in the gas station office, pointing his weapon at the mechanic and the driver. Ivan was leaning in the doorway, smoking a cigarette, when they saw a car pull up to the pumps. The major told Ivan to go and serve them. Ivan put his cigarette out and walked out to the pumps. The car had out of state plates, so the driver didn't find anything strange about Ivan pumping his gas. Ivan returned to the office and plonked a twenty dollar bill down on the counter. The major looked at his watch and wondered how long it was going to be until they were picked up. Ten minutes later, a black sedan pulled up in front of the gas station building. The major told Ivan to go and get in the car and turned his attention to the hostages.

"Gentlemen, through no fault of your own, you have become mixed up in this. I ask that you tell no one about any of this or I guarantee you will both be hunted down and killed like dogs. Do you understand?"

They both nodded nervously still facing the wall.

When they heard the car pull away, the driver and mechanic, still very scared, began to discuss what they should do.

"I think we should just forget this ever happened, as we have just been requested to," said the mechanic.

"You really think so?" said the driver.

"Yes. Don't you think he meant what he said? If we contact the police, they will kill us and they obviously know where to find me. I would really appreciate it if you would forget it ever happened. It will likely be harder for them to find you, but I have no doubt they will. How did you come to be with them anyway?" asked the mechanic.

"They were involved in an accident west of here, on Highway 2. The guy with the gun said they hit an animal and it had run off, but there was an automatic weapon and numerous shell casings in the road. Their car was badly damaged and it looked like the driver and the passenger in the front seat may have died in the accident. They asked someone to help them find a telephone, so they could call the police and I believed them, even though I was suspicious because of the weapon and their foreign accents."

"So I don't need to tell you to keep your mouth shut! You should already know that after what you've just told me," said the mechanic.

"Yes, you're right. I was on my way to work this morning and I haven't had a chance to call in yet to say I'll be late. Can I use your phone?"

"Sure go ahead, but please let someone else worry about catching up with these people. I certainly don't want to die," the mechanic said.

"Don't worry, I'm with you."

"I hope there weren't too many people at the scene of the accident or you may have some explaining to do to the police. Anyway, I'm sure you'll have a good story ready, like you dropped them off and went to work. Please don't mention me. You know there's another service station just up the road and there's a phone there too. Just say you dropped them off there," said the mechanic.

"Thanks. I'll check it out. Don't worry - if anyone contacts me, I won't mention you."

The mechanic waited until the driver had phoned his work and driven off, then went back to the oil change he was doing when he had been interrupted.

Now back on the road heading west, Major Trsenkov figured they were several hours behind the Americans. They soon got back to the scene of the accident and as they sped by, could see several highway patrol cars, a fire truck and two ambulances. The wrecked Lincoln was off to the side of the road behind a tow truck. There was a Medivac helicopter there too, so the major thought perhaps there was hope for Sam and Anton - maybe they hadn't been fatally injured after all. The major didn't give the scene a second thought once they had passed by, understanding it was just part of the job. His only interest once again, was to catch up to the Americans and kill them. He wondered where they might be heading.

Williams and Shelby got lucky and found a gas station just opening up. Williams pulled up to the pumps and a young mechanic, wiping the grease from his hands, came out to help them. Williams asked him if he had any gas cans he could buy. The mechanic said he didn't think so, but he'd check. Williams asked him how far it was to Spokane from here and which was the best way to get there. The mechanic told him to stay on Highway 2 and then take Interstate 95 south and Interstate 90 west. He said he figured it was just over two hundred miles and it would take them, three to four hours to get there. After gassing up the truck the young mechanic found an old gas can, filled it up and placed in the back of the truck. Williams paid him and thanked him for his help.

They pulled out of the gas station and continued to head west. Fifteen minutes into

Idaho they were traveling south on I 95, past a sign indicating that Spokane was one hundred and ninety five miles ahead. Williams was pushing the truck as hard as he could, but it was still only going just over sixty miles an hour. They were driving through blowing snow again and finding some of the lanes on the interstate closed. Williams figured they should find a motel and lie low once they got to Spokane, making it almost impossible to track them down.

At a Tuesday morning conference call, SAC Chief of Staff Callaghan told Base Commander Maty that the permanent solution for the compromised missile was to remove the complete nosecone containing the nuclear warheads, then fly it out and ditch it in the Pacific Ocean. Scientists from the Department of Energy had apparently already looked into exploding the warheads in the desert but had rejected this because it would be observed by too many people living in nearby communities and would lead to too many questions. An underwater explosion in waters deep enough to cover Mount Everest seemed to be by far the best option. The scientists said that although there would be a significant spray dome, it should dissipate very rapidly, leaving no trace of the explosion. The water displaced would be radioactive, but the particles would start to break up almost immediately. They had put the Pacific Tsunami Warning Center in Honolulu on alert and would be alerting the United States Air Force weather stations on Midway and Wake Islands also. Callaghan told the base commander that information about the incident at Minot had been relayed to all the other missile bases in the United States and they were all on high alert. Also, the President had informed the Prime Minister in England and he had put all the missiles sites over there on heightened alert also.

Callaghan informed the base commander that the President had been briefed and although he had a few concerns, had approved the plan to ditch the nosecone in the Pacific Ocean. He said that the President was very pleased to see how well contained everything had been so far, which, besides stopping the detonation and finding those responsible was his highest priority.

At Warren Air Force Base near Cheyenne, Wyoming, the base commander had been informed by SAC that his ICBM Emplacer-Extractor, currently being used to replace Minutemen with Peacekeeper missiles, was needed at Minot Air Force base as soon as possible. He was ordered to have his men work around the clock to dismantle it and have it ready to be transported to Minot. Cranes were already lifting the large steel structures onto flatbed railway cars, their high booms swinging backwards and forwards. Trucks with banks of floodlights in the back were lighting up the whole area. It was estimated that within the next five to six hours, the train should be ready to begin its journey to Minot, North Dakota. Some of the flatbed railcars carrying parts of the ICBM Emplacer-Extractor were already covered with tarpaulins, with the stamp of the United States Air Force visible. The military train was going to be given priority over regular freight trains, but not over passenger trains, they didn't want any undue attention drawn to it. It would be taking the main northerly rail line through the western parts of the states of Nebraska, South and North Dakota.

Williams had changed his mind about finding a motel and suggested they ditch the truck and hop a westbound freight. Shelby was surprised at this but agreed. The idea of heading for Australia had come to Williams a few miles back, while they were sitting at a railway crossing, waiting for a passenger train to speed by. He put this to Shelby, who said he guessed they had to go somewhere to get away and that sure would be getting away. Williams said he figured they could hang out with his sister and her husband for a while. Shelby became quite excited about the idea and asked Williams if he really thought they could make it there. Why not said Williams I've wanted to go there to visit my sister since she moved down there a few years back.

Williams found a trail leading down to the railway tracks and drove into some snow-covered bushes to hide the truck. After about half an hour, they could see the bright headlight of a train off in the distance. It turned out to be a freight train with a variety of container railcars. As it was approaching, it seemed to be going quite slow, but as it began to pass by them, they realized it was actually going quite fast and they needed to be running at the same speed as the train to stand any chance of getting on board. There were only a few cars left by the time they got up the needed speed. Williams managed to scramble up onto a container car and helped Shelby get on board. It was most uncomfortable. There was a lot of vibration and the railcar they were on was coated in ice. They moved to the next railcar which seemed less icy and offered more shelter from the bitterly cold wind. The railcars were screeching loudly as they maneuvered around the curves along the track. Williams was thinking "iron horse" was a good name, because it felt like you were riding one. They wished they had purchased gloves and jackets with hoods back in Cold Water Falls, because their hands and ears were already freezing cold. They were trying to warm their hands by keeping them in their pockets, but had no way of warming their ears. Shelby suggested they tie their socks together and loop them around their heads, over their ears, but Williams rejected this idea saying their feet would freeze. The only option they had was to keep taking their hands out of their pockets and putting them over their ears. Shelby's ears hurt so much that he took his jacket off and used it to cover his head. Williams did the same thing, worrying that his ears might be getting frostbitten. They had frozen snow in their hair and their faces were turning reddish blue. Shelby couldn't stop his teeth from chattering and his nose hurt if he breathed in too quickly. Williams suggested they jump up and down to try and get warm. They tried it, but their bodies ached so much from the cold that they were unable to do it for very long. Besides, standing up also exposed them to the cold wind.

"Think warm thoughts," said Williams. "Pretend you're sitting on the beach on a tropical island somewhere."

Shelby said, "I've got an idea. Why don't we hug each other?"

"You know, that's not a bad idea. I'm willing to try anything."

They looked like fully-clothed wrestlers, their hands tucked into each other's sleeves, each having the other in a headlock. The train continued on its journey as the men huddled together, both soon falling asleep.

A number of hours later they awoke as numerous railway tracks and railcars were coming into view on either side of them. They had arrived in the port of Seattle.

As the train began to slow down, the two men jumped off and began to explore their new surroundings. They found a boxcar in one of the sidings that was unlocked and as soon as they got inside started to feel warmer almost immediately. Although there was no heat inside the boxcar, it felt warm just to be out of the wind. Within an hour or so they were feeling much better, now that they were sheltered, rather than outside directly exposed to the elements.

Base Commander Maty began a Tuesday afternoon conference call with the FBI, state and local police authorities with an apology for not being able to meet with them before now. He explained that since very early the previous morning, he had been focusing all his attention on stopping the potential detonation of the missile in the damaged silo. On the call were Ken Harris, Deputy Director of the Federal Bureau of Investigation; several of his senior federal agents; Minot Police Chief Grogan; Director

McNally of the North Dakota State Police; and a number of other high ranking state and local police officials. The base commander said he understood that the FBI would be providing backup support to the state and local police authorities, even though this was not officially an inter-state matter.

He asked Minot Police Chief Grogan if he had made any progress in apprehending those responsible for the break-in. Grogan said there had been an incident at the border early on Sunday morning and that on Sunday afternoon, a warrant had been obtained for the arrest of two men staying at the Elk Motel, close to the border. The men were suspected of crashing the border. But when troopers went to serve the warrant, the men had already left the motel. The previous day he had been contacted by the Tollesbury police about a statement from someone who had been forced to drive a paratrooper from the north side of the base up to Ebdon ski resort on Saturday afternoon.

"That's interesting because a group of local people came to the base on Saturday afternoon, saying they were looking for one of their friends.

He may have been the one who was forced to drive the paratrooper up to the ski resort," said Base Commander Maty. Then he asked Director McNally if he had anything to add. He said he was aware of the incidents at the border crossing, Elk Motel and the ski resort but didn't have anything else to add.

Base Commander Maty then asked Deputy Director Harris if he would chair the remainder of that meeting and future meetings. Harris said he would and also said that as of that morning, this had become an FBI case. He informed the others that information had been received from the police in Cold Water Falls, Montana, that they had received a call the previous day about two strangers who had spent most of the day in a local restaurant there. They were also checking on another incident early that morning, west of the town of Liberty, Montana. A vehicle with province of Ontario license plates was involved in a serious accident. According to witnesses, an automatic weapon and shell casings were found at the scene and two of the occupants who were in the badly damaged vehicle quickly left the scene of the accident. Two other occupants in the vehicle were fatally injured. There are suspicions that the two suspects may have been involved in the accident, because the timeline fits. He said that the police were following up on both of these leads and would provide further information on them as it became available.

"Thank you," said the base commander. "As I mentioned at the outset of the meeting, I am sorry that this is the first time we have been able to get together. I suggest we meet again tomorrow at the same time, to discuss our progress." He ended the call.

After scouring the city of Spokane for several hours, Soviet agents located the Americans' pickup truck. Based on where they'd found it, Major Trsenkov figured the Americans must have hopped a train. He found a payphone and phoned an agent in Seattle and asked where trains go upon entering the city. He was told that most passenger trains normally terminate their journeys at the main downtown train station, and container freights usually terminate their journeys in the port of Seattle. All other freight trains get routed to different industrial areas via a central hub, north-east of the city. Even though it was very unlikely the Americans would have managed to climb aboard a passenger train, the major requested agents be sent to all three locations. After he got off the phone with the agent from Seattle, he phoned General Ulanov.

When one of the general's regular telephones rang, he stood up, reached over and picked it up. Major Trsenkov informed him they had lost the Americans and because it was not a secure line, hung up immediately. The general, who was already quite despondent that the mission had failed and that the Americans were being hunted down to be killed, suddenly felt very faint and collapsed to the floor of his office. It was snowing lightly in Moscow that night and sixty-four-year-old General Vladimir Ulanov of the Strategic Rocket Wing of the Soviet Department of Defense was dead.

Williams and Shelby waited until dusk before leaving the boxcar to look around the port area. Huge container ships, most of them almost as long as a football field, were well lit and they were able to determine that there were at least a dozen of them in the port, all in different stages of being unloaded or loaded. There were groups of men everywhere on the dockside and they were careful not to let anyone see them. They had seen enough for now and made their way back to the relative safety of the boxcar under the cover of darkness.

Base Commander Maty hadn't slept for almost two days since first being informed about the potential nuclear explosion and was totally exhausted. He asked Lieutenant Colonel Smith to take over command while he went to get some sleep. His wife was surprised to see him as he came through the front door and asked him if he wanted anything to eat. He said he was too tired to eat and just wanted to go to bed. His wife followed him up the stairs and helped him get undressed and into bed. Although he was extremely tired, sleep wouldn't come. He couldn't stop going over the events of the last two days. The whole situation seemed so unreal. How could this have happened here at Minot? He couldn't stop thinking about who could have done it. He wouldn't have thought many people knew how to trigger the detonation countdown of a nuclear warhead! He was starting to run through the possibilities, when sleep finally overcame him.

Suddenly, outside the bedroom window, there was the deafening sound of a huge explosion and blinding flashes of white light, which turned night into day. The curtains, blinds and furniture were all swept against the far wall. The air was thick with dust and debris and a mushroom cloud could be clearly seen, forming high up in the night sky. A massive crater slowly came into view as the smoke began to clear. Fires were burning everywhere.

The base commander awoke, sweating profusely. He jumped out of bed, ran over and looked out of the bedroom window. Outside it was dark, with a few dim lights visible off in the distance. His wife burst into the bedroom and asked him if everything was alright.

He turned towards her and said, "Yes, everything's alright. I was just having a nightmare about the end of the world - nothing too serious."

His wife helped him get back into bed and told him he had only been asleep for about an hour. He fell back to sleep instantly.

Wednesday February 17

Williams and Shelby awoke early on Wednesday morning feeling really hungry, but there wasn't much they could do about it. They dry shaved using a razor Shelby had brought with him to the ski resort. Although their hair was greasy and their clothes soiled, they both looked reasonably presentable. Upon leaving the boxcar, they could see huge cranes and gantries loading a monstrous ship with containers from the train that they had arrived on yesterday. The containers were multi-coloured, with large, meaningless letters like CSL, APL and POL painted on them.

As they approached a gang of men on the dockside, a tough-looking dock worker greeted them saying, "Good day."

"We're looking for passage across the Pacific and we're willing to pay top dollar and work if need be," said Williams.

In a very deep voice, the dock worker told them that these were box ships that didn't take passengers. He suggested they go and check with the passenger shipping lines, located near the port entrance.

"We're working men, not tourists and would feel much more at home on one of these ships," insisted Williams.

The dock worker figured Williams wasn't going to take no for an answer and said he would take them to meet one of the container ship skippers.

Following the nightmare, Base Commander Maty had slept well and the following morning, after eating a home-cooked breakfast, headed back over to the base headquarters building. It was a bright sunny morning and he felt refreshed after having had a good night's sleep.

He chaired a very brief ten o'clock conference call with SAC and told everyone on the call that the train carrying the ICBM Emplacer-Extractor extractor tripod should be arriving at the base that night. He said that was all the new news he had to report at the moment and he ended the call.

At an even briefer conference call with the FBI and different police authorities that afternoon, FBI Director Harris said he didn't have anything new to report and that call also ended quickly.

Dusk was rapidly approaching as one of the last containers was being lowered into place on the massive container ship. It would be another four hours before the ship would be slowly towed out into Puget Sound and make its way through the Sound's straits, channels and narrows to the Pacific. Williams had paid handsomely for the one-way trip to Singapore and had agreed that he and Shelby would stay out of the way. Although initially reluctant to allow them aboard, once Williams had offered him five thousand dollars cash, the captain had quickly agreed to take them. The captain told the crew that Williams and Shelby were industrial financiers, representing the interests of the shipping line's major shareholders. This was a bit of a stretch, given the way they looked, but the crew seemed to have accepted the explanation. They were on board the *Asian Trader*, a container transporting ship, operated out of the port of Hong Kong. The ship was carrying hundreds of containers, all stacked high in rows on the main deck. There was a multi-storey superstructure at the stern of the ship which looked like one of the numerous white apartment complexes you see along the beaches in Florida. This structure took up less than ten percent of the space on the ship; the remaining ninety percent was completely filled with containers. All the way up the side of the accommodation block were catwalks. They jutted out like balconies, each one enclosed with high railings. Hanging off the side of the accommodation block were two impressive looking lifeboats, one larger than the other, both orange.

Williams and Shelby were given a tour of the ship by the communications officer, Hugh. They climbed up to the top floor of the accommodation block and were taken down a passageway onto the bridge. It overlooked the containers. They were told the ship was over three hundred metres in length, but all they knew was it seemed to be an incredible distance from where they were standing to the bow of the ship. The captain welcomed them to the bridge and told them that once the ship's manifest had been reviewed, they would be on their way. He seemed excited to have them on board and took great pride in showing them the ships navigational instruments. Williams and Shelby tried their best to show genuine interest, as he showed them barometers, barographs, radar screens, chronometers, compasses and all kinds of other instruments. He described in detail what each one of them was for – measuring atmospheric pressure, calculating wind speed, determining the ship's position, speed and heading. They could tell by the enthusiasm he showed when describing each one of them that this was his playground. There were microphones, numerous telephones and what looked like old fashioned walkie-talkies everywhere. There was a large display panel on the wall, showing the entire layout of the ship. Small lights were lit up on the display, all of them green. These apparently alerted the crew to fire or water problems anywhere on the ship. He introduced them to some of his officers and the helmsman, who were reviewing a large chart. He jokingly told them the ship pretty much steered itself, while poking the helmsman in the ribs. He said it stayed on course by itself once it entered the major east-west shipping lanes. He said the tricky part was navigating in and out of harbors. He told them a pilot would soon be coming aboard to assist them to manoeuvre the ship up through Puget Sound. Away from his officers, he told them they were lucky to be on his ship, because his crew was from Hong Kong and they all spoke good English. He said most of the other container ships in the port were from Shenzhen or Shanghai and the crews on those ships spoke very little English. One of the telephones on the bridge rang and the captain politely excused himself.

This was Williams and Shelby's chance to leave the bridge. Hugh took them down to the "communal floor", as he described it. They were shown the galley, which was very clean and the crew lounge, which was very well furnished. They were surprised to find a movie theatre, swimming pool, sauna and hot tub on board. There was also a recreation room with a table tennis table and pool tables. They were not shown the captain's quarters, which was on the same floor, but were told he had an office, bedroom and his own bathroom.

Just as they were completing the tour, an officer handed them some keys and asked Hugh to show them where their cabins were. Their cabins were quite small and everything was bolted down. They had a window, not a porthole, a wall sink and toilet, which gave the cabin the look of a prison cell. There was a bed attached to the wall and Hugh told them there were communal showers and washrooms on each floor.

You don't get much of a room on a container ship for five hundred dollars a day, thought Williams.

As he sat in his sparsely furnished office in the base headquarters building, Base Commander Maty was thinking about the lack of progress being made by the FBI-supported police authorities. Never having worked with the FBI before, he hadn't realized how dependent they were on the state and local police authorities. Essentially all they were doing was providing information whenever it became available. From what he could tell, the FBI was best suited for long-term surveillance and evidence collection, on major criminal activities. They did not seem to be well suited for situations that required immediate action. Anyway, it was only a few days after the infiltration and these things probably took time, so he would cut them some slack.

The train carrying the ICBM Emplacer-Extractor had arrived at Minot Air Force base and cranes were already beginning to load large sections on to flatbed trucks. It had been years since there had been so much excitement on the base. People were constantly arriving and a makeshift parking lot had been set up close to the damaged silo. The engineers from the missile manufacturer who had reset the detonation countdown variable were still on the base and would be staying until the nosecone had been detached and was on its way to be ditched. Engineers from the silo manufacturer were working on repairing the main missile cover hydraulics control system. A number of local contractors had been brought in to provide the required scaffolding and floodlighting around and above the damaged silo. It was a hive of activity.

By now the Soviet agents in Seattle had discovered that the Americans had left a few hours earlier, on a container ship bound for Singapore. Although consummate professionals themselves, they had to admire the resourcefulness the Americans had shown so far, in eluding them.

Major Trsenkov was not happy when he was given the news about the Americans. He had set up his headquarters in a downtown Seattle hotel. Since the death of General Ulanov, he had been reporting directly to one of the Deputies to the Chairman of the Supreme Soviet and had been recently directed to instruct the agents in North America to return to their normal duties.

Because a replacement for General Ulanov had not yet been appointed, agents in Singapore had been contacted directly by the same Chairman's Deputy and given orders to kill the Americans upon their arrival. The agents in Singapore were given the Americans' descriptions, the name of the ship they were on and its expected time of arrival; that was all.

Thursday February 18

By early Thursday morning, the ICBM Emplacer-Extractor was in place, straddling the damaged silo. Crews had worked through the night to make sure it would be ready on time. It would still be several hours until the main missile cover's hydraulic control system would be fully operational once again. A base maintenance crew, with the help of engineers from the silo manufacturer, were completing the repairs as quickly as they could.

Hundreds of camp beds had been set up in one of the giant hangers next to the main airstrip and all essential base personnel had been ordered to remain and sleep on the base. Most people on the base only knew there was a problem with the missile in the damaged Bravo Charlie four silo; they had no idea of the extent of the problem.

When Williams and Shelby awoke early on Thursday morning, they could feel that the motion of the ship was very different from the night before. After slowly making their way to the galley, steadying themselves by pushing against the walls along the corridor, they heard there was a storm blowing up from the south-west and less than twenty-four hours into the voyage, a ferocious storm hit. Never having sailed in such rough seas before, both Williams and Shelby became violently seasick. The captain insisted that they go and stand out on a balcony below the bridge, facing into the wind and rain. This was his tried-and-true remedy for seasickness. The men had been given rain slickers and rubber boots and looked like a pair of Boston whalers, as they stood facing directly into the blowing wind and blinding rain. Water was sloshing all around them and it periodically felt as if someone was throwing buckets of water over them. *Some remedy*! thought Williams; it was more like the Chinese water torture, whatever that was. However, with the wind and rain blowing in their faces, they were actually beginning to feel better. They were soaking wet and wondering what was worse - being seasick or drenched from head to foot. The captain had been checking on them periodically and on his last visit, was very pleased when they told him his remedy seemed to be working. He commented to them, in his comical broken English, that they would soon be hardened seaman.

At a very brief ten o'clock conference call with SAC that day, Base Commander Maty told everyone that the countdown variable had been reset again and the nosecone of the missile was about to be removed. He answered several questions about the nosecone removal and then said he needed to leave to go a briefing with Deputy Secretary of Defence Craig and ended the call.

Since Monday, the base commander had been periodically briefing Deputy Secretary of Defense Craig and senior officers from the Department of Defense and the Pentagon. It seemed to Secretary Craig that everything was going well, so he didn't want to interfere and as long as good progress was being made, he didn't see any reason to involve the White House either.

Representatives from the missile manufacturer were focusing on removing the nosecone from the upper stage of the missile. Those on the base who were assisting with the removal were told it was being flown to the missile manufacturer's plant in California, where they could further investigate a problem with the missile's nosecone. The local contractors had been thankful to get the extra work at this time of the year and had asked very few questions. They really had no interest in the reasons they had been contracted to do the work; they were just happy that they were needed and were being very well compensated.

During a conference call with FBI, state and local police Thursday afternoon Deputy Director Ken Harris told everyone on the call that it had been determined that two men matching the descriptions of the suspects had left Seattle on a container ship bound for Singapore. He said INTERPOL had been provided with the descriptions and I have just been informed that the Central Intelligence Agency has received reliable information from inside the Kremlin as to the identities of the suspects. This information has also been passed on to INTERPOL. As in the meeting in the morning, Base Commander Maty told everyone on the call that the detonation countdown variable had been reset, gaining them another three days.

Late on Thursday, the nosecone was gently lifted off the lower stages of the missile rocket and out of the silo. Although it was swaying backwards and forwards in the wind, it was skilfully lowered onto a concrete skid on the back of a flatbed truck. Following this, forklifts and cranes maneuvered other concrete sections into place, fully encasing the nosecone. It was being encased to ensure when jettisoned it would drop to the bottom of the ocean. An explanation for doing it wasn't given to those doing the work. While this was going on, the remaining stages of the missile rocket were disengaged from their support systems. The flatbed truck carrying the encased nosecone slowly encircled the base and drove out onto the main runway where a huge B-52 Stratofortress was waiting. A crane lifted the heavy skid off the flatbed truck, onto a special truck, which was in turn slowly winched up into the rear cargo bay into the cavernous cathedral-like interior of the giant aircraft.

By late afternoon, the ferocious storm in the Pacific had passed and the sea was calm again. Williams and Shelby were told by some crew members that there were always storms in February during the crossings.

It would be late Thursday afternoon before Wolf's truck was repaired.

Friday February 19

On the morning of February the nineteenth, flashing beacons were all that could be seen through the darkness as the giant B-52 aircraft lifted skywards. The big aircraft slowly gained altitude and began to fly towards the sparsely populated states of the US north-west. As the plane flew west through one time zone after the next, time almost stood still. The area selected for the detonation had already been designated as a no-fly zone and several United States Navy ships were patrolling in the area.

The President had been briefed and was happy with the way things were going, although he was disappointed that those responsible had not been apprehended yet. International protocol required that nuclear tests be announced at least six months in advance and an unannounced nuclear explosion was going to lead to all kinds of questions, in the United Nations Security Council. What the President didn't know was that the Soviets would already know exactly why this unplanned nuclear test had taken place. For them, it would bring closure to the late General Ulanov's failed mission. The President had already decided to explain the unannounced test as being unavoidable due to a malfunctioning nuclear missile - which was actually very close to the truth.

On board the B-52 that had taken off from Minot Air Force base, co-pilot Captain Gregory Marks asked, "What time is the detonation planned for?"

"Saturday morning, local time, by which time we should be back at the base," said the pilot, Captain Javier Garcia.

Studying a map, Marks asked, "So where are we heading?"

"Out towards Japan; then, at the International Date Line, we'll head south towards the equator. The drop zone is several hundred miles south of the Johnson Atoll," Garcia explained.

"I see it; you've marked it with an X, south west of Honolulu and south of the Midway Islands."

"Yes, so get comfortable. It's going to be a long haul. I hope you got plenty of sleep last night," said Garcia laughing.

"This sure was a close one!" said Marks. "It really shows how vulnerable we really are, if someone can do this on one of our missile bases."

"Yes. You know, it also shows that no matter how good you think you are doing, it's never enough. I hear that from now on, they're doubling the security patrols along the perimeter of all US missile bases."

"Did you hear if they arrested anyone yet?" asked Marks.

"No, and I was told it is very unlikely they will now," responded Garcia.

"Who do you think did it?"

"Hard to say, but from what I have heard, it seems whoever it was, flew to the base on the way in," said Garcia.

"I heard there was an incident at a border crossing north of the base last weekend," Marks said.

"Yes, they figure it was likely related to the infiltration, but are being tight lipped about it. Do you realize we are among a very small number of people who even know what's really going on?" said Garcia.

At seven o'clock Friday morning, local time, the B-52 and the two escort F-16 fighter aircraft reached the Pacific.

"Only a few thousand more miles to go," said Garcia.

Unbeknownst to Williams and Shelby, while they were playing cards below decks on that Friday morning, they were almost being over-flown by the B-52 on its way to ditch the missile's warheads. Even though it was only their third day out, they had already got into an onboard routine. They would wait until the majority of the crew had finished their breakfasts, then go down to the galley. There was always lots of food left. After breakfast they would go to the crew lounge and read magazines and books until lunch time, when they would follow the same routine, eating after most of the crew had eaten. Lunch was usually a cold buffet. In the afternoon they would watch a movie. They had watched two Sylvester Stallone *Rocky* movies so far. They had been going to dinner after the crew had eaten and last night found they were eating at the same time as the captain and his officers. He had invited them to his table and seemed to be most interested in both of them. Williams had done most of the talking and had told the captain they both used to work for IBM, being careful not to say where, because they were supposed to be Canadians, and they had recently quit to go on an around-the-world trip, likely heading for Australia first. The captain told them he had been to Australia on a number of occasions and the Aussies who worked on the docks were the toughest men he had ever encountered in any of the ports in the world and he had been to most of them.

At a very brief ten o'clock conference call with SAC on Friday morning, Base Commander Maty informed everyone on the call that the plane carrying the nosecone was on its way to ditch the nuclear warheads, then ended the call.

Approximately seven hours after leaving Minot Air Force base, the B-52 had reached its destination. It was seven-thirty in the morning local time. The aircraft was flying quite low, at less than two thousand feet, as the rear cargo bay doors opened. The aircraft climbed and the nuclear cargo tumbled out, end over end into the white-capped sea below. It made a splash as it hit the water and quickly disappeared into the depths below. It would be another twenty hours until the explosion was expected to occur. The huge B-52 gained altitude slowly circled and headed eastward. Captains Garcia and Marks high fived each other, Garcia saying, "Mission accomplished!"

They were both extremely relieved to have successfully delivered their cargo and very happy to be heading for home.

That same Friday, Wolf and Carol drove from the northern base perimeter road where Wolf had met the paratrooper coming off the base, to the ski resort, in an effort to try and locate Wolf's hunting rifle. They were now getting close to the ski resort and had not seen any sign of it or anything the paratrooper had thrown into the trees. All the trees they had passed had snow right up to their lowest branches. Carol suggested they should come back in the spring when the snow would be melting and they might be able to find it then. Wolf said it would be rusted by then, so there was no point; he would have to buy another one.

At a brief two o'clock conference call with the FBI that afternoon, everyone on the call was informed that the suspects were expected to arrive in Singapore a week from today and INTERPOL had been formally requested to apprehend them upon their arrival. Deputy FBI Director Harris stated that now that apprehending the suspects was in the hands of INTERPOL, this would be the last of these daily calls. He thanked everyone and ended the call.

William's plan, which he had already discussed with Shelby, was that once they reached Singapore, they would make their way to Australia. It seemed to be as far away as you could get and he wondered how many other people on the run had escaped to there over the years. As soon as he could, he would get a postcard off to his sister in Sydney, letting her know he and a friend were on their way to visit her and her husband. At least that way she wouldn't be totally surprised when they showed up on her doorstep. He felt confident that he and Shelby would be able to make a new life for themselves there, even though he was still worried that the Soviets would continue to hunt them down. He didn't know General Ulanov was dead.

It was just after six o'clock local time, when the huge B-52 touched down back at Minot Air Force base. The return flight had only taken six hours due to the strong tail winds. Base Commander Maty was very pleased to hear that everything had gone as planned and the warheads were now sitting safely at the bottom of the Pacific Ocean.

News of the successful ditching quickly spread up the chain of command and the President was also very pleased and very confident that he could handle the political fallout following the detonation. He slept well for the first time in a week.

Saturday February 20

At a very brief conference call with SAC on Saturday morning, Base Commander Maty told everyone on the call that in six hours from now, the warheads should detonate in the depths of the Pacific Ocean and ended the call when there were no questions.

Just after nine o'clock local time in the Samoa time zone, six hundred miles south of the Midway Islands, there was a massive underwater explosion.

At four o'clock Saturday afternoon in Washington, the United States government released a statement saying that they had carried out a nuclear test in the Pacific Ocean.

Major Trsenkov, now back at the farm, heard the news and knew for sure the mission had failed. He and some of his agents were in the process of putting the farm back the way it had been before it had been rented for the mission. The small light aircraft had already been torn down and its numerous parts buried in one of the unused fields on the farm. He was thinking that there may well soon be another black mark in the KGB's file on him.

Sunday February 21

While strolling around the deck of the *Asian Trader* early Sunday morning, Williams and Shelby overheard some crew members chatting about a nuclear explosion in the Pacific.

"Did you hear that?" asked Shelby.

"Yes. It finally makes sense," said Williams, as they walked on.

The captain planned to keep the call he had just had with INTERPOL to himself. He felt the matter could be dealt with when the ship docked in Singapore. So far, the two Canadians hadn't caused him any trouble.

Williams and Shelby were in the crew's lounge, studying an atlas of the world open to a page that showed a map of the Asian and Australian continents.

"You know, Singapore is right at the bottom of the Chinese mainland," said Williams.

"Yes, I see that. So how are we going to get to Australia from there?" Shelby asked.

"Either by ship or plane. I think ship would be better, just like the one we're on. Security tends to be tighter at airports than at seaports," said Williams.

"I wonder which route ships take when they're going to Sydney?" said Shelby pointing at the map. "Along the top, around and down. Or right down the west coast, past Perth, along the southern coast and up? Either way it looks like you have to go right around Australia to get to Sydney."

"There should be some really good sight-seeing, depending how close we get to the coastline," said Williams. "By the way, don't forget to remind me to send a postcard to my sister."

The captain knew he was breaking shipping company rules by providing the Canadians with a passage. He really wanted to ask them why INTERPOL was looking for them, but held back, thinking it was better not to confront them in case they reacted violently. He realized he had made a serious mistake allowing them on-board, which could cost him his job, but it was too late to worry about that now. If it came down to it, he would have to come up with a plausible explanation, but he wasn't in the mood to be inventive at the moment.

At a very brief ten o'clock conference call with SAC on Sunday morning, Base Commander Maty told everyone on the call about the announcement by the President the previous day and said he hoped that apart from political condemnation by a handful of world leaders, this would be the end of the matter. He genuinely thanked everyone on the call for all their help and support during the last week and said this would be the last of these conference calls and when there were no questions ended the call.

The following Friday February 26

Finally the day dawned when Williams and Shelby were due to arrive in Singapore. They were very excited and had risen early on that Friday morning. They were standing on the highest deck of the accommodation block, looking out to sea.

Shelby said, "You know how people wonder how it is that an aircraft made from tons and tons of steel can fly. Well, it's the same for a ship made from tons and tons of iron. You wonder why it doesn't sink like a stone."

"You're right. I've never seen anything made of so much iron as this ship we're on," said Williams.

"It's truly amazing, given how much planes and ships must weigh; it really is quite a phenomenon. It seems to go against everything we know about heavy objects and gravity. Aerodynamics and buoyancy have got to be among the greatest discoveries ever made by man, but you never hear them mentioned."

Just then, the captain put his head around the corner and shouted to them to come and join him on the bridge. When they got there, he handed Williams a pair of binoculars and asked if he could see the dark outline of a long irregular shape far off on the horizon.

"I see it," said Williams, passing the binoculars to Shelby.

Shelby looked through the binoculars just as the captain said, "That's the coast of Singapore off in the distance. I hope you've enjoyed the voyage?"

"Yes, we're hardened seaman now, thanks to you," laughed Williams

Williams shook Shelby's hand and said, "We made it."

"Feels good," said Shelby.

Several hours later, as they were coming into Singapore harbor, Williams knew this would be the time when they would be at their most vulnerable. He figured Soviet agents would be waiting for them. He didn't know that the port of Singapore had been completely closed by Soviet agents who had concocted a bogus story about the *Asian Trader* having to be quarantined due to a serious outbreak of the Asian flu on board. Soviet agents, posing as senior representatives from Singapore's Health Department, had presented a fake Medical Bulletin to the Singapore port authorities, which, among other things, required the complete evacuation of the port six hours before, and twelve hours after, the scheduled arrival of the *Asian Trader* from Seattle.

All incoming road and rail traffic was to be stopped and no other container ships were allowed to enter the harbor. The port authority chairman and harbormaster strongly objected to the closure, indicating that such extreme measures had never been taken before for an outbreak of the Asian flu. They said thousands of tons of cargo would be impacted and they would be contacting the Minister of Health to protest the requested closure. The agent in charge pointed out to them that the Minister of Health had signed the Medical Bulletin, so there was no point in them contacting him or the Health Department. The agent in charge also showed them a fake letter from the Minister of Industry, stating the port authority would be fully compensated for any loss of revenue during the closure. This had calmed the situation.

"Well I guess we have no choice" said the chairman. "We will comply with the Minister of Health's wishes."

The port was cleared of all dock workers hours before the *Asian Trader* was due to dock.

No one, including agents from INTERPOL, was allowed to enter the port. Only the Soviet agents, posing as ministry medical personnel, were allowed to move freely throughout the port.

Soviet agents had been summoned from all over the Malaysian peninsula. Among them were some of the most ruthless Soviet operatives in the world. Life meant very little to them and the death of others even less. Being a Soviet agent in south-east Asia meant that their families enjoyed a better standard of living than most of their fellow Malays, even though they led secluded lives, socializing with only other Soviet-sponsored families. The Soviets took full advantage of the Malay culture of subservience, as even though Malay society was gradually changing, it was still very colonial and a culture that still respected those in authority, who were obeyed without question.

As the huge container ship was making its way towards its wharf within the harbor, there was all kinds of vessel traffic, primarily small craft and coasters, sailing around it. Many of them were criss-crossing in front of the massive ship. From up on the bridge, Williams and Shelby could see a panoramic view of the brightly lit skyscrapers of downtown Singapore through the heavy rain. They left the bridge, telling the captain they were going to get ready for their arrival.

As the ship was coming into its berth, Williams and Shelby were looking over the side at the dark choppy water below. It looked to be very dirty, with streams of green and yellow surface oil illuminated by the bright dockside lamps. The ship's bow thrusters were churning up the dirty water as they helped move the ship into its berthing position. It looked like all kinds of equipment had been readied along the dockside for their arrival; cranes, huge forklifts and large container moving gantries were everywhere, but strangely, they noticed there were no dock workers anywhere, in contrast to the port of Seattle, where they had been everywhere.

As the ship was about to dock, the captain asked his first officer to find the Canadians and confine them to their cabins. The first officer went down to their cabins, but didn't find them there. As he began to make his way down the accommodation block catwalk, he saw them both. He hurried down to where he'd seen them, but when he got there, they'd gone. He looked all around but they weren't anywhere to be seen. He made his way back up to the bridge and reported to the captain that he couldn't find them anywhere. The captain told him to round up as many crew members as he could and search the ship from top to bottom, the fact that his first officer couldn't find the Canadians didn't bother the captain too much. It wouldn't be good for his reputation to be seen assisting INTERPOL. There was frequently trade in goods other than those that were listed on the ship's official manifest.

Williams and Shelby had got lucky arriving in Singapore on a rainy evening. Seeing no one around, they jumped over the side of the ship, hoping their splashes wouldn't attract any attention. They swam as fast as they could through the dirty smelly water until they reached a concrete jetty. They scrambled up and made their way up a set of concrete steps. Williams peeked up onto the dockside and seeing no one, waved to Shelby to follow him. They ran into the doorway of an old warehouse and stood there, dripping wet, watching the rain come down in the gathering fog. Even though it was raining, they could feel the thick, warm humidity of the tropics. They had made it ashore in Singapore and were now only four thousand miles from the comparative safety of William's sister, in Sydney.

Unbeknownst to Williams and Shelby, Soviet agents were hiding everywhere throughout the port and many of them had seen them run across the dockside into the warehouse doorway.

After several minutes standing in the doorway, Shelby said, "We can't stand here all night; we're going to catch pneumonia."

"Give me a minute," said Williams.

"There doesn't seem to be anyone around," said Shelby.

"I know. Hold on a minute," Williams repeated.

While they had been talking, a huge gantry had been making its way past them.

"Why don't we move along with this big thing?" said Shelby, pointing to the gantry.

"Alright," said Williams, rather impatiently.

They stepped out of the warehouse doorway and moved underneath the giant gantry. It was transporting containers and making a loud squeaking noise as it moved along on top of a set of rusty rails.

Looking up, Shelby said, "Hey, look at the way those containers are swaying right above us! Shouldn't we get out from under here?"

"No, this is an excellent way to leave the dock area. We look like dock workers," said Williams.

"Well, I don't know about you, but I'm scared."

"The gantry operator can't see us, so why are you worried?"

Unbeknownst to them, a Soviet agent was operating the gantry and as it continued to slowly move along, the agent in charge gave the order for the containers it was carrying to be released. As the huge containers thudded to the ground all around Williams and Shelby, they only just managed to avoid them. Williams looked around and noticed that there was gantry upon gantry, lined up along the dockside, all with containers hanging about twenty feet off the ground. It was a trap for sure! Every gantry in the port was in the vicinity of their newly arrived container ship. It was a veritable minefield of hanging containers.

"So what do we do?" shouted Shelby, almost out of breath.

"We need to get away from here. There's something badly wrong!"

Just as Williams said this, shots started to ring out all around them. Automatic gunfire was coming from cranes, gantries and numerous dockside building windows. Williams got his pistol out of his backpack and loaded a new ammunition clip. They could see a train slowly approaching them from behind and Williams thought this may also be part of the trap. Hiding behind the legs of a gantry, they waited for the train to reach them and began to run alongside it, using it as a shield between them and the buildings. Williams scrambled up into the cab of the lead locomotive and pointing his pistol at the driver, told him to speed up. Shelby scrambled up into the cab right behind Williams and heard the driver say he couldn't go any faster because he was getting ready to take a side track. Gunfire was now being directed into the cab of the locomotive. The agent in charge was mystified as to where the train had come from; all rail traffic was supposed to have been stopped. Shelby could see one of the monstrous gantries moving towards the train in an attempt to cut it off. It was clearly on a collision course with the train.

The lead locomotive that Williams and Shelby were standing in squeezed past the on-coming gantry, but the gantry crashed into the locomotive behind, pushing it off the tracks and down onto its side. Several railcars behind it and the lead locomotive also eventually toppled over, falling sideways. Although thrown down, Williams, Shelby and the driver weren't hurt and managed, with great difficulty, to climb up out of the locomotive's cab. Once out, Williams and Shelby ran as fast as they could towards the train terminal area. Containers were being released from numerous gantries as they ran under and past them. The automatic gunfire had started up again and there was nowhere to hide, except behind the legs of the giant gantries. A few seconds later, they heard a loud scream of agony as the locomotive driver was gunned down. Williams managed to clear some falling containers and changing direction, headed for a ramp leading up into a massive container ship.

Shelby wasn't so lucky and got snagged by a falling container. Fortunately, the edge of the container had snared him in such a way that the heel of his boot was taking the weight. Although he was pinned and lying on his stomach, he somehow reached back and managed to remove the lace from his snagged boot. Pulling his leg with both hands, he tried to pull his right foot out of the boot. Bullets were pinging and dinging off containers all around him, making loud metallic sounds. Because his foot was being squeezed within his boot, he couldn't pull it out. He painfully twisted his body around, so he was now lying on his back, rotating his leg in the process. This did the trick and his foot popped loose. He could see row upon row of containers ahead of him and got up and ran towards them. His bootless foot really hurt and he couldn't put any weight on it, so he was hopping along as best he could on his good foot. It was still raining and very dark.

Shelby was wondering what had happened to the gunfire, when suddenly it started up again and he could actually hear bullets flying past his head. Two Soviet agents came around the corner behind him and started chasing after him. He came to the end of a row of stacked containers, turned the corner and ran back in the direction he had just come from. As he was hopping along, he felt something hit him at the back of his right thigh and he stumbled. He felt the back of his right leg and when he pulled his hand away, it was covered in blood. As he hobbled forward, he was hit high on the left shoulder and he went down. The agents who had been chasing him caught up to him.

One of the olive-skinned Malay Soviet agents, standing over him, said, "Do you have anything to say before we blow you away, you American dog?"

Looking up and in pain, Shelby said, "Yes, stop watching so many American movies and get your own lines."

Just as Shelby said this, Williams, who was kneeling about twenty yards away, shot both Soviet agents and they both went down screaming, writhing in pain. Shelby crawled over, grabbed one of their handguns, pointed it at them both, and sarcastically said, "You were saying?"

Williams lifted Shelby up off the ground and they slowly made their way to the end of a row of stacked containers. Shelby's wounds were bleeding badly and Williams could see his jacket and pants were covered with blood. Shelby asked Williams to let him sit down for awhile and Williams helped him down to the ground. He ripped Shelby's pants away where most of the blood was and after checking could see an entry and exit wound; that was a good sign. It looked like a bullet had passed through the outside of Shelby's right thigh, likely causing muscle and blood vessel damage. Seeing more blood on Shelby's left shoulder, he pulled his jacket and shirt down and looked at his shoulder. It looked like he had just been nicked and it was only a flesh wound.

Williams shifted his attention back to Shelby's leg. He took the ripped off pant leg and tied it as high as he could around his leg, cutting off the blood flow as well as best he could. Shelby complained to Williams that he had tied it too tight and he was starting to lose the feeling in his foot.

"It won't be for long, just until I can rig something up around the wound," said Williams.

Williams ripped one of the sleeves off his own jacket. He tied it around Shelby's leg to try and stop the bleeding and to keep the wound clean and then loosened off the tourniquet, much to Shelby's relief.

After Williams had finished with Shelby's leg wound, Shelby asked him if he would look at his foot. Williams could see it was swollen at the back of the heel and could also see a lot of bruising below the ankle. He could see why it would be painful for Shelby to put any weight on it. Williams said there wasn't much he could do for his foot right now.

Shelby was thanking Williams for stopping his leg from bleeding, when they heard voices close by.

"Stay down!" whispered Williams, kneeling down with his pistol cocked.

A Soviet agent came running around the corner. Williams shot him and he went down quietly in a heap. Shots were now being fired at

Williams and Shelby from behind and they turned and saw two more Soviet agents running towards them out of the darkness. *Are these people crazy?* thought Williams, as he aimed and shot both of them, knocking them side-ways into some containers. This was five agents he had shot and he wondered how many more of them there were. He took another ammunition clip out of his backpack.

Shelby was looking very pale and was having trouble getting his breath. Williams helped him to sit up, which seemed to help with his breathing. "We need to get you some medical attention."

Shelby just nodded, looking very tired.

"I'm going to carry you," said Williams. "I need you to stand up and lean over my shoulder as I squat down."

Williams helped Shelby to his feet, standing him up on his one good foot. Then he crouched down and Shelby leaned over his shoulder. Williams slowly got to his feet and set off carrying Shelby. All Williams could see were containers ahead of them and they began to hear voices again, which seemed to be off in the distance. Williams was thinking how they could get out from within the containers, even though they were providing cover for them at the moment. He stopped, squatted down and sat Shelby down, leaning him against a container. He climbed up the bars on the container doors of a stack of containers, high enough to peek over the top. Even though it was dark and still raining, he could see they were on the edge of where the containers were stacked and could see the lights from the container ships along the dockside. He jumped down, swung Shelby over his shoulder again and began to make his way to where the container ships were. He was thinking about the men he had just shot, telling himself it was him and Shelby or them - he'd had no choice. As he came to the end of a row of stacked containers, he could see a brightly lit ramp leading up into a container ship. He figured this was the only option they had, so he made his way towards the ramp, shooting out the bright light that was illuminating it. As he was struggling to carry Shelby up the ramp, gunshots started to ring out again and bullets began to ricochet all around them.

Williams turned to see where the shots were coming from and could see flashes lighting up the darkness, high up in the cabs of cranes and gantries. Summoning up all the strength he could muster, he ran up the ramp onto the ship and sat Shelby down on the deck. There didn't seem to be anyone around. Williams knew Shelby needed medical treatment and opened a door at the bottom of the ship's accommodation block. He managed to manhandle himself and Shelby through the door and along a corridor. As they turned the corner, they could see a storage room, which turned out to be unlocked. Once inside, Williams turned on the light and helped Shelby get comfortable, wedging him between some metal buckets. Williams said he was going to see if he could find a medical kit but just as he was about to leave the room, heard voices. He helped Shelby get up, turned off the light and as they were both standing behind the door holding their breath, it opened. Someone looked inside and seeing only cleaning equipment and supplies quickly closed the door, leaving Williams and Shelby standing in the dark. Williams turned the light back on and helped Shelby get into a comfortable position again. Shelby looked like he was getting the color back in his face, which Williams thought must mean the makeshift dressing was working.

Shelby said, "If you find a medical kit, please make sure you bring me some painkillers too; my foot is killing me."

"No problem," said Williams. "I'll bring the whole thing; don't worry."

Not hearing voices anymore, Williams opened the door and looked into the corridor. He couldn't see anyone in the corridor. He shut the door and asked Shelby if he could remember where the medical kits were on the ship they had just been on. Shelby said he thought there was one on the bridge and another in the galley; they were the only places he remembered seeing them.

"Wasn't there one on the wall in the showers, too?"

"I don't remember."

"I think there was. Anyway, that's where I'm heading."

Several minutes later, Williams returned with a medical kit.

"Where did you find it?" asked Shelby.

"In the washroom on this floor, I guess all the washrooms have them too," said Williams. "You know, I think the crew must all be ashore. I didn't see anyone around."

Williams opened the medical kit and there was a box of something called Aspo. He read the information on the side of the Aspo box and it said it was a form of aspirin, only stronger. Williams opened the box and popped out three tablets.

"Here take these; this is what you need. Hopefully you've got enough saliva to swallow them down; if not, I can go and get you some water, if I can find something to put it in."

Shelby quickly swallowed the pain killers.

"Can you lay down on your side?" asked Williams.

Shelby got down on his side and Williams, straddling him, removed the jacket sleeve from around his thigh. The wound looked very clean and uninfected. He wrapped a real bandage around Shelby's leg, covering the wound. Then he looked at his shoulder wound, which he covered with some gauze, secured with strips of plaster. Shelby asked him to check his foot which he said still really hurt. Williams could see it was badly swollen.

"I can bandage it up if you like, to try and give it support." Shelby asked him to do that and Williams strapped it up as best he could with a tensor bandage.

"What now?" asked Shelby, sitting up.

"I think we should stay here for now. You need to rest and I need time to figure out what our next move should be. Try and sleep for awhile," said Williams.

The pain killers were kicking in and Shelby was soon asleep. Williams, sitting next to him, was thinking about the welcome they had just received upon their arrival here in Singapore. It looked as if the Soviet agents had taken over the whole port. Williams hadn't seen one dock worker and wondered how the Soviets could have taken over one of the busiest ports in the world. This was obviously also why no one was aboard the ship except the Soviet agents.

Williams figured that he and Shelby should perhaps wait it out until the crew returned, then make their move, because this would likely mean the Soviet agents had left. Shelby was snoring softly, which seemed like a good thing to Williams. He made some space for himself and using the edge of a mop as a pillow, fell asleep.

Soviet agents were now gathered on the dockside at the bottom of the ramp leading up into the container ship that Williams and Shelby were hiding on. The agent in charge was doing most of the talking, or shouting, which might be a better way to describe it, and was not happy. He was telling the large group of Soviet agents gathered around him that finding the Americans was their highest priority, not looking after the agents who were either wounded or dying among the stacked containers, so none of them were very happy either. He told them to search the ship from top to bottom, because the Americans were hiding somewhere.

Saturday February 27

Williams awoke staring down the barrel of a gun. A Soviet agent was standing over him. Williams quickly moved his head out of the line of fire and brought his right boot up between the puny-looking agent's legs. The gun went off and the agent fell on top of Williams, gasping for air, a pained look on his face. Williams hoped no one had heard the gunshot and grabbed the agent's wrist, shaking the gun loose. As he pushed it away, he brought his knee up into the agent's face. Blood started to stream from the agent's nose as Williams pushed him away and stood up, pointing his own pistol at him. He gave the pistol to Shelby, who was awake now, and told him to keep it pointed at their unwelcome visitor while he found something to tie him up with.

Most of the Soviet agents were searching through the rows of containers stacked high on the main deck, but some of them who were searching the accommodation block heard the muffled gunshot, but had no idea where it had come from. They figured that an agent searching between the containers may have fired at a rat, they seemed to be everywhere on the ship.

Williams tied a bandage around the agent's bloodied mouth, making sure he could still breathe through his nose, which might not be so easy now that it was likely broken. Either way, Williams really didn't care. These people were trying to kill him and Shelby, so all bets were off; it was dog eat dog now. He tied the agent's hands and feet together and moved him into a corner of the storage room, under a row of hanging mops and brushes. The room was very cramped now, with the three of them in it.

Williams figured the room was unlikely to be searched a third time, so they should still continue to sit tight until the crew returned. Shelby got comfortable again and fell back to sleep. Williams noticed the Soviet agent was sleeping too and after a while he dozed off also.

Williams awoke with Shelby whispering in his ear, telling him to listen. They could hear voices talking in Chinese. Williams sat up and whispered to Shelby that he would go and see what was going on. Shelby helped himself to more painkillers as Williams was leaving the storage room. He could see the agent still sleeping.

Williams couldn't see anyone in the corridor, so he quickly made his way to the door that led out onto the deck. Once he got out onto the deck, he could see it was beginning to get dark and wasn't raining anymore. He could hear men shouting and the sounds of machinery being operated. Obviously things were getting back to normal again. He went to the side of the ship, looked down and saw a great deal of activity, similar to the way it had been when they were in the port of Seattle.

Someone approached him while he was looking over the side railing and spoke to him in Chinese. Williams nodded and quickly made his way down the ramp leading down from the ship. When he got onto the dockside, he looked around to see if he could find someone who didn't look Chinese or Malay. He could see a big black man driving an oversized forklift and ran over and asked him if he spoke English. Finding out that he did, Williams asked him how he could get to downtown Singapore from there. The forklift operator told him trains left every hour for downtown from the train terminal. Williams thanked him and made his way back to the ramp leading up into the ship. Before walking up the ramp, he picked up an empty clipboard, a pen and a piece of paper, off a table close by. As he walked up the ramp, he scribbled a few numbers onto the piece of paper to make it look like he was working, taking inventory or something. He made his way back to the storage room and when he got inside, told Shelby, who was sitting waiting for him, to take the Soviet agent's clothes. Shelby left the agent, now awake, in his socks and underpants and asked Williams what they were going to do with him.

"Let's leave him here to surprise whoever comes to do the cleaning."

Shelby was limping badly and had to be supported by Williams as they came down the ramp in the gathering darkness. Williams was carrying the clipboard and a handcart, which he had found hanging in the storage room. Shelby was dressed in the Soviet agent's clothes, which only just fit him. He only had one boot on; his right foot was still too badly swollen and he couldn't get a boot on it. Williams's clothes were still very damp from being in the water the night before but there wasn't much he could do about it.

When they reached the dockside, Williams put the clipboard back on the table where he had found it and told Shelby to stand on the handcart. Shelby put all his weight on his good foot while

Williams pushed him along the dock, starting to run, making it look like they were playing a game. Dock workers watched them as they ran by, but no one confronted them.

When they reached the train terminal, there were very few workers waiting on the platform. Williams pushed the cart along until they came to a bench seat where Shelby hopped off and sat down. There was a ticket dispenser on the platform which only took coins. Williams figured it must be an honors system, so they would have to take their chances, because he only had large, American dollar bills. They waited about fifteen minutes and a train pulled in. Williams helped Shelby get on board and they sat and waited. There was only one other person in their car and he was reading a newspaper and paying no attention to them. Ten minutes later, the doors closed and the train started its journey into downtown Singapore.

The Soviet agents had left the port late on Saturday morning, after being unable to locate the Americans. One of their agents was missing, three were wounded and two were dead. The wounded and dead had been picked up, but there was no trace of the missing agent. Once he got to his base, the Soviet agent in charge phoned Moscow and told the Deputy to the Chairman of the Supreme Soviet that they had lost the Americans. The Deputy told him to wait for new orders. Not happy with the performance of the Singapore agents, he did not thank him for the information. The Chairman was not at all happy to hear the news and told the Deputy to continue to track the Americans down and kill them. He said their escape was unacceptable because the knowledge they carried must never be allowed to get out.

Soon after leaving the train station in downtown Singapore, Williams and Shelby found a small hotel close by, the Peninsula Mandarin. With Shelby not able to walk far, they figured this hotel would be good. When the hotel clerk asked Shelby what had happened to his foot, he said he had twisted it falling down some steps the night before.

Once they got to their room, Williams removed the dressings from Shelby's wounds and bathed them in warm water. The bullet wound on his leg showed no signs of infection but the flesh wound on his shoulder had quite a lot of redness around its edges. Williams assured Shelby this was a normal part of the healing process. He dried Shelby's wounds and suggested that he leave them uncovered to let the air get to them which should help them heal quicker.

Williams took a quick shower and when he came back into the room, he asked Shelby what his clothes measurement and shoe size was. He said the stores should still be open so he would go and buy them some new stuff. Shelby took some more painkillers and went to bed.

About two hours later, Williams came back to the room with an assortment of jackets, pants, shirts, socks, underwear and shoes. He'd also got some sandwiches, drinks and a bag of ice for Shelby's foot.

After waking Shelby up they both ate, after which Shelby tried on some of the new clothes Williams had bought which fitted perfectly. Williams already knew his fit because he'd tried most of them on in the store.

Williams sat down on the bed next to Shelby and realized he was tired. "Well, I sent a postcard to my sister and tomorrow I'll go and see if I can find a container ship to take us down under to Australia," he said.

Shelby was trying to find a comfortable sleeping position and didn't say anything in response. Williams wrapped the ice pack around Shelby's swollen foot, slumped down onto his own bed, turned off the bedside lamp and was asleep almost immediately and snoring softly. Shelby, still in a lot of pain but feeling groggy after taking some more pain killers, turned his light off and was soon snoring too.

Sunday February 28

Williams woke Shelby up and told him he was going to see if he could find them a passage to Australia on another container ship. He went to the train station, just up the road, and found the port shuttle train platform, where there was a train waiting to leave. Now having some change, he bought a return ticket from one of the machines. When he reached the port, it was very quiet there; he thought it was probably because it was a Sunday. He found his way back to where the container ship berths were and asked one of the few dock workers who was around, if any of them were sailing to Australia. The dock worker said he didn't know; all he knew was that this one they were looking at was bound for Shanghai in a few days. He told Williams to go and check at the harbor master's office. Williams didn't want to do this; he wanted to pay one of the captains again. The harbor master would only tell him container ships didn't take passengers.

He walked up and down the berthing piers, looking at the names of the massive container ships. Nothing jumped out at him, until he came to one named *Pride of Perth*. He figured this had to be Australian with a name like that and looked for a flag, but couldn't see one. There was a ramp leading up into the ship but no one seemed to be around. It looked like the ship was either half-loaded or unloaded; there were cranes towering over it and gantries straddling it. Still not seeing anyone around, he walked up the ramp and looked around on the deck. He still couldn't see anyone and wondered what he should do. He went back down the ramp, sat on some shipping crates and waited.

He waited for about an hour and still not seeing anyone on the pier or on the ship, thought he had no choice but to go to the harbor master's office. When he got there, he found the door locked. Not seeing anyone else around he thought to himself he'd have to come back the next day.

While he was walking towards the train terminal, he saw two Malay dock workers coming towards him. They approached him and asked him what he was doing. He said he was looking for a passage to Australia and asked them if they knew anything about the container ship *Pride of Perth*. One of them said he thought it sailed to a number of Australian cities. Williams asked if it went to Sydney and the Malays said they thought it did. They suggested he should come back tomorrow and check with the passenger lines, because container ships didn't take passengers. Williams thanked them and continued walking towards the train terminal where he caught a train back downtown.

When he got back to the hotel, he told Shelby that he had found a ship that looked like it was going to Australia, but he hadn't been able to meet with the captain.

Shelby said he was feeling much better; his wounds didn't hurt as much and seemed to be getting better and the swelling in his foot had gone down quite a bit since he had iced it the previous night. He also said he was able to get both of his new shoes on.

"That's great!" said Williams. "How about going to get something to eat?"

Shelby said he was feeling very hungry and would like to, so they set off to see if they could find a western-style restaurant.

After walking around the downtown streets for almost half an hour, sweating in the high humidity, all they had seen were food stalls with picnic tables set up in front of them. They were amazed at how unbelievably clean Singapore was; it was spotlessly clean with no garbage anywhere. As they walked around, they stood out from the majority of the short, stocky Malays; they hoped no one singled them out or recognized them. Shelby said his foot was starting to hurt again and he couldn't walk much further, so they decided to eat at one of the cooking stalls. They ordered chicken curry with steamed rice and were given a pot of green tea to take to their table while they waited for the food to be prepared.

As they sat at the picnic table in downtown Singapore, Williams said, "You know, we're pretty close to getting to Australia."

"Good!" said Shelby. "How much money do you have left?"

"At least ten thousand of the Soviets' money and about four thousand of my own. How about you?"

"I have about two thousand pounds and a few dollars."

"I guess neither of us spent much during our training - not really having anything to spend it on, except cheap cigarettes and booze."

After eating the food which tasted pretty good and filled them up, they made their way back to their hotel. Once back in the room, they both took showers to try and cool themselves down in the tropical heat and humidity. Williams told Shelby that tomorrow morning they should check out of the hotel and assume they would be getting a passage to Australia. They were both still feeling quite tired and slept well for the second night in a row.

Monday March 1

Williams and Shelby took the train back to the port of Singapore first thing on Monday morning, crowded in with noisy Malay dock workers. Once they got into the port, Williams led the way to the container ship named the *Pride of Perth.* All the heavy equipment that had been silent the previous day was in full operation. Williams asked one of the dock workers if he knew if the ship's master or captain was onboard and he told him he was. Williams and Shelby walked up the main ramp onto the ship and asked the first person they met where they could find the captain. He told them to wait out on the deck and he would go and call him and asked why they wanted to speak to him.

"Tell him we would like to speak to him about some special cargo we would like him to take to Sydney, Australia," said Williams.

The dock worker went through one of the doors at the bottom of the accommodation block and within a few minutes, returned and asked the men to come with him. Once they got inside the accommodation block, he directed them to a phone hanging on the wall.

"Hello," said Williams.

"Hello, this is Captain Fletcher speaking. I understand you have some cargo you want taken to Australia?"

"Yes, Sydney actually, but I would rather discuss this in person with you, because it's quite unique."

"Wait back out on the deck where you were and I'll be down soon," said the captain.

The captain was a big man, with a thick Australian accent. He shouted to Williams and Shelby as he was climbing down the catwalk on the side of the accommodation block. Soon after stepping down onto the stern deck, he walked over and shook their hands.

He said, "Did you see me come down the catwalk? I like to climb down them sometimes, to see what shape they're in. The ship often gets inspected by the Australian port authorities and my neck is always on the line. Anyway what is this all about?"

"We are the cargo that would like to travel with you to Sydney," said Williams.

"Well, we go there, but why do you want to travel there on a box ship?" asked the captain.

"We are working men, not tourists and will make it worth your while. We already paid for a passage from Seattle to here on a container ship, similar to this one, so we already know the routine."

"You know, this is quite unusual," said the captain.

"We'll pay you eight thousand dollars cash," said Williams.

"Is that US dollars?"

"Yes."

"Let me see," said the captain. "I'm pretty sure we have room for you both. Are you ready to go today? We're leaving tonight."

"Yes," said Williams. "We've just got this backpack, no other luggage."

"You boys are travelling light. Where are you from?

"We're from Winnipeg, in Canada," said Shelby, speaking for the first time.

This didn't seem to register with the captain and he said, "Come with me," opening one of the doors leading into the accommodation block. The men followed him up to the second floor where he stopped and said, "Here, you can have these cabins. They have their own shower stall, sink and toilet. I will get someone to give you the keys. Can we settle up, before I take you up for breakfast?"

Williams reached into his backpack, took out a handful of bills and gave them to the captain. The captain counted the money and put it in his back pocket.

"Thanks," he said. "Now let's go eat."

Williams and Shelby met a number of the crew in the galley, all Australian. While they were having breakfast with the captain and some of his officers, Williams asked him when they expected to get to Sydney. The captain said the ship would be going to Perth, Adelaide and Melbourne first. He said if the ship left as planned that night, they should be arriving in

Perth in a week and should be in Sydney a few days later.

After breakfast, the captain asked a young, tough-looking, member of the crew, called Tony, to get the keys for Williams and Shelby's cabins and to give them a tour of the ship.

Already the accommodations seemed newer and more modern to both Williams and Shelby.

It wasn't long until the Soviet agent in charge in Singapore heard from the Deputy to the Chairman of the Supreme Soviet in Moscow. He was ordered to send agents to all the airports and seaports in Singapore. The Soviet leadership assumed that Singapore was not the Americans' final destination. The agents who had been dispatched to the port of Singapore soon learnt that the Americans had left the day before on a container ship bound for Australia. This information was reported back to the Deputy in Moscow.

The Deputy immediately put his intelligence staff to work in researching the Americans' backgrounds. Within several days, it had been determined that Williams had a sister living just outside Sydney. The Soviets didn't have a very extensive network of agents in Australia but did have a number in each of the large cities.

The Deputy contacted the agent-in-charge in Australia and told him what he wanted him to do. The Soviets plan for killing the Americans had changed significantly after what had happened in Singapore harbor.

Williams and Shelby spent most of Monday reading in the lounge, sitting on big comfortable sofas. There was quite a collection of paperback novels on the ship in bookshelves all around the lounge, making it more like a library than a lounge. They found their cabins much more roomy and comfortable than on the *Asian Trader* and figured it was probably because Australians were bigger and required more space than the Chinese.

The next day, Tony joined them while they were watching the shipping traffic sailing around the big ship. He told them they were currently sailing south through the Singapore Strait and would soon be going through the Sunda Strait, between the Indonesian islands of Sumatra and Java. He said this would be in about three hours from now and they shouldn't miss it.

Several hours later, Tony knocked on their cabin doors and told them they were starting to sail into the Sunda Strait and they should come and see it. As they were on their way up to the top deck of the accommodation block Shelby said, "You know, this is already a better voyage than the last one; we didn't see anything except ocean."

"Yes, it's much better when there are things to see," agreed Williams.

They were amazed how close the coast was on either side; they could see hilly jungle-like terrain, dotted with tall palm trees. They were also surprised by the number of off-shore oil rigs in the Strait itself. Tony told them to look over to their right where they should be able to see the remains of a famous volcano. He told them that it was called Krakatoa and when it had become highly active, a hundred years ago, had killed thousands of people and had devastated the whole area. He told them that the Strait was a passage to the Indian Ocean and that they were leaving the Java Sea and the Pacific Ocean behind. Once they had passed by the Indonesian islands of Sumatra and Java, there wasn't much to see for the next few days - just the usual expanse of ocean. The next day, however, Tony told them that they would be passing Christmas Island, which didn't mean much to them. Tony explained to them that the name was interesting because the first explorers, the British he thought, had apparently discovered the island on Christmas Day and thus had named it Christmas Island.

Williams and Shelby followed a similar routine to the one they'd had on the *Asian Trader*. They ate after the crew and spent most of the days reading and watching movies.

The following Sunday March 7

On the sixth day out, Williams and Shelby could see the continent of Australia off in the distance. It was really only an outline and it was not until they were approaching Perth and the port of Fremantle several hours later that they could see the rocky and rugged coastline.

As the *Pride of Perth* was moving into its berth, Williams and Shelby were sitting in the galley; Tony came in and told them they could go ashore with him later that night if they wanted to. Feeling there wasn't much point in sitting in a dock-side tavern, drinking and singing old sea shanties into the early hours of the morning, they both declined, saying they'd found a good movie to watch. Subconsciously, neither of them had been able to get over their experience in the port of Singapore and they didn't want to draw any attention to themselves.

The next day, while containers were being taken off the ship and more were being loaded, Williams and Shelby spent most of the day reading on the balcony of the accommodation block. They were enjoying the sights and sounds of the busy port and watching the large container ships manoeuvring their way in and out of the harbor. The weather was much better in Australia than in Singapore, with warm sea breezes and no noticeable humidity. They were told it was still summer and the temperature was a very warm 85 degrees.

Williams and Shelby repeated the same routine while the ship was tied up in the ports of Adelaide and Melbourne. They still didn't see any point in going to some seedy working man's bar in the dock area. This was not their thing; although they noticed the crew didn't waste any time leaving the ship once their duties had been taken care of. The captain and his officers didn't seem to leave the ship while it was in the harbor. Williams had seen them in the corner of the galley, playing cards and drinking late into the night on several occasions.

Shelby's wounds were almost healed now and he felt no discomfort from them anymore. His foot no longer hurt and the only sign it had been injured was a dark blue line of blood along the bottom.

Williams, always thinking, was wondering what the Soviets were doing to try and find them and wondered if the police authorities were still looking for them also. He figured it would have to be INTERPOL who would be looking for them now and didn't know too much about them. There didn't seem to be any Soviet or INTERPOL agents at the port of Singapore on either the Sunday or Monday before they left. He thought perhaps it was a master stroke to be taking another container ship, because this might be the last thing either the Soviets or INTERPOL would have anticipated.

INTERPOL were still actively searching for Williams and Shelby, even though their trail had gone cold. On the previous Saturday, when they were allowed to get into the port of Singapore, they met with the captain of the *Asian Trader*. He told them that his crew had been quarantined under false pretences and that the two Canadians had disappeared. He was asked if the Canadians had been confined to their cabins and said they had, but they must have found a way to get out. The captain asked the INTERPOL agents what the Canadians were wanted for and was told this information was classified. This greatly upset the captain and he said that anything else they wanted to know was also classified and asked the INTERPOL agents to leave the ship.

The senior agent in the INTERPOL office in the Singapore reported to the FBI that the suspects' whereabouts were currently unknown at this time. The FBI was not surprised at this, never having had much success working with INTERPOL in the past. Because the situation had been dealt with, the interest in finding those responsible had waned and it had now become more a matter of national security, than law enforcement.

Life had pretty much gone back to normal at Minot Air Force base. A new missile had been installed in the repaired silo. SAC and Base Commander Maty had made use of the ICBM Emplacer-Extractor while it was still at the base. It was now on its way back to Warren Air Force base in Wyoming.

Thursday March 11

As the *Pride of Perth* was coming into its berth along one of the piers in a large container port, several miles south of Sydney's famous harbor, Williams and Shelby were looking for any signs of anything unusual. It was a bright sunny day and nothing looked out of place. There were dock workers everywhere. Forklifts were shooting along the dockside, and cranes and gantries were in full operation. This was a relief to both of them after their port of Singapore experience. It was now almost a month since they had left Moscow.

They said their goodbyes to the ship's crew and left the deck as soon as the first ramp was moved into place. When they got down onto the dockside, they asked a dock worker if he knew where they could get a taxi. He told them they would have to telephone for one and they would find telephones in the Customs Services building a few hundred yards south of where they were.

When Williams got through to a taxi company, a dispatcher asked him for the address where he wanted to be picked up and the address where he wanted to go. Williams read out his sister's address and looked around and seeing a sign said he was calling from the Port Hobart Customs building. The dispatcher told him it would cost approximately a hundred dollars. Williams said that wasn't a problem, as long as the driver would take US dollars. The dispatcher told him this could be arranged, but there would be a conversion fee. Williams said that wasn't a problem and was told a taxi should be there within fifteen minutes.

Williams joined Shelby sitting on a bench outside the Customs Services building and watched planes landing and taking off from what he guessed must be Sydney airport. As they were sitting there Captain Fletcher and one of his officers came by on their way into the Customs Services building. A short time later, a taxi pulled up in front of where they were sitting and the driver yelled out Williams' name.

As Williams and Shelby approached the taxi, the driver asked, "Are you Mr. Williams, for the taxi for Hornsea?"

"Yes that's us," said Williams.

"Jump in the back. Do you have any luggage?" the driver asked in a heavy Australian accent.

Williams said he just had a backpack which he wanted to keep with him. He and Shelby scrambled into the back of the not-so-clean taxi. The driver said Hornsea was quite a way from where they were. Williams acknowledged that this was where they wanted to go and said his sister lived on a street off Junction Road in a place called Waroga.

"You mean Waroongaa," said the driver.

"Well yes, if that's how you pronounce it. It's 26 Derwin Ave, supposedly off the Pacific highway."

"I know roughly where that is and have a map book if we can't find it. You know, I usually work around the harbor area, so this is really going to take me out of my way."

"Don't worry," said Williams. "There will be a nice tip for you. We'll make it well worth your while, if you get us there in one piece. We were told we could give you US dollars; I hope they told you that?"

"Yes, that's alright. It happens all the time, especially around the airport."

The driver asked them if this was their first time in Sydney and they said it was. He told them they were currently south of Sydney, near Botany Bay, where Captain Cook first landed. He said that Hornsea is where two major motorways converge, north of Sydney; it's a nice area, close to a coastal national park.

"Anyway get comfortable. It's going to take us a while to get there."

The driver asked the men where they were from in America and as usual, Williams did the talking. He said they were from Canada, keeping up the pretence, and were taking an extended vacation and coming to visit his sister.

The driver said, "Like most working Aussies, I've never been anywhere, but if I did go somewhere, I'd like to go to Canada."

"It's a big country," said Williams, "but I think Australia is, too, isn't it?"

The driver said it was, but there wasn't much to see in the interior. Williams and Shelby weren't sure what this meant, but didn't say anything.

Williams and the driver continued on a discussion about the two countries for awhile. After about an hour, they had reached Junction Road. The driver pulled over to the side of the road and checked his map book.

"Here it is, just north of here."

When they reached the house, the taxi driver told Williams it would be one twenty, with the conversion fee.

"No problem," said Williams, taking two one hundred US dollar bills out of his backpack and telling him to keep the change.

"Thank you, thank you very much. That is very generous of you!" said the taxi driver. "Here, please take my card. If you need a ride back to the harbor or airport, give me a call. Enjoy your stay in Australia and thank you again."

They knocked on the front door of number 26 and when it opened, Williams' sister greeted them winking and frequently shifting her eyeballs to the right. Based on what she was doing with her eyes, Williams figured something must be wrong. She invited him and Shelby in. As they moved inside, she asked them if they would like something to drink.

"A beer for me," said Williams. "This is Peter, my friend and fellow globetrotter; this is my sister, Sue."

"Pleased to meet you, Gerry mentioned you'd be coming too in his postcard," said Sue.

"Good to meet you," said Shelby.

"Can I get you a drink, Peter?"

"Yes, I'll have a beer too, if you've got one."

"This is Australia; everyone's got beer in the fridge."

Sue returned with the drinks, followed by two clean cut men, pointing guns at Williams and Shelby.

"Welcome to Australia," one of the men said.

"Who are you?" asked Williams.

"We are your Australian welcoming committee. We're going to make up for the welcome you missed in Singapore," said the other man.

William's sister was dumbfounded as she looked at her brother.

"So you work for General Ulanov?" asked Williams.

"General Ulanov, no, he's dead. I guess you didn't hear," said the man who had spoken first.

Williams was trying to keep a conversation going with the Soviet killers. His pistol was in his backpack beside the chair he was sitting in, but there was no way he could get to it. He still had the hunting knife strapped to his leg but didn't know how to get to it quickly. He had to create a diversion of some kind, but how?

"General Ulanov is dead?" said Shelby, not knowing how much he was helping Williams by also engaging in the conversation.

"Yes, he died several weeks ago."

Williams chipped in, "So what have you got planned for our welcoming party and why are you pointing those guns at us?"

"You will find out soon enough," said the agent who had spoken first.

Williams' sister, who was still standing in front of the two agents, put down the tray of drinks on the coffee table in front of Williams and started to step away. All in the same movement, Williams kicked the coffee table and drinks towards the gunmen and pushed his sister towards them. As he slid off his chair sideways, he pulled his knife out of its sheath and threw it. It embedded high in one of the agent's legs. The lead agent pushed Williams' sister aside and fired at him, missing him, as Williams was rapidly crawling towards him on his hands and knees. Williams grabbed his legs and tackled him to the ground; the agent hit his head on one of the upturned legs of the overturned coffee table.

Shelby was also involved now and was wrestling the gun out of the hand of the agent who had Williams' knife sticking out of his bleeding leg. The Australian Soviets proved to be much tougher than the Asian agents. Williams was trying his best to wrestle the gun out the first agent's hand, but could see it was pointing directly at him when his sister came to the rescue and hit the agent directly in the face with a large bronze statue. The Soviet went limp immediately, blood appearing from different parts of his face. Shelby got the better of the second agent and was pointing the agent's gun back at him.

"Are you both alright?" asked Sue. Both Williams and Shelby said they were. "I think I killed him!" she said.

"No," said Williams. "He's still breathing, but he's unconscious by the look of it."

"I need to go to Kevin. He's tied up in our bedroom."

"Go! We're fine," said Williams. "So what do we do with you?" he said, looking at the second agent.

"There will be more agents here soon," the Soviet snarled.

"Not if you tell them we're dead," said Williams. "Do you have a way to communicate with them?"

"By telephone."

"Right then, I'll tell you what. If you phone whomever and tell them we're dead, I won't pull my knife out of your leg and let you bleed to death."

"Yes, I can do that," the agent said, looking down at his leg and at his unconscious colleague.

"Let's wait for my sister and hopefully she can give you a phone to use," said Williams.

Just then Sue and her husband came bursting into the room. "Who are these people?" asked Williams' brother-in-law, Kevin.

"It's a very long story and I'd rather not go into it right now. Do you have a telephone?"

"Yes, in the kitchen."

"Will the cord reach into here?"

"I don't know; I'll go and see," Sue said. She came back into the doorway of the room saying the cord would only reach that far.

Williams pulled the unconscious agent out of the way and helped the other one manoeuvre his way to the doorway.

"What is the number?" Williams asked.

The agent gave him the number and Williams' sister dialled it.

While Williams gently held the hilt of the hunting knife embedded in the Soviet's leg, he listened as the agent told the person on the other end of the line that the Americans were dead and that he and George were leaving. Then Williams whispered to Sue to hang up the phone.

"Good, so now what about you and your friend? What should we do with you?" asked Williams.

"Just let us go. We'll continue to say you're dead. I've already told them you're dead so we can't change our story or we'll be killed," said the agent.

"Just know that if you come back here, you will be killed for sure," said Williams, reaching into his backpack and bringing out his pistol.

Sue and her husband just looked at each other.

Williams asked them if there was a hospital nearby. Sue said there was and Williams asked Kevin if he would drive there so that the Soviets could be dropped off. The agent who had been unconscious was starting to come around.

Williams and his sister's husband bundled the two Soviet agents into his car with Shelby's help. Williams told Shelby to stay with his sister.

When they got to the hospital, Williams pulled the two agents out of the car and sat them down next to Emergency, then reached down and pulled his knife out of the agent's leg and he screamed out loud. Williams wiped the blood off his knife on the man's shirt and quickly ran and jumped into the car and told Kevin to floor it. He looked back and could see someone standing talking to the two wounded men.

Once Williams and his brother-in-law got back to the house, Williams sat him and his sister down and along with Shelby, told them as succinctly as he could why these men had tried to kill them.

"So these were Soviet agents?" said his brother-in-law.

"Yes, but I'm pretty sure this is the last we will see of them. As of right now, my friend Peter and I are dead as far as the Soviets are concerned. Now how about that beer?"

"Yes, I think I'll have one too," said Sue, getting up and moving towards the kitchen.

Red Shadows On Liberty's Soil

Kevin just sat looking at Williams and Shelby with a wide-eyed stare.

Lyon, France—October 1985

The late afternoon sun was illuminating the impressive looking headquarters of INTERPOL, the International Criminal Police Organization, beside the river Rhone in Lyon, France. On the records floor of the multi-storey glass-fronted building, a newly recruited intern was sitting in a brightly lit cubicle updating database information on persons of interest from around the world. Although officially not a fully-fledged member of the staff, new intern, Jean Paul Broussard was already being asked to undertake numerous routine staff duties, making him feel like a glorified data entry clerk, as he entered endless amounts of information from highlighted sections of copies of official letters and documents. His boss had told him to try and understand the significance of the information being entered and it would make the work more interesting, which he'd been trying to do, but was still finding most of the information very mundane, like changes to upcoming court appearance dates, mailing addresses and phone numbers.

That afternoon he was studying an official letter in reference to a person by the name of Peter Shelby. He keyed in the name and a long list of people with the same name appeared on his display and not knowing which one to select he re-read the letter to see if there was any other information that could help identify the person in question and found a date of birth. After entering this only one Peter Shelby was displayed and the information indicated his whereabouts were currently unknown. The letter was from the Royal Canadian Mounted Police to the Australian Department of Immigration and Citizenship. Two of the sentences in the letter had been highlighted for entry into Shelby's online file. The first indicated there was no record of a Canadian passport ever being issued to a Peter Shelby with this date of birth. Jean Paul duly entered this information into the online file. The second highlighted sentence indicated that no record of Australian parentage had been found for a Peter Shelby with this date of birth. Jean Paul entered this information and saved the updates. From the data he had just entered Jean Paul had deduced that this particular Peter Shelby must be living in Australia and had recently applied for Australian citizenship. He hoped his boss, the internship co-ordinator, would be pleased with what he'd found because according to the online file Shelby's whereabouts had been unknown since March nineteen eighty two, nearly three and half years ago. Jean Paul made his way down the corridor to his boss's office and saw that he had already left for the day and although he knew where he would probably be, in the small bar at Lyon's Des Congres Hotel quite close-by, news of what he had uncovered would have to wait until tomorrow. He went back to his cubicle and picked the next document off the top of his work pile. He was trying to control his need to tell his boss about what he'd discovered knowing he had no one else to tell. To those busily working around him it would mean nothing, they were probably continually determining the whereabouts of missing persons. This was his first one and he just had to let his boss know about it. He put all the relevant papers in a folder, shut his computer down, locked up the documents and letters in his work pile and grabbed his coat. This didn't go unnoticed by his co-workers but no one showed any outwardly signs that they had seen what he was doing. He quickly made his way to the elevators hardly able to control his excitement.

The afternoon sun was still shining brightly as he left the building. As he got closer to the hotel he began to have second thoughts about what he was doing and his pace slowed considerably as he mulled over whether he should wait until tomorrow and if anyone mentioned he had left early say he hadn't been feeling well. However, he was still very excited about what he'd found and decided to continue on to at least see if his boss was actually there. If he wasn't then the news of what he had discovered would definitely have to wait until tomorrow morning.

He went into the hotel bar finding it to be very dark, so much so that he was having difficulty making out people's faces. He was looking all around but couldn't see his boss. His boss however had seen him as he had come in through the door and stood up and called out to him. Jean Paul made his way over to where he was standing and saw a pretty dark haired woman sitting across from him in the booth they were occupying. His boss asked him if there was something wrong at work and Jean Paul responded saying that there wasn't and that he had come to tell him something. His boss asked him if it couldn't have waited until tomorrow and Jean Paul reluctantly said he really wanted to tell him what he had discovered. His boss leaned over to the attractive woman he was with, whispered something in her ear then he put his arm around Jean Paul and led him over to the bar.

Sounding very angry his boss said "You don't come looking for me outside the office to discuss work. Firstly, it is a violation of company security policies, secondly, I assume there are confidential papers in the folder you are carrying another violation of company security policies and thirdly I am off limits to you once I leave the office, so whatever you have come here to tell me will have to wait until you and I are back in the office, which in my case will be tomorrow morning."

Jean Paul started to say "But . . ."

"No buts, come to my office first thing tomorrow morning, now go back to the office and lock up the papers you've brought with you" said Jean Paul's boss still angry.

On his way out Jean Paul glanced over at the woman sitting patiently waiting for his boss to return and thought he recognized her from the office but wasn't sure.

Disappointed Jean Paul made his way back to the office and stayed there until his normal quitting time. He was scared that he may have upset his boss so much that he might even get fired in the morning. That night he couldn't sleep worrying about what might happen and what his parents and extended family would say if he was let go.

He got up early and went to the office to prepare for the meeting with his boss. He didn't want to cause any more problems so he wasn't planning on taking anything with him to his office. He knew his boss always arrived at eight o'clock sharp so a few minutes after eight he made his way to his office and knocked on the open door.

"Good morning Jean Paul, come in" said his boss while still unlocking his desk draws.

"So what was so important for you to risk your internship and very future with INTERPOL yesterday afternoon?"

"I'm very sorry sir, I hope I didn't cause you any problems, I wasn't thinking, I am really sorry."

"Please, enough with the apologies what was it you wanted to tell me?"

"That I had found where a fugitive is living whose whereabouts have been unknown for several years."

"Good work but you didn't have to hunt me down outside the office to tell me this, carrying confidential papers, tell me more."

After Jean Paul had told his boss what he had found out about a person by the name of Peter Shelby his boss asked him to investigate the matter further. As Jean Paul was leaving his boss's office, his boss said "Please don't ever do what you did yesterday again, it was most unprofessional and unnecessary, I will put it down to youthful exuberance and will overlook it this time, keep up the good work."

This is exactly what it had been and nothing more was ever said about the incident again even though Jean Paul saw the woman his boss had been with in the elevator a few days later. She looked away when she saw him.

Jean Paul was very excited now that he was doing investigative work. He learned that Peter Shelby had applied for Australian citizenship furnishing false Canadian passport information as evidence of his existing citizenship. He had applied for Australian citizenship under the born overseas to Australian parents' provision. What Jean Paul didn't know yet but soon would was that Shelby's close friend Gerry Williams whose whereabouts had also been unknown since March nineteen eighty two had applied for Australian citizenship at the same time. They had in fact signed each other's application forms in the proof of identity section. It seemed that two Australian men with the same last name as Williams and Shelby listed in a directory of Australian persons living overseas, specifically in Canada, had been indicated as being their fathers.

Several days later Jean Paul received faxed copies of their application forms and from these was able to determine where they were living in Sydney, Australia.

Sydney, Australia—November 1985

It had been another raucous night at the famous Lord Nelson close to Sydney harbour. Gathering there on Thursday nights had become a weekly tradition for Williams, Shelby, their girlfriends and a number of their mutual friends and tonight had been particularly enjoyable as one of their friends had been celebrating a birthday. The obligatory birthday cake had been brought out and they accompanied by the bar staff had just finished belting out happy birthday.

Thursday was the busiest night of week at the Lord Nelson with patrons usually two or three deep around the bar by five o'clock in the afternoon. It was now approaching midnight and the bar had almost emptied out, Williams, Shelby and their girlfriends had just said their goodbyes and were making their way to the exit when several clean cut looking men in suits stepped in front of them blocking their way.

"Peter Shelby?" asked one of the men blocking their way. "Yes" responded Shelby.

"Who wants to know?" demanded Williams pushing in front of Shelby looking very angry.

"You must be Gerry Williams" commented one of the other men blocking their way.

"What is this?" snarled Williams.

One of the men flashed an INTERPOL badge saying "Peter Shelby you are under provisional arrest for crimes committed against the United States of America."

Pushing out at the men blocking their way Williams shouted "Back off you've got the wrong people."

"But your friend just admitted to being Peter Shelby?" replied one of the INTERPOL men.

"I don't care" shouted Williams taking a swing at him and only just missing.

Their girlfriends ran back to tell the few friends that were left about what was going on and the several men still at the table made their way to where Williams and Shelby were tussling with the men in suits. One of their burly Australian friends began pushing the plain clothed INTERPOL men back out towards the street, while another INTERPOL man was talking into a microphone on his jacket lapel. Very soon after, numerous uniformed police officers began to appear converging where Williams and Shelby were brawling and it took the INTERPOL agents and the police quite a while to get the situation under control by eventually getting the better of Williams, who had been doing most of the fighting. Williams and Shelby were pinned up against an outside wall and frisked as several of their friends were led away in handcuffs. The INTERPOL agent going through William's wallet looking for identification shouted "Bingo! Mr. Gerry Williams we figured you and Shelby would be together being the dynamic duo you are supposed to be!"

"Gerry Williams you are under provisional arrest for crimes committed against the United States of America" stated the agent while shoving William's wallet back into his jacket pocket. Williams and Shelby were manhandled towards unmarked police cars and shoved in the back. They already knew instinctively that this was the beginning of another nightmare.

Since the day they had arrived at William's sisters several years earlier they had been making new lives for themselves in Sydney. They'd been using their real American identities with anyone they met even though they still only had false Canadian passports for official identification. Locally in Sydney this had not been a problem because as soon as anyone heard their accents they could tell they were Americans. Getting jobs had been fairly easy based on their impressive education and experience even though they didn't have college transcripts or letters of reference, as soon as they talked about their education, previous job experience and significant accomplishments it quickly became obvious they would be an asset to any organization, so much so that they were offered jobs during their interviews. Once employed, it had been easy to get dates usually with the most attractive single women in the company. Because they had become so close and had stuck together since their fateful coming together in Moscow several years earlier they had found they really liked to go on double dates and had found two women, life-long friends, who liked to double date too. The dates had led to steady relationships and they'd been living in one of the swankier neighbourhoods in Sydney for the last three years with these stunningly good looking Australian women, both professionals in their own right. They were both blondes with pleasant personalities and figures to die for which would not have looked out of place in the centrefold of Playboy. Neither the women nor Williams or Shelby were interested in a long term commitment so it had been working out perfectly. On Sunday mornings Williams and Shelby had been regularly getting together for a pick-up game of American football with a number of other Americans they'd met in Sydney. Life had been good, almost idyllic and they had naively thought their past was behind them however they had just found out this certainly wasn't the case.

After a long drive to the outskirts of Sydney they were driven into an abandoned warehouse and taken into an office area where they could see a group of tough looking men playing cards. The men turned in unison and looked in their direction some of them standing and coming over to where they were and as one of them was coming towards them he said "So this is Bonnie and Clyde? Welcome to the Heartbreak Hotel!"

"Funny guy" muttered Williams "Looks like you guys fit in well here. Too bad you don't have better things to do than run around arresting innocent people."

"Innocent people surely that doesn't apply here? We know who you are and what you tried to do so cut the crap with the innocent people stuff" added another one of the men who'd been playing cards.

"None of you know the real story just what you've heard" responded Shelby emphatically.

"Whatever?" said one of the agents, as he led them to the cots lined up along the wall where they were told to sit down on different metal cots and double handcuffed to the headboards by the same wrist and ironically told to get comfortable. Williams was thinking who do they think we are the Houdini brothers? They had been situated several cots apart so couldn't speak to each other without shouting. Williams checked his watch under the extremely bright florescent lights and saw it was almost two thirty in the morning. The men who had arrested them gradually drifted over to the cots and lay down and one of the last men to come over mercifully turned off the fluorescent lights where they were. The four tough looking men who were playing cards when they'd arrived were still at it and Williams figured these must be the night watchmen. He was having difficulty getting comfortable due to the way he had been handcuffed to the headboard. He could see Shelby already sleeping while he lay observing the INTERPOL men who all seemed to speak with Australian accents were all around the same age mid to late thirties and were probably the best INTERPOL had in this part of the world. These were William's last thoughts before he dosed off.

Williams was shaken awake by one of the INTERPOL agents and was feeling very groggy as he checked his illuminated watch seeing it was twenty to six. He'd had very little sleep, had a splitting headache and was hung over.

Amazingly the card game was still going on and it appeared that he and Shelby would be on the move again soon. They were released from their handcuffs and on their way back to the cars Williams asked if he could go to the washroom and was taken into a dirty dilapidated washroom that had obviously been totally vandalized. He said he needed to sit down and was told as he could see he'd have to wait until they got to their next destination, which he was told wasn't going to take very long, Williams knew escape was not an option. He could see Shelby in the back of one of the cars as he was shoved into the other one. He wasn't sure why they were being kept apart.

Ten minutes later handcuffed to each other they were walking through Sydney International Airport being directed into the first washroom they came to. One of the INTERPOL men broke the locks off adjacent stalls removed their handcuffs and shoved them inside. While Williams was sitting in his stall he was thinking about how they could escape, but couldn't come up with anything. There were four INTERPOL men who he assumed were armed waiting for them only a few feet away. Shelby was thinking that the situation they were in was crazy once again and was wondering why this was happening to them all over again. While they were sitting in the stalls they heard a great deal of talking going on and when they came out found that several additional men had joined the men from INTERPOL. Williams and Shelby were handcuffed to two of the new men and led out of the washroom the INTERPOL men had made the handover.

"How did you boys like Australia?" asked one of the new men with an American accent.

"Who wants to know?" asked Williams testily.

The new guy got right in Williams face "Listen pal, we can play games if you like, but why don't we just be buddies, we're going to be spending the next twenty hours within inches of each other while we get you boys' home safely?"

Williams responded that he liked living in Sydney, didn't want to go anywhere else and wasn't interested in being any ones buddy.

They were whisked through Security, the men they were with only having to flash their, what looked like Central Intelligence Agency badges. They checked in at the gate and after a great deal of paperwork was exchanged and reviewed at the counter they were led down a Qantas Airlines passenger ramp on to a large commercial airliner and taken to the back of the plane where their handcuffs were removed. They were seated on opposite sides of the aisle wedged between two CIA agents, one of their legs cuffed to the seat they were sitting in, Williams thought they certainly were being treated like precious cargo.

It took almost an hour for the rest of the passengers to board the plane after which the giant aircraft began to slowly back away from the ramp. The Boeing 747 took off into bright sunshine starting its ascent to its cruising altitude beginning its long journey to the northern hemisphere. Up until now, Williams and Shelby hadn't given much thought to what might lay ahead for them and they both began to think about the possibilities. Shelby figured they'd be put on trial and wondered what evidence would be used against them, Williams couldn't believe that after almost three and a half years they had been found and he wondered how, they obviously weren't wearing military uniforms and wondered if they were being arrested as civilian or military combatants and whether this would make a difference whenever they were brought to trial and also wondered if the knowledge he had gained about the Soviet Union's nuclear program would be of any value to the United States government and whether he could somehow use it to make a deal of some kind. He like Shelby had a feeling of foreboding having been thrust into the unknown once again.

To Williams and everyone else's surprise about an hour into the flight Shelby yelled out loud enough that most of the passengers in the rear of aircraft could hear what he'd said which was he was being forcibly abducted by the CIA and should be set free. Within seconds of the outburst he had been stabbed in the ribs with a hypodermic needle and had slumped down in his seat as if he was dead.

The CIA agents on either side of Williams looked at him and one of them commented "How about you, are you going to yell out too?"

Just as this was being said a passenger sitting in the aisle seat in front of Shelby stood up with a concerned look on his face and looked back to where he was slumped down, the CIA agents on either side of him just smiled at the inquisitive man who quickly sat back down. Shelby's outburst had created a lot of chatter at the back of the plane with several people turning and looking back to where he was slumped down. Gutsy move thought Williams thinking that he never knew Pete had it in him. Unfortunately, it looked like he had been sedated with something that would have brought an elephant to its knees.

After not being able to relax or sleep very much since being dragged from the Lord Nelson Williams dozed in and out of sleep until he eventually fell into a deep sleep waking up only a few hours before their scheduled arrival in Los Angeles, Shelby was being revived with smelling salts around the same time. They ate a meagre airline breakfast which was still most welcome given that it was almost twenty four hours since either of them had drunk or eaten anything. The remaining hours passed quickly and once the plane landed and began taxiing towards the terminal building they were un-cuffed from their seats and re-handcuffed to the CIA agents who made their way to the front of the plane and were the first ones off when the door was opened. They climbed aboard a waiting airport shuttle cart and sped through the terminal building to a departure gate where they boarded a flight to Washington, DC ahead of all the other patiently waiting passengers. Once again being the first ones onto the plane they had to wait until the rest of the passengers boarded. They were shackled to their seats again and wedged between CIA agents. The flight to Washington took nearly four hours during which time they were able to eat several times which was most welcome to them both. During both flights they had spoken very little to their escorts not really having anything in common with them except being American. They were feeling jetlagged and depressed not knowing what the future held for them except it wasn't going to be pleasant whatever happened. As in Los Angeles they exited the plane as soon as the door at the front of the aircraft was opened each handcuffed to an agent, they were led down several flights of stairs and pushed into a small shuttle bus which transported them to a waiting helicopter. It was a short ride to a small suburban airport where they were shoved into a minivan and within a few minutes had joined a major highway. They learned from one of the agents that they were being taken to the CIA's headquarters in Langley, Virginia, the journey taking less than fifteen minutes likely because it was quite late in the day. In order to enter the parking lot one of the agents had to phone through to someone and the gate was opened remotely and once through they drove through a massive parking lot to the back of an impressive looking building. They were pulled from the minivan and as they were making their way towards the entrance to the building to their surprise one of the agents bent down and pulled a trap door up out of the grass and they were pushed down some steep steps leading to a basement area where they were locked in separate cells reminiscent of the cabins they'd been assigned to on the Asian Trader container ship which they had travelled from Seattle to Singapore on while making their escape to Australia several years earlier. Locked in adjacent barred cells they were finally able to talk to each other, Shelby started off the discussion panicked about their apartments and cars, Williams assured him that Carol and Stella, their girlfriends, would take care of everything, but it really didn't matter anyway because they likely wouldn't be going back there any time soon.

"So what do you think?" asked Williams.

"What do I think? I think maybe this is the end of my life as I've known it, yet again" replied Shelby.

"I agree it doesn't look good but it is not a totally cut and dried situation as far as I'm concerned, no one has heard our side of the story yet."

"Do you really think they care about what we have to say?" asked Shelby.

"They should, after all, in the United States you are considered innocent until proven guilty."

"Maybe so, but I'd be surprised if that applies to us."

"I'm sorry to hear you are so resigned to your fate but I guess time will tell" responded Williams trying to get comfortable.

Shelby just sat on his hard bed sobbing.

Early the next morning handcuffed to each other they were taken to meet John Reynolds, of the CIA they assumed who was sitting in small interrogation room. He came straight to the point.

"You have two options you can spend the rest of your lives rotting away in a federal penitentiary or a military prison depending on how you're brought to justice not to mention you might even get the death penalty or you can assist the United States government in any way we see fit to utilize your apparent talents."

"Is it that clear cut?" enquired Shelby.

"Trust me you are going to pay heavily for what you attempted to do guilty or not will not be relevant if they are lenient you might get life if they're not the chair."

"But what about our side of the story?" enquired Shelby.

"You'll be lucky if they even let you testify believe me I am aware of the feelings towards you all the way up the chain of command which by the way is the same as it was in the winter of nineteen eighty two."

"It's a no brainer for me" responded Williams. "Me too" chipped in Shelby.

"I will assume you have both chosen option two." They both nodded.

"As you probably realize with option one assuming you don't get the death penalty you are almost guaranteed a long life even though you'll be incarcerated for the rest of it. With option two there is no such guarantee. It is hoped you're both not too rusty and have retained most of your skills and expertise and I can assure you Mr. Williams that you won't need any of your nuclear physics knowledge for what we have in mind. You both still seem to be in pretty good physical shape you must have been working out down under this bodes well for the training you will soon be required to undertake. I think that's all I have to tell you. You should be on your way within the next day or so good day gentlemen."

With that Williams and Shelby were escorted back to their cells.

The next afternoon they were taken from their cells by the same CIA agents who had escorted them from Australia, taken back to the same small airport they had arrived at a few days earlier and asked to scramble aboard a small rough and ready looking military plane, they weren't aircraft buffs so they didn't know or really care what kind it was. Several hours later they were bundled off the uncomfortable and cramped plane into the back of an old van and driven to a non-descript two-storey building off to the side of the landing strip. They had no idea where they were and it was getting dark as they were locked up in individual cells once again. The only thing they knew was the weather seemed to be a little warmer and they soon heard a profusion of bugs starting up their nightly cacophony so figured they were definitely off the beaten track somewhere.

Sleep didn't come easy to Williams these days being preoccupied about what the United States government could want them to do, he figured it had to have something to do with what they had been forced to do during the Minot mission for the Soviets probably payback of some kind.

Early the next morning Williams and Shelby ate breakfast which neither of them was very impressed with comprised of shrivelled up bacon, dried-up fried eggs, cold toast and a glass of water. Following this they were taken to a cluttered office where they were greeted by a distinguished looking gentleman wearing army fatigues.

"Good morning I'm Dave Wiltshire I understand from John Reynolds, you are my special new recruits" he said laughing. "Welcome to Harvey Point, North Carolina. Where are you both originally from?"

"I'm from Bismarck, North Dakota" replied Shelby. "Albany, New York" responded Williams confidently.

Both state capitals if I'm not mistaken you must both be men of some metal. Anyway you're here to be trained in what are known as black operations however before your training begins you will need to undergo physical fitness evaluations" offered Wiltshire.

"We've had them before so we know what they entail" responded Shelby.

"You might find ours a little different from the Soviets but the briefs I have read so far indicate that you are both already in pretty good shape. Once you've had your physicals assuming all goes well you will begin your training in earnest. Do you have any questions for me?"

"Only one" replied Shelby. "Shoot" responded Wiltshire.

"How long will we be locked up in cells?" asked Shelby "You can probably imagine how confining and depressing they are."

"I understand and as soon as you both demonstrate you are committed to working with us and are not contemplating escaping we will integrate you into the general training center population. How about you Mr. Williams any questions?" asked Wiltshire.

"As Pete told you the sooner we can get out of the cells the better our frame of mind is going to be and speaking for myself I can assure you I have no intention of trying to escape I am very thankful to be here and to have been given this opportunity it has already been made very clear to us what the other option is" replied Williams.

"I'm glad to hear you appreciate where you stand because I would agree you are very lucky to have been given this chance. We'll try and get you out of the cells as soon as we can. Is there anything else?" asked Wiltshire.

Williams and Shelby shook their heads.

"We're done here then" advised Wiltshire signalling they were to be taken back to their cells.

Following successful physicals Williams and Shelby began their training spending their first day being given a high level overview of the Special Activities Division and its role within the CIA. They were told they were going to be trained to be Paramilitary Officers within Special Operations and began to learn what would be expected of them including swearing an oath of secrecy. They learned that although the other officers would be assisting the Pakistani Intelligence Services training and preparing Muslim Mujahideen freedom fighters to fight the Soviets in Afghanistan they would have a different mission but weren't told any more than that. They found out that they were in extremely elite company training with officers from the ranks of the Army's Rangers, the Navy Seals and the Air Force's Special Operations Aviation Regiment and the following day joined the other trainees in a defensive driving classroom training course which seemed most bizarre to both of them. Following this they participated in hand to hand martial arts combat training which seemed like it might be much more useful. Their training continued with communicating using codes, leadership skills and target practice. Following this was jump school where Williams excelled resulting in him assisting the drill instructor with the jumps. Shelby not having had previous parachute training initially had to get over the fear of jumping and badly sprained his ankle on his second jump and had to have it strapped up for his next series of jumps which were very painful if he wasn't able to put all his weight on his good foot when landing. It was amazing to Shelby how Williams stood out from the rest of the class, he figured it was because he was super intelligent, a natural leader and had an innate ability to think on his feet and time and time again he had proved himself to be more resourceful than anyone else during the tough training exercises. Williams couldn't stop thinking about fact that he and Shelby weren't getting the full training because he knew that other men were being trained on helicopters because he had seen them frequently taking off, hovering and landing over on the ocean side of the camp. He couldn't understand why he and Shelby weren't getting the same training as everyone else and decided he'd ask Wiltshire about it the next time he ran into him and several days later he had a chance meeting with him. When they greeted each other as he always did Wiltshire asked Williams how the training was going and before he could answer told him he had been getting excellent reports about him and Shelby and was about to walk off when Williams asked him why he and Shelby weren't getting helicopter training.

"I don't have time to discuss this right now I'm already running late for my next meeting but if you come to my office at five this afternoon we can discuss it then" replied Wiltshire as he was hurrying away.

"See you then" shouted Williams after him.

Williams spent another afternoon being bored stiff sitting through training on the use of different weapon systems in various combat situations and couldn't wait for five o'clock to roll around when he could meet with Wiltshire. Shelby could see Williams was preoccupied thinking about something other than the weapons training and asked him what was on his mind and Williams told him about his upcoming meeting with Wiltshire and asked him if he wanted to come along but Shelby said he had already arranged to play pool when this afternoon's class ended so thanks but no thanks. Just after five o'clock Williams took a seat in Wiltshire's outer office after seeing he wasn't in his office and a few minutes later Wiltshire came striding in and told Williams to come into his cluttered office following him in closing the door and making his way behind his polished mahogany desk where he slumped down into a well-worn brown leather chair. "Chopper training do you know something I don't?" asked Wiltshire.

"I doubt that!" responded Williams.

"Why do you think you and Shelby need helicopter training?" asked Wiltshire.

"For a start it would be a darn sight more valuable than defensive driving classroom training also isn't it likely that helicopters will be involved in whatever we will be doing when we get to wherever we're going?" asked Williams tongue in cheek.

"That may be so but I am giving you the training I have been ordered to give you nothing more nothing less I myself don't know what's planned for you and Mr. Shelby once you leave here no one has told me yet" stated Wiltshire.

"So we are being setup to fail I guess?" replied Williams. "You said it not me" offered Wiltshire.

"So the reason we are being trained to be good drivers, good leaders and weapons experts is because that is what you have been ordered to train us in?" asked Williams.

"I'll tell you something else Reynolds doesn't want you and Shelby getting too close to the other men who don't know anything about your history. He wants to keep it that way and he doesn't want you to get hurt and has asked that you be kept in a class room setting whenever possible funny though it may sound. Welcome to the United States military. Is there anything else? I have a dinner appointment at six o'clock and don't want to be late like I usually am. By the way I've also been told that you and Shelby are so capable that you'd be ready to go anywhere at the drop of a hat so don't sweat not getting helicopter training now if you would excuse me I need to close up shop for the day" replied Wiltshire.

Williams got up and was moving towards the door when Wiltshire mumbled "You'll be on your way sooner than later so make the most of the rest of your stay here."

"Yea right" commented Williams opening the door still feeling very frustrated after the disjointed conversation he'd just been part of.

He headed for the mess hall in the hope he'd still find

Shelby there and it turned out he was still there. Williams helped himself to a coffee and sat down at a table close to where the pool tables were and heard a tough looking guy with a shaved head who he didn't much like say "Hey, want to be my partner hotshot and play the winners?"

"Why not" responded Williams.

It turned out Shelby and a guy known as Sniffer because he always seemed to be sniffling were the winners.

Shelby asked Williams how his meeting with Wiltshire had gone and Williams said he'd tell him later. The pool didn't last long with shaved head quickly clearing the table several times before taking off with Sniffer. Shelby sat down with Williams at the table where he had left his half-drunk coffee and Williams told him all he got was a load of bullshit from Wiltshire and that he actually thought he was better than that.

"What do you mean?" enquired Shelby.

"What I mean is the impression I got is we're just going through the motions here killing time while they decide what to do with us."

"What do you mean?" asked Shelby again.

"We just have to keep doing what we're doing and one day we'll be whisked off somewhere and that's when the fun will start."

As they were making their way to their billets along a dimly lit path they were startled by someone behind them shouting "Hey you two we know who you are and what you did."

"Traitors!" shouted someone else.

Williams and Shelby turned around and although it was dark could make out a group of men some of whom they recognized as being the hard men of the class including the tough guy with the shaved head, who had earlier partnered with Williams at pool.

"Please do tell us more?" responded Williams sarcastically as he and Shelby held their ground facing the angry tough looking men.

"You don't belong here with us" replied a burly young man.

"Which means exactly what?" asked Williams.

"It means this" said one of the men running at Williams and taking a swing at him. Williams evaded his lunge as the rest of the men came a few steps closer moving towards where and Shelby were standing in a threatening way.

"So" responded Williams "What else is on your tiny minds?"

"Why you" said one of the other men as he and two others rushed towards Williams in unison.

Williams turned away from them pulling a small iron pipe away from the Velcro straps securing it inside his jacket and used it expertly to fend them off putting all three of them down on the ground with some mighty cracking blows. By now Shelby was embroiled in the melee and had just kicked another man where it hurts the most who was writhing around on the ground making whimpering sounds.

Williams moved and stood over the men on the ground saying "You gentlemen were saying?"

The leader looked up and in a gravelly voice said "We were told what dirty fighters you are and from now on you better watch your backs."

"Oh I'm scared how about you Pete?"

Shelby didn't respond and started to walk away.

"Any of you boy's still want a piece of me?" asked Williams looking down at the men lying on the ground some of them spitting up blood.

"As I thought" commented Williams slowly turning and running to catch up to Shelby.

As Williams lay in his bunk that night he began to think about what might have been if he hadn't made the decision to give up everything and go over to Moscow several years ago to try Communism and thought that from now on whatever happened he would use all of his guile and cunning to stay alive until he was free again. He decided this is what would drive him to eventually escape from those trying to unjustly punish him and Shelby, escape was all he had to look forward to and the quicker he managed to achieve it the better, sleep eventually overtook him.

It was already obvious to Dave Wiltshire that Williams was a natural leader and would be able to handle any situation he found himself in and the training he was currently being given was really superfluous to requirements. He had been recording Williams's and Shelby's progress and had been very complimentary about them in his reports to Reynolds at Langley. Reynolds in turn had passed the information on regarding Williams's talents and Shelby's abilities to his superiors but they were not interested in utilizing their talents elsewhere and had pointed out that regardless of how good they were they were both traitors.

Williams completed his paramilitary officer training at the head of the class, Shelby did very well too even though he hadn't had any previous parachute training, both Williams and Shelby had shown themselves to be equal to if not better than the majority of the elite officers in the class. The training was over and it was a Harvey Point tradition to have a celebration upon its completion before everyone dropped off the face of the earth travelling to hostile countries where they would have little or no opportunity to celebrate. It was also important that the new paramilitary officers arrive at their destinations in an excellent state of mind and the celebration weekend over the years had ensured this, these men were in the prime of their lives in perfect physical condition and obviously in need of natural relief. When they are told what the celebration was Williams and Shelby couldn't believe it, it had been arranged that tomorrow at noon a bus load of single women would be arriving at the camp and staying for twenty-four hours and they had been told they could participate. Private accommodations had been arranged for each of the would-be couples. On Friday night Williams and Shelby were shown their quarters for tomorrow night which were the same as everyone else's. They had been allocated a Quonset hut which looked like an aluminum can that had been cut in half lengthwise and set on the ground and had discolored perforated steel planking for the floor and a single bed inside which they would have to make do with, it was up to each of them how they decorated and arranged the inside. Williams although he had been sleeping better over the last few days found it difficult to get to sleep that Friday night thinking about what these CIA people had in mind for him and Shelby. He figured they would be going to Afghanistan to fight the Soviet invaders and was thinking it was amazing how military people think in that they always seem to do things to get revenge. Just after two o'clock he finally dozed off which was just as well because he had to be up at six o'clock to help get the mess hall and his hut ready for the arrival of the women.

The morning flew by with all the cleaning and food preparations not to mention all the self-grooming that was going on. It was almost time for the women to arrive and Williams was already wondering how they would be paired up he hadn't seen a list or anything all they had been told was to be in the mess hall at noon wearing civvies. Williams, Shelby and the others were looking out of the mess hall windows as a bright yellow school bus pulled up at the entrance. Women hurried off the bus most of them scantily dressed to show off their considerable womanly attributes even though it was the middle of the winter. They were each carrying an overnight bag and were asked to leave these inside the entrance door. They came into the hall in groups talking and giggling nervously, most of the men were standing over by the windows at the front side of the hall not quite sure what to do as the women came in. Williams being the true leader he was began to break the ice with some initial introductions after which it didn't take long until all the men and women had joined together talking in small groups around the bar. Williams couldn't help noticing that without exception the women were all very attractive and appeared to be very personable so whoever had selected them should be complemented on doing an exemplary job. Williams and Shelby were paired up with two attractive brunettes one called Sally and the other Brenda. After getting the women and Shelby drinks Williams began quizzing them about where they lived and what they did. Sally said she worked in real estate and Brenda in advertising. Shelby and Brenda seemed like a match made in heaven already, Shelby was describing some of his most successful advertising campaigns and she seemed to be most impressed. Williams was making small talk with Sally about what an interesting concept this whole thing was and she was telling him how excited all the women were and that she had been looking forward to it since she'd signed up several weeks ago. Williams asked her who had contacted her and she told him someone had come to her club and had asked for volunteers, he was in uniform and explained that single women were invited to spend Saturday night at the camp. Some of the women said they had done it before and it had been great fun and signed up right there and then so I did too. She said half the women were from her club and the others from a similar club.

So that everyone could get to know each other a murder mystery or "whodunit" game had been arranged and everyone was asked to gather at a long table in the middle of the hall that had been especially set up. Williams had all the details and suggested that they would likely be playing the game up until and after dinner if this was alright with everyone. No one objected, each person was asked to take one of twenty four name tags from a bowl on the table each name tag represented a character in the game. There were ten murder suspects, three investigators and eleven witnesses. There was also a pile of sheets which were currently being rifled through indicating what each character could reveal and what each player had to do. The game quickly became great fun with the investigators asking all the suspects and witnesses what they knew until each murder was solved. As time moved on Williams found he was attracted to a vivacious blonde called Suzy and made his move. She seemed mesmerized by his wit and it was obvious to all of the other men including Shelby that she would be his for the night. Shelby was now paired up with a soft spoken woman called Maggie and they seemed to be really getting along, laughing and joking a lot. It was not until close to midnight that the last murder was solved and by then everyone was well relaxed from a combination of drinks and the fun they'd been having all afternoon and evening and everyone appeared to be paired up. Williams and Suzy made the first move and within minutes the mess hall had emptied out. As they were making their way to William's makeshift quarters he was thinking how he would like to make this night very special. It had been several months since he'd been with a woman and since leaving Australia he hadn't had any opportunity to even get close to a woman although he'd tried and failed on a couple of occasions with two of the women who worked behind the bar in the mess hall finding out fairly quickly that they were both happily married.

He'd readied his quarters for romance, had a selection of flowers, several candles, a cassette player and some slow soul songs. All these things had been provided to him by members of the mess hall staff, they had been freely provided to him because he had shown a genuine interest in their lives often asking about their families. Williams had learned long ago that if you showed interest in other people's lives they would be interested in yours. Now as he walked hand in hand with Suzy on this moonlit night he was thinking how he wanted whatever they did to last, however, as soon as they got through the door of the hut Suzy kicked of her high heels and began to discard her clothes while excitedly kissing him. He quickly realized making anything last with Suzy was going to be a challenge she was all woman, her smell, how she felt in his arms, the way she kissed. Williams was wild with desire for this Venus wrapped in his arms but whispered "Can we slow down a bit and make the atmosphere just right" letting go of her to light some candles and starting the cassette player soft soul music beginning to play.

"No rush" said Suzy sulkily as she reached down for her blouse covering herself up as she moved and sat on the end of the bed. Williams moved to where she was sitting reached down along the side the bed and lifted a dripping bottle of champagne out of a bucket of cold water and asked Suzy if she could reach the glasses on the makeshift bedside table which she did offering them to him to fill.

"You sure know how to treat a lady" she said sarcastically "I don't know what I'm allowed to do first, smell the roses, enjoy the candlelight, listen to the music, drink champagne, make love or maybe you'd like to play cards?"

Williams said nothing while he removed the wire from around the cork of the Champagne bottle and manoeuvred it out until it popped spilling champagne on him, Suzy, the bed and the floor while thinking things hadn't gone exactly as he had planned and was wondering what he could do to make them right.

"I'll tell you what" said Williams excitedly "Have a little champagne and then we can do whatever you want?"

Suzy held the champagne glasses up as William's poured the bubbly into them, she took her glass and chinked William's glass, saying "Cheers" and they both took sips from their glasses.

"Will you be participating in whatever I decide I want?" asked Suzy sarcastically.

"Of course I will. I just wanted to create the right atmosphere because I want tonight to last forever" replied Williams, putting his glass down on the floor and taking his shirt off.

"I think you know what I want" said Suzy "But you seem to have been doing all you can to stop me from getting it."

"Please don't view it that way I just wanted the night to be perfect and didn't want to rush anything."

"I understand I get it so let's just take our time even though I am sure like me you have been looking forward to this."

"You must understand it has been a while since I have been this close to a gorgeous woman and it may be a very long time until I am this close again."

"So why are you wasting time? Everything is perfect let's get it on I'm not leaving until tomorrow we've got all night and actually I'm really glad you slowed things down but now come here so I can thank you for being so considerate and going to so much trouble."

They embraced gently kissing each other Williams slowly removing the rest of her clothes and exploring her warm voluptuous body knowing the longer it lasted the more enjoyable it was going to be. He was soon driving Suzy wild, she was cursing out loud and gasping for air until she pushed him away. It was Suzy's turn now and after fully undressing Williams she slowly took him to the brink on several occasions they were entwined, sweating and crying out in unison as together they reached the first of several climaxes that night. They took a short break and started all over again taking their time going slowly listening to the soft music in the candlelight, it was very romantic and after one last successful attempt to reach paradise on earth Suzy fell asleep. Williams turned the music off, blew out the candles and as he got back into bed could smell her perfume and hear her breathing softly. He stared up at the corrugated steel sheets that formed the structure of the hut and thought about all the other passionate and mutually fulfilling love making that was going on along the row of huts, men and women all experiencing wonderful highs. He eventually fell asleep.

Williams who was used to getting up early awoke before Suzy who he could see and hear snoring softly next to him, she didn't look quite as good as she had the night before but neither did he probably. She had definitely given Williams a night to remember and as he lay there he was thinking to himself that despite the circumstances you find yourself in during your life something good usually always happens looking back on the previous mission he recalled many exciting things that had happened so hopefully there were more adventures ahead no matter where he and Shelby ended up, Suzy was certainly a good start. He was thinking that most people live fairly ordinary lives like he had up until he had gone to Moscow and they would likely jump at the opportunity to swap places with him and Shelby. Suzy began to stir pulling him towards her telling him she had missed him and they began to make love again for almost an hour until Williams suggested they needed to make a move as it was after ten and breakfast would already be being served. He told her she could wash-up at the mess hall and she reluctantly agreed. They got dressed and after hugging and kissing inside the doorway of the hut headed to the mess hall where Suzy made use of the facilities while Williams found out that Shelby had enjoyed his night just as much as he had but without all the trimmings. The only thing Shelby had done that Williams hadn't was to get coffee for him and Maggie earlier that morning. Shelby still not the great romantic had enjoyed a wonderful night talking and making love with Maggie her telling him how sorry she felt for him after he had told her about his current situation which was most pleasing to Shelby who still felt hard done by not being able to escape from the nightmare that had begun several years before upon his arrival in Moscow. It was apparently of great comfort to him to have someone understand his current plight in a kind of motherly way. Shelby and Maggie were already well into their breakfasts and when Suzy reappeared Williams asked her how she took her coffee and liked her eggs and went over and joined the food line as she sat down with Shelby and Maggie. Suzy looked around and saw everyone was having breakfast and likely talking about how they wished their rendezvous' weren't coming to an end so soon, she felt the same way.

"Did you sleep well?" enquired Shelby trying to make small talk.

"If I had it wouldn't have been much of a night would it now?" laughed Suzy loudly.

"No I guess not" muttered Shelby.

Maggie burst out laughing too just as Williams came back to the table with the coffees and two plates stacked with eggs, bacon, sausages and pancakes which he and Suzy began to dig into.

"What were you all laughing about?" asked Williams. "We were comparing notes" replied Shelby sheepishly. "What!" asked Williams "Not in detail I hope?"

"Oh no" mumbled Shelby "Just how well we had slept last night."

Williams started to laugh "Now I know why you were laughing, I don't think sleeping was on the agenda last night." "Can we change the subject?" asked Shelby without looking up. "Where are you guys going?' asked Maggie complying with Shelby's wishes.

"We've been so well trained we could go anywhere but they haven't told us specifically where we're going but you can bet it will be a hot spot somewhere" responded Williams.

"Wow, that must be exciting?" replied Maggie.

Williams and Shelby looked at each other and Williams agreed with her saying "Yes it is."

Red Shadows On Liberty's Soil

They had just finished their breakfasts and coffees when the school bus came into view slowly pulling up outside, it was approaching noon and couples were kissing in every corner of the mess hall.

Williams stood up and looking around the hall said "Well ladies I'm sure I don't need to tell you all how wonderful it's been to have you visit us this weekend, I just hope it was just as wonderful for all of you?"

Tears welled up in Suzy's eyes as she stood up and grabbed Williams putting her arms around his neck and kissing him so hard her teeth were banging against his. Pulling away Williams said jokingly "Well I guess I know Suzy's answer."

Shelby and Maggie got up and kissed hard and long before following the others out of the mess hall.

As Suzy and Williams were making their way to door she said "I guess last night was the infamous one night stand? The best one I've ever had by the way. I guess there's no point in giving you my number?"

"I'll take it if you're giving it" whispered Williams "You just never know in this life."

Suzy fumbled around in her purse found a pen and an old envelope and wrote her name and number on the back and handed it to him. She hugged him around the neck and kissed him as tears rolled down her cheeks "I guess this is it. Thanks for everything. I will never forget last night" she said grabbing him again and kissing him tears streaming down her face.

"I think you're going to miss the bus if you don't go now" said Williams slowly pulling away from her vice like grip.

It took a while to get all the women on the bus many of them showing signs of being emotionally distraught. All the men were standing outside the mess hall entrance as the school bus slowly pulled away. Waving hands could be seen all the way along the inside of the bus before it turned the corner of the building and disappeared out of sight.

The men all looked forlorn as they trudged off to attend a final meeting to get envelopes with details of their assignments inside. The meeting didn't last long Williams and Shelby had not been given an envelope and once the meeting was over the men quickly dispersed leaving them and two Navy Seals comparing notes from last night. Williams learned that two Army Rangers had got into a fight over the two women who were left at the end of the night but apparently it hadn't lasted very long once one of the women made it clear who she wanted to take to bed. This was the only negative thing that seemed to have happened and after briefly sharing experiences for a few more minutes Williams told the others he was going to get his stuff out of his hut and bunk down early to try make up for the sleep he didn't get last night. They all laughed and went their separate ways Shelby following after Williams.

Unbeknownst to Williams, Shelby and the other men the women who had visited them were all army officers from an elite airborne division at Fort Bragg army base within easy driving distance. This had been a final test to see if the men could be trusted to keep their mouths shut under relaxed circumstances and as it turned out all but three of them could. The three men who had divulged information that was considered classified were severely reprimanded and reminded of their obligations and the oath of secrecy they had been sworn to and all three still graduated.

On a chilly morning in late January nineteen eighty-six a sleek Gulfstream jet took off from runway number one at Harvey Point headed for Dulles International Airport near Washington, DC. Once on board and buckled up Williams and Shelby were introduced to CIA Overseas Station Chief Doug Brown who leaning forward started talking to them from the seat opposite them.

"My safe house is located in north-east Afghanistan I have been operating from there covertly for a number of years now, I understand we will be working together soon?" offered Brown.

"So that's where we're going?" exclaimed Williams "I knew it!"

Brown ignored the outburst saying "I will try and give you as much information as I can I work closely with the local maliks, mullahs and rebel commanders providing them with whatever they need which is generally information about how the occupation is going in different regions of the country and any significant developments in regard to the overall Soviet invasion. In return they provide me with information about what is happening in their town or village. I don't mean to bore you, just shout out if you have any questions."

"I have a question?" mumbled Shelby "What is a malik and mullah?"

"Maliks are usually the largest landowners in a particular area who are called on to arbitrate local conflicts, oversee tax collection, and head up the town or village council and are also usually delegates to the provincial and national parliaments. Mullahs are local Islamic clerics or mosque overseers essentially the religious leaders within the community" responded Brown.

"Now what do you know about the war currently being waged in Afghanistan?"

Williams mentioned that he knew the Soviets were in Afghanistan but really didn't know much else, Shelby volunteered that he'd heard the Soviets were fighting Muslim rebels who were trying to stop them from taking over the country.

"Wc have a lot of ground to cover by the sound of it which is what I expected" continued Brown.

"Are we actually going to Afghanistan?" asked Shelby.

"Yes" answered Brown "You and your buddy are going to be the CIA's newest men in north-eastern Afghanistan.

Now that you are fully fledged members of the CIA's Special Activities Division it is planned that you will be leading cross-border raids into the Soviet Union, one of your favourite places I understand?"

"Yea right" hissed Williams, "We had no choice. We were forced to do what we did!"

""Let's get back to why the Soviets are in Afghanistan shall we?" suggested Brown.

"You know in a way it's actually good that you don't know anything about the history because many reasons have been put forward for the Soviet occupation most of them incorrect, for example they are after middle-east oil or have always wanted an all-year-round warm water port and by going into Afghanistan they would be closer to one in either southern Pakistan or

Iran. Other reasons given are the continued expansion of the Soviet empire into Asia or to protect their considerable natural resource interests from the west particularly natural gas, uranium and copper. Plausible though most of these sound, the real reason the Soviets are in Afghanistan is actually somewhat anti-climactic the Marxist Afghan government, the Democratic Republic of Afghanistan or DRA, asked the Soviets to provide security and assist them in their fight against the Mujahideen the name given to the rebel freedom fighters a coalition of Muslim guerillas who from their perspective are fighting a Jihad or Holy War against the DRA and now the Soviets."

"Doesn't seem like much of a contest given the might of the Soviet Union?" commented Williams.

"Maybe so but the Afghan government was in big trouble even before the Soviets rode into town like the cavalry and since then even with their support they haven't been doing much better. I just wanted you to have some perspective on the overall situation over there because you will be working with the rebel freedom fighters and Afghans to hopefully make the situation even worse for the Soviets, by the way you know the conflict is being referred to as the Soviet Union's Vietnam which might put it into better perspective for you" advised Brown.

Just at that moment a voice came over the aircraft's public address system telling them the aircraft was on its final approach and would be landing shortly.

"Let's pick this up again on the next flight" said Brown leaning back in his seat.

Once they had transferred to the much larger Boeing 737 and it had reached its cruising altitude, Brown rejoined them and continued the briefing.

"Where were we? Let me see, the Soviet Union is in big trouble these days they have had another change at the top, a new General Secretary has just been appointed. The revenues they have been getting from their very significant natural resources are way down, they are fighting a war in Afghanistan and there is a lot of civil unrest in their Republics. A turning point came recently when the religious leaders in Afghanistan called for an all-out Jihad or Holy

War against the new Afghan communist regime and the Soviets requesting all Afghans fight alongside the Mujahideen freedom fighters in defense of the Islamic faith. Something you should understand is that the Afghan government has only ever controlled the larger cities in Afghanistan and tribal leaders and clan chiefs have always controlled the rural areas of the country and as the new communist state of Afghanistan began to slip away from Moscow's control the then aged Soviet General Secretary Brezhnev decided direct military intervention was the only way to keep the new government in power. This was similar to the way the Soviets invaded Hungary in nineteen fifty-six and Czechoslovakia in nineteen sixty-eight. Once the Soviets went into Afghanistan they dissolved the existing government removed those who had been in power and put their own people in place their names won't mean anything to you. At the time I don't think the Soviet's even realized that they would only be able to control the larger cities not the whole country, their plan was to quickly stabilize the current situation by strengthening the Afghan army and be out of

Afghanistan within a short period of time with any fighting being done by the new DRA government's army. So far the overthrow of the old regime has proven to be much easier than fighting the literally thousands of guerilla freedom fighters spread throughout the country. In the early years of the war a succession of Soviet General Secretary's, Brezhnev, Andropov and Chernenko all died while trying to get the better of the Mujahideen rebels. Their military leadership in the field had recommended withdrawal on several occasions but it had fallen on deaf ears back in Moscow and when Mikhail Gorbachev came to power he ordered a Soviet military victory within one year."

"I think you are saying the Soviet Union is itself in a tenuous position these days and it obviously underestimated what it was getting into when it went into Afghanistan?" commented Williams "Pete and I know first-hand that the Soviets were in bad shape several years ago when they sent us off on a mission to speed up nuclear disarmament, they were having expenditure issues even back then trying to sustain their nuclear arsenal."

"Anyway that's what we were told at the time" mumbled
Shelby.

"How about we take a break" sighed Brown not really listening to what they had been saying.

Before he could move off Williams asked him what kind of raids he and Shelby would be expected to undertake.

Brown laughing said "That's up to you two geniuses to figure out but you need to start slowly building up capable teams and gradually attacking bigger and bigger targets. Now let's take that break!"

Once Brown had left Shelby asked Williams how he felt about this whole thing and Williams suggested they would have to do their best while always trying to escape.

Brown returned about half an hour later and resumed the briefing saying "The Pakistani's and Iranians are very concerned about the potential advance of the Soviet Red Army into their countries and have been training and supporting the Mujahideen rebels along with many other countries including the United States who have been providing significant aid via Pakistan. The

United States have been supporting the anti-communist rebel factions in Afghanistan for a number of years now and multitudes of foreign Muslim rebels have joined the fight, at last count there were well over thirty-five thousand from at least forty different Islamic countries fighting in Afghanistan, quite astounding don't you think? The CIA's Special Activities Division paramilitary officers have been authorized by the United States Congress to carry-out covert operations against the Afghan communist government and their Soviet backers and have been working closely with the Pakistani Intelligence Services to train and equip the Mujahideen rebels. I think it is planned that you will meet with some of their leaders before you leave Pakistan for Afghanistan and it has also recently been agreed by the Brits, us and the Pakistani's that we will help the rebel guerilla fighters to take the war into the Soviet Union itself where any damage done could significantly affect the morale of the troops and those supporting them. Members of the Pakistani Intelligence Service are embedded with the Mujahideen rebels providing direct assistance to them and there are currently over four thousand rebel bases in Afghanistan. In addition we have begun to distribute subversive literature and thousands of Qur'an's into the Soviet Union's southern republics of Tajikistan, Uzbekistan and Turkmenistan, which are predominantly Muslim, many Soviet Muslims living in these bordering Soviet Republics have family in Afghanistan and are sympathetic to their cause. We are already attacking Soviet military garrisons, munitions factories, storage depots, power stations, railways and any other places where we can cause significant disruptions. However in carrying out these raids we have found every incursion sparks an immediate retaliatory response from the Soviet's in the form of aerial bombing or helicopter gunship attacks so they are not being undertaken without a cost to the Mujahideen rebels and the Afghan people."

Although Williams and Shelby were beginning to experience information overload Brown continued telling them that each rebel commander is leading as many as three hundred men sometimes more. There are usually cells in each district and a significant number of cells in each province many operating from underground bunkers and in some areas there are large networks of tunnels invisible from the air containing numerous adjoining rooms. In some cases they are heated by hydro-electric power from mountain runoff water. Do you have any questions?" asked Brown.

"Yes why do all these countries end in "Stan"?" enquired
Shelby.

"It's a Persian word meaning land or place" said Brown knowingly

"Here is a piece of trivia for you, Afghanistan is the only official nation whose name begins with an A but doesn't end with an A. Check it out!"

"Any more questions?" enquired Brown.

"Not for me" responded Shelby wearily. "Me neither" offered Williams.

"Good I'll see you both in Afghanistan and don't forget to remember I'm your lifeline while you are there so always maintain contact with me and you'll likely find nothing more valuable in Afghanistan than donkey dung and poppies. Now I'll let you gentlemen get some down time before we arrive in Pakistan" said Brown getting up and moving towards the back of the plane.

"Wow" whispered Shelby "That was a lot of information to take in all at once."

"I don't know if it was for our sake or his to try and impress us with how much he knows about the conflict in Afghanistan I guess some of it might be useful" responded Williams.

"He does seem to be very egotistical" responded Shelby. "No kidding. Anyway as he suggested let's get some down time" sighed Williams leaning back and closing his eyes.

A few hours later they had arrived at Peshawar Air Station in Pakistan where they emerged into the heat and humidity as soon as they stepped out of the plane. Below them they could see a group of American's in military fatigues, several Pakistani's in light blue uniforms and several men with shaggy beards dressed in long flowing robes.

"Welcome to Pakistan" said one of the Americans greeting them as they came down the mobile stairs.

"Thanks" responded Shelby not sure what else to say.

"I would like to introduce you to Colonel Khalid Mahsood he is the commander of the base you will be staying on until your transportation to Afghanistan is arranged" one of the Americans offered.

The Colonel shook hands with them saying "Two fine looking American specimens if I may so."

"Thank you Colonel" responded Williams

Just at the moment Station Chief Brown came striding by stopping to greet them saying "I'll see you boys in Afghanistan" before walking on.

After some more welcoming greetings Williams and Shelby were directed towards an old looking vintage Jeep and asked to get in the back where they were handcuffed to the Jeep's rusty frame, their bags tied on the back. As they exited the airport they could already tell it was going to be a bumpy ride. They sped through narrow streets and it didn't take them long to see what a poverty stricken country Pakistan was in contrast to where they'd been living for the past several years in Sydney which had exuded prosperity and was bright, clean and well maintained. The streets they were currently passing through were dirty, in a total state of disrepair and they could see garbage strewn around everywhere.

"Welcome to the Third World" commented Williams. "Talk about culture shock" replied Shelby.

As the Jeep continued to navigate its way through the pot-hole filled streets they passed numerous low powered motor cycles, the occasional small car and many strange looking multi colored severely overloaded motorized vehicles. There were many men, women and children walking along by the side of the road pulling hand carts piled high with furniture, suitcases and what appeared to be all their worldly possessions and stray dogs and chickens were running wild everywhere. Williams wondered why there were so many people on the move and figured they must be displaced refugees from the Soviet occupation of Afghanistan. After driving through crowded bustling streets for what seemed like hours they eventually came to the gates of a military base where their driver waved at the guardhouse and the bar was raised to let them onto the base. They were driven around the base until they arrived in front of a collection of small white huts where they and their bags were freed from the Jeep and they were ushered through the door of one of them. It was very hot in the hut, there were bunk beds against one wall, a table and chairs in the middle of the hut and a round mirror hanging on the wall above a sink beside a toilet, their first impression was that the only other thing the hut seemed to have going for it was that it was spotlessly clean.

"So these are our new digs or should I say our new cell" commented Williams "Talk about the bare essentials."

Shelby checked the door and found it had been locked from the outside, he also noticed the windows had bars on the outside.

"It looks like they even know who we are in Pakistan!" said Williams laughing.

"Why wouldn't they aren't they working with the CIA?" replied Shelby.

"It was just a joke, how about playing cards to kill some time? I brought some with me" responded Williams.

"Let me get changed first and I'll be right with you, don't go anywhere" replied Shelby getting a tee-shirt and shorts out of his kit bag."

"Hold on while I get changed too by the way didn't Brown say we'd get more training from the Pakistani's I wonder what they're going to teach us how to make curry?" quipped Williams.

"Who knows" commented Shelby shuffling the playing cards "I assume we're going to play Gin?"

They played cards and although they were thirsty were reluctant to drink the water from the tap over the sink. After playing cards for a while they heard the door to the hut being opened and a Pakistani in uniform came in carrying a tray full of Styrofoam containers which they found out contained rice and a curry of some kind. There was also some flat bread, paper plates, paper cups and plastic spoons on the tray.

Shelby asked if there was anything to drink and the Pakistani told him the tap water was safe to drink before leaving.

"What did I tell you" commented Williams "Our Asian vacation sure is starting off with a bang, Pakistani cuisine, rice, curry, bread and tap water, inside a steaming hot wooden hut."

After they'd eaten the rice, some of the cauliflower curry, the bread and drunk some tap water having nothing else to do they climbed into their bunk beds, Williams had lost the cut of the cards so he'd had to take the top bunk. They had brought some novels with them that Dave Wiltshire had given them, two by Ken Follett and two by Robert Ludlum, they both already knew boredom was going to be one of their worst enemies on the mission and were both feeling jet lagged and tired from the change in time zones. Williams started to read Triple one of Follett's bestsellers and Shelby, The Bourne Identity, another popular bestseller. There was an electric light bulb hanging from the ceiling in the middle of the hut which shed enough light for them to read by and they both eventually fell asleep with it on not needing it to be dark to sleep.

They were woken early the next morning by a different uniformed Pakistani officer who asked them to join him at the small table in the middle of the hut.

"I have come to give you some information" commented the uniformed officer.

He laid out a torn and wrinkled map of Afghanistan on the table and pointed out the Soviets bases which were circled on the map and seemed to be close to cities like Kabul, Kandahar and Jalalabad. He showed them the area it was planned they would be located in way up in north-eastern Afghanistan there were no Soviet bases in this area. He pointed out a garrison in Termez on the Soviet-Afghan border in the Soviet Republic of Uzbekistan which he said was what the CIA wanted them to attack. He told them they could keep the map and suggested they should always be in uniform when they were on a raid so that they would be treated as prisoners of war if they happened to be captured.

Williams asked him how long it would be until they left for Afghanistan and he said he didn't know but it shouldn't be too long. They asked him several more questions after which he left them still studying the map.

Red Shadows On Liberty's Soil

Later that afternoon Williams and Shelby were driven to a restaurant in a town they were told was called Badaber. With them in the roomy Mercedes were two Pakistani officers that they hadn't seen before one in the front next to the driver and one sitting beside them in the back. When they arrived at the restaurant they were introduced to a paramilitary officer from the CIA's Special Activities Division Graham Weekes. They were also introduced to a senior Pentagon official Bill Matheson and about a dozen or so nameless Mujahideen rebel leaders who greeted them warmly. The Mujahideen leaders explained the makeup of the rebels in Afghanistan which Williams and Shelby were already familiar with following their briefing by Station Chief Brown. They were told that many of the men were foreign freedom fighters who were happy to be waging a Jihad against the atheist Soviet communists and that the arrival of the Soviets in Afghanistan had incensed the Afghan people so much that they were doing all they could to help the Mujahideen freedom fighters to defeat them and the puppet Marxist government they were propping up.

Another leader stated "We along with regional tribal warlords are fighting both the Soviet and DRA troops and America is helping us in any way they can."

"We can't thank you enough" said another leader.

The discussion was very disjointed with most of the Mujahideen leaders talking among themselves including Williams and Shelby occasionally. One of them told them to watch out for the Afghan secret police the KHAD who were infiltrating the regional tribes and spreading false information while trying to gather intelligence. Someone else said the land of Afghanistan is ours and it will be ours again. Our cause is right and Allah is on our side added another leader. While these discussions were going on the big round table they were sitting at was gradually being filled up with dish after dish, there were large bowls of salad and rice, different meat dishes, bowls of curry and several plates of flat bread. Matheson began to offer tea to anyone who held their cup out while one of the Pakistani officers was explaining to Williams and Shelby what the different dishes were, he suggested they might like the aloo gosht, chicken with potatoes and shashik marinated lamb chops with herbs. He suggested they might also like daal, roti, yogurt, pickles, salad, pakoras and papadums. This was the first time Williams and Shelby had ever been offered so much Pakistani food and they were reluctant to take too much of anything apart from rice, which they figured wouldn't cause them any intestinal problems. While they were carefully choosing what to eat Matheson began to talk about where they would be going in Afghanistan a town called Zadian, in Balkh province a mostly mountainous region close to the Soviet Union's southern border. Suddenly they heard the sound gunfire and the Mujahideen leaders seeing the shock on Williams and Shelby's faces burst out laughing and one of them said don't worry its Saturday night the men are just letting off steam if there is a loud explosion then start to worry.

Matheson continued "The village where you will be staying is far enough from any main roads so as not to be noticed by Soviet troops moving down from the north but it is close enough to launch raids across the border. Termez in Uzbekistan is where the largest Soviet staging garrison is located. It's about ten miles north of where you'll be staying, you will find the summer months are quite hot and the winter's cold. Weekes joined in, telling them that the Station Chief in the area is Doug Brown and they told him they'd already met him on the plane coming over. Weekes continued telling them that Brown was a good man who had been in northern Afghanistan for several years now and he was confident he would help them with anything they needed. He told them they would be working closely with the Mujahideen and Afghan rebels and living with them. Williams asked what it was going to like for them.

"We don't really know ourselves" said Matheson "But it'll definitely be a new experience for both of you."

"Yea right" responded Shelby sarcastically.

After eating what they could and listening to the many different stories being told by the Mujahideen rebel leaders the Pakistani officers indicated it was time to go and as Williams and Shelby were getting up from the table the Mujahideen leaders started shouting and waving their hands in the air.

Matheson said apologetically "Sorry I forgot to tell you before you leave the table you have to thank Allah, their God, for the food you have just received in this part of the world grace is always said at the end of the meal."

They sat back down put their hands together and along with the Mujahideen leaders quietly thanked Allah for the food."

The Mujahideen leaders acknowledged what they had done and ran to shake their hands and wish them well as they got up from the table gently patting them both on the back. Once they got outside away from the Mujahideen leaders Matheson and Weekes who had accompanied them out of the restaurant told them they would be coming to see them next week to discuss what's currently going on in northern Afghanistan.

"Good" said Williams "We'd also like to discuss our current living conditions among other things with you."

But before they could say much more they were bundled into the back of the Mercedes and driven off into the night.

Red Shadows On Liberty's Soil

Weekes and Matheson kept their word and late on Monday morning met up with Williams and Shelby in a large meeting room in one of the main buildings on the military base, it felt really good to be out of the hot hut and to be with fellow Americans who appeared to care about them.

"We know why you're here and would suggest you do your best to stay alive when you get to Afghanistan" said Weekes.

"I don't think you really know why we're here" replied Shelby.

Weekes ignored Shelby continuing on "This occupation will end eventually and depending upon the deal you have you could possibly go free."

"But that's the thing" responded Williams "Nobody has told us what will happen if we survive, we were given two options, go to trial for treason or do whatever the United States government wanted us to do which looks like fight the Soviets in their own country no one has told us what will happen to us if we survive."

"I think you can figure out why" conjectured Matheson. "But what if we do?" asked Shelby.

"To be honest I don't know what is planned for you if the war ends and you survive" offered Weekes.

"We understand" said Williams agreeably.

"We do?" queried Shelby.

"We'll discuss it later" said Williams's looking quite agitated "Now can we discuss what you guys came here for?"

"We really only came here to allow you to ask us any questions you may have about the situation you find yourselves in" offered Weekes.

"Let's start at the top then, why are we being kept captive by the Pakistani's and not you guys?" asked Williams.

"I think I can answer that" replied Matheson "We're not setup to keep anyone captive we have no facilities for this we are all advisors living in hotel accommodations. I guess I could lock you in my bathroom what do think Graham?"

"We could take one each" laughed Weekes.

"Surely you must be based somewhere?" enquired Shelby. "We're spread out in different parts of north-west Pakistan along the Afghanistan border" said Weekes more seriously. "That explains why the Pakistani's seem to be reluctant hosts" replied Williams.

"Why do you say that?" asked Matheson.

"Well they are keeping their distance not being very friendly and the accommodations we are being held in are funnily enough not much bigger than a hotel bathroom and sweltering hot."

"Leave it with me I will speak to them about having you moved" responded Weekes assuredly.

"When we get into Afghanistan will we be imprisoned like we are here?" asked Shelby.

"No you will be just like a Mujahideen freedom fighter surviving day to day anyway you can, I think as you probably know from talking to Doug Brown you will be required to plan and lead raids into the Soviet Union in conjunction with the local rebel commanders who already know you're coming" commented Weekes.

"Well at least that's something to look forward to" replied Shelby.

"You'll find the Mujahideen rebels to be better educated on the whole compared to the local Afghans but don't underestimate the desire of these locals to fight and die for the cause. You will need to prove yourselves to gain their respect." stated Weekes.

"What happens if we get injured or fall sick" asked Shelby. "Brown is your lifeline, make sure you keep in contact with him" offered Weekes.

"Where will we live once we get to where we're going?" asked Shelby enjoying finally being able to ask questions on the things that had been bothering him for a while.

"We think you will live near the town of Zadian which I believe we mentioned to you the other night, exactly who with, we don't know" commented Weekes.

Shelby was on a roll, "Knowing what is going on in Afghanistan what do you think our chances of survival are?" "From what I understand about the current situation it seems to me the war has almost reached a stalemate so I would say your chances of survival are pretty good the Mujahideen freedom fighters and Afghan rebels are well-practiced in guerilla warfare. The Soviets although better equipped have not been able to get a stranglehold on the rebels who are spread throughout the country they control several of the larger cities and other smaller urban centers but overall they are not making many inroads" advised Weekes.

"Interesting" muttered Williams "Any idea when we will be deployed?"

"We hear you should be on your way before the end of the week" suggested Matheson.

While tea and biscuits were being brought into the meeting room Weekes was drawing out a rough map of Afghanistan on a flip chart.

"I think you both know the geography of the country by now but as a refresher Afghanistan is here in the middle, Pakistan is here off to the east and south, the Soviet Union's southern border is up against Afghanistan's northern border and Iran is off to the west. Kabul is the Soviet equivalent to Moscow or so they like to think but the Afghans in general are impossible to control primarily due to the ruggedness and lack of infrastructure in the country as a whole which really only allows for local control. The Soviets probably had no idea when they crossed the border how difficult it was going to be to take control of Afghanistan but if nothing else it has allowed them to field test their latest conventional weapons in a theatre of war unfortunately at the expense of the Afghan people whose country is currently in total turmoil" advised Weekes.

As mentioned you need to gain the respect of the people you are working with as soon as you can then you should be able to control them rather than it being the other way around.

We would be interested to know the full story as to why you find yourselves in this situation we've only heard what you tried to do not why?" enquired Weekes.

"You can tell them Pete" mumbled Williams while pouring himself a cup of tea.

"Let me see, Gerry and I had arrived in Moscow in the middle of the winter of nineteen eighty one, I was on vacation and he was planning to give Communism a try, if you can believe that. It seems the Soviets were looking to find a way to halt the nuclear arms race the cost of which was severely impacting their floundering economy anyway this is what we were told by an old Soviet general. They were looking for two suitable Americans to help them achieve this and we were unfortunately the chosen ones. We were given a choice between spending the rest of our lives doing hard labor in Siberia or undertaking a mission to rid the world of nuclear weapons and we opted for the latter and by the time the mission got underway I think we both believed we were doing the world a huge favor unfortunately having to sacrifice American lives in the process. As it turned out our brilliant fellow countrymen managed to find a way to stop the detonation of an armed nuclear missile in its silo and we were able to escape to Australia where we'd been living up until a few months ago."

"That is an amazing story" commented Matheson.

"Yes I hope you will be able to get revenge on the Soviets which may actually help your cause in the long run" offered Weekes "Do you have any other questions of us?"

"I don't" replied Shelby looking a little sad.

"I'm good" added Williams "But please try and find us somewhere else to stay and thank you for taking the time to help us better understand the situation we'll find ourselves in soon it's most appreciated."

"Good luck to you both" said Matheson getting up to leave the room with Weekes.

They shook hands and Williams and Shelby were left alone in the large room.

"Let's hope they keep their word on getting us better accommodations which would help a lot right now" commented Shelby.

"Well they came here to see us today as they promised so I don't see why they won't help us if they can" replied Williams.

Still locked in the hut two days later Williams and Shelby had no idea why they had stayed in Pakistan as long as they had, William's theory was that it must be to acclimatize them to the pace of life in central Asia and begin to slow them down. In the west everyone expects things to happen instantly but in this part of the world everything happens at a much slower pace and Pakistan of all the countries in this part of the world was perhaps the most like the west so it was a good place to begin to get acclimatized with life in the east. Williams had shared this theory with Shelby and his opinion was their master's in the CIA couldn't give a hoot about them so why would they be trying to be nice to them and didn't agree with him. Williams couldn't think of any other reason to delay them so long so he was sticking to his theory and suggesting to Shelby that the CIA did care about them because it was in their interests for them to be successful because it would mean they had impacted the Soviets if only in a small way. Williams already realized it was futile to try and convince Shelby of this so he stopped talking about it. Shelby on the other hand couldn't stop talking about them being stuck there unless it was to further punish for them. It certainly wasn't helping his state of mind not being able to understand why this was happening to them again. He kept telling Williams that perhaps they had changed their minds and they were going to be brought back for trial in the United States and he humored him by saying it was a possibility never really thinking it was. Discussion about William's theory had almost created a rift between them which was most unusual because they had always managed to get along even under the most stressful circumstances and it was only when Williams suggested they try and break out of the hut that Shelby re-engaged with him again.

Shelby got excited about this and was full of ideas on how they could do it, attack the next Pakistani who brought them food, cut a hole in one of the walls of the hut or pretend one of them was sick. Williams went for the last idea and thought he could pull it off the next time food was brought in, he planned to exercise until he was dripping with sweat which would hopefully be just before their food was about to arrive and it would look like he had a raging fever which was making it difficult for him to breathe. He had only just begun to exercise when the door of the hut opened and two Pakistani officers entered and told them to get their stuff and come with them. It took all of two minutes for them to get their "stuff" together because they couldn't get out of the swelteringly hot hut quickly enough. They were escorted to an open Jeep and told to get in the back where they were handcuffed to the legs of the backseat. By where the sun was located in the sky directly above them they figured it must be around noon. It was swelteringly hot as they drove through busy streets reaching a deserted sandy dirt road which they drove along for mile after mile creating a dust cloud behind them. The sun was beginning to set as they arrived alongside a collection of dilapidated buildings where many men some in uniform were milling around, it didn't look much like a border crossing but they both suspected it was because there were various official looking signs along the side of the road. They came to a stop outside one of the buildings and were immediately surrounded by angry looking long shirted men. After being freed from the Jeep they were roughly shoved by many filthy hands towards one of the old buildings and after going through a door were introduced to someone who they were told was the district rebel commander a tough looking man with a shaggy beard, turban and fierce darting eyes. He welcomed them to Afghanistan in English saying he was pleased to meet them. After this brief greeting he signaled to one of his men and Williams and Shelby were taken down a dark hallway to a room with no windows at the rear of the building where a lone candle was providing the only light. There were some well-worn Persian rugs on the floor, a pile of blankets and a small table in the small room. Although they were not impressed by what they saw, the room was cooler than the sweltering hut they'd been locked in for the last week or so. Their bags were brought into the room by a young skinny man who dumped them down and quickly left.

"Not exactly the Holiday Inn" laughed Williams. "You're not kidding" said Shelby "Why the hell have we been brought to this godforsaken place?"

"I guess its' part of the handover but at least we're on the move again" suggested Williams taking in his new surroundings "You know I haven't been sleeping well lately so I think I'll have an early night."

"May as well there's nothing else to do, it looks like the biggest decision we've got to make is who's going to blow the candle out" responded Shelby.

"Don't blow it out I want to find something to use as a pillow" replied Williams feeling around in his bag "I guess some of these dirty clothes will have to do."

Shelby asked Williams if he thought he should use the spare blankets in the room as a pillow and Williams said he wouldn't because they might be infested with something but it was up to him. After thinking about it for a few seconds Shelby followed Williams lead and grabbed some dirty clothes from his kit bag to use as a pillow.

"Can I blow the candle out now?" asked Shelby.

"No" said Williams "Just let it burn itself out it doesn't belong to us, if the long shirted men want it out I'm sure they'll take care of it."

"That's alright" replied Shelby "It doesn't bother me." "Sweet nightmares" whispered Williams while he was trying to get comfortable.

They were woken by several men talking loudly in their room in what sounded like Pashto from the language training they'd been given, it seemed they were required to get their stuff and follow them. They were led outside where men were gathered around a different Jeep from the one they had arrived in, the rebel commander was there too. He shook hands with them and directed them to get into the back of the Jeep, two men were sitting in the front of the Jeep and introductions were made. The man sitting in the passenger seat introduced himself as Kaleem who said the driver was Akbar.

"I'm Gerry and this is Peter" responded Williams.

"Good to meet you" said Kaleem in reasonably good English.

The driver showed no reaction and remained silent as he slowly drove the Jeep away from the large gathering of long shirted men.

"Please get comfortable you have a long journey ahead of you to one of the remotest parts of Afghanistan" said Kaleem turning around and talking to them.

"Wouldn't have it any other way" replied Williams "Pete and I always like a challenge so bring it on."

"You Americans really are crazy" said Kaleem.

"No not crazy just confident in our own abilities that's all" laughed Williams.

Kaleem laughed as he turned away settling into his seat. After he'd turned away Shelby commented to Williams "These CIA people really do want to torture us I don't think they could have sent us anywhere worse on the planet?"

"How about to the chair or a penitentiary!" responded
Williams.

"You know what I mean anywhere worse than that" mumbled Shelby.

"It's early days yet you never know you could have more tales to tell your grandchildren before this is over" laughed Williams.

"If I live that long" replied Shelby.

Williams leaned forward touched Kaleem on the shoulder and asked him how long it was going to take them to get to where they were going.

Kaleem said "About a day depending on how many times we get stopped by unofficial checkpoints."

This didn't register with Williams or Shelby.

They had only been travelling for just over an hour and Williams and Shelby already couldn't imagine having to travel like this for another twenty-four hours even though the weather was clear at the present time and they were excited to finally be in Afghanistan. An hour or so later they were stopped by a group of men blocking the road it didn't look like an official checkpoint so they figured it must be one of the unofficial checkpoints Kaleem had mentioned earlier. The men were wielding AK-47's and other fearsome looking weapons including rocket propelled grenade launchers apparently known as RPG's according to Kaleem. They were talking so loudly amongst themselves to the extent that it was almost comical arguing with each other in deep guttural tones and after several more heated discussions a rough looking long shirted man waved them on without even looking at them. The weather was still good with blue skies and clear mountain vistas as the same unofficial checkpoint scene was repeated numerous times as they journeyed north the inspections varying in scope from a brief glance to an all-out search for weapons and valuables neither of which they had which was probably making their journey go a lot smoother. They'd been told by the Pakistani's who had driven them to the border that any money or the like that they might need would be provided by Station Chief Brown once they got to their destination. Brown obviously knew Afghanistan well and didn't see any point in subjecting them to any potentially life threatening situations prior to the start of their mission. The Afghan rebels were scary enough if you didn't have concealed weapons or valuables and he obviously knew the danger Williams and Shelby might face if they had been in possession of either. The constant stoppages and searches were adding time to their journey but at the same time allowing them to become familiar with the men they would soon be working with. Obviously these were very rough and ready mountain men whose lives appeared to be very primitive especially if all they did all day was stand around and wait for opportune booty.

So far they had not seen or encountered any Soviets but had already been told what to do if they did which was to keep their mouths shut and say nothing, Kaleem would do all the talking and provide identification papers if required. Williams and Shelby wondered how the Soviets dealt with the constant interference by the Afghan rebels or whether they melted away whenever a Soviet convoy came into view. To think they had been living a life of luxury only a few months ago and were now making their way across one of the most impoverished countries in the world on a mission that likely had no way of being remotely successful. But it was what it was and they would have to figure out if there was an upside, in Williams experience there always was.

It was beginning to cloud over and they could see dark ominous looking clouds up ahead as they seemed to be approaching a particularly large gathering of men blocking a mountain pass up ahead. Several vehicles had already been stopped and surrounded and men, women and children seemed to be being pulled out of the vehicles and thrown around.

"What's happening?" asked Shelby as they were getting closer.

"It looks like these might be relatives of some of the men" said Kaleem straining to see what was going on.

"Wow, they sure have a funny way of greeting relatives. I'd love to push and pound my relatives around like that, it brings a whole new meaning to family feud" laughed Williams.

Kaleem turned back to them "This is what I think is happening I'm not totally sure but relatives are usually greeted in this way especially if it has been long time since they last saw each other. Afghans are very emotional, huggy, feely people!"

They were now very close to the gathering and were wondering what was in store for them and they didn't have to wait long before several men came running towards their Jeep firing their weapons in the air.

Kaleem turned around to Williams and Shelby "Don't worry this is a sign they're happy."

The men stopped firing their weapons as they approached the Jeep and indicated the Jeep could go on through past the strange celebrations that were still going on. Once they were past Shelby commented to Williams that some Afghan customs are going to take some getting used to.

Kaleem turned back to them "You have picked the coldest time of the year to come to Afghanistan."

"That figures" responded Shelby "The people who sent us here don't like us very much."

"Anyway don't worry we'll be stopping and lighting a fire to keep warm soon and Akbar can rest he's been driving for many hours."

Without warning it began to rain hard and Kaleem provided Williams and Shelby with an old umbrella which amazingly kept most of the rain off them. It was still raining heavily as they approached another unofficial checkpoint that would become particularly scary, there were only about a half a dozen men standing in the road but apparently Akbar hadn't slowed down sufficiently as they had approached them and they fired several shots at the Jeep cracking the windshield. Williams and Shelby were not happy about this and Akbar was even more upset as they were just about to find out, he jumped out of the Jeep and ran at the men with a scary looking dagger in his hand and had just about reached them when Kaleem caught up with him tackling him to the ground jarring the dagger loose.

"What the hell" shouted Shelby from the backseat of the
Jeep "Now who's crazy?"

While Kaleem was wrestling with Akbar the men in the road surrounded them shouting, pointing and poking at them with their weapons.

"Just what we need" muttered Williams as he started to get out of the Jeep.

Kaleem straining his neck to look back at the Jeep yelled at the top of his lungs telling Williams and Shelby to stay in the Jeep. One of the men hit Akbar in the face with the butt of his rifle cursing at him and Akbar's face was soon covered in blood. Kaleem now up on his feet was yelling and waving a bunch of papers at one of the men who seemed to be the leader as several of the men came over to the Jeep and looked Williams and Shelby over saying something neither of them understood.

"I think they just called us pussies" whispered Williams. "What?" responded Shelby.

"I'm only joking but they said something like that."

Akbar covered in blood stumbled back to the Jeep and slid behind the wheel releasing a stream of obscenities. The leader walked over to the Jeep the rest of the men following after him and to their surprise told them they could go on through and Kaleem jumped into the Jeep as Akbar slowly drove past the men who were now in loud animated conversation with the leader who seemed to be admonishing them for firing at the Jeep.

"What are the papers you were waving?" asked Williams enquiringly.

"In your language they would be "safe passage papers". They were provided by Station Chief Brown for your journey. They indicate that whoever detains you will be killed by the local warlord in the area, which they know will happen because it already has on a number of occasions, these warlords are like medieval kings and what they say goes if they want someone killed they will be."

Akbar his face still covered with dried blood was still cursing.

Shelby commented to Kaleem "Akbar doesn't appear to have the right temperament for this kind of work?"

"Like all men in this part of the world he has a hot temper if that is what you mean?" replied Kaleem "You must be careful here, every man and boy has a dagger or a gun in Afghanistan and if they don't, they are willing to die to obtain one. Where you come from every man and boy has money in their pocket here they have a deadly weapon."

Several hours further into their journey they were forced to stop by another large gathering of men and were told to get out of the Jeep which was searched. Kaleem was trying to show the person he thought was the leader the "safe passage" papers but he wasn't paying any attention to him meanwhile Akbar still with an angry scowl on his bloodstained face, Williams and Shelby were directed over to a structure by the side of the road while Kaleem continued to move amongst the crowd of men waving his papers and yelling in the hope that someone would show some interest in them. Eventually at gunpoint he too was directed over to the structure where the others were standing, Shelby asked him what was going on and Kaleem told him they wanted money to let them go through that's why they were searching the Jeep.

"Do you have any?" enquired Williams.

"Yes" responded Kaleem "But I don't plan to give it to them."

"What choice do we have?" asked Shelby. "We need to tell them we don't have any." "What if they search you?"

"They won't." "Why?"

"Because we don't do that we are men of honor who take your word for it."

"What about the safe passage papers?" asked Williams. "They told me the local warlord wants money to let vehicles through papers don't mean anything to them." Williams had already observed that Afghans avoided direct confrontation keeping their distance always talking loudly amongst themselves. It seemed you had to approach them if you had anything to discuss with them or give them, this was a trait he had noticed with eastern Europeans who also acted similarly like your very existence was irrelevant unless you had something to offer them and Williams was thinking to himself that this was certainly going to be a most difficult mission because Afghan men seemed to be constantly in conflict about one thing or another and to make matters worse they all seemed to be armed to the teeth.

It was beginning to get dark and turn cold and Williams asked Kaleem what he was planning to do and he was still adamant he wasn't going to give them any money. The men in the road continued to ignore the four of them as night fell and Williams and Shelby could only hear loud voices in the dark now. About an hour past and they asked Kaleem again what he was going to do and he said that they needed to wait. So perhaps William's theory had been correct, perhaps it was patience training they had undergone in Pakistan after all. A raging fire was now burning on the other side of the road from where they were huddled the flames lighting up the night. Not long after off in the distance they could lights approaching from the same direction they had come in. Kaleem told them he thought it was probably a convoy of Soviet trucks coming.

"This is our chance to escape" said Kaleem.

The four of them ran to the Jeep where Kaleem pushed Williams and Shelby into the back while shouting at Akbar to get them out of there. He turned the engine on and they rapidly sped off up the road past the big fire, the men who had stopped them completely ignoring them as they drove by, fortunately the Soviet convoy had stopped by the fire and it didn't take them long until they could only see darkness behind them and Akbar turned the Jeep's lights on.

Soon it began to snow and they huddled in the back of the Jeep under a blanket. Kaleem told them they would be stopping soon to light a fire and told them the bad news was that they didn't have anything to eat or drink because the men who had just stopped them had taken all their supplies of fruit, flat bread and water but there was some good news they were only a few hours from reaching their destination.

"So why don't we keep going? Akbar has just had a break so he shouldn't be tired" responded Williams.

Kaleem spoke to Akbar who grunted something then turned back to Williams and Shelby and told them Akbar agrees so we will keep going and hope there are no more unofficial checkpoints between here and Kheyrabad.

Somehow William's and Shelby had managed to make it through the unofficial checkpoints and were in a clearing surrounded by high mountains where many men were gathered standing around talking. Here we go again thought Williams as they got out of the Jeep and were introduced to a tall bearded man who Kaleem told them was the local district rebel commander who didn't seem particularly pleased to meet them and after greeting them whispered something to Kaleem and rudely turned his back on them and walked away talking to a group of newly arrived men. Kaleem told Williams and Shelby to get back in the Jeep where they sat there for over an hour before Kaleem told Akbar to drive until eventually they came to a large compound containing a number of dilapidated buildings.

Kaleem told Williams and Shelby to collect their stuff and while they were doing this Akbar was saying goodbye to them. Kaleem asked them to follow him as he led the way between two deserted windowless buildings to some rocks piled up against a compound wall where he removed the dirt from on top of a wooden hatch lifted it up and Williams and Shelby could see a large hole. Kaleem shouted into the hole and voices shouted up after which Kaleem told them this was the end of the line for him and Akbar now they had been delivered to the headquarters of the Northern Alliance guerrilla fighters.

"Thank you" said Shelby shaking Kaleem's hand, we really appreciate your help in getting here, are we in Zadian?"

"Just outside" replied Kaleem.

"I agree with Pete we couldn't have got here without you" replied Williams shaking Kaleem's hand and thanking him. "The rebel commander will take it from here, good luck" said Kaleem as he began to walk away.

The descent into the hole was very tight requiring them to lift their kit bags up over their heads as they descended into a dimly lit tunnel. They were greeted by several armed men who led them down another tunnel, there were no ceiling supports above their heads just packed mud. The tunnel ended in a large spacious area where they could see a familiar sight armed long shirted men standing around talking vociferously. They could see the rebel commander who had been unfriendly to them when they'd first arrived but this time he was much friendlier and invited them to sit with him on a plush Afghan rug.

"Welcome to Northern Alliance headquarters" stated the rebel commander.

"Thanks" said Shelby "Great to be here."

"Tell us about your trip?" enquired the rebel commander. "It took us all day and night to get here, we came through many unofficial checkpoints or roadblocks we're actually not sure what to call them and all kinds of weather imaginable, torrential rain, freezing rain and a snow storm" responded Shelby.

"More like a blizzard if you ask me!" chipped in Williams. "Well you must be tired I suggest we find you something to eat and you can rest, we should meet in the morning to discuss your plans" suggested the rebel commander catching the eye of one of his men.

The man asked them to follow him and they left the open area and went along a different tunnel until they came to a small room that was lit by a solitary candle in a holder on the wall, it seemed to be a storage room of some kind. There were large wicker baskets stacked high against one of the walls and a long bench with piles of what looked like clean shirts. Another man came into the room carrying a number of colorful Afghan rugs which he spread over the dirt floor. Williams commented that it looked like they were taking over the laundry room and hoped that wouldn't be a problem but didn't get any reaction from the men in the room who soon left.

"The accommodations just keep on getting better" commented Shelby sarcastically.

"I must say it's an improvement on being huddled under a blanket in the back seat of a Jeep during a raging blizzard so don't complain too much" replied Williams.

"That's true I guess it sure looks like we won't be sleeping in a real bed anytime soon perhaps it will be good for our postures" remarked Shelby.

"Now you're being a little too positive I wish they had real pillows they would really help, but I guess they're too bulky to lug around and would soon get dirty lying in the dirt oh well such is our penance!" sighed Williams.

Several minutes later a long shirted man came through the door carrying a tray with two large bowls of rice, some flatbread and two cups of what looked like tea. He put the tray down on the end of Shelby's rug and said what sounded like pilau, naan and tea before quickly leaving.

"I really need something to eat or I'm going to pass out I feel very light headed" said Shelby grabbing for one of the bowls.

They both devoured the food finding that it didn't actually taste too bad the rice concoction seemed to include onions, raisins, orange peel, nuts and stringy meat of some kind the tea was hot and sweet and the bread very filling.

"Wow that really hit the spot" remarked Williams after he finished eating.

"It was real good" replied Shelby.

After discussing their new surroundings they both got comfortable and were soon asleep even though it was the middle of the day.

They had slept right through to the next morning and were awoken by loud shouting which didn't seem to be being directed at them. From what they could tell there had been a cave in.

"Great" commented Shelby "That's all we need."

"Let's go and see what we can find out" suggested Williams moving towards the doorway and could see the tunnel was full of long shirted men shouting and yelling, one of them shouted to them to stay in their room so they settled in for the wait. They discussed what they planncd to tell the rebel commander once the situation was under control and agreed they needed a better way of describing the freedom fighters rather than "long shirted" men.

"What else can we call them?" asked Shelby.

"They're Mujahideen so how about Muja's for short?"

"No that is probably very derogatory how about Mojo's that's different enough for them not to know we are referring to them?"

"I like that" said Williams "Mojo's!"

Shelby looked out into the tunnel and couldn't see anyone and shouted it looks like they've gone.

"Alright let's go and see if we can find the rebel commander" responded Williams.

They could see where the cave in had happened and had to crawl over several mounds of dirt to get down the tunnel eventually coming to the ladder that led up out of the tunnels. After climbing up they could see a familiar sight, long shirted men or Mojo's standing around in animated conversation the tall rebel commander saw them and shouted to them to come and join him. It was snowing lightly in the winter sunshine as they made their way to where he and his men were gathered.

"What happened?" asked Shelby.

"It seems there was a minor earthquake in the mountains which caused the tunnel cave-in it happens quite often and is nothing to worry about" replied the rebel commander.

"Are we going to discuss our plans today?" asked Williams.

"Yes some of the other Mujahideen chiefs should be joining us shortly so let's wait for them" mumbled the rebel commander. Suddenly the decibel level went up as a large group of Mojo's broke through the crowd striding towards where they and the rebel commander were standing. The rebel commander greeted the newly arrived men kissing and embracing them after which they immediately got into animated conversation with him. Williams and Shelby stood and waited patiently for the conversations to die down the rebel commander beckoning them to follow him and the large group of Mojo's who had begun to walk off. They walked along a snow covered mountain pass eventually ending up in what looked like a village square where the large group of men split up leaving Williams and Shelby huddled with the rebel commander and the Mujahideen chiefs. The rebel commander turned to Williams and Shelby and with a mock bow indicated the floor was theirs. Williams explained as best he could in Pashto that the two of them were there to assist, he was careful here, knowing their mandate was to actually lead cross border raids into the Soviet Union and explained what this would involve at a very high level. Before he'd finished talking one of the Mujahideen chiefs stepped out of the group and called to some other men. One of the men came running over and joined the group and listened intently to what Williams was saying.

One of the Mujahideen chiefs introduced the man who had joined them in broken English saying "This is Yusuf he is one of our most experienced fighters and has already led several raids across the border into the Soviet Union the men respect him and listen to him you will assist him."

"We would very much like to do that" offered Williams

"We feel we can be most helpful to him and all of you."

"Let Yusuf be the judge of this" responded a now seemingly angry Mujahideen chief.

The huddle broke up leaving Yusuf, Williams and Shelby standing together the rebel commander and Mujahideen chiefs walking away in deep conversation.

"Can we go somewhere to talk further?" asked Williams. "Yes, to my home" replied Yusuf "You need somewhere to stay, right?"

Williams and Shelby acknowledged they did and agreed to go with Yusuf hoping the accommodations where he was taking them might be better than the ones they'd stayed in so far in this part of the world but weren't betting on it.

Yusuf told them he lived north-east of Zadian and accompanied them while they got their belongings out of the tunnels, then led the way along a steep snow covered mountain pass that eventually descended towards an iced over lake where they could see numerous tracks of footprints in the snow going in all directions across the frozen lake. The view had a festive look to it, trees coated with snow, a mountainous backdrop with a light sprinkling of snow in the cool air but the sound of sporadic gunfire off in the distance quickly brought them back to reality. They were about to start living a life similar to a sheep herder and Williams was once again thinking about how they could escape even though Yusuf seemed a cheerful enough fellow and was whistling as the three of them began to make their way across the snow covered lake. So far Yusuf hadn't tried to make small talk so Shelby started some asking "How far is it to your home?"

"It shouldn't take us more than an hour to get there, the lake being frozen over will take some time off the journey" replied Yusuf, in English good enough for Williams and Shelby to understand.

"That's not too bad" commented Williams, who was already feeling the cold through his un-insulated clothing.

He and Shelby didn't have gloves but neither did Yusuf who was wearing a sheepskin vest which looked to be keeping him warm the long scarf he had wrapped around his head was helping to keep his head and the tops of his ears warm also. Williams and Shelby didn't have any head gear of any kind talk about strangers in a strange land thought Williams, we might not even make it to Yusuf 's and if we do we'll probably have frostbite by the time we get there. Just as Williams was about to mention this to Yusuf, he preempted him saying "We'll stop at my parents place they live on the other side of the lake and they should have some warm clothes you can borrow."

Within minutes of crossing the lake they had arrived at a collection of buildings behind a high wall. There was an archway leading inside and several armed men greeted them on the other side and recognizing Yusuf offered them cigarettes which they declined. Yusuf asked them if his father was home and they nodded affirmatively pointing over to what looked like a pig pen. It turned out to be exactly that and a spritely looking older Afghan man waved to them as they approached it.

"This is my father Kaaseb" said Yusuf.

Yusuf's father made his way around to where they were standing and greeted them in a very friendly manner after which he and Yusuf began to walk towards the expansive looking buildings in the compound Yusuf beckoning to Williams and Shelby to follow. They soon reached an impressive looking white building and after taking their boots off were greeted by a woman fully cocooned in flowing black silk garments, she bowed down to them pointing to a plush looking colorful Afghan rug in the middle of the floor.

Yusuf said "This is my mother Alia she would like you to sit down while she gets us tea."

This is the first women Williams and Shelby had been introduced to since their arrival in Pakistan and they promptly sat down on the rug as requested, Yusuf and his father joining them. To their utter disappointment it was no warmer in Yusuf 's father's house than it had been outside and hoped this was just an anti-room of some kind and there would be a raging fire burning in the house somewhere. Yusuf began speaking to his father in a language Williams and

Shelby didn't understand and almost immediately his father got up and left the room.

"I just asked my father if he could find some warm clothes for you and he's gone to look" commented Yusuf.

Not long after this Yusuf got up excused himself and left the room which was a welcome development as it gave Williams and Shelby a rare moment alone to talk.

"So what do you think so far?" asked Shelby.

"It is just about what I expected nothing more nothing less we are in a civilization that is a hundred years or more behind the west" responded Williams.

"Scary isn't it?" whispered Shelby.

They don't even have railways!" whispered Williams just as Yusuf came back into the room his father following him carrying a collection of jackets. Each one of them looked very warm but none of them fitted either of them, disappointed Yusuf asked his father if he had any bigger ones and Kaaseb left the room again as Yusuf went through the discarded pile of jackets and vests holding one of them up "Maybe it would fit if it was worn open?"

Yusuf 's mother came into the room carrying a tray full of cups and a pile of flat bread and indicated to Williams and Shelby to take some bread and a cup of tea off the tray. Yusuf 's father came back into the room carrying some blankets giving Williams and Shelby one each.

"Don't worry" said Yusuf "We'll visit some of my friends not far from here they're all big people and they should have some warm clothes that will fit you that we can borrow."

Yusuf, his parents, Williams and Shelby sat quietly drinking tea and eating the flat bread. Williams looking at Yusuf 's parents said a heartfelt "Thank you."

Yusuf 's parents both smiled but didn't say anything.

"They speak Old Persian" said Yusuf "So they won't be able to understand you but they know you are good men because you're with me."

When they'd finished their tea, Yusuf told his parents they had to leave and Williams and Shelby now wrapped in blankets followed Yusuf back out to the mountain trail. They soon reached another collection of buildings inside a high wall, this time there was a gate in the wall which was closed but not locked. Just like at Yusuf 's father's compound, there were armed men standing around just inside the gate. They greeted Yusuf, who asked them if a friend of his was home and they told him he wasn't. Yusuf asked them if they had any warm jackets his friends could borrow and they immediately rushed off in different directions. A few minutes later they returned carrying several jackets each. Williams and Shelby picked through them until they found several that fitted well eventually selecting two and thanking the men. Yusuf told the men he would return the jackets the next time he came to visit his parents and the men acted like it was no big deal offering friendly toothless smiles. Williams and Shelby rather sheepishly asked Yusuf if it would be possible for them to get hats and gloves and these were quickly provided also the Afghan men smiling and patting Williams and Shelby gently on the back, Yusuf thanked the men and they left the compound to continue their journey. Yusuf seemed to be oblivious to the cold, although he did have his head scarf and large pockets in his sheepskin jacket to keep his hands warm. After travelling several more miles Shelby's feet were beginning to feel very cold. Shelby and Williams were wearing regular army issue boots with no lining of any kind and when Shelby told Yusuf about his cold feet he said not to worry because they would be passing his brother Hamasa's house soon and they'd stop and get him to light a fire even though he told them fires were usually only lit at night. When they reached Hamasa's he lit a fire for them and gradually their feet began to thaw out and warm up while they drank several cups of hot Afghan tea and found they needed to relieve themselves so Yusuf took them out to the back of the house to a hole in the ground and told them to do it in there. When they got back inside Yusuf's brother who seemed to speak and understand English better than Yusuf told them he was looking forward to going on skirmishes and raids with them. This indicated to them that their mission in Afghanistan had already been discussed ahead of their arrival and it appeared great things were expected of them. They set off again on what they hoped would be the final leg of the journey and already one thing had become very clear to them was that although Afghanistan was one of the poorest countries in the world the hospitability and generosity of the people was second to none apart from the men they had encountered on their journey there. They even liked the hot spicy Afghan tea which they'd been given wherever they'd gone. By now they had come to another collection of buildings surrounded by a high wall which Yusuf indicated was where he lived, they had finally arrived at their home in Afghanistan.

It was almost dark now and they wondered what the night might have in store for them and as it turned out things started to look up their new accommodations were quite warm thanks to a wood stove in a large central room. They were welcomed by Yusuf's wife, Nadia and her sister Rashida who were shrouded and cocooned from head to toe. They would soon learn the flowing robes that Afghan women wore were called chadri's. Williams took a long look at Rashida making eye contact with her through the small concealing net covering her dark wild piercing eyes which looked to be beckoning him until she and her sister scurried out of the room upon a signal from Yusuf. Williams had always been fascinated by the way Muslim women were always covered up when in public or with men other than those of their own family, he had been intrigued by this whenever he'd seen them on the news or in documentaries, it was obviously something he and Shelby would need to get used to. Having only briefly seen Nadia's sister he already had a desire to find out what was hidden beneath the flimsy flowing robes she was wearing and one evening after they had finished eating Rashida came into the room fully covered up and picked up their empty bowls all the while staring at Williams with her tantalizing green eyes. Williams got up to assist her even though she gestured that he shouldn't, carrying his bowl he followed her into a room at the back of the dwelling where Yusuf 's wife was kneeling over a large bowl washing dishes. After handing the dirty dishes to her sister Rashida went outside William's startling her as he joined her standing very close to her. There were fires burning in all directions around them, outdoor fires at night seemed to be a way of life in Afghanistan, maybe it was safer to cook outside than inside.

Williams trying to make conversation said "Beautiful night don't you think?"

Rashida looked at him and shook her head as if she didn't understand what he'd said but he knew she could understand English just like her sister and brother-in-law. He said the same thing in Pashto and she looked at him and nodded her head in concurrence. As she turned to go inside Williams moved to block her way rubbing up against her body, she jumped back and shook her head indicating her disapproval, Williams reached forward and put his hands on her breasts gently touching them, she jumped back again shaking her head making no sound.

"This is where you are I wondered where you'd got to?" commented Shelby as he joined them.

"Look at the stars up there I don't think I've ever seen them so clearly" responded Williams.

Rashida brushed past Shelby and went back into the dwelling and when Williams and Shelby came back inside she was sitting next to Nadia and Yusuf on the rug next to the wood stove fingering prayer beads. Yusuf asked them how they liked Afghanistan so far and they both acknowledged it was very different from what they were used to. Rashida's darting eyes continued to intrigue Williams he envisaged an extremely attractive woman under her silk garments. He hoped one day those tantalizing eyes and much more of her would be revealed to him until then he would have to be patient. He had a feeling that under Afghan law it was the woman who normally got punished for indiscretions of any kind and the last thing he wanted to do was to put her in a compromising position even though he knew he would not be able to restrain himself if the situation ever presented itself to him. Just from the looks she was giving him he knew she felt the same way but he'd have to leave it up to her to make the first move. He was aroused just sitting close to her and much to his disappointment she got up saying she was tired head in concurrence. As she turned to go inside Williams and was going to lie down. Williams knew it was going to be an unbelievable challenge to try and seduce her not knowing that within a few weeks' she'd make it easy for him. Soon after Nadia and Yusuf got up and said they were going to lie down too, Williams and Shelby followed soon after them.

Early the next morning there was no sign of Nadia or Rashida and when Yusuf appeared Williams asked him where they were. Yusuf said they had probably gone to get water from a nearby mountain spring. Williams, Shelby and Yusuf, his brother Hamasa, known as Hami, who they had already met and another relative Jawid, who was called Jawi met later that morning to discuss ideas for raids on the Termez staging garrison, north of the border up in the Soviet Union. Williams and Shelby were finally doing what they were being forced to do by the CIA it was amazing how long it had taken them to get to this point thought Williams he remembered what Brown had told them that it was up to them to decide on and plan the raids according to what they thought would be most disruptive to the Soviets always asking the rebels their opinion and getting their buy-in.

Williams asked Yusuf, Hami and Jawi if they were young Soviet troops preparing to enter the conflict in Afghanistan what would be most disruptive, disturbing and unnerving to them?

Yusuf spoke up first "For me it would be bad water and food, unsanitary toilets and perhaps no electricity although that might not be such a hardship because many of them probably don't have electricity where they come from." "What about their sleeping quarters surely we can disrupt them somehow?" chipped in Shelby.

Yusuf commented that they should steal weapons and ammunition too which were needed badly by the rebels.

"Let's look at each one of these" suggested Williams "Let's start with the water supply."

Hami spoke up "If we dump donkey dung in the water tower tank it should make the water smell bad."

"That sounds like a good plan" offered Shelby.

"Is there a water tower and supply just for the garrison?" asked Williams.

"Yes they have their own" replied Yusuf.

"So that would seem possible, do you know if the tower is guarded?" asked Williams.

"No" added Jawi "But there is a high fence around the garrison itself."

"Contaminating the water shouldn't be a problem then" suggested Williams "What about the weapons?"

Yusuf said "There is an armory in the garrison which is regularly stocked!"

Williams asked Yusuf if he had ever stolen weapons or ammunition before and he said he hadn't but was willing to give it a try. Williams agreed that this was also possible.

"How about the food this seems like it might be harder to get at?" asked Williams.

Yusuf said "Why not spread donkey dung where the food is prepared and stored?"

"Yes that would work" said Williams "What about the latrines we'll need to block them so they back up and are not easy to unblock."

Yusuf said "We could fill the toilet bowl drains with cement and smear donkey dung everywhere."

"Wow" said Shelby "I never realized that donkey dung was such an amazing weapon!"

"What about the electricity. Are there generators on the garrison?"

"There must be" said Yusuf.

"Can we use donkey dung to disable the generators too?" asked Shelby tongue in cheek.

"I doubt it" replied Williams "But we'll have to look into how we can knock them out."

"Next is your suggestion Pete disrupting their sleeping quarters any ideas?" asked Williams.

"We could catch some camel spiders although they are not venomous they have quite a bite and look very scary, they are big and foreign soldiers are terrified of them" said Jawi "I'm sure we could collect a bag of them and let them loose wherever the soldiers sleep this would definitely be most disturbing to them and will create a great deal of commotion."

"Sounds good" chipped in Shelby.

"So let's include the camel spiders in our plans" suggested Williams.

The meeting broke up with them feeling satisfied that they had come up with some good ideas for the raid.

The following day Station Chief Doug Brown accompanied by several local maliks dropped in at Yusuf's to see how Williams and Shelby were doing and what they had planned. He told them that overall the covert operations in the north-east quadrant of Afghanistan were going really well now they were getting reliable information about Soviet troop movements in the area. The CIA had been getting information from spy satellites and with it the rebels were attacking Soviet convoys coming down from the north on a regular basis. Williams told Brown and the maliks about the ideas they had come up with for the raid and Brown suggested they might be taking on too much to start with and they should spread their ideas out over a number of raids allowing each one to be successful while they assessed the capability of Yusuf and the others. Williams agreed and suggested they could contaminate the garrison water supply on the first raid. In the second they would steal weapons and ammunition and in the third pollute the kitchens, toilets, disable the generators and release the camel spiders. Brown said this sounded good for a start and said that although these initial raids may seem small and insignificant they are sending a message to the Soviets that the rebels are everywhere including in the Soviet Union and it is only a matter of time until the raids become bigger and more catastrophic and after drinking some more tea Brown and the maliks left.

Williams and Shelby spent the next few days studying maps and generally getting familiar with the town of Termez,

Yusuf and his brothers were most impressed with how clearly Williams and Shelby explained things and the detailed planning they were doing. Williams had already begun to take on a leadership role with his innate ability to analyze and suggest different approaches to potential obstacles. Very often Williams and Shelby would see Yusuf, Nadia and Rashida kneeling on prayer rugs praying normally whenever they heard the guttural call summoning Muslims to the Mosque for mandatory prayers. Williams and Shelby accepted this was part of their culture and could see how important it was to them. They had heard that Muslims faced Mecca when they pray paying homage and giving thanks to Allah numerous times during their prayers. Their prayers come from their holy book the Qur'an and from an early age they are required to pray five times a day just after dawn around noon in the afternoon after sunset and before they go to bed. When they were praying their clothes, hands and feet have to be clean. Williams had joked it was like having a wash and brush-up and putting on your Sunday best but instead of doing it once a week it is thirty-five times a week which really seemed excessive to him and Shelby.

On Saturday night, Yusuf took Williams and Shelby to Kheyrabad for the first time to meet up with the Mujahideen freedom fighters and Afghan rebels in the area. They gathered every Saturday night in the large hall in the center of the town and Williams and Shelby were taken aback as they entered the hall and saw a huge collection of sandals piled just inside the door They took their boots off and went into the main hall where they saw a gathering of bare-footed, armed, shabbily dressed, un-shaven men who all seemed to be rough and ready for pretty much anything and becoming particularly raucous after drinking several Chai's the locally brewed Afghan tea. It was a dark spicy drink containing among other things crushed cloves, cardamom, cinnamon, ginger, black pepper, goat's milk and sugar, it was quite a pungent concoction and even though it was non-alcoholic it seemed to affect the men as if it was, Williams and Shelby didn't really care for it but drank it to be hospitable and fit in. The men seemed to be very happy to be together and all seemed to be talking at the same time an Afghan trait Williams and Shelby had noticed and they were finding the multiple conversations difficult to follow. Williams and Shelby were called upon to talk to the gathered group about life in America with Yusuf doing the interpreting even though very few men in the group took the time to listen but instead carried on with their own loud boisterous discussions. Williams and Shelby soon found out the highlight of these gatherings was the dancing, the men formed a large circle and each man danced in the center to music provided by sitar like instruments and a collection of drums. Each man tried to do a different dance but they all seemed to consist of very similar moves, twirling, leg stomping and arm waving, their robes swinging all about them. It was great fun especially when it came to William's and Shelby's turns which created a great deal of excitement, Williams went first gyrating around to the music much to the delight of the men circling him, Shelby was next and started with a Cossack type dance which didn't seem to go over too well until he began to spin on one leg like a figure skater and showed great agility while swirling and zigzagging from side to side which even surprised Williams. Towards the end of his dance everyone in the circle was clapping and shouting for him to keep going and he went on for a few more minutes before flopping down to the floor completely exhausted. Several men hoisted him up on their shoulders and paraded him around inside the circle as all the other men cheered and whistled their appreciation. These gatherings happened every week and were certainly a great opportunity for Williams and Shelby to get to know the men they would be working with. The gathering ended with everyone down on their knees praying including Williams and Shelby, who knelt down and kept quiet.

Five of them walked into the snow covered clearing and waited, the waning moon providing their only light. Williams and Shelby were accompanied by Yusuf, Hami and Jawi. The bearded Afghans had multi-colored head scarfs, long white shirts, vests, white baggy pants and sandals, Williams and Shelby were wearing khaki desert fatigues and army boots and looked very much out of place. Several minutes later they could hear the chop, chop, chop sound of a helicopter heading towards them and after briefly hovering and blowing snow up all around them it touched down. Ducking down covering their eyes from the blowing snow they scrambled aboard with their sacks of donkey dung. Once they'd taken off Yusuf shouted to Williams and Shelby that the helicopter was a captured Soviet Mi-8 transport helicopter, which didn't mean anything to either of them. All they hoped was it would get them to where they were going but did think it was a great idea to be using a Soviet helicopter to fly into the Soviet Union. Twenty minutes later the helicopter had touched down in a flat deserted snow covered field. They quickly unloaded their stuff and the helicopter took off disappearing into the night sky. They planned to make the garrison water supply taste unpleasant by dumping non-toxic donkey dung into the reservoir tank located high up in the water tower.

They hoped that once the tainted water supply was discovered it would send a scare through the garrison resulting in other sources of water having to be brought in involving a significant number of resources that would otherwise have been dedicated to the occupation. They cut through the garrison perimeter fence carrying the dung onto the garrison grounds. They quickly found the water tower and Yusuf, Hami and Jawi relayed the sacks of dung up to the top, Shelby acting as lookout at the foot of the tower while Williams went to find the armory, kitchens, latrines, generators and troops sleeping quarters. When he returned looking up the water tower he couldn't hold back his laughter remembering what he and Shelby had been told jokingly by Brown on their way to Pakistan that they would likely find no more valuable assets in Afghanistan than donkey dung and poppies.

While they were waiting they heard vehicles approaching and Williams yelled up to Yusuf, Hami and Jawi telling them to stay out of sight. He and Shelby laid flat on the ground as a small convoy of trucks passed by, once they'd gone by Williams shouted up the all clear and Yusuf shouted down that they were almost done and not long after the three of them climbed down. They now needed to find somewhere to hide until it was time to be picked up by the river barge that had already been arranged that was going to take them across the river that separated the Soviet Union from Afghanistan. After they'd got through the perimeter fence Yusuf told Williams he knew where there were some abandoned buildings down by the river where they could hide out.

"Let's head there" responded Williams.

It was dark and they couldn't see very far ahead of them but were able to make out the river and found the buildings which looked like they had been abandoned for a long time only one of them still had some of its roof left. William's and Yusuf checked out the other buildings and decided to hide in the one that still had some of its roof left. They cleared out the garbage and settled down to rest before sunrise. William's thoughts wondered to escape he couldn't get it out of his mind but eventually like most of the others dosed off. He was awoken by Yusuf whispering that there was a vehicle approaching where they were hiding. It was dark so they couldn't see what kind of vehicle it was but it seemed to be quite large from the outline they could make out so figured it must be a truck of some kind. Everyone was awake by now looking over the window ledge at the approaching lights. As the vehicle was getting closer they could see it was an army truck which appeared to be patrolling along the river. It moved slowly past the building they were hiding in and its rear lights slowly disappeared into the darkness.

"It looks like they're checking to see if anyone is crossing the river during the night" whispered Yusuf.

Nobody responded to Yusuf's comment all wanting to get back to sleep.

The sun came up much too quickly for Williams liking. Hami had got a fire going with the garbage collected the night before and was heating up a can of soup and while Shelby was warming his hands he commented to Hami that he didn't think a can of soup would go far.

"At least it will put something in our empty stomachs" responded Hami stirring the dark colored concoction "Its brown barley which is quite filling."

"I must say it smells good" responded Shelby "What's in it?"

"Barley, rice, vegetables, fruit and nuts" replied Hami.

While the soup was heating William's made his way down to the river where he could see high sand dunes over on the other side and not much else apart from withered straw like tall grass growing along the river bank. Yusuf startled him as he joined him asking him what they were going to do next, Williams said he thought they should try and find out if the troops in the garrison had detected the contaminated water supply. Yusuf suggested Jawi and Hami could go to the Termez market to see if anyone was talking about it and Williams thought this was a good idea so after they'd had some soup, Jawi and Hami set off for the Termez market. They returned several hours later with the news that there was talk about a water problem at the garrison and that water was already being trucked in.

"Mission accomplished!" shouted Shelby excitedly shaking everyone's hand.

"Now comes the tricky part" responded Williams

"Getting across the river back to Afghanistan."

The plan was for them to hide out until they knew the raid had been successful then meet up with the barge up-stream from the border crossing bridge, it was now evening and the barge was nowhere to be found. While they were waiting Williams observed the Termez-Hauireton river bridge border crossing which seemed to be very busy with numerous donkey carts, trucks of all shapes and sizes most of them military and many people on foot moving in both directions. After waiting for several more hours Yusuf suggested they should probably cross the border river bridge because it didn't look like the barge was coming. He said it could have broken down, got delayed or run out of petrol which apparently happened quite frequently. He told Williams and Shelby that the Soviet border crossing guards checked people and vehicles both leaving and entering, there were also handlers with Alsatian dogs and there were no border guards on the Afghan side of the bridge. Somewhat apprehensive Williams figured it was time to make a move, he and Shelby turned their khaki fatigues inside out and asked Yusuf if he and Hami would mind swapping their sandals for his and Shelby's boots and let them borrow their head scarfs. Yusuf and Hami un-wrapped their head scarfs and slipped off their sandals somewhat begrudgingly, while Williams and Shelby took off their boots. The sandals were a little small for both Williams and Shelby but they managed to get them on, conversely the boots were a bit big for Yusuf and Hami. Yusuf helped Williams and Shelby tie their head scarfs and they now looked more like Afghans and Yusuf and Hami still looked like Afghans.

"I think we're ready" said Williams.

Yusuf asked Williams and Shelby if they wanted to borrow their daggers and they both said no.

As they approached the border crossing they could see that most people seemed to be passing through the barrier in either direction without being stopped by the Soviet border guards who seemed to be more interested in searching vehicles than people. Yusuf told Williams and Shelby to stay behind him and just as they were about to pass through the barrier one of the guard dogs began growling and pulling on its leash.

"Halt" shouted a Soviet border guard as he walked towards them, Yusuf started talking immediately telling the guard they were returning home after delivering donkeys. The guard catching a whiff of donkey dung stepped back and waved them on holding his nose shouting back to the handler that the dog had probably smelt the shit that most Afghans smell of and they both burst out laughing.

Once they got across the bridge Williams and Shelby swapped the sandals for their boots and returned the head scarfs to Yusuf and Hami after which they trekked back to Yusuf's place, along several snowy mountain passes, saying goodbye to Hami and Jawi along the way.

Nadia and Rashida both fully covered were waiting to get them anything they wanted, Yusuf said he'd like some tea and bread after he'd changed his smelly clothes. Shelby said he would like the same and went to change also, Nadia left the room leaving Rashida alone with Williams and she came up so close to him he could smell the tangerine like fragrance of her perfume. She whispered that she had missed him and was pleased he was back and as she moved away from him she tripped and almost fell backwards on top of him and he had to break her fall briefly holding her slim body. Just as she regained her balance Nadia came back into the room with a pot of boiling water and they all had tea and bread after which Williams and Shelby said they were going to lie down leaving Yusuf, Nadia and Rashida to their prayers. Before Williams fell asleep he was thinking how amazing it was how Rashida had reached out to him and was extremely encouraged by this she obviously felt the same way about him as he felt about her.

He was gently woken out of a deep sleep and was most surprised to see it was Rashida fully shrouded kneeling down over him. She whispered to him to come with her, stood up and beckoned to him to follow her, already fully clothed he pulled his boots on and followed after her. They quietly left the dwelling through the back entrance Rashida picking up a water container as they were making their way out of the compound. It was very dark as Williams followed behind her as she walked into the darkness his eyes gradually beginning to adjust to the lack of light. He could make out hills in the distance and after walking for quite a while they began to climb up one of the them, Rashida leading him towards a stand of trees. On the other side of the trees they came upon a den like structure which Rashida pulled him into behind her. Once inside she removed her head covering and began to kiss him like he had never been kissed before her. What she was doing with her lips and tongue was sending shivers up and down his whole body. He couldn't believe how good it felt, was this the same shy, say nothing, don't come near me woman. There were sleeping mats scattered on the floor and Rashida pulled him down on top of her still kissing him, pulling away from her Williams gasped "Hey, what's going on?"

"I thought you wanted me, now you have me is there something wrong?" responded Rashida looking hurt.

"No, nothing is wrong, I just hope you know what you're doing, that's all" said Williams, taking Rashida in his arms and kissing her hard on the lips feeling her hot breasts pushing against him. She pushed him away and pulled her chadri up over her head and was naked apart from a black bra and panties. They grabbed for each other kissing more gently this time her loose jet black hair falling across his face, it smelt like roses. Williams wasn't sure how far he could go but was soon given a signal when Rashida felt down between his legs. He put his hand down her panties and gently began to rhythmically rock her as she gasped and began to breathe heavily as she pulled his baggy pants down and touched him gently. He unfastened her bra releasing her large breasts with dark nipples which he took turns sucking and couldn't hold back pulling her panties aside and as he penetrated her a feeling of euphoria immediately fully enveloped his body making him tingle all over as he made love to her. She was pulling him closer her nails digging into his back her legs pointed up in the air. Traces of sweat appeared on their brows and shoulders as they were wholly emotionally embraced in love making. Williams wanted the feeling to last forever but it came to an end much too soon leaving him with a most satisfying sensation.

"No, no" Rashida cried out "Not finished?"

"I'm sorry" gasped Williams pulling her head towards him and kissing her "I couldn't help it."

Suddenly, they heard a woman's voice and looked at each other as Nadia entered the den before either of them could react. Rashida covered herself up with her chadri and Williams turned away from Nadia who was whispering something to Rashida, from what Williams could tell she was telling her to come with her. Rashida quickly got dressed grabbed the water container and left the den with Nadia. Williams got dressed and followed after them, it was still very dark and he wasn't sure where to go except back the way he and Rashida had come through the stand of trees. He was very relieved to know that Rashida wasn't a virgin and wondered what had happened to her husband who had never been mentioned. He managed to find his way back to Yusuf's house and was surprised to find Nadia waiting for him. She shooed him away with her hands and he went to lie down on his sleeping mat hoping

Shelby and Yusuf hadn't heard anything. As he lay there he still wasn't sure why Nadia had come to find them and figured it had to be to protect her sister but wasn't really sure as he fell asleep.

The next morning when Williams awoke he could see Shelby reading one of the books Wiltshire had given them. He whispered to him quietly "You know although we are being punished big time for what we were forced to do three or so years ago by the Soviets this is a very different situation we find ourselves in here. For starters nobody is watching our every move so instead of coming back here after the next raid, why don't we stay on the other side of the border and start our escape from there?"

"What about Yusuf and the others?" whispered Shelby quietly.

That is a problem I agree we'll need to figure out how we can get separated from them" whispered Williams.

"Where do we go in the Soviet Union?" asked Shelby "Are we going to surrender?"

Just at that moment Yusuf called to them to come for breakfast.

Yusuf's wife Nadia to their surprise was not wearing her chadri this morning but instead a long silk dress and she looked extremely attractive, she said Rashida had gone to get water which was somewhat unusual because they always seemed to go together. Yusuf told them it was the custom to wear the chadri when out in public but in the home it wasn't necessary to wear it with family which he now considered them to be. Only if Afghan headmen like the local maliks, mullahs or strangers are visiting is it only really necessary to wear the chadri in the dwelling.

"The local maliks seem to be very important?" suggested Shelby.

"They are, they usually own the majority of the land and many of the buildings in the local area and are called upon to make judgments whenever there is a serious incident. They in conjunction with the mullah's have the power to put people to death or severely punish them" replied Yusuf.

"Scary people!" responded Shelby.

"Yes, it is most important to keep on their good side" replied Yusuf.

"Why don't you both just relax today you have been working non-stop since you arrived here" suggested Yusuf.

"Actually I was thinking we could fix the shutters in our room because whenever it rains or snows it gets blown into the room" responded Williams.

"You can try but it is difficult to find building lumber in this part of the country" replied Yusuf looking quite serious.

"But there seems to be a lot of deserted buildings in the village surely some of them have old shutters?" asked Williams.

"They do but the penalties are very severe for stealing which is what it would be considered. People have lost hands for stealing less. Please be very careful and let me know if you see anything that would work for you then I can try and get permission from the maliks" replied Yusuf looking very pensive. "That's good to know" replied Williams "I am kind of fond of my fingers and hands and have heard stories about people getting them chopped off."

After eating a breakfast of scrambled eggs and flat bread Yusuf and Shelby went out the back to chop wood, Williams stayed behind thinking about ways to escape and wondered if anyone was actually keeping track of their whereabouts, he did remember being told that a number of Pakistani intelligence agents were embedded with the Northern Alliance rebels. It was still winter and he wondered if they should perhaps wait until late spring or early summer before trying to escape, they could try and make their way through the Soviet Union's southern Republics and across the Caspian Sea to Turkey, this would be a herculean challenge though requiring them to pass through four or five different Soviet Republics. Williams had been studying maps of the Middle East and Asia and was thinking that an escape through southern Iran or Pakistan to the sea might be a better alternative however getting to southern Pakistan would be another significant challenge given they were currently in the most northerly part of Afghanistan. They wouldn't want to go to northern Pakistan because they'd be near the Peshawar Air Station and CIA operatives, travelling south through Afghanistan would also be a great challenge having to cross the Hindu

Kush mountain range on the way. Williams began to realize why they were probably located where they were it was pretty much escape proof and it must have been planned this way by a CIA think tank. William's was thinking escape may be too greater challenge right now so maybe they should focus their attention on the raids and take advantage of escape opportunities as they arose. This seemed to make the most sense and he went out to find Yusuf and Shelby who were still chopping wood.

Spurred on by the success of the first raid when they had polluted the garrison's water supply resulting in significant problems for the Soviets in Termez, Williams, Shelby, Yusuf, Hami and Jawi began to plan their next raid. During the last raid Williams had determined where the armory was located, in a building off on its own away from the other barracks buildings not far from the water tower. New weapons and ammunition were almost impossible to come by, so this would be an unprecedented opportunity for Williams and

Shelby to prove their worth to the rebel commander and his men. It was pretty obvious from the collection of weapons Williams and Shelby had seen when they'd first arrived, daggers, swords, flint lock muskets and various bolt action rifles, newer more modern automatic weapons would be hugely appreciated, however, for this raid they were going to need a helicopter for the duration of the raid to transport the weapons back to the village. Williams asked Yusuf if he would ask the rebel commander if they could get the use of the helicopter for an hour or so.

"You can ask him yourself on Saturday night" laughed Yusuf.

We are also going to need a lot of help to relay the weapons from the armory to the helicopter and Yusuf quickly calculated that they would likely need at least forty men, he also wanted to take some additional men on the helicopter to help them when they got onto the garrison so it would probably take about fifty men altogether. Williams said he was concerned that with so many men involved there was a chance someone might talk. Yusuf assured him that the men who he would ask to participate were all trustworthy and fully committed to the Jihad against the Soviet infidels. Williams accepted Yusuf 's assurances not wanting to upset him in any way and listened as he told him how long he figured it would take to get the additional men in place, at least a week for that many men to cross the border unnoticed into Uzbekistan.

"Where will they stay?" asked Williams.

"With business owners in Termez that they either supply or purchase goods from, this will not be a problem" suggested Yusuf. "They'll meet up with us on the night of the raid?" asked Williams.

"Yes, don't worry they will be like shadows in the night, you won't know they're even there until the raid begins" responded Yusuf.

"Great" said Williams "What's next?"

"What do you want the five of us to do during the raid?" asked Yusuf.

"Let's see" replied Williams thoughtfully "What do you think?" Yusuf said "I would suggest Hami and Jawi be the lookouts, we should be in the armory and Peter can stay on the helicopter with the pilot."

"Sure whatever you want me to do" replied Shelby. "Sounds good" responded Williams wanting to keep the flow going.

"So we'll tell everyone on Saturday night?" asked Yusuf sounding very excited.

Hami commented "But we will only tell them where to meet on the night of the raid, nothing more."

"Will that be good enough for them?" asked Shelby.

"This is normal, some may ask questions, but we'll tell them that this is all they need to know. They are used to working like this. They don't care what is planned as long as it is for the Jihad. Living or dying is of no consequence to them, doing whatever they can to defeat the Soviets is all that matters" explained Yusuf excitedly.

"What kind of weapons can we expect to find?" asked Williams.

"Russian automatic assault rifles, hopefully new AK-74's and Makarov pistols. We should also make sure we get lots of ammunition clips, but any weapons we can get will be a great improvement on what we're using today, British Lee-Enfields, Russian Mosin-Nagants, Chinese 56's and German Mausers.

We also have some American M16's, but we're very short of ammunition for these."

"So we'll be doing the freedom fighters a great service and the Russians a great disservice, it sounds like the perfect raid" commented Shelby.

"Do we have any weapons we can use during the raid?" asked Williams.

"Daggers!" said Yusuf still sounding excited. "Will these be enough?" asked Williams.

"Yes, if we have to kill anyone it will need to be in silence" suggested Yusuf.

"We're all set then, so long as we can arrange for the helicopter and the additional men" commented Williams sounding excited himself.

Saturday night rolled around and as soon as the local rebel commander arrived, Yusuf, Williams, Shelby, Hami and Jawi asked if they could briefly meet with him. Williams told him about their plans for the raid on the armory and he got very excited about getting a stash of brand new Soviet weapons and ammunition but was concerned about the helicopter having to stay on the ground in Uzbekistan for an hour. This was the only operational helicopter he had and it was being used frequently to rescue guerrilla fighters in tight situations and transport supplies throughout the region, it was also no match for the latest Soviet helicopter gunships which often patrolled southern Uzbekistan, but after much discussion it was agreed Williams and Yusuf could have the helicopter.

The usual Saturday night revelry was well underway by the time it was agreed they could have the helicopter. After this Yusuf, Hami and Jawi went to speak to the men whose services would also be needed on the night of the raid. About an hour later Yusuf came over to where Williams and Shelby were standing waiting for their turn to dance and told them everyone they needed had been informed and had agreed. That night Williams and Shelby danced with renewed energy the thought of the upcoming raid exhilarating them. After much Afghan tea and merriment they made their way back to Yusuf's totally exhausted but very happy that they were now playing a key role in the Jihad against the Soviets.

On the night of the raid Williams, Shelby and Yusuf had to assume the forty men they needed to assist them were already across the border and would be in place. They had no way of confirming this. Williams did a quick count and there were sixteen waiting for the helicopter. Williams thought it was supposed to be fifteen. Yusuf told him the brother of one of the men had insisted he come along and the helicopter could easily carry an extra man. Williams didn't make a fuss about it. They were a bedraggled bunch with beards of different lengths and assorted clothing, some had bullet belts slung across their chests over their long soiled shirts, they were all wearing sandals apart from Williams and Shelby. Most of them had scarves wrapped around their heads like turbans and all of them except Williams and Shelby had fearsome looking daggers stuffed in their belts. They could hear the helicopter making its way towards where they were waiting and within a few minutes it came into view its bright light shining down on them. As soon as it touched down they scrambled aboard and it took off. Yusuf's men were sitting on both sides of the noisy vibrating helicopter staring away from each other avoiding eye contact. Talking was out of question due to the loud noise the helicopters engines were making so they all sat in silence. From the previous raid Williams and Shelby knew it wasn't going to be a long ride and they felt relaxed and confident about what they were about to do and it didn't take long before they began to hear a difference in the sound the engines indicating the helicopter would soon be touching down. The pilot's voice came over the public address system asking someone to open the side door which was quickly opened the ground rapidly rushing up to meet them. Within a few seconds the helicopter had landed its rotors coming to a stop.

"Don't be too long" shouted the pilot to anyone within ear shot as he came out of the cockpit.

Most of the men had left the helicopter and were following Yusuf as he headed towards the garrison. As they got near the perimeter fence they were joined by the additional men appearing like ghosts out of the darkness. Yusuf shouted to them to form a line from the garrison perimeter fence to the helicopter and to their surprise get ready to pass weapons and ammunition to one another. Shelby stayed on-board the helicopter and was asking the newly arrived men closest to the helicopter to try and get as close as they could so they could pass the weapons directly up to him once they started to be passed along the line. Williams, Yusuf, Hami and Jawi and the other men who had come on the helicopter were cutting their way through the perimeter fence where it had been recently repaired and once they got onto the garrison, although it was dark, they soon got their bearings and made their way to the armory. Yusuf told the men around him to watch out for signals from Hami and Jawi once the relay had started. When they got to the armory they discovered it was locked with a padlocked chain and Yusuf immediately began sawing through the chain with the rusty hacksaw he had brought with him for this very purpose. It took Yusuf quite a while to cut through the thick chain during which time everyone in the line was wondering what was going on until the news spread that the chain locking the armory door was being removed. The chain finally gave way and when they got inside Williams and Yusuf could see stacks of boxes many already opened. There were rifles with tags on them in racks on the walls which Williams figured must have already been assigned out and were back in the armory for safe keeping. There were two rows of boxes stacked five high full of automatic weapons and after opening one of the boxes marked Ammunition found bundles of thirty round magazine clips which would make it a lot easier to pass them along the line thought Williams. He estimated there were over five hundred brand new assault rifles and a more than an adequate amount of ammunition for each of them. He figured it would take several hours to move all of these weapons and ammunition and suggested they shouldn't spend more than one hour in the armory which Yusuf was non-committal about suggesting they should wait and see. Yusuf and Williams started taking the weapons out of the opened boxes. They were brand new Russian AK-74 assault rifles as Yusuf had hoped, there didn't appear to be any new pistols. Yusuf brought several rifles out of the armory and handed them to the first man in the line, the relay had begun.

He looked around and could see Hami and Jawi watching the armory from a distance. William's had determined the optimum number of AK-74's that could be passed along the line easily were three anymore and the men were having trouble passing them to each other but three allowed the relay to keep moving smoothly. Some of the men had to walk a few paces to pass the weapons to the next man and then quickly get back into position to receive the next three but the relay was working well. The most difficult hand-offs were through the perimeter fence but this was still being accomplished without too much trouble or any significant slowdown. Williams figured at a rate of approximately six per minute they could move about two hundred and fifty rifles in just over an hour surely this would be a sufficient enough haul. On-board the helicopter the pilot and Shelby were stacking the rifles and ammunition as best they could and finding it difficult to keep up. Hami and Jawi were watching both the troop and officer barracks and as soon as they saw someone they would signal to those in the line using a dim flash light and the relay would stop. The men on the garrison weren't going to the latrines very often that night so the relay had only been stopped two or three times so far but a man on his way to the latrine caught a glimpse of a reflection from Jawi's flashlight on the weapons being relayed. It was only a very brief flash but enough to make him detour to investigate. Jawi on seeing this stealthily made his way across the parade ground to where the soldier was. The soldier could see several automatic assault rifles lying in the grass and was starting to back away as Jawi reached him and immediately cut his throat with one swipe of his menacing looking dagger. Blood was spurting out everywhere as Jawi dragged the blood soaked body behind the latrines while at the same time shouting to the men to continue passing the weapons again.

While this had been going on someone had come out of the officer's barracks and was making his way to the officer's latrines in the now quite heavy rain. Hami signaled to warn those working around the armory which created a reflection on one of armory windows which the officer on route to the latrines saw and he began to make his way towards the armory and as he got closer thought he could see men moving around inside. Thinking he shouldn't investigate the situation alone he ran over to the garrison headquarters building where he knew several officers were on duty.

The officers all looked up as he flew through the door one of them saying "Miroslav what are you doing here you are too early for your shift?"

"I think there's something going on over at the armory" replied Miroslav out of breath.

Two of the officers seeing Miroslav was really distressed put their great coats on and made for the door.

From the path leading to the armory they couldn't see any lights or any one through the heavy rain. As soon as Hami had seen the officer quickly heading over to the headquarters building he had run over to the armory to warn Yusuf, Williams and the others in the line close-by. They quizzed him on whether he thought the officer had seen anything and Hami said based on where he had hurried off to he figured he had so they all left the armory Yusuf reattaching the chain and padlock before they moved behind the armory lying down in the long grass near the perimeter fence. It was still raining hard as the three Soviet officers arrived at the armory and still couldn't see anything unusual.

"I must have been seeing things" suggested Miroslav.

"Well it's twenty to four in the morning and I'm getting soaked to the bone out here" quipped one of the officers who'd accompanied Miroslav to the armory.

"Let's get back" suggested the other officer trying the door as he said it and surprisingly it opened the chain and padlock falling to the ground.

"What's this?" he said looking confused as they all went inside.

Jawi saw the three men go into the armory as he was coming out from behind the troop latrines. This confused him and he made his way over to where the men forming the line were and asked if they knew what was going on over at the armory. They said they didn't but weapons and ammunition were no longer being passed along the line anymore. Jawi followed the line of men towards the back of the armory where he found Yusuf, Williams and Hami hiding. He told them he had just seen three Soviets go into the armory and Yusuf jumped up immediately telling Hami and Jawi to come with him.

"I'm coming too" whispered Williams, as he was beginning to get up. "No" said Yusuf we can take care of this stay here which although it hurt Williams he agreed to stay where he was.

The three Soviet officers could see packing materials strewn throughout the armory which was most unusual.

"Mikhail and his boys are not keeping this place very tidy we'll have to report this" commented one of the Soviet duty officers.

"You know this is most unusual, this place is usually immaculate, everything in its place?" replied the other officer.

"Why would the door be unlocked?" enquired Miroslav. "Perhaps someone has broken in" replied one of the other officers.

"I'll find Mikhail and let him know what we've found here."

As the three officers were making their way to the door to leave, Yusuf, Hami and Jawi burst in slashing out at them with their gruesome looking daggers two of the officers quickly going down gurgling blood Yusuf and Hami straddling them. Miroslav tried to fight back as Jawi stabbed him repeatedly in the neck until he fell to the floor grasping his throat. A few minutes later Williams came in and saw the carnage, blood splattered everywhere. Yusuf said they should leave before the men were missed. This was alright with Williams still in a state of shock after seeing such butchery. They all grabbed as many bundles of ammunition as they could carry and led the rest of the men off the garrison. On the way to the helicopter Williams turned to Yusuf and asked him why they had murdered the Soviets and Yusuf stared at him with wild eyes and Williams knew the answer it was an opportunity to kill Soviets nothing more nothing less. He now knew first hand this was a cold blooded conflict to the death this was not a game it was the real thing there was true hatred here. Williams was not happy that three Soviet officers had been murdered in cold blood. He didn't know Jawi had also murdered a soldier. It was not planned that anyone would be killed during the raids, they were planned to be only disruptive.

On the trip back to Zadian they tallied up the haul, they had been in the garrison for about fifty minutes including the ten minutes it had taken to cut through the chain, the several stoppages due to men going to the latrines and the murderous attack on the three Soviet officers. They had spent only thirty minutes in total actually moving weapons and ammunition and William's initial estimate of six guns per minute had been significantly reduced when they had decided to alternate between the guns and ammunition and in the end less than a hundred guns and the ammunition for them had been taken. Yusuf, Hami and Jawi were most excited about the haul despite William's apparent disappointment. They said they had never captured this many weapons and ammunition in a raid before and thought the rebel commander would be most pleased. Williams was not convinced of this but considering there had been no casualties on their part it was perhaps worth celebrating. Williams was amazed how the men who had formed the relay had disappeared back into the night once the raid was over. He thought to himself that Afghans were certainly very resourceful and resilient people, heavily reliant on their wits and cunning and was beginning to understand why it had been so difficult for invaders to make incursions into Afghanistan throughout the recorded span of history. It seemed every Afghan man, women and child were defiant always doing their utmost to make life as miserable as possible for would-be invaders.

Once back at the drop-off point Williams, Shelby, Yusuf, Hami, Jawi and the other men who had come with them and the pilot unloaded the guns and ammunition as quickly as they could and the helicopter left. The morning sun was just appearing over the nearby mountains as Yusuf sent Jawi off to get some donkey carts to haul the weapons cache back to the local rebel commander's hideout. The guns and bundles of ammunition were temporarily buried in the sand in case a Soviet helicopter gunship passed overhead and noticed something unusual. It didn't take long for Jawi to return with several donkey pulled carts and more helpers and the guns and bundles of ammunition were quickly dug out of the sand, dusted off and loaded onto the carts and covered up with old potato sacks. Yusuf, Hami and Jawi walked triumphantly ahead of the carts as they made their way to the entrance to the underground tunnels, where Williams and Shelby had spent their first night. Upon their arrival there they were greeted by men kissing and hugging them including the rebel commander who greeted them with a big smile across his craggy bearded face. As the guns and ammunition were quickly being unloaded and taken below the rebel commander grabbed one, slotted a high capacity magazine clip into it and fired several rounds into the air shouting "Allahu Akhbar God is great" a number of times. He asked Yusuf, Williams, Shelby, Hami and Jawi to have tea with him but Yusuf declined saying he needed to change his blood soaked clothes which hadn't gone unnoticed and taking Yusuf's lead Williams and Shelby said they needed to go with Yusuf in order to find their way back to his home. Neither of them had any desire to go back down into the tunnels again. Hami and Jawi took up the offer even though their clothes were blood stained too.

There was no one home at Yusuf's but there was tea in small thermos bottles and naan flat bread that had been left for them. Within a few minutes the bread had been devoured and the sweet tea drunk after which Williams and Shelby went to lie down.

Once they got comfortable Shelby whispered "We got lucky again."

"What do you mean?" asked Williams.

"Don't you think it was more luck than judgment that we pulled off another successful raid last night?" whispered Shelby.

"I don't know but until we can figure out how to escape from here let's hope our luck holds out" responded Williams.

Williams hadn't told Shelby about the murdered Soviet officers even though he had asked Williams why Yusuf, Hami and Jawi's clothes were covered in blood. Williams had told him they'd cut themselves getting through the perimeter fence which he seemed to accept.

After this brief exchange Shelby began to snore and unknowingly Williams soon joined him.

Williams awoke to the strong aroma of curry and saw that Shelby was already up and could hear laughter and got up to find out what was going on. He found Shelby, Yusuf, Nadia and Rashida playing cards and Nadia and Rashida were not covered up with their Chaderi's and both looked very attractive.

"When did the party start?" asked Williams looking somewhat hurt.

"Not long ago" said Nadia laughing. "Can I play" asked Williams.

"After this round" responded Rashida.

He pulled up a stool and asked what smelt so good.

Nadia still laughing said "It's a surprise!"

"No problem" said Williams "I didn't mean to crash the party."

"Come on" said Yusuf "Peter just joined us and I got up just before him you haven't missed anything."

Williams looked over at the big simmering pot and said

"I'm so hungry I could eat a horse."

"How about a goat?" laughed Rashida.

"So that's it curried goat" responded Williams.

Shelby hadn't said anything since Williams had joined them and he quietly asked him why he was so quiet when everyone else seemed to be in such a good mood.

Shelby told him he'd speak to him later but never did.

Hami and Jawi had almost reached Hami's house that afternoon when they both saw a dust cloud off in the distance. They watched it until they knew for sure it was a Soviet convoy and waited until it passed by on the way to Zadian they presumed and they took off to let Yusuf know.

The latest game ended with Yusuf winning and Williams being invited to join in, he'd played the game before but wasn't quite sure of the rules so they played a trial hand for him. They had just started the first real hand when Hami and Jawi burst in breathing heavily.

Jawi blurted out "We just saw a Soviet convoy heading for Zadian and on the way here we heard the Soviets are looking for two Americans".

"Don't worry" commented Hami looking at Williams and Shelby "No one will tell them anything we never do."

"Well someone must have talked for them to even be here?" replied Williams rather angrily.

"It must have been one of the men on the raid" suggested Shelby.

"Perhaps" added Yusuf.

"What should we do?" asked Shelby.

"Go with Nadia and Rashida they know where you can hideout, I will go and see what's going on I'm sure the local maliks will handle the situation they normally do whenever the Soviets come here, don't worry said Yusuf.

He told Hami and Jawi they should go and tell the local maliks and the rebel commander what was going on.

Peering into the town square Yusuf could see a number of military vehicles, diesel fumes spewing out of their exhausts while they were parked idling. Soviets were standing around in groups, the smell of their strong and pungent cigarettes noticeably present in the air. Yusuf was reluctant to let the Soviets see him in case they recognized him.

Red Shadows On Liberty's Soil

After they had changed into their chaderi's Nadia and Rashida led Williams and Shelby to the same place where he and Rashida had made love. Once they were settled in Nadia and Rashida shuffled off leaving them on their own. They began to conjecture about who might have tipped the Soviets off beginning with Station Chief Doug Brown for some reason.

"Do you think we've been too successful given we were probably sent here to fail miserably?" asked Shelby.

"I don't think so surely the more damage we inflict on the Soviets the better it is for the US backed Afghan cause?" responded Williams.

Why they had both thought of Brown first neither of them knew except they obviously didn't trust him because he was CIA.

"So if not him who else?" asked Shelby "Surely not any of the men who had helped us on the raid?"

"Yusuf assured us they could all be trusted" responded

Williams "So I don't think so".

"The next question is why?" commented Shelby "What would anyone have to gain by telling the Soviets we were here?" They hadn't given much thought to double agents since arriving in Afghanistan.

"You know double agents have been present in every other war or conflict so why not this one" replied Williams.

"But what was to be gained?" asked Shelby.

Williams replied "There are snitches everywhere so why not here, remember what the Mujahideen rebel leaders told us when we met them in Pakistan to watch out for the Afghan secret police who they said were infiltrating the regional tribes and clans spreading false information and gathering intelligence information."

Unbeknownst to Williams and Shelby and everyone else coincidentally the local maliks were meeting with Brown that afternoon to discuss the state of the conflict. This was a scheduled monthly meeting to see how they could help each other, Brown had planned to check in with Williams and Shelby while he was in the area but upon hearing the news that the Soviets were in the town square looking for two

Americans he said he had better get back to his safe house.

Alone in the hiding place Williams and Shelby got around to talking about escape again.

"Have you figured out where we can escape to yet?" asked Shelby.

"From the maps I've looked at the choices are very limited the Soviet Union, Pakistan, Iran or China" replied Williams.

"What if we commandeered the helicopter we've been using?" asked Shelby.

"How far do you think that would get us, we've already been told they hardly have any fuel for it."

"Let's say we could get fuel, what then?"

"Well I guess it's a possibility it would certainly get us well on our way to wherever we decide to escape to we will need to speak to the pilot about the fuel situation anyway let's say we could get sufficient fuel where do you want to go?" asked Williams.

"I don't know but we should start to figure this out I'm sick of living like this, crapping in a hole, eating curry and drinking Afghan tea all the time. We don't even have one home comfort, it really stinks" responded Shelby adamantly.

"OK we'll need to get serious about escaping then" replied Williams.

"I wonder what's going on in Zadian there's been no gunfire so hopefully they're still talking" suggested Shelby.

"I still don't understand how they're on to us it has to be the double agents none of the rebels would give them any information surely?" asked Williams.

"What about the two Afghans who brought us here?" responded Shelby.

"That's quite a long shot it was quite a while ago" replied Williams.

"But things move very slowly here so this might turn out to be the only explanation in the end" responded Shelby.

Williams and Shelby were feeling tired after losing a night's sleep so they piled up cushions to try and get comfortable but neither of them slept worrying about what might crawl on them. While they had been talking they had noticed several strange looking different sized insects moving around in the sand near them.

After being kept waiting by the local maliks the Soviet commander was in a foul mood and when they finally did arrive with their big beaky noses, sallow completions and dark eyes the Soviet commander told them he planned to take Zadian apart reducing it to rubble if the whereabouts of the two Americans who he knew were here weren't provided immediately. The maliks told him they didn't know what he was talking about because there were no Americans here maybe in Pakistan but not here.

After they had informed the maliks about the Soviets, to remind the Afghans who was in charge and that nothing was going unnoticed. However it was pretty much impossible to get a reaction from the Afghans regardless of the issue. They were consistently defiant always making it clear that Afghanistan was their country and not the Soviets. They seemed to be fearless and had proven to be a most formidable enemy always willing to embrace death ahead of life itself. The Soviets had been in the town square since late in the afternoon so by the time Williams and Shelby got back to Yusuf's it was quite late. Yusuf told them he still didn't know how the Soviets knew about them but still planned to find out. He suggested someone in the Soviet garrison might have heard their accents even though they had killed anyone they had encountered during the raid so there should have been no witnesses. Nadia asked Williams and Shelby if they wanted something to eat and they both said they didn't but grabbed some warm naan bread off the table before going to lie down. Williams couldn't sleep thinking about Rashida while listening to Shelby's light snoring, he was thinking she was probably the most beautiful women in all aspects that he had ever encountered and here she was living in a house made of mud bricks in the middle of one of the poorest countries in the world and wondered if this had perhaps contributed to her overall beauty, no stress. Then he thought that probably that wasn't true because there had to be a lot of stress being a woman in Afghanistan. They had no rights, weren't permitted to be educated and seemed to have to do most of the work both inside and outside the home. It was obviously a different kind of stress from that of the women living in the competitive western world. There were certainly no waistline or junk food issues, food here was very basic, rice, bread and meat occasionally. There were no packaged foods or alcohol that he'd seen, there was only thick Afghan tea which everyone seemed to drink a lot of even though clean water was in short supply and it took significant time to fetch it. It was unclear how women bathed perhaps that is why they went for the water every day to bath at the same time. He was also thinking that if he and Shelby did escape in the Soviet helicopter she could perhaps come with them which was probably a stupid idea but who knew what the right thing to do was. He could be dead tomorrow so why not try and live life to the fullest while he still could. He wondered if he should speak to Yusuf about the way he felt about Rashida but was scared it might destroy their friendship. He thought to himself why was it that men from the west were so weak and always had to have whatever they wanted? It was obviously the way they were brought up, spoiled. Why were men from the east so strong willed, letting things be, not wanting to change them for their own fulfillment? Why did westerners think they could just take whatever they wanted? If nothing else this was making Williams think about his own life where he was used to getting what he wanted, that is what he was up against. It wasn't just about a stunningly beautiful women, it was about getting what he wanted. Getting what he wanted had been instilled into his sort for centuries. He was just the latest edition of this ancestry. It was not his fault he was weak, cowardly and would do anything to get what he wanted. For centuries his race has been the scourge of native civilizations, always taking and never giving. The world would be a lot different place without his race, it might even still be as it originally was paradise, sleep overtook him as he was continuing to pursue these thoughts.

The following morning when he awoke he found Station Chief Brown, Yusuf and Shelby talking about the recent raid on the armory. He joined them and gave his perspective on how the raids had gone. Brown told them that even more troops than had previously been estimated were being assembled at the Termez garrison. Williams told Brown they were still working out the details for their next and most ambitious raid and that he and Shelby were growing beards and planning to wear sandals and head scarfs which they hoped would allow them to escape back across the border bridge without incident. They figured it would take a few weeks to grow the beards and during this time Yusuf suggested they wear Afghan clothes to get them soiled so they would be dirty like everyone else's. Brown said he was pleased with what he had heard and after drinking more tea left.

Seven of them walked into the now familiar snow covered clearing to wait to be picked up. Williams, Shelby and Yusuf would be leading the three two-man teams planning to sabotage the garrison kitchens, latrines and generators. Williams was paired with Padi, short for Padshah, another of Yusuf's relatives. Shelby was teamed with Jawi and Yusuf with his brother Hami. Osi whose name was apparently Osman, a friend of Yusuf's, was bringing the scary looking camel spiders. It was a cloudy night, the moon and stars nowhere to be seen. As they stood waiting for the helicopter they looked like any other band of freedom fighters. The only thing that separated Williams and Shelby from the other Afghan men were their teeth, they still had them. They all had beards and were wearing head wraps of different colors, brown, light blue and black and white squares. Yusuf was wearing a long brown shirt and baggy trousers of the same color. Williams, Shelby, Osi and Jawi were all wearing long white shirts, black baggy trousers and dark grey waistcoats. Padi and Hami were wearing light blue shirts and baggy white pants. They were all armed with new AK-74's with thirty round clips and the Afghans also had their frightening looking daggers in sheaths in their waistbands. It wasn't long until they could hear the helicopter approaching and a few minutes later it had touched down obscured by the cloud of sand and snow it was churning up. They all scrambled aboard with their sacks of donkey dung, cement and camel spiders. The helicopter lifted off heading north rattling and shaking all the way to the drop off point close to the garrison. Once on the ground they quickly unloaded their stuff and set off the helicopter almost immediately taking off and disappearing into the night sky.

Jawi and Hami were carrying the sacks of dung and Yusuf had a small bag of cement. Osi didn't seem to have a care in the world as he trudged along behind the rest of them keeping a watchful eye on his sack of camel spiders. From the information they had collected on the previous raids they knew which buildings they needed to head for. They cut their way through the perimeter fence and once on the garrison grounds split up into their teams.

Williams and Padi started to skirt around one of the buildings heading towards where Williams knew there was a generator. Yusuf and Hami headed for the troop latrines, Shelby and Jawi made their way to the kitchens while Osi got comfortable sitting below a slightly open window at the back of the troop billets, his sack of spiders on the ground beside him. The spiders were planned to be released at the very end of the raid because as soon as the first big scary camel spider was spotted the whole garrison would likely be alerted by panicked screams.

Shelby and Jawi had found the kitchen and were busy spreading dung in the sinks, on the counter tops and in the pantries. There were large walk-in refrigerators which contained large quantities of various kinds of meat and poultry which they spread dung all over too. They finished up by hiding the leftover dung where it would be difficult to find to ensure the smell would remain in the kitchen even when the visible dung had been cleaned up. It hadn't taken them long to fully contaminate the kitchen and they were soon running to meet up with Osi.

As Williams and Padi passed the end of a barrack block they could see a security light over the entrance door and Williams wondered if the troops paid much attention to these lights because they and many others would soon be going out once they began to disable the generators. He could see the main gate house off in the distance which was very brightly lit up and wondered if the generators they were planning to disable were feeding it too and hoped not. He knew disabling the generators was going to be the trickiest part of the raid.

Yusuf and Hami checked the latrines and finding no one inside went to work blocking the toilet bowls with the quick drying cement and smearing donkey dung throughout. Someone surprised them as he entered the latrine they were working in.

"What the . . ." was all the soldier was able to say before Hami rushed at him stabbing him in the throat blood spurting out everywhere as he fell to the floor dying.

"Let's get out of here" yelled Yusuf and they ran to meet up with Osi and the others.

"We won't say anything to the others about the soldier?" asked Hami.

"No they don't need to know" responded Yusuf.

Williams and Padi heard a whistle, the signal that both Yusuf and Shelby's teams were finished and waiting for them. So far Williams and Padi had only managed to disable three generators but most of the lights on the garrison had gone out and they could hear men shouting so they too set off to meet up with the others.

As soon as Williams and Padi arrived Shelby helped hoist Osi up to the window that was slightly open, which he quickly fully opened peering inside. He could see beds lined up along the wall under the window and realized he would need to be careful where he dumped the camel spiders he didn't want one to land on anyone's head. Hearing more shouting Williams whispered to Osi to hurry up. Shelby passed the bag of spiders up to him and he untied the cord from the top of the sack and shook it until one large spider after another appeared and was gently pushed off the window sill into the room. All Osi could hear was snoring and once the sack had been emptied Osi jumped down and ran as fast as he could after the others who were already heading for the perimeter fence. With some of the garrison generators disabled it was eerily dark everywhere.

As they were making their way towards the abandoned buildings by the river they began to hear the scared screams of the troops and as soon as they got inside one of the familiar abandoned buildings they began to hear the chop, chop, chop sound of a helicopter getting progressively louder. They could see a bright light in the night sky heading towards where they were hiding. The helicopter came into view and hovered close-by as men in army fatigues rappelled down and once they hit the ground ran towards where they were hiding. Automatic weapons fire lit up the night sky as they were quickly surrounded and heard someone shout "Put your weapons down and your hands up" in English.

Realizing their chances of surviving a fire fight with what William's assumed were Soviet Special Forces killers were very slim he told everyone to drop their weapons and put their hands up. Williams moved over to one of the windows and shouted into the darkness that they were ready to surrender.

On hearing this several Soviets burst through the doorway and quickly herded everyone up against one of the walls. They were all searched, their daggers taken and all their automatic weapons thrown in a heap in the middle of the room. While this was going on they could hear vehicles coming to a halt their brakes squeaking outside the abandoned buildings. The Soviet who had spoken previously entered the building and directed them to sit down. He picked up one of the new AK-74's off the pile of weapons and commented "Interesting the garrison armory was broken into a few weeks ago and new AK-74's were stolen!"

That's all he said.

Williams was thinking how efficient the Soviets had been in capturing them and wondered who had tipped them off and what was ahead for them. He knew it wasn't going to be pleasant. Soon the order was given for everyone except Williams and Shelby to stand up and leave the building. Yusuf, Hami, Jawi, Padi and Osi were pushed up against an outside wall and Williams and Shelby suddenly heard a tremendous amount of automatic gunfire not far from where they were sitting. When the gunfire stopped they were told to standup and were led out towards some army trucks and told to climb up into the back of one of them. They had both been trying to look over their shoulders to see if they could see anything in the almost pitch black darkness but couldn't. The bulky Soviet leader and two other armed men climbed up into the truck after them.

"Take a seat" ordered the Soviet leader "I have some good news and bad news for you, the good news is you are not going to be shot like your Afghan friends because you are Americans and may have information that might be useful to us. The bad news is you are going to be taken to

Sheberghan prison where guaranteed you will die a slow miserable death."

"You mean everyone else is dead?" gasped Shelby jumping up.

One of the armed guards pushed him back down.

The Soviet leader replied "Yes some more Afghan vermin have been exterminated just be thankful that you're still alive." "But these men were prisoners of war they shouldn't have been killed like this?" pleaded Shelby.

The Soviet leader replied "Like they were worrying about that when they cold-bloodily murdered the men on the garrison a few weeks ago. I know it wasn't you two because you could never butcher men like the Afghans do."

Following this exchange the Soviet leader left the truck leaving Williams and Shelby sitting across from the two guards who had their automatic weapons pointed at them. The truck began to move off followed by the other trucks in the convoy which were transporting the storm troopers.

Williams immediately began to think about how they could escape from their Soviet captors.

He figured the prison they were being taken to would be an absolute hell-hole and knew they needed to do whatever they could to avoid going there as being imprisoned there would undoubtedly result in their eventual deaths as the Soviet leader had suggested. Williams hoped it would be a long ride the guards becoming fatigued and was most disappointed when he found out the guards changed on the hour, every hour, to ensure this wouldn't be a problem. However Williams did notice there was a short time interval during the change of the guards and was racking his brains as to how to take advantage of these few moments when they were left unguarded but nothing had come to him yet. The new guards had taken up their positions by the time Williams thought of something but it would have to wait until the next shift change. What he had in mind was to pretend that one of them was sick the newly arrived guards not knowing how long this had been going on. The new guards might become concerned and want to get a closer look at the sick person which could provide an opportunity for the other one to overpower them. Williams thought it was worth a try and discussed it quietly with Shelby so they would be ready at the next shift change and Shelby agreed to fake not being able to breathe. During the next shift change as the new guards were climbing up into the truck they could see Williams kneeling over Shelby. Williams indicated to them that Shelby was having trouble breathing and as the truck began to move off one of the guards took the bait and leaned down to take a closer look at Shelby. The other guard sat down pointing his automatic weapon at Williams. After looking at Shelby the concerned guard asked the other guard to take a look and as he leaned down over Shelby, letting his guard down, Williams grabbed him around the neck and pushed his head down towards the floor of the truck. Shelby reached up and pulled the other guard down on top of him getting him in a headlock. The guard Williams was trying to hold down managed to fire off several rounds and the unmistakable sound of gunfire caused the truck to brake and come to a halt.

While Williams was struggling with one of the guards he noticed Shelby was bleeding likely from being nicked by one of the small bayonets attached to the guards' automatic weapons and began to hear loud voices shouting outside. The canvas flap at the back of the truck was pulled aside and someone peered in asking if everything was alright. He immediately took the situation in and yelled out at the top of his lungs dropping the flap and disappearing out of sight. Almost immediately Williams and Shelby could see a number of gun barrels pointing directly at them from under the flap. Williams looked down at Shelby and could see blood streaming down his face from an ugly gash and told him to release the guard he'd been holding down. Williams put his hands up deciding that in a shootout he and Shelby would have no chance. He was also very concerned about the cut to Shelby's face. The two guards were in control again pointing their weapons at Williams and Shelby as they moved towards the back of the truck. One of them pulled the flap back and shouted something and the husky Soviet leader climbed up into the truck and quickly handcuffed Williams and Shelby to the metal bar running along the side of the truck. He could see the blood seeping from the cut on Shelby's face and left the truck and returned a few minutes later with a handful of bandages which he handed to Shelby who held them up against the wound on his face with his free hand to try and stem the flow of blood. Shelby said his face really hurt and Williams said he thought he needed stitches but knew under the current circumstances he wouldn't be getting any.

"Well gentleman I must say you are most resourceful overpowering two armed guards. We could use men like you on our side." quipped the Soviet leader.

"Do you blame us?" asked Williams "Too bad you didn't kill us it might be better for us to die here rather than rotting to death in an Afghan prison and what are you going to do about my friend, he is badly cut."

"I wish I could help you, but you know how it is I can't be seen to be aiding the enemy now can I?" replied the Soviet leader.

"Why not what about the Geneva Convention?" asked Williams.

"A fine agreement which unfortunately is not being adhered to here in Afghanistan mainly due to the ugly nature of this conflict and the inhuman treatment of our troops when captured by the barbaric Afghans and Mujahideen. I would suggest you try and get as comfortable as you can they have a prison Infirmary at Sheberghan prison where I am sure your friend will be looked after" replied the Soviet leader.

The leader shouted at the two guards who were still recovering from the fighting they'd just been involved in and they quickly climbed down out of the truck and were replaced by two new guards. The guards sat down across from Williams and Shelby pointing their weapons at them and the Soviet leader said something to the guards as he was leaving the truck and they acknowledged whatever he'd said. Shelby looking out from behind the bandages told Williams in a muffled voice that he was alright. Williams told him he didn't look alright with blood dripping from his face but needed to hang on until they arrived at the Sheberghan "holiday camp".

They arrived at the prison just as the sun was coming up and looking through the flap at the front of the truck they could see high metal gates as they drove into the prison yard. All the trucks apart from the one they were in pulled over and stopped at what looked like a command post. The truck they were in continued on deeper into the prison complex driving across an open field towards several long dirty white looking buildings which they figured were cellblocks. The truck stopped at the entrance to one of them where their handcuffs were removed and after getting down from the truck they were pushed towards some scruffy looking men wielding battered looking Kalashnikovs. These men were talking loudly amongst themselves pointing to Shelby's blood soaked clothes and the bloody bandages he was holding up to his face. One of them walked over and opened the rusty cellblock door and waved them over. As they were entering the cellblock Williams turned saying "My friend needs stitches and we were told he would be taken to the Infirmary once we arrived here."

The man pushing them into the cellblock shrugged his shoulders as if to say no one had told him or didn't understand what Williams had said. Williams was still adamant as he continued to be shoved forward almost falling over realizing there was nothing he could do. There was a terrible stench and piles of human faeces in the gutters running along either side of the long corridor they were being pushed down. They would find out that the prisoners in the cellblock were protesting the conditions in the prison by pushing excrement out to where the guards had to walk. It appeared the protest wasn't working and the smell was overpowering. They couldn't believe human beings were being imprisoned under such abhorrent conditions. As they were prodded further along the corridor they could see overcrowded cells jammed full of emaciated looking, half naked, unshaven men staring at them.

Shelby mumbled to Williams "Can you believe we're going to be locked up in here?"

"I think I've been in cleaner cattle markets" remarked Williams, laughing "I wonder if they have room service?" "How can you joke about such filth, this is absolutely ridiculous, how can anyone survive in here?" mumbled Shelby angrily.

'Well right now it doesn't look like we have much choice" responded Williams.

Red Shadows On Liberty's Soil

Towards the end of the corridor there was a narrow empty cell which they were pushed into, the door locked behind them. Men of all ages were reaching their arms through the bars of the cells on either side yelling and screaming at them. They were already frightened for their lives not knowing what kind of diseases or infections these crazed men might have. Shelby had temporarily forgotten about the pain from the wound to his face as he and Williams stood in the center of their narrow cell avoiding the many filthy hands reaching out to touch them. They weren't sure what to do except stand side by side in the middle of the cell and wait until gradually the excitement caused by their arrival subsided and they were able to sit down still in the centre of the cell. The prisoners surrounding them had stopped trying to touch them and were no longer shouting at them. As they sat there the stench in the cellblock began to overpower them again and they had to cover their mouths and noses with their sleeves. This was difficult for Shelby because he was still holding blood soaked bandages up to his face.

"You'll get used to it" said someone in a soft voice.

They both turned and saw an old man who was just skin and bones holding onto the bars in the next cell.

"Welcome to hell on earth" whispered the old man.

"Great to be here" responded Williams "Wouldn't have missed it for the world I guess there's no washrooms in here?"

"The closest we have are overflowing toilet pails and a hose down every few days, you have your own a pail over there against the wall. Perhaps you could speak to the prison authorities and get toilets and showers installed" laughed the old man his skeletal body shaking.

"This is ridiculous" mumbled Shelby "These unsanitary conditions will kill us all in no time!"

"I think that's the idea" commented Williams.

"Yes you are correct Mr., three or four men die in here every day and it's getting worse and they only come and remove the corpses when they feel like it. From your accents you sound like you're Americans what are you doing in a place like this?" asked the old man.

"Believe me we didn't seek this place out Soviet Special Forces brought us here after we'd been captured doing our best to help the Afghan cause" replied Williams.

"Well you're not unique either the Soviets or the DRA brought all us here to die miserable deaths we're all considered to be Afghan or Mujahideen rebels whether we actually are or not it doesn't matter to them" said the old man.

Not having anything else to do Williams and Shelby carried on a dialogue with the old man learning all they could as quickly as they could about the prison. While they were talking they heard the sound of more men being brought into the overcrowded cellblock and cell doors creaking as they were opened and closed and could hear the new arrivals being questioned by those already in the cells. Williams and Shelby learned a lot of things from the old man, they found out that the prison was designed to house roughly eight hundred prisoners but most of the time was holding well over three thousand. The cellblock they were in contained thirty-six cells, eighteen on each side of the corridor. There were at least sixty or seventy men locked in each cell built to accommodate less than a quarter of that number. Apparently outside between the cellblocks was a water tap where the prisoners were allowed to drink and wash themselves whenever the cells were being hosed down. Williams and Shelby later found out that they weren't going to be let out to drink or wash from the tap. The only way they could get water or wash themselves was by grabbing one of the hoses being used to wash the faeces and urine out of the cells. While they were talking to the old man they were taking in their appalling surroundings, many of the men were wrapped in thin soiled blankets and had sores on their faces and dirty feet. Many of them had shaved heads apparently to avoid lice infestations which were rampant throughout the prison. Most of the prisoners had unkempt beards were gaunt and skeletal looking and appeared to be naked under the thin blankets. They could see several toilet pails overflowing with faeces and urine in the cells on either side of them. The rusty tin roof covering the cellblock was about fifteen feet high and they were soon going to find out the cellblock got unbearably hot whenever the sun was shining down on it. The concrete walls of the cellblock rose up about ten feet above which it was open to the roof and covered with narrow vertical metal bars. These barred openings permitted light and air into the cellblock but exposed the prisoners to the cold temperatures in the autumn and winter months sometimes going as low as twenty degrees Fahrenheit. Today the weather was around sixty degrees but they could still feel a cool breeze coming in through the bars. William's first instincts had been right cattle were definitely treated better than this in most civilized countries and was really worried about the excrement that was being pushed into the corridor by the prisoner's with their bare feet. How lucky they were not to have had their boots confiscated. The conditions in this prison were far worse than they could have ever imagined.

Shelby commented that he wondered if Station Chief Brown knew about the absolutely appalling conditions in here. "He must" said Williams talking into his sleeve. "I reckon he's probably heard about the conditions but unless he's actually been here he wouldn't believe it."

"The average life expectancy in here must be only months" mumbled Shelby in a muffled voice.

"I reckon there'll come a time fairly soon when we'll actually be looking forward to death" sighed Williams.

Williams and Shelby spent the first night sitting in the center of their cell leaning back to back and didn't sleep much even though the cellblock became quiet once the strange music stopped. They found out that at dusk every day music was played on some very weird musical instruments for an hour or so, pieces of thread tied across small wooden boxes, whistles made from hollowed out pieces of wood and drums made by stretching human skin taken from dead rotting corpses across hollowed out pieces of wood.

Early the next day a tall dark skinned man called to them through the bars of the cell beside them and introduced himself as Mohammad Jaffer and jokingly said in impeccable English

"Let me be the first to welcome you to the Sheberghan resort and spa."

"Things are looking up Pete we've found another man with a sense of humour, I'm Gerry Williams and this is my good friend Peter Shelby we're pleased to meet you Mr. Jaffer."

"Mohammad will do fine."

"So will Gerry and Peter" replied Williams.

Mohammad asked if he could take a look at Shelby's wound and he slowly took the bandages away from his face and found the gash was open, dark red in colour along its edges and looked like it must be very sore and painful.

"You definitely need stitches I just hope it's not too late I'll see what I can find to stitch you up with before it gets any more infected" offered Mohammad.

While Williams, Shelby and Mohammad were talking they were being watched intently by many of the other men in Mohammad's cell, Mohammad told them that there were very few men in the prison who understood or spoke English just him and the old man they'd talked to yesterday, they were the only ones in his cell. He told them if they needed to speak to anyone he would translate for them and told them he was fluent in five languages and a medical doctor.

"What if anyone wants to speak to us?" mumbled Shelby.

"I will translate for them and you. You have probably already realized there isn't really much else to do in here but talk so let me know whenever I can be of assistance to either of you." "I'm sure there are a million things I would like to ask you and the other prisoners about but right now I have just one question?" asked Shelby "When do we eat?"

"Ah a good question" replied Mohammad "There are actually no regular meals in here those of us without friends or family have to rely on other prisoners who do. Food is brought in by relatives and friends, they try and bring in as much as they can on each visit and what they bring in is shared, we are all brothers in here. Sharing your food also gets you protected from the many violent men in here. I have a good friend Tahir who shares whatever food he gets with me. He has a sister who visits him several times a week and gives him as much food as they will allow I will share whatever he gives me with you both."

"This is ludicrous" commented Shelby "No regular meals. This is totally inhumane no wonder most of the prisoners have ribs protruding out?"

Williams spoke up "It's Bridge on the River Kwai stuff oh well I guess I could use to lose a few pounds."

"We also sleep on the concrete is that right?" asked Shelby. "Yes you sleep where you can whenever you can at least there is only two of you in your cell there's nearly seventy in mine. Men sometimes get robbed if it is known they have anything valuable and it is not uncommon to find men have been murdered during the night" whispered Mohammad.

"No food and nothing to sleep on this is unbelievable we have to do something" whispered Shelby quietly.

"I'd like you to meet my friend Tahir I'll get him to come over to the bars to meet with you and I'll translate for you as he only speaks old Persian" said Mohammad.

A very pale and sickly looking man appeared on the other side of the bars.

"This is Tahir" said Mohammad introducing him to Williams and Shelby who reached out to shake his hand until Mohammad shouted "No we don't shake hands in here there is far too much sickness and disease I recommend you never touch anyone."

Williams and Shelby looked at each other thinking how close they had come to being touched by dozens of prisoners when they had arrived yesterday.

Tahir spoke forcefully to Mohammad for several minutes and when he'd finished Mohammad said to Williams and Shelby "Tahir says he can help you escape as long as you take him with you."

"We're in" replied Williams.

Tahir said something to Mohammad who in turn told Williams and Shelby "He is feeling tired and wants to rest but will speak to you again tomorrow."

Following this very brief exchange Tahir disappeared back into the overcrowded cell. Tahir's words were all Williams needed to hear to become preoccupied with escaping and Williams and Shelby talked to Mohammad and Tahir every day after this and after giving it a lot of thought Williams explained that he and Shelby's only option was to escape to China. He explained why they couldn't escape to Pakistan because the authorities there were working closely with the Americans and if they were captured who knew what would happen to them. They couldn't escape to Iran because the Iranians were no longer friendly with the west since the Shah had been deposed. The three Soviet Republics bordering Afghanistan to the north were out of the question because if the Soviets found out who they were they would be taken to Moscow and executed or sent to Siberia. This information surprised Tahir and Mohammad. Tahir through Mohammad told them he knew the route to China. Mohammad said Tahir says you need to make your way to the Wakhan Corridor located in the remotest part of north-eastern Afghanistan. They found out that it is a long narrow strip of land between high mountain ranges that links Afghanistan to China separating the Soviet Union in the north from Pakistan in the south. Williams asked Mohammad who in turn asked Tahir how they could get there and via Mohammad Tahir told them they would have to go north-east to Feyzabad then go east from there which didn't really didn't help them very much. Another man who Mohammad apparently called Pazhwaak kept coming over when they were talking, smiling at them nodding his head from side to side. Mohammad told them he had gone mad from being imprisoned here.

Williams jokingly said "I'm surprised he's stayed alive in here long enough to go mad he must have a strong constitution or lots of relatives who feed him well."

Williams asked Mohammad if he knew anything about the terrain surrounding the prison and he told him there was scrub and uncultivated plants that stretched all around for miles until they eventually thinned out and became desert. He said it was low growing and very dense and had been cut away from around the prison due to the potential danger of it catching fire during the very hot months.

"It doesn't sound too bad" offered Williams.

"The thing about it is" responded Mohammad "There is nowhere to hide if you're standing up in the middle of it you can be seen from miles away."

"Well I guess we'll have to take our chances when the time comes" replied Williams.

While they were talking a man Williams and Shelby hadn't seen before came up to Mohammad and handed him something. After he'd left Mohammad said he could stitch up Shelby's wound if he wanted and asked him to put his face up against the bars. Mohammad threaded a needle, licked its end and slowly began to stitch up Shelby's wound the edges of which were now a yellow and dark reddish color.

"Let's hope we're closing it up in time open wounds are obviously very vulnerable to infection in here" commented Mohammad.

"Better late than never" responded Williams.

Shelby was tolerating the pain well as Mohammad expertly stitched up the wound even though it was difficult working through the bars and due to the weakened skin all around the wounds edges.

"There" said Mohammad "Now at least you'll have a fighting chance of avoiding serious infection and the healing process can begin to get a foot hold."

"Thank you, thank you so very much" said Shelby as he moved away from the bars feeling like his face was on fire. He laid down resting his head on his arm trying to get comfortable on the concrete floor and soon fell asleep.

Williams thanked Mohammed saying he'd speak to him and Tahir later and went over and tried to comfort Shelby.

Later that night when everything had quietened down Williams was mulling over what he had learned about escaping since he'd been at Sheberghan. He'd never stopped thinking about it night and day and already figured he'd got the basic information he felt he needed with the exception of how to get out of the cell which had been eluding him so far given they were never being let out. This was going to be his focus from now on and figured everything else would fall into place once he'd figured out this first step and he eventually dozed off.

Nadia was doing her best to cope without Yusuf but was finding it extremely hard. Rashida had already moved back in with their parents but Nadia still held out hope that Yusuf would come home. Yusuf had always provided for her and not wanting to go to her parents she had no choice other than to go to the local malik's for help and they had been arranging food for her. The malik's knew who was doing well in the village and should have food to spare and she was sent there. This was very humiliating for her and she was frequently propositioned by the man of the house wanting sex in exchange for the food. If this happened she'd leave and go without food for several days. Her future was now completely in the hands of the malik's and she knew if Yusuf didn't return they would soon be requiring her to take up with another man which was customary under such circumstances. The community could only be expected to provide for her for so long and in fact they had already suggested a man who could provide for her.

She was missing Yusuf so much he had been such a caring husband and an unusually kind man in a country where most men were brutal beasts especially behind closed doors. Nadia was afraid she would be forced upon a cruel man making her life a nightmare and not worth living. She had looked for work in the village but the malik's were not going to allow this because they wanted a man to be responsible for supporting and more importantly controlling her. Nadia knew exactly what was happening and couldn't do anything about it and knew she would eventually have to do what the maliks wanted and take up with another man or return to live with her parents who now with Rashida to support were struggling to survive themselves. This was just the way it was, she just hoped whoever the man was she ended up with would be kind to her and not be like most men in the village uncaring and prone to violence. She wouldn't have to wait long because the local maliks wouldn't allow the situation to go on for much longer a few more weeks at the most.

When Brown and the local maliks arrived at her dwelling one day she flew at him pleading with him for any news of Yusuf. Brown said he hadn't heard anything and that was why he was there to see if she had received any news.

Brown said "The Pakistani's are being hounded by Langley for any information on the whereabouts of Williams and Shelby and in turn the Pakistani's had been calling him constantly for any news. He hadn't been able to give them any so far. He was one of only a few western diplomats still operating in Afghanistan and was concerned about what Williams and Shelby might be forced to tell the Soviets if they'd been captured. Nadia said she understood his concern about the Americans but she was very worried about Yusuf because he had never been gone for so long before and she feared something had happened to him, his brother and the others. Brown asked the maliks to continue to arrange food for Nadia and he would see what he could find out and left. When Brown got back to his safe house he asked one of his assistants to find out if anything unusual had happened in Termez. The next day Brown's assistant arrived at the Termez border crossing and started asking questions of anyone who would speak to him. It didn't take him long to find out that a number of dead bodies had been found down by the river near the old abandoned buildings not far from the garrison. That was all he could find out. When he returned and told Brown he knew the news wasn't good but didn't comment he knew how brutal the Soviets could be with captured rebels. Finding out exactly what had happened was going to be almost impossible especially with it happening inside the Soviet Union. There were skirmishes almost every day with the Soviets resulting in rebel deaths and casualties, war was always ugly. Brown didn't hold out much hope for Williams, Shelby, Yusuf and the others but would keep making enquiries. He reported in to the Pakistani's that Williams and Shelby were still missing in action and that he would provide further information as it became available. News that Williams and Shelby were MIA which in most cases meant dead was passed up the chain of command to the President who was still a most interested party knowing these were the perpetrators of the nuclear missile detonation incident at Minot, North Dakota several years earlier.

As the days turned into weeks, Williams and Shelby couldn't believe it was possible that they were being treated worse than the other malnourished prisoners who like them were rapidly heading towards a miserable death. They often talked about the conditions in the prison being worse than those Dickens wrote about in nineteenth century London, it seemed they had both enjoyed his somewhat depressing novels. They wandered if the Soviets knew who they were other than Americans. Surely in one of the remotest parts of the Soviet Union the men who had captured them couldn't have any idea that they had been apprehended in Moscow and trained by their masters several years earlier. Also surely if these Soviets had known who they were they would have been taken to Moscow.

They had been trying to maintain their strength by doing daily sit-ups and push-ups but with food in such short supply they had been losing weight at an alarming rate which was weakening them despite their daily exercise regime. They had developed rashes and some of their teeth hurt which was most likely due to malnutrition. They were also finding it hard to quell their thirst even though Mohammad smuggled water in whenever he went out to the tap. The cellblock continued to reek of excrement and rotting corpses, the only escape from the stench was to cover your nose and mouth with rags ripped from what was left of their clothes. There was no doubt they were in an absolute hellhole where death seemed to be the only way out, it was obvious the conditions in the prison were designed to eliminate the inmates as rapidly as possible. No one in authority had spoken to them yet which they were still hoping would happen given they had been spared the night Yusuf, his brother and the other Afghans on the raid had been killed.

The days continued to pass very slowly in Sheberghan and today Williams was watching a small spider spin a web. The spider was a reddish brown color on top, black underneath and had striped black and reddish brown legs. It was amazing how quickly it spun its web in a symmetrical oval pattern.

The partially completed web was supported by several solitary strands attached to the top of one of the barred windows and reinforced by other strands running perpendicular across it. The spider would spin several strands at a time its legs working feverishly then rest sitting in the middle of the web on the strands strung across the unfinished web. While waiting in the center of the web the spider made itself as small as possible as if it was waiting for some unsuspecting prey even though the web was only half completed. The strands of the web got closer together as the web was nearing the center. It was anchored so well that even when a strong gust of wind came it still held firm. It was surprising how long the small spider rested until it started to spin the web again. Up until now the spider had spun approximately thirty circular strands and it looked as if it had another twenty or so to go before the web would be completed. As the web gently swayed in the wind the sun was lighting up different parts of it giving it a silvery sheen. It was truly nature at its most basic, the spider, the web and eventually the entangled fly.

It came to Williams very early one morning as he lay awake getting out of the cell was simple they'd become corpses themselves that way the hose down crew would have to open the cell to remove them. That was it the timing was about right too especially given the way he and Shelby had been treated you would expect them to die anytime now. He had finally found a reason for the hose down crew to open the cell however before they could fake their deaths Shelby almost became a real corpse coming down with a fever that severely weakened him as a result of prolonged sweating that couldn't be alleviated. He kept drifting into a deep sleep and whenever he awoke would shake uncontrollably recollecting the flashback dreams he'd had. A reoccurring dream or nightmare was from several years earlier when he and Williams had left two women tied up in the woods near a US-Canada border crossing. He would visualize a large brown grizzly discovering the women and whenever it approached them the women screaming loudly making the huge drooling animal back away. The women still tied up were terrified and fearing for their lives and were almost hoarse from screaming. This time it was not backing away from their screams and just kept on coming and would soon be right on top of them. They had both shut their eyes and were listening to its heavy breathing as it approached and was about to maul and bite them to death. This was where Shelby's dream always ended with him waking up and going into a spasm with sweat pouring off him. He'd had the same dream many times and it always ended the same way with the women still alive which he was always thankful for. He hoped they were still very much alive and it was just his fever fuelled imagination running wild. Mohammad told Williams he thought Shelby had contracted bacterial meningitis and after much protestation from the prisoners all around him he was taken to the Infirmary leaving Williams alone in the cell. However it wasn't as if Williams didn't have any company he was surrounded by dying men. Williams couldn't figure out why they even had a prison Infirmary because surely they weren't purposely trying to keep the inmates alive. They were treating everyone like shit and then trying to save them when they got sick it didn't make sense he'd have to ask Mohammad if anyone had ever returned from the Infirmary. The diseases Mohammad had previously told them inmates were taken the infirmary with hepatitis, dysentery, typhus and malaria all sounded pretty deadly.

He'd been in the cell by himself for several days now and knew from the way he was feeling it wouldn't be long until he would be on his way to the Infirmary or Crematorium so he needed to escape soon. Mohammad and Tahir had decided not to escape with him and Shelby, Tahir wasn't feeling well, Shelby was also sick and Mohammad thought it would be impossible for the four of them to escape together at the same time. Being alone in the cell for the last few days was the impetuous Williams needed and he had decided to make his move the next time the hose down crew came into the cellblock. As it turned out they started cleaning early the next morning and as they were making their way along to the end of the corridor they were surprised to see Williams wasn't waiting for them. They already knew Shelby had been taken to the Infirmary so hadn't expected to see him. Both he and Williams were usually waiting to grab one of the hoses to drink and wash themselves with. When they got to their cell they could see Williams lying up against the back wall which made the members of the crew feel sad because they had liked the two Americans. One of them unlocked the cell door and pushed a wheelbarrow half full with dead bodies into the cell close to where Williams was lying. He pushed Williams with his foot and getting no reaction knelt down and robbed him of his boots tying them onto his belt by the laces. Then he and another member of the crew picked Williams up and slung him up onto the wheelbarrow. Once on the wheelbarrow the smell was almost too much for Williams and it was all he could do not to immediately throw up. He was holding his breath trying not to make a sound which was helping him to avoid the terrible smell. In Mohammad's cell two more dead bodies were lifted up and thrown onto the wheelbarrow on top of Williams which was both good and bad. Bad because the smell was even more overpowering and good because it hid him further down in the pile. The cleanup crew picked up several more corpses from the cells at the end of the cellblock after which one of them pushed the wheelbarrow back down the corridor and out of the cellblock. The fresh air Williams was now beginning to breathe was wonderful compared to the air he'd been breathing in the cellblock for the last several months. Although he was trying not to he threw up the stench being just too much and soon some of what he had thrown up started to drip down the side of the wheelbarrow. The guard pushing the wheelbarrow saw it and thought it was strange and stopped and looked to see if he could see where it was coming from. It seemed to be coming from the middle of the pile and he wasn't going to poke around in the stinking pile of rotting bodies. He figured he'd wait until he had dumped the bodies into the fire pit and see if he could see where it was coming from then. Williams head was covered by a dead body so he hadn't been able to see what the guard was doing when he had stopped so was relieved when the wheelbarrow began to move again, there wasn't anything he could do if he attempted to move he might dislodge the bodies on top of him and expose himself. A few minutes later the wheelbarrow stopped again and he felt himself being dumped out along with all the other dead bodies, which was very painful upon impact. Fortunately he'd landed face down with dead bodies on top of him, God he thought this must be the worst experience of my life and for some reason he wondered how many Jews had escaped the Nazi concentration camps this way. The guard poked around in the pile of dead bodies with a stick but couldn't see anything and very quickly the smell began to overpower him forcing him to step back and no longer worry about it. Some Crematorium thought Williams lying in the pile of the stinking corpses. Out of the corner of one eye he could see another cleanup crew member coming around the corner pushing another wheelbarrow full of dead bodies. These were dumped on top and beside him and were now a very heavy weight on top of him even though they were just skin and bones. He figured he knew what would happen once the dead bodies had all been dumped they would all be burned. He laid there for as long as he could then not being able to take it anymore pulled himself out from under the pile of stinking dead bodies. He couldn't see any members of the cleanup crew around and figured they would probably be waiting for dark before burning the dead bodies that way the dirty black smoke would not be too obvious.

After getting his bearings he headed in the direction of a building off by itself which he figured had to be the Infirmary. He could see the high prison wall behind it. There was a garden shed close to the Infirmary which he managed to squeeze behind and crouch down out of sight. He stayed there until it got dark and when he began to see flames and smoke rising from the fire pit this was his cue to make a move. Stretching his now stiff legs he made his way to the Infirmary and as he got closer he could hear cries of pain and suffering so he knew for sure it was this was it and wondered what he would find inside. He opened one of the double entrance doors as quietly as he could and stepped into a narrow front hallway which was being lit by candles in fixtures on the wall. He peered around the corner into a small room off to the left side of the hallway and could see two men in white coats sitting at desks talking. He walked over and looked into the larger room off to the right side of the hallway and could see a number of sickly looking men in cots most of them moaning and groaning in pain. He hoped the men in white coats hadn't seen him and realised he would have to wait until they left the building before trying to find Shelby. He quietly left the building and waited near the prison wall off to the side of the Infirmary where he had a clear view of the double entrance doors even though it was now quite dark. He didn't have to wait very long until he saw the two men no longer wearing white coats coming out and locking the double entrance doors of the Infirmary with a thick chain and large padlock. Once they'd left Williams walked over to the padlocked doors checking the door handles the chain was threaded through. They were only screwed into the doors and Williams thought it wouldn't take much force to pry one of them loose. He went and got the rusty shovel he had seen behind the garden shed and used it to pry one of the handles away from the door the screws popping out. With the door handle, chain and padlock hanging down from the other still attached door handle he entered the Infirmary.

He could make out about a dozen men lying in cots in the dim candlelight who all appeared to be very sick most of them looking like they were close to death lying motionless with their mouths open. They were covered with dirty stained sheets and blankets and all had dry and swollen lips most likely due to dehydration and malnutrition a few of them appeared to have fevers and were sweating profusely. It was hard to tell what was ailing them they all looked deathly sick and Williams wondered what kind of care they were getting if any. No doubt they like many others before them would soon die from dysentery or pneumonia which was known to be responsible for most of the deaths in the prisons in Afghanistan. Williams found Shelby although it was hard to recognize him, the wound on his face had become badly infected, his face was horribly swollen and his eyes puffed up and closed. Around Mohammad's stitches the swelling was a dark red and blue color and he was either sleeping or heavily sedated and his breathing was noticeably labored. He was in the very back corner of the room next to a man who had bright red blotchy spots all over his face and was groaning constantly and had been vomiting over the dirty blanket covering him. Neither Shelby nor anyone else for that matter was hooked up to an intravenous drip or any other kind of medical monitoring equipment and was still dressed in the clothes now rags he had been wearing when he and Williams had been captured. He had a soiled sheet partially covering him and Williams reached down and picked up a soiled blanket off the floor and covered him up with it. He then shook him to try and wake him and Shelby stirred opened his swollen eyes and looked up at him.

"Hi Pete" whispered Williams "You look like you went ten rounds with Mohammad Ali which is ironical given where we are anyway how are you feeling or is this a really stupid question?"

Shelby tried to speak through the part of his mouth that wasn't swollen but all Williams heard were some undecipherable sounds. Shelby looked terribly sick so much so that Williams didn't hold out much hope that he would survive very much longer without medical treatment. Before seeing him Williams had no idea how close to death he was and he was obviously much too sick for Williams to consider taking him with him.

He took Shelby's hand and squeezing it hard whispered into his ear "I will get word to your family somehow now rest." Tears formed as Shelby closed his eyes.

Williams kissed him on the forehead saying "Hang in there partner" wishing he could do more for him but knew he couldn't.

He did also wonder if he should end it right here and now but didn't feel he had the right even though he had been his very best friend for the last few years. Williams figured that perhaps they might somehow make him better and he should at least give him a chance to recover no matter how slim. After looking around for Shelby's boots and not finding them he reluctantly left his side.

Just being in the Infirmary was tough, men were crying out in pain throughout the dimly lit room and all their cries were in vain because no one was listening. As he had suspected the Infirmary was being used to temporarily locate the very sick until they died giving the outward appearance that prisoners were being treated humanely. He couldn't see any medical equipment or medication anywhere but this made sense. It was just like the rest of the prison where death seemed to be the primary goal and it was certainly working. Prisoners were dying all the time whether they were in the Infirmary or not,

Williams more than ever knew it was time to put on his game face and make his escape.

It was very dark outside the Infirmary but he could still make out the high prison wall and was amazed there were no guards around. He wasn't sure what it meant, did they all go home at night? The only people he'd seen were the two would-be doctors. He moved over to the wall and hoped he'd find it falling apart like the rest of the prison but it was solid and there was no way to climb up it that he could see. It looked to be about three men high and had no barbed wire along the top. A long extension ladder might do the job but where was he going to find one of those. They may have them to make repairs to the roofs of the cellblocks but more than likely being the government they had a company under contract who did any needed repairs and they would have their own ladders. A ladder was probably out of the question so he began to think about what else he could use. He thought a trampoline might do the job even though he'd only ever been on one once and had found it very difficult to even get more than a few feet in the air. A rope could well do the job also if he could find one long enough and somehow anchor it on top of the wall. The Infirmary was really the only place open to him so he went back in and looked around for something he could use. He couldn't help checking on Shelby again finding him in a deep sleep, then moving into the smaller room he went over to the desks the doctors had been sitting at and wondered if he could use several of them stacked one on top of another to climb up the wall. There were four of them altogether and he lifted one of them up and found it was incredibly heavy. He checked inside the draws and apart from a few pens and some disheveled papers there was nothing heavy in them. He removed them anyway but the desk was still extremely heavy and he knew it was going to be almost impossible to stack them one on top of another. While he had been lifting the desk he had noticed a number of cots stacked up in the far corner of the room. He walked over to them and pulled one of them off the stack and it was nowhere near as heavy as the desks. The frame was bolted to the head and foot boards and there were sturdy slats at intervals to support the mattress. He figured it would only take two of these to allow him reach up to the top of the wall and started dragging the cot towards the double doors making a loud scrapping sound. He dragged it out of the Infirmary and over to the prison wall and propped it up with the foot board end on the ground. He went back into the Infirmary and dragged another one out and leaned it up next to the other one. He figured he would need to secure the two cots together and went back into the Infirmary to see what he could find for this. He located a small storage closet and found a bundle of electrical cable which although not ideal he thought it might do the job. He slung the heavy cable over his shoulder and on his way out took one last look over to where Shelby was and was just about to leave through the door when he heard voices outside and he quickly hid behind an empty cot in the larger room. He figured they must have found the broken handle and continuing to hear voices became concerned that he might be locked in the Infirmary so he crawled out from where he'd been hiding to try and hear what was being said. While listening he heard the static of a walkie-talkie and figuring he had no choice but to confront whoever was outside so as not to get locked in kicked the double doors open and rushed out surprising a lone guard standing just outside. He pushed him to the ground and viciously kicked at him repeatedly the guard dropping the walkie-talkie on impact finding it impossible to fight Williams off. Blood began to flow from a wound to the guard's head and trickle out of his left ear as Williams continued to pummel him until he looked to be unconscious. Williams dragged the guard's limp body into the Infirmary hallway, the guards face and clothes were covered in blood as were William's hands. Williams wiped his hands on the guard's shirt. He pulled the flimsy well-worn sandals off the guard's feet and tried them on and they were too small. He went over and picked up the bundle of electrical cable and as he left the Infirmary heard someone talking on the discarded walkie-talkie. He picked it up and in his best Pashto said everything was alright and he was signing off. The person on the other end didn't know what to make of this because they'd been discussing the damage to the Infirmary door when he'd heard the walkie-talkie thud to the ground followed by a lot of commotion now he was being told everything was alright. This was most confusing and he wasn't sure what to do, Mustafa had also said he was signing off which was very strange because they normally stayed in constant contact. He and Mustafa were currently the only ones in the prison and he knew he couldn't leave the command post. He did sometimes but not very often and he couldn't chance it right now with more prisoners scheduled to arrive at any time. He and Mustafa usually took turns patrolling the cellblocks and Infirmary at night so he figured Mustafa must have solved the problem with the Infirmary doors and would be back at the command post at the top of the hour. He put the walkie-talkie back into his hip holster and went to make some tea while he waited for the new prisoners to arrive and Mustafa to check-in.

Williams anchored the end of the electrical cable to the foot of the first cot and carrying the rest of the bundle climbed up the outside of the second cot the slats cutting into his bare feet. Standing on top of the first cot and making sure it was stable he pulled the second cot up on top of the first which didn't leave much room for him then as best he could he tied the foot of the top cot to the bottom cot and threw what remained of the cable up over the wall. He climbed up to the top of the top cot and summoning up all the strength he had left pulled himself up and straddled the top of the high prison wall. He perched there briefly to get his breath then slowly lowered himself down the outside of the wall burning his hands on the electrical cable in the process but the cots had held.

Once he reached the ground Williams was in two minds what to do, it wouldn't be light for several more hours and he was very reluctant to move away from the prison wall until he could see where he was stepping however on the other hand getting away under the cover of darkness made sense too. The problem he was wrestling with was that the whole of Afghanistan seemed to be mined so around the prison was probably no exception and would probably be worse. On the other hand he knew he should get as far away from the prison as quickly as he could because once they found the cots propped up against the wall it would be obvious someone had escaped.

He already knew what the terrain was going to be like from the discussions he'd had with Mohammad and human nature told him when they started looking for him it would be on the side where he had gone over the wall.

At the top of the hour when Mustafa didn't show up Abdul got on the walkie-talkie and tried to contact him but got no answer. It was just after three o'clock in the morning and he didn't quite know what to do, he conjectured that Mustafa had perhaps had to deal with more issues at the Infirmary the last place where he knew he was. New prisoners had arrived and been locked up so this was no longer a worry as it approached four o'clock. It was two hours since he'd seen or heard from Mustafa which was most unusual and he still didn't know what to do he couldn't leave the command post knowing he could lose his job or even worse if his superiors found out he had so he decided he would have to wait until six o'clock when the day staff came back in and report Mustafa missing if he hadn't shown up by then.

In the darkness still fearing there might be land mines Williams carefully made his way around to the other side of the prison and started to slowly move away from the wall. Although he was still most concerned about the mines he'd decided to take his chances, he still had at least three hours before the dawn and needed to make the most of these while it was dark. His eyes were beginning to adjust to the lack of light and he was able to make out shapes where he was stepping in the bushes. He had found a path and was following it as it snaked its way through the tangled vegetation and at least he was finding the ground between the bushes quite sandy which was good for his bare feet but hadn't gone much further when it felt as if he'd trodden on something hard, a branch, root or something. He felt down under his foot and it was moist so figured it must be bleeding, this was all he didn't need based upon his experiences so far in Afghanistan most cuts or sores soon became infected unless they were treated, he figured the reason for this was that most Afghans were undernourished resulting in them having weak immune systems. He was now the same as them after being locked up in the Sheberghan prison for several months and while tending to his foot he began to think how he had never ever felt so all alone and vulnerable in his life.

"They" had finally broken him which should make "them" very happy knowing their plans had almost been accomplished, Shelby was very close to death and might even be dead by now and he was fighting for his life. He could see a sliver of a moon and a profusion of stars which weren't helping to light his way very much and he'd come to the end of the path he'd been following the undergrowth becoming incredibly thick and un-penetrable.

"Now what" he thought?

He couldn't chance struggling through this thick tangled undergrowth with a bad foot but he didn't want to go back but he really had no choice. He remembered not far back there had been a path crossing the one he'd been on so decided to backtrack and see if he could find it.

As the sun was coming up over the eastern horizon a rusty old bus transporting sleepy prison workers rumbled through the gates of Sheberghan prison pulling up at the command post. Workers quickly got off the bus fanning out to take up their daily duties. Abdul was already explaining to the just arrived prison supervisor that he hadn't seen Mustafa since two o'clock when someone burst in shouting that Mustafa's been found dead inside the Infirmary and it looks like those responsible have escaped over the wall. Abdul banged his head on his desk and began to sob uncontrollably he and Mustafa had been life-long friends. The prison supervisor tried to console him by telling him to go home to his family and take the rest of the week off. The prison siren sounded and gradually the prison workers began to assemble outside the command post. Once they were assembled the prison supervisor told them it looked like Mustafa had been murdered trying to stop an escape last night and that the Soviet authorities had been informed and would soon begin to search for whoever had escaped. He made it clear that it was not any of their responsibilities to search for those who had escaped and that they should all go back to their posts and resume their normal duties.

Williams was waiting to see the beginnings of the sunrise and hoped when the sun appeared it would confirm he was heading east because he'd found the other path and wasn't sure what direction it was going in. When the sun did begin to turn the night into day it seemed that he was heading in a northerly rather than in an easterly direction where the sun had risen. He needed to be going towards the rising sun and left the path despite his bad foot and started to make his way through the tangled undergrowth heading directly east. It was like wading through knee deep water and he thought wouldn't that have been nice as he struggled on pretending the bushy undergrowth was the turquoise shallows of a warm sea. This thought helped him deal with his current circumstances as he slowly navigated his way east. All around him were low bushes for as far as he could see just like Mohammad had told him, he couldn't see the prison but his bad foot felt like it was on fire and he figured it wouldn't be long until he'd have to stop to check it. Knowing that he was free was driving him on even though he was in a lot of pain. When he came to an area that was almost clear of bushes he slumped down, even though the sun had just come up it felt like he had been making his way through the bushes for many hours already. Sitting on the ground he felt down under his foot and he could feel a puncture wound under his big toe. It was still bleeding and he needed to cushion his foot somehow so he tore a piece of rag off what remained of his pants and tied it around his toes. As he sat there in the clearing he realized he was feeling very fatigued and tired.

The Soviets arrived at the prison later that morning their armored all-terrain vehicles coming to a stop outside the command post. The Soviet commander entered the command post and asked if anyone spoke Russian. The prison supervisor replied in Russian that he did. The Soviet commander asked where the Americans were and was told one of them was in the Infirmary and that the other had been found dead and cremated the night before.

"Take me to see the American in the Infirmary" demanded the Soviet commander not able to control his anger as he shouted out a stream of obscenities in Russian mentioning something about incompetent Afghans.

"Please follow me" said the prison supervisor.

The Soviet commander and several of his men followed him out of the command post past the fire pit to the Infirmary. Once inside they could hear men crying out in pain. The prison supervisor told the Soviet commander that one his men had been murdered during the escape attempt. The Soviet commander told him he was sorry and commented he knew how hard it is to lose someone. The prison supervisor took the Soviet commander over to Shelby's cot where he could see a very sick man barely alive his face badly swollen, he had a corpse-like pallor and was having trouble breathing. The Soviet commander asked if Shelby was receiving any medical treatment for his ailments and was told that he wasn't because the prison had run out of medical supplies several months ago. The Soviet commander shouted something to one of his men and he quickly left the Infirmary and soon returned with a suitcase-like medical kit from which he removed a large syringe which he filled from a small bottle. Antibiotics were injected into Shelby's arm and he had no reaction at all to having a needle stuck in him.

The Soviet filled another syringe from another small bottle and injected Shelby once again getting no visible reaction. While this was going on the Soviet commander was asking the prison supervisor about the circumstances of the other Americans death and was told he had been found dead in his cell yesterday by the cellblock cleanup crew. The Soviet commander asked the officer dispensing the drugs to Shelby to stay with him and asked the prison supervisor to show him where the escape had taken place. They went out to the wall and he could see the two cot frames piled one on top of the other leaning up against the high prison wall and he thought to himself how most ingenious.

"How many men escaped?" he asked.

"We don't know we don't keep a count of the prisoners here" said the prison supervisor rather sheepishly.

"So you have no idea who or how many men may have escaped is that what you're telling me?"

"Yes that is correct."

Following this exchange the Soviet commander's attention returned to the Americans as he made his way back to the Infirmary.

"How long have the Americans been imprisoned here?" "Roughly three months" replied the prison supervisor

"They were kept in a small cell away from the rest of the prison population because we were told they were special prisoners when they arrived."

"They were but unfortunately the officer who delivered them got transferred to a different part of Afghanistan very soon after and although he'd told us about their capture and imprisonment here we obviously forgot about them due to the numerous other pressing matters we've been dealing with." The prison supervisor commented "I was told they were going to be interrogated but they never were."

"Like many other things during our occupation here in Afghanistan they dropped through the cracks" said the Soviet commander off handedly.

While the Soviet commander, his men and the prison supervisor were discussing the Soviets failure to interrogate the Americans Shelby suddenly came awake, the antibiotics he had been given had already begun to take effect. The

Soviet commander told Shelby he was going to do all he could to make sure he got better and that his men were going to stay with him until he was in good health again. Shelby understood most of what the Soviet commander had said and this was wonderful news he was already feeling a lot better and wondered what super drugs he had been injected with. He was told they were different forms of penicillin which were killing the micro-organisms that had been trying to kill him. The Soviet commander left the Infirmary with the prison supervisor and the men who hadn't stayed behind to care for Shelby and once he got back to the command post he and his men joined the other men milling around the armored ATV's and soon they headed off to begin the search for those who had escaped. Helicopters were already searching and as Williams had anticipated they had started their search on the side of the prison where he had gone over the wall. The Soviets in armored ATV's also had to be wary of the land mines that were scattered around the prison to foil those who might try to storm it in an attempt to release the rebel prisoners and less than an hour into the search one of the ATV's back axle and wheels were blown off catapulting into the bushes leaving the vehicle disabled and those inside shaken up.

Back in the prison Infirmary Shelby already feeling much better didn't realize he was being revived to be interrogated into telling the Soviet's what he and William's were doing in Afghanistan. His face was still badly swollen and flies were landing and taking off on his wound constantly. He still had meningitis which had been causing him to have terrible headaches, fevers and altered states of consciousness but he was feeling much more positive about his future and hoped he would now get better rather than die a horrible painful death.

After resting for a while Williams set off again limping through the still thick undergrowth, his foot was feeling a little better now that he'd wrapped a rag around it. He could make out hills far off in the distance and hoped the dense bush would come to an end sooner than later. His knees were hurting and raw after constantly brushing up against the tops of the bushes. He took his shirt off ripped it in half and tied the two halves around his knees and set off again and could immediately feel the difference so much so it put his focus back onto his bad foot which was still very painful. He came to another clearing and stopped and retied the rag which had come slightly loose around his toes then continued on. His other foot was holding up well considering he had no idea where and what he was stepping on. As soon as it started to get dark he began to look for a clearing eventually finding one. The ground was sandy and soft and he hadn't seen any rodents or animals all day long so figured he should be safe here through the night. With the light fading quickly feeling dog tired as soon as he laid his head down he dozed off flashing back to when he was in the silo on Minot Air Force Base several years earlier. He began to sweat profusely as he remembered what he had tried to do and still didn't know why the missile in the silo hadn't detonated and was wondering how it could have been stopped. He knew his fellow countrymen could be unbelievably inventive especially during a crisis and must have figured out which wires to cut or which affected hardware modules to remove and had managed to unarm the missile somehow? He had been told any attempt to modify the software would cause the warheads to detonate but what was this based on? Perhaps it had been an incorrect assumption on the part of the Soviets. But as quickly as the flashback had come it had gone and he awoke and in the darkness and could see stars everywhere. He was back in the moment the reality setting in that he had come to the end of his first day of freedom in quite a while feeling sore and tired he fell asleep.

That afternoon another Soviet armored ATV picked up the stranded Soviets who had run over a mine and after hearing the news that one of the search vehicles had hit a land mine the Soviet commander responsible for the search immediately called it off.

He said it wasn't worth risking any more vehicles or men looking for worthless rebels whose chances of survival were very slim given the shape they were probably in and the uninhabited lands they would have to make their way across. It was also the first escape from Sheberghan prison in all of its years of operation so it was unlikely to happen again very soon. Also if those who had escaped did manage to survive and reunite with their rebel friends hopefully their story of the misery in Sheberghan prison might act as a deterrent to them.

William's was woken by the chop, chop, chop, sound of a helicopter and quickly crept under some nearby bushes hiding until he couldn't hear it anymore. He was feeling really thirsty and standing up shirtless his trousers in tatters and rags wrapped around his knees and foot he didn't feel very much like his old confident self. He wondered what the Pakistani Colonel who had met him and Shelby at the Peshawar Air Station would say if he saw him now. He was obviously no longer a fine looking American specimen but he still had strong survival instincts.

Once they got word that the Soviet commander in the area had called off the search the Soviet High Command were furious and immediately ordered it be resumed. The search continued the next day still on the side of the prison where the escapees had gone over the wall. Several armored ATV's crisscrossed the bushy desert terrain south-west of the prison and helicopters circled at different distances out from the prison. The Soviets continued to assume the escapees had not got far.

The sea of brush continued off into the distance as far as Williams could see as he doggedly kept heading in an easterly direction and without warning stepped on a stick or something and felt immediate pain in his leg. He looked down and saw a large snake poised to strike it was brown with black beaded eyes and as thick as one of his arms. It kept flicking its forked tongue as its tail quivered wildly and he could already feel the pain from the bite but continued to stand as still as he could until the snake decided to slither away under the bushes. He looked down to see if he could see where he'd been bitten remembering his father telling him on a hiking trip once what to look for if you were ever bitten by a snake. If there were fang marks in addition to teeth marks the snake was likely poisonous. If there were no fang marks just teeth marks the snake was likely to be not poisonous. Williams couldn't see any fang marks just small teeth marks so he figured he should be alright. The marks were very small so the snake likely hadn't bitten him very hard but the bite still hurt.

He also remembered that it was important to keep the wound as dry as possible to minimize bacteria build-up and infection. He could still hobble along even though now he had an almost intolerable stinging sensation coming from his right leg. Limping he continued to make his way through the bushes wondering if they were ever going to end. Several hours later as he was getting closer to the hills the bushes finally began to thin out the terrain becoming desert like. He struggled on as best he could but wouldn't be able to go much further with his knees, foot and leg hurting like they did. The sun was almost down and darkness was about to envelope him as he sat down on a large rock protruding out of the side of a hill, it looked like he would be spending the night here at the end of his second day of freedom. Once it became dark looking up at the stars he began to reminisce about his childhood which was a common occurrence whenever he was feeling really down.

He thought back to when he was a boy growing up in a clapboard row house in Albany, New York, which was great fun because of all the friends he'd had back then. He remembered asking his father why it was called a clapboard house and he'd told him that when you carried two or more boards together they made a clapping sound, it was as simple as that. He began to think about the name Albany itself and remembered learning at school that it was named after a Duke who later became a King of England but he couldn't remember which one. Another discussion he'd had with his father was why the main road close to where they lived was called a turnpike. His dad had told him that turnpikes were toll roads and were named after an old English word for a gate with spikes a tollgate. It still didn't make much sense to him as he sat in the darkness somewhere in the middle of Afghanistan looking up at the incredible star filled night sky and knew there were still turnpikes in many states even today. He remembered going up to Sarasota Springs to watch horse races in the summer and camping at Lake George named after another English King he guessed. There was a fort, penny arcades, boat cruises, mini-golf, beaches and lots of other fun things to do there. He remembered his sister and him being allowed to pick out T-shirts which their mother would buy for them. The memories of these things made him feel a little bit better but he was still very thirsty. He wondered if he could drink his own urine if he could produce any, he remembered seeing a TV program once where someone had drunk his own urine and thought he'd said that it was at least ninety-eight percent water. He'd also heard somewhere that it was recommended for people who were lost at sea to drink urine rather than sea water so it must be alright to drink as a last resort. This was the last thought he had before sleep overtook him.

The guards at the prison didn't know Williams had faked his death and it was him who had escaped but Mohammad and Tahir did once they heard they were searching for escapees and heard how they'd escaped. Life in the prison was going on as normal again if you could call it that new prisoners arriving and old prisoners dying horrible deaths every day. It had become a predictable cycle from capture to death to which the Soviet's and the Afghan government continued to turn a blind eye. People were dying every day in the Soviet Union's Republics and in other parts of Afghanistan at an alarming rate from a lack of food and shelter so why should they worry about a few imprisoned rebels who had been trying to kill them and still would if they had the opportunity to.

Williams was woken by the sound of a motorcycle and saw that the sun was already high in the sky. His throat was parched and he was having trouble swallowing what saliva he could generate. It felt as if he had no moisture left in his body as he made his way towards where the sound was coming from. After climbing up the slope of a nearby hill and looking down he could see someone on a dirt bike riding around a circular track and started to make his way down towards the motorcyclist. As he got closer he could see it was a boy who had a checkered head scarf over his face to protect him from the flying sand dust. The boy could see Williams making his way down the hill. There was a small stand of trees halfway down the hill and when Williams came out of these the boy stopped riding around and took a good look at him revving up his motorcycle showing off. Williams waved to him trying to be as friendly as he could meanwhile the boy was noticing the state Williams was in and was scared never having seen a man so naked and rough looking. He thought he looked like someone out of the bible some tortured religious figure. William's mouth was so dry that although he was shouting no sounds were coming out. The boy shouted something out loud and took off towards the dirt road running along the base of the hill leaving a cloud of dust behind him. Williams figured it wouldn't be long until others came to check him out as he could see a number of houses within walled compounds not too far from where he was but couldn't see any people. It was the most encouraging thing he'd seen since he'd escaped from Sheberghan prison. There were cultivated fields for as far as he could see and he was wondering how he could make himself less Robinson Crusoe like but didn't have anything to work with. He just hoped there were no Soviets in these parts as he could be either shot or taken straight back to Sheberghan prison. When he reached the dirt road at the bottom of the hill he hid in some bushes at the side of the road and waited.

Red Shadows On Liberty's Soil

While hiding in the bushes at the bottom of the hill, a tractor, three donkey carts and two trucks passed by within a short period of time so Williams figured if he lay on the side of the deeply rutted dirt road it wouldn't be long until he would be spotted. It only seemed to be peasant traffic if there was such a thing and there didn't seem to be any Soviet presence here from what he could tell. He heard a vehicle approaching, checked to make sure it wasn't a military vehicle and crept out of the bushes and lay down in the road. It turned out the vehicle was a tractor pulling an empty cart. The driver stopped, jumped down from the tractor and went over where Williams was lying. He shook him and Williams acted like the driver had revived him and gestured he needed water by making a drinking motion with his hand. The driver helped him up onto the back of the cart turned the tractor around and drove in the direction he had just come in towards one of the compounds Williams had seen from up on top of the hill. They entered through the open gates, pulled up beside one of the houses and the driver ran inside. Within a few minutes a woman covered from head to foot in a silk shroud came rushing out carrying a large jug. She handed the jug to Williams still sitting on the back of the cart and he drank the water spilling a lot of it down his chest and immediately began to feel better. While he had been drinking the water the driver and the woman had been having an argument yelling at each other. Williams figured she was upset with the driver for bringing him here and he had already made the decision to say nothing until he knew who he was dealing with and seeing he had finished drinking the woman snatched the jug out of his hands and hurried back into the dwelling. The driver helped Williams down from the cart and into the dwelling where the woman was waiting for them just inside the door. She helped Williams into a dimly lit bedroom where the driver motioned to him to lay down on the bed. Williams was still half naked and was surprised to finally be in a bed and so totally exhausted that he fell asleep once his head hit the pillow.

About an hour later the local maliks' with hooked noses and long pale faces arrived to see

Williams. They had been told he had been found lying in the road almost naked, they had never heard of anything like this in these parts. This was most unusual almost like an Alien having landed and they were most suspicious. The driver told them the stranger was sleeping and asked them to come back later. Williams had heard the conversation between the maliks' and the driver and was concerned knowing they would be coming back later. Although he tried not to fall asleep again he did and was woken by someone gently shaking him. He looked up and found himself surrounded by old men in cloaks staring down at him in the dim candlelight. Realizing they were crowding him they all stepped back in unison. None of them quite knew what to say and in what language so Williams helped them out.

"Hi I'm an American who got lost touring your beautiful country."

This started a tremendous amount of agitated discussion between the maliks. They were speaking Pashto which Williams was familiar with but even so he still couldn't follow their multiple conversations. One of the maliks spoke and everyone immediately stopped talking.

"You say you got lost but you must have started somewhere?"

"Yes you are right in Pakistan we entered into Afghanistan through the famous Khyber Pass" offered Williams.

"You are a very long way from there how did you get here?" another malik asked.

"A good question" laughed Williams "I was travelling with friends in an off road vehicle in I think its called Jowsjan province when we hit a mine. I was the only one who survived all of my other friends were killed and somehow I got from there to here."

This created a great deal more discussion until the head malik spoke up again.

"We find it difficult to believe that you and your friends were touring Afghanistan during our war with the Soviets?"

Williams faked he was tired closing his eyes very often and the head malik seeing this said "We will come back and speak to you again in the morning now please rest."

The maliks and driver all left the room.

Williams was relieved the questioning was over because he really did feel very tired and soon dosed off again. A few hours later he was woken by the shrouded woman holding a bowl of rice and a large earthen jug out to him. She had also brought him some clothes and a pair of sandals. As he sat up he noticed a youngish looking armed man standing outside the door and figured he was probably the driver and woman's son. He hungrily ate the rice mixture with his hands and drank the water in the jug. He handed the bowl and jug back to the woman who was waiting just inside the door thanking her as she bowed as she left the room locking the door behind her. Williams was left in the dim light being provided by a solitary candle in an attachment on the wall and wondered what time it was. Feeling refreshed he was thinking more clearly now and was wondering how he could get out of there before the local maliks returned in the morning. Knowing he was being guarded troubled him and would make whatever move he made to escape riskier even though he figured escaping from a house had to be a lot easier than from a prison. He looked around at his surroundings and it seemed the only furniture in the room was the bed he was lying in. There was a shuttered window, a collection of different sized pots on the rug covering the dirt floor and a wall rack with hooks on it on the wall at the foot of the bed. He listened and not hearing any sounds coming from anywhere in the house got out of the bed. He untied the rags from around his knees, leg and foot and discarded what was left of his old clothes. He checked his wounds which weren't hurting as much anymore and put on the long shirt and baggy pants he'd been provided with and tried on the sandals which were a bit small but would do. He went over to the window to see if he could open the shutters and found he couldn't. They were secured on the outside by a horizontal piece of wood inserted into two metal holders on either side. He would need to dislodge the piece of wood somehow. He went over and leveraged the rack off the wall the screws coming off with it and went back the window and quietly banged one of the screws between the slats below the securing piece of wood but the screw was not long enough to lever it up and dislodge it. Seeing there was nothing else in the room he could use he went over and lifted the heavy patterned blanket off the bed and got a surprise. An air bed was taped to the top of a wooden box that had been turned upside. He remembered when he had first time laid on the bed he thought it felt like an air bed. He turned the bed over and pulled one of the wooden legs off and using the rack he'd pulled off the wall quietly banged one of the long nails out. He went over to the window shutter and using the rack banged the nail though the slats below the piece of wood securing them. Not hearing anything he banged the nail down with the rack as quietly as he could, dislodging the piece of wood securing the shutters. He opened the shutters and looked out into the dark night and standing on one of the pots under the window he went out through the window head first like a modern day high jumper. Unfortunately the pot toppled over as his foot left it and it smashed on the packed dirt floor making a loud bang. Once he got to his feet he ran as fast as he could out of the compound.

He had been running as fast as he could for quite a while now and no one seemed to be chasing after him so he hid in a ditch by the side of the road to catch his breath. He waited a little while longer but no one seemed to have come after him so he got up and started walking towards some houses off in the distance. He came to a crossroads where there were several branches leading off towards the houses and decided to stay on the main road which seemed to be skirting a village. He figured he still had three or four hours before the dawn.

Walking along in the dark he occasionally saw oncoming lights and ran and crouched down in the fields by the side of the road and had not been detected yet so it had been working. The road he was walking down seemed to be taking all kinds of twists and turns and he hoped he was still heading in an easterly direction and this was one of the roads that led to the Chinese border but he wouldn't know for sure until the sun began to appear over the horizon. He didn't have a passport or any papers only his accent which he hoped would be sufficient crazy though it sounded. As he walked on he was surprised how good he was feeling the food and drink he'd recently been given had really invigorated him and the fact he didn't have an ounce of fat on him was helping too. He felt so light footed he could have skipped along the road if he wanted to.

Suddenly he heard a vehicle approaching from behind its headlights shining past him so he knew it was already too late to try and hide. An old Jeep with two men in it pulled up alongside him and the passenger started speaking to him in Pashto. William's responded in the best Pashto he could muster trying to make out he was an Afghan. The driver leaned over towards where he was standing and said that they weren't going far but would be glad to give him a ride and asked him where he was going.

Williams had been thinking about the number of times he was going to be asked this question and had prepared a pat answer and responded "To the next village."

Although Williams didn't know how far the next village was the answer seemed to be acceptable the driver who told him to get in the back. Because it was still dark it wasn't obvious to the two men that Williams wasn't an Afghan with his shaggy beard and all. However when the man in the passenger seat turned around and asked him why he was walking along the road in the middle of the night he thought he might be in trouble. He told him he needed to get an early start to the day because he had a lot of business to take care of. Obviously the next question followed along the same theme what kind of business? William's said he had to see a malik in the next village about several parcels of land that were in dispute and just as he finished answering the Jeep hit a large pot hole with quite a jolt and the driver started cursing at the passenger as if it was his fault and the questioning abruptly came to an end. Williams really wanted to ask how far it was to the Chinese border but was worried it might lead to more questions. It was great that he'd got a ride in the direction he thought he needed to go in because riding was always better than walking wherever you were travelling in the world and hoped the ride would continue for a while longer. The passenger turned back to Williams and offered him a beaten up old thermos telling him it contained hot tea. Williams took a long drink of the hot thick black sweet tea which almost immediately started to have an effect on him oh know he thought it's been spiked. The driver and passenger were talking and laughing about the rape of a boy the week before and Williams started to get a bad feeling.

Not long after they came to an intersection and the driver turned off the main road and they hadn't gone far when the driver pulled the Jeep over to the side of the road and turned the engine off.

He looked back at Williams and said "Get out" in a quite hostile tone while pointing an old pistol at him. As Williams was getting out of the back of Jeep the passenger ran back to where he was and physically dragged him out telling him to put his hands on the hood of the Jeep. The driver came up behind Williams and held the pistol to the side of his head while the passenger tugged and pulled Williams baggy trousers down and saw he wasn't wearing any underwear.

"Me first?" demanded the passenger expectantly.

"Go ahead" said the driver still holding the pistol to
Williams head.

The passenger unbuckled his belt and let his trousers fall. This was Williams cue and as quick as a cat he grabbed the pistol out of the driver's hand and praying it was loaded shot him between the eyes and he crumpled to the ground. The passenger still standing with his pants down around his ankles just stood there staring at Williams as he raised the pistol and shot him between the eyes too and he dropped to the ground. Williams pulled his trousers up feeling no remorse for either man whoever they were they had been about to rape him. He was shaking after having murdered these two men in a matter seconds. He'd had no choice in the circumstances they were about to rape him then probably murder him so it was a true case of self-defense. He was amazed how quickly and efficiently he had dealt with the situation and thought to himself that he was definitely someone to be reckoned with when it came down to the crunch. After he'd stopped shaking he checked to make sure both men were dead and noticed the driver was wearing a new pair of boots and after pulling them off him found they were a good fit. He dragged both bodies into the nearby bushes and threw the old pistol into the bushes over on the other side of the road. He got behind the wheel of the Jeep and drove back to the main road noticing that the fuel gauge was registering on empty even though the engine was running and figured it must be broken so he would drive until he ran out of gas thinking there were so many things he didn't know about Afghan life like where to get gasoline. He figured he'd gone about ten miles before the Jeep slowed and came to a stop out of gas. As he was getting out of the Jeep he checked inside to see if he could find anything that might be useful but only found a rusty dagger under the passenger seat which he saw no use for so left it where he'd found it. He abandoned the Jeep right where it had stopped in the middle of the road and set off on foot.

As he walked down the road the sun began to rise signaling the start of another day of freedom and from the direction it was rising he was able to confirm he was pretty much heading in an easterly direction. He could see a vehicle way off in the distance coming towards him and crouched down in the field beside the road until it passed. At the start of this new day Williams figured he had to stop hiding in fields and be bold enough to tell the truth about who he really was. Not too long after he heard what sounded like a horse and cart clopping along behind him. It turned out to be a donkey and cart carrying sacks of potatoes.

A black and white dog was sniffing at his feet as the driver was asking him if he could give him a ride. Williams said he could and the driver told him to jump up on the bench seat next to him in English which surprised Williams. Once he'd sat down the driver asked the inevitable question where was he was headed? Williams told the driver in English to China which didn't get much of a reaction to his surprise and he wasn't sure why. Was it so far away that it wasn't worth discussing or was the driver heading there too? Williams had to find out and asked the driver how far it was to China and the driver said he thought it was about one hundred and fifty miles but no one ever went there because the border was closed. They soon got to talking about themselves the driver introducing himself as Daoud and Williams introducing himself honestly as himself. Daoud said he was surprised to find an American walking along a dirt road in Afghanistan. Williams didn't respond. As they bounced along Williams was wondering if the people from the dwelling he had escaped from were bothering to look for him or just glad to be rid of him. He was also thinking about the men he had killed an hour or so before and wondered how soon their bodies would be discovered. The ride hadn't lasted long they had stopped outside a small dwelling on the outskirts of what looked to be quite a large town. Daoud asked Williams if he would like to come in and have some breakfast. After his recent experiences Williams was reluctant but really having no choice followed Daoud into the dwelling. It was dark inside until Daoud lit some candles and started a fire and once the fire had taken hold hung two large pots over it. One looked like it contained water and the other a stew of some kind, it looked like they were going to have Afghan tea and warmed up stew for breakfast which was different but didn't surprise Williams after all this was Afghanistan. Williams figured Daoud must live alone and looking at him close up wasn't surprised, he had an unkempt shaggy salt and pepper beard, very few teeth and a weather beaten complexion, it would be hard to love such a face but perhaps someone had once. Williams was offered a bowl of stew and cup of tea both steaming hot which he enjoyed immensely. He was reluctant to tell Daoud his story in case it turned him against him so he'd just have to speculate about what he was doing here in north-eastern Afghanistan. Daoud seemed very happy to have company and had been doing most of the talking until Williams told him he had to leave to continue on his journey. Daoud got upset and said he was welcome to stay with him for a few days and he would take him further east towards China. Williams wasn't sure how to respond. He could certainly use some rest but was concerned if he stayed he might be found out having escaped from another residence or for killing the two men along the road. He already liked Daoud and more importantly his instincts told him he could trust him so he decided to take a chance and take him up his offer and stay with him to recharge his batteries. Trying to reach China would take all the energy he had and if he could boost it in some way and get a ride all the better. Daoud offered him the floor in another room and gave him cushions, a blanket and a well-worn sleeping mat. Even though it was still quite early in the day as soon as Williams lay down he fell into a deep sleep. Daoud seeing Williams sleeping left the dwelling and took his load of potatoes to barter with the merchants at the local market. He didn't return for several hours and found Williams still sleeping when he got back. He left him to sleep and the following morning when he got up still found him sleeping. Daoud let him sleep. Williams eventually woke up later that afternoon and could hear Daoud talking to someone in the other room and immediately became concerned. He looked into the room and saw Daoud with another man who resembled him. Daoud seeing Williams asked him to come and meet his brother Fahran who also spoke English. After the introductions Daoud told Williams he'd need an identification card to travel east with him as there were normally Soviet and Afghan government patrols along all the main roads during the day. He told Williams his brother could provide these for him but it would take a day or so. Williams thinking it made sense and the likelihood of him being found here at Daoud's was most unlikely agreed and Daoud's brother Fahran said he would come back tomorrow to take his photo.

"How does Aaron Hassan sound for a name I believe Aaron is quite a common name in

America which hopefully you can remember easily and Hassan is a very common last name in Afghanistan. What language do you want to speak?"

"Pashto" said Williams "I am familiar with that."

Williams told him his date of birth and Daoud's brother got up and said he had to go and would be back first thing in the morning. Daoud offered Williams some hot stew and he had gobbled down several bowls before he realized he hadn't left much for Daoud and apologized for eating so much and Daoud told him not to worry he would make some more. It was already dark outside and Williams periodically throwing logs on the fire was beginning to relax for the first time in months which was a very good feeling especially knowing he was still free. Early the next morning Fahran arrived to take Williams photo waking him and Daoud up. He asked Williams to wrap the black and white checkered scarf he had brought with him around his head like a turban and trimmed his shaggy beard. There now you look like an Afghan. Fahran took several photos with a big Polaroid camera and about an hour later presented Williams with an identification card with the name they had agreed on Aaron Hassan. Daoud said he just needed to do a couple of things then they could be off so Williams stayed inside drinking tea with Fahran while Daoud went to load his cart.

They left Feyzabad just after nine o'clock that morning heading east towards the famous Wakhan Corridor, the first leg of the journey to China had begun. Daoud's rickety old cart rattled through the streets of the old town with Williams sitting next to his new best friend Daoud whose cart was being pulled by a tired looking donkey called Gita. Daoud's dog Feddy a black and white sheepdog was running up ahead occasionally stopping to let them catch up. Williams had been formally introduced to Gita and Feddy just before they'd set off. Daoud had let him feed Gita some carrots and play fetch with Feddy and he'd almost lost a finger in the process. They were making their way through potholed streets manoeuvring around the bigger ones and Williams was thinking that everything is better with two plus a dog. He wasn't sure about the donkey yet as they trotted past bleached sun-dried mud brick homes, overgrown playing fields and neglected gardens. Williams was listening to Daoud's continuous monologue about how hard life was in Afghanistan periodically nodding and looking his way to indicate he was listening. Under his blue and white checkered head scarf Daoud was dressed in an old thread bare woollen jacket, a long dirty white shirt, thick black baggy pants and open toed sandals which showed off his grimy feet. Williams was dressed in a very similar fashion due to the fact Daoud had provided him with some of his old clothes. He was also wearing the black and white checkered scarf Fahran had let him keep after the photo shoot. Daoud seemed to be in a cheerful mood periodically showing off the few yellow teeth he had left whenever he laughed following something he'd said about the hardships of living in Afghanistan that he thought was funny, he hadn't stopped talking since Williams had climbed up beside him. They hadn't gone too far when they came to the end of the paved road leading out of the town the tarmac coming to an abrupt end. Williams remembered as a kid going on bike rides to subdivisions under construction and reaching the end of newly paved roads the fields beginning again this was like that. This seemed to be the only road east whether it was paved or not and as they started down it Williams realizing what a formidable journey it was going to be. They were beginning to make their way across flat desert like landscape dotted with the occasional bush or shrub and Williams was thinking what a contrast this landscape was compared to the three days he'd spent escaping from Sheberghan prison when all he had seen were bushes and shrubs. The path had become quite uneven now with deep ruts from the numerous cart wheels that had passed along it. It was causing the cart to jerk and bounce around making for a very bumpy and uncomfortable ride. Blowing snow was in air even though it was a hot and sunny day and Williams could occasionally see towering mountains way off in the distance. From time to time a truck would come up behind them slowly overtaking them, forcing Daoud to move Gita and the cart over to the side of the road as it moved by. A few more hours into the journey the terrain began to change from desert to rugged rocky foothills. The change was quite startling and Williams assumed it must be because they were heading into the mountains.

Daoud could see Williams looking somewhat mystified and said "You're the one who wants to go to China."

"Yes I know" said Williams "I guess now I'm getting close it is beginning to seem like a daunting task."

"Daunting?" said Daoud "What is daunting?"

"Oh it means intimidating or discouraging if you know those words in English?"

"You sure have some funny words?" laughed Daoud "Anyway this is nothing, wait until you get into the real mountains that will be really "daunting" as you say."

The path was gradually becoming snow covered as it wound its way through various rock formations. The journey had turned into an obstacle course and was becoming most interesting. It reminded Williams of the canyons he had seen in westerns as a kid, but instead of the rocks being red and brown they were grey.

Daoud looked over at Williams and said "You like going through these rocks don't you, it really excites you!"

"It's because I've never been in such a strange landscape before, it's all new to me, that's why I'm enjoying it so much" responded Williams.

They were travelling between huge rock formations towering high above them on either side completely in shadow the sun now nowhere to be seen. Daoud reached behind him and grabbed a small scratched and dented metal flask which he offered to Williams, excitedly shouting "Russian vodka you like?"

Williams pushed it back at Daoud saying it was a too early in the day for vodka even if it was Russian.

Looking somewhat hurt Daoud replied "It's never too early to drink good Russian vodka" and told Williams to keep the small beaten up flask and reached behind him and grabbed a well-worn leather bottle.

"Here try this it's Afghan tea!" said Daoud handing the bottle to Williams.

Williams took the top off the bottle and took a swig, Daoud had been true to his word it was hot spicy Afghan tea. Williams took several large gulps trying to repair their friendship because he knew it was an Afghan tradition to share tea with family and friends.

"Look over there" said Daoud pointing.

Williams could see figures carved into the rock face. They were grotesque and contorted figures of animals and men. They all had small bodies and large heads that reminded Williams of some of Picasso's sculptures and paintings

"What are they?" asked Williams.

"They were carved in the rocks by the Mongols centuries ago on their way to ravage Persia. You can tell they were barbarians from these carvings, mindless maniacs if you ask me." "They must have carved these in the rocks with very primitive tools. It is really amazing what man can do" responded Williams.

"You Americans really are romantics you see the positive side of everything. Anything and everything is a great feat to you even rock carvings by barbarians!"

Williams asked Daoud if they could stop so he could get a closer look of the rock carvings but Daoud refused, saying they wouldn't reach their destination before dark if they stopped. Williams understood Daoud's reasoning, Donkeys don't have headlights, but was sad to only get a brief glimpse of the extremely unique and historical carvings.

The path was getting narrower and darker the further they went.

"Is this the Wakhan Corridor?" asked Williams.

"No not yet, the corridor is much wider this is just a mountain pass on the way they are numerous in this part of the country I am sure you have heard of the famous Khyber

Pass. Williams didn't comment. They continued on through high rocky passes for several hours until they came back into bright afternoon sunshine and could see a wide valley up ahead with a river running through it.

"I guess you could call this the start of the Wakhan Corridor which I know you have been anxious to reach" laughed Daoud.

"You're right, I really appreciate you bringing me all this way" replied Williams.

"This is just the beginning of your journey my friend" responded Daoud.

Williams had been trying to remember what Tahir and Mohammad had told him about the different routes through the corridor he thought they'd said he should take the southern route following the Wakhan River to the Wakhjir Pass leading to China. He also remembered they had said he should be careful taking this route because there were often avalanches in the Hindu Kush Mountains on the Pakistan side. He also remembered being told to avoid the northern route because it was close to the Soviet Republic of Tajikistan and the border guards up there were trigger happy shooting anything that moved. Just then the cart hit a rut and bounced up and down wildly and because he had been bounced around so much William's backside was becoming sore and he noticed Daoud was sitting on an old cushion and asked him if by any chance he had another one. Daoud said he didn't and suggested Williams take his jacket off and sit on it. Williams did this and found it did soften the bench seat a little. It reminded him of going on a long bike ride sitting on an uncomfortable seat which gradually chafed you and became so painful that you were frequently riding standing up on the pedals. After bumping along for several more miles Williams was about to ask Daoud if he could sit on the sacks in the back of the cart when a Soviet armored all-terrain vehicle suddenly appeared out of nowhere pulling up beside them. Daoud moved the cart over to the side of the road while the Soviets were getting out of their ATV blocking the road.

"Papers please" said one of the uniformed Soviets in Pashto while he was approaching Daoud's side of the cart. Williams pulled out his identification card and handed it to Daoud who passed both cards to the Soviet. The Soviet checked the id's and briefly glanced up at each of them and gave Williams card to the other Soviet to look at it.

The other Soviet commented that the card looked very new and asked Williams where he had got it. Williams was not sure what to say and Daoud seeing this chipped in saying he got it at the registration office in Feyzabad because his old card had expired, I took him.

They both took a close look at Williams and at the ID card and there was no doubt it was him.

"What's wrong with your friend, hasn't he got a tongue?" asked one of the Soviets.

"What else would you like to know" responded Williams in his best Pashto.

"What's in the cart?" asked the other Soviet. Williams was struggling to tell them when Daoud said "Grain and poppies for trade."
The Soviets seemed satisfied with the answer and handed both ID cards back to Daoud and made their way back to their ATV and sped off.

"Wow that was a close one" commented Williams.
Daoud said he agreed and told Williams he could sit in the back of the cart if he wanted and sitting on the grain sacks did provide some relief as the rickety ride continued. After they'd gone several more miles Daoud turned back to where Williams was sitting and told him they should be in Eshkashem by nightfall which didn't mean much to Williams. He was thinking how easy it had been when they were stopped by the Soviets

because he had papers and how different things might have been if he hadn't had them.

They were gradually getting closer to the higher mountains and it was getting colder the blowing snow becoming thicker. Williams asked Daoud if there was a way through the corridor to China and Daoud said there must be because illegal smuggling had been going on through it for centuries. The light was beginning to fade and up ahead Williams could see a collection of strange looking huts off to the side of the snow covered path. Daoud told Williams that this is where they'd be staying tonight with the headman of the settlement who Daoud said was a Mongol Kyrgyz called Azat who he would be trading his grain and poppies with for livestock which he planned to sell back in Feyzabad. They passed a number of well-dressed young women in bright green skirts and long sleeved red velvet tunics tending to sheep, goats and yaks. Daoud pulled Gita to a stop outside the entrance to what Williams assumed was the headman's hut which looked like it was made of felt like material. Almost immediately an old man with Mongolian features rushed out of the hut and embraced

Daoud as he was climbing down off the cart. They exchanged greetings and Daoud pointed to Williams who was still sitting in the back of the cart saying this is a friend of mine and Azat ran around to the other side of the cart and offered his hand to Williams who reached out and shook it. Azat seemed genuinely pleased to meet him seemingly welcoming him in a language that was totally foreign to Williams who struggled to climb out of the cart and surprised Daoud by walking over and hugging him while at the same time thanking him for bringing him here. Daoud pushed him away saying something Williams didn't understand but figured it wasn't complimentary.

Williams followed Daoud into Azat's hut while Daoud was explaining that these structures were called yurts. They joke it's like living and sleeping in a sheep because it's made of wool and smells like mutton which sounded really gross to Williams. Once inside looking up Williams could see a wooden wheel high up in the roof, poles supporting the overall structure the walls of which were richly adorned with bright wall coverings, multi-colored quilts and stretched furs. The floor was covered with beautifully colored and patterned Persian rugs and a small fire was burning in the center of the yurt the hole in the middle of the wheel in the roof allowing the smoke to escape. Several kerosene lamps were providing light and over the fire hung a large pot which Williams assumed would probably contain water for tea and other things. Azat looked nothing like Daoud who had an Arab look to him. Azat looked Chinese. A small woman who Williams assumed was Azat's wife offered him and Daoud some warm naan bread and tea and fussed over them motioning to them to sit down on some large cushions. Williams was mesmerized watching the smoke drift up from the fire to the central smoke-hole of the yurt and Azat came over and sat with them chinking his cup to theirs. The hot sweet tea tasted wonderful to Williams.

"You know it only takes Azat a few hours to take his yurt down and put it up somewhere else" commented Daoud.

"Oh really I think it would take me several days to take it down and several more to put it back up. Does he move around a lot?" asked Williams.

"Not a lot maybe three or four times a year depending on the season" said Daoud.

Williams left it at that not really knowing what Daoud meant.

When they'd finished their tea Daoud said he had to go and see to Gita and Feddy and asked Azat if there were any wolves around.

"No. Nobody has seen any so far" responded Azat apparently. Williams couldn't understand what he had said and Daoud translated. "Don't worry Feddy will let us know if there are any around" commented Daoud boastfully.

When Daoud had left using sign language William's indicated to Azat's wife that he wanted to lie down and she found him a sleeping mat, a blanket, some different sized cushions and showed him where in the yurt he could stretch out and as soon as he lay down he felt the need to go the bathroom. Azat's wife pointed to a bucket in the corner not far from where he was but Williams indicated he would rather go outside. As he was going out of the door he nearly banged into Daoud coming back in from outside and he told him to go over next to where Gita was tied up. Williams didn't want to do that and walked past Gita and relieved himself about twenty paces further on, he didn't see Feddy. It was dark thankfully so no one could see him as far as he knew. When he came back in Daoud was lying against the opposite wall from where he had been lying and Azat and his wife were sitting next to the fire. Williams lay back down and closed his eyes but couldn't sleep for a long time worried about sleeping with Afghan-Mongol people he hardly knew even though he trusted Daoud. They didn't seem like they would kill him but he was reluctant to go to sleep all the same and lay awake wondering if wolves might come and attack Gita during the night until he finally fell asleep.

Williams was woken by Daoud offering him a cup of hot tea. Williams asked Daoud if he thought Azat would lend him a donkey.

Daoud laughed saying "Those days are gone my friend but you could ask him if you could borrow a horse as long as you don't take it into the mountains and get someone to bring it back to Azat."

"A horse sounds much better" replied Williams excitedly. "I'll ask him for you" offered Daoud.

"Thank you" replied Williams still excited.

"The key is to find someone to ride it back" muttered Daoud.

"Right" said Williams "Would I be able to get some skis and camping stuff as well?"

"I'll ask" replied Daoud.

The sun was already high in the sky as Williams was tying camping equipment, skis and ski poles to the saddle bags on each side of the big horse. Daoud, Azat and his wife were waiting quietly to wish him well on his journey but before he got up on the horse Williams hugged Azat and his wife, thanking them for their hospitality and then Daoud thanking him for helping him to get there. Daoud, Azat and his wife were waving as he slowly trotted off towards the most untraveled part of Afghanistan if not the world.

Looking up the valley Williams could see multiple layers of rugged terrain, the highest layer being a ribbon of bright white snow-capped mountains and he wondered if one of them might even be Mount Everest. Below this layer were darker mountains with no sign of any snow.

Underneath these were foothills with sparsely spaced trees and below these a layer of hillocks with lush multi-coloured vegetation it was a truly majestic sight the kind you often see in scenic landscape paintings. The only thing missing was a lake to provide a perfect reflection of the towering snow-capped mountains. He already had the feeling from here on in the journey was going to get a lot tougher. He'd been told to make his way to where the highest mountain passes began and started to pick up the pace even though the terrain was not ideal for travelling on horseback at speed. Apart from along the riverbank the ground was very uneven with rocks protruding up everywhere through the plentiful fescue. Surprisingly though it was warm enough to allow him to temporarily shed a layer of clothing. After travelling for what seemed like several hours Williams stopped at a naturally formed ramp leading down to the river, he dismounted and led the horse to drink from the river. The water was absolutely crystal clear. He could see different sized fish swimming past and shoals of tiny fish darting off in all directions. Once the horse had finished drinking he continued his journey galloping along beside the river. As the light was starting to fade he began to see a high mountain pass up ahead and figured he had reached the point where he needed to find someone to ride the horse back to Azat. He had passed a yurt settlement a mile or so back and figured he should probably return there. After travelling at a slow trot for a while he came to a yurt where an old man was sitting smoking in front of it. He trotted up to the yurt and using sign language indicated he wanted him to take the horse. The man pointed to another yurt close by and Williams made his way over to it. There wasn't anyone there so Williams began to whistle quite loudly which soon brought several people running out of nearby yurts to see who it was. He dismounted and pointed to the horse then in a westerly direction and one of the men nodded that he understood what he was saying and after making sure the man knew who the horse belonged to Williams handed him the reins. His name was Bashir and he kept saying Azat's name pointing west and nodding indicating he knew exactly what Williams wanted him to do. Williams removed his stuff from the horse after which Bashir tied the horse up and gave it water. After he'd looked after the horse Bashir invited Williams into his yurt and soon they were sharing tea Bashir toasting Williams with the words "Kha sehat walary! Cheers! Good health!" after which although it wasn't very late Bashir offered Williams somewhere to sleep in the yurt. Williams made himself as comfortable as he could with the cushions and blankets Bashir had given him and already felt very comfortable with Bashir and fell asleep as soon as his head hit the cushion and found himself back in Sheberghan prison on a bright sunny day standing just inside the high prison gates. There was no one around. He had already checked the cellblocks and Infirmary and they were all deserted there were no prisoners or guards anywhere. The only sound he could hear was a door banging and as he began to walk towards where the sound was coming from after turning a corner saw Shelby walking towards him, he was smiling and calling his name excitedly and Williams awoke and found Bashir standing over him saying what sounded like the word Soviets. Williams was surprised by this news. He thought it would probably be better to remain where he was which Bashir seemed to agree with gesturing to him to do exactly that. Bashir indicated he was going to find out what was going on and soon found out that Soviet's had arrived overnight and setup camp right next to the yurt settlement. Apparently they had travelled down from the Kyzylrabot garrison north of the Tajikistan-Afghanistan border and were looking for an American. It was amazing how quickly the news spread by word of mouth throughout the yurt settlement. Bashir came back and told Williams as best he could that the Soviets were looking for him and he should remain in the yurt. They could hear a lot of shouting going on outside as the Soviet leader gathered his men telling them to go to every yurt remove all the furnishings and belongings and mark it as having been searched. Within a short time his men had carried out his orders using the blood of a butchered goat to mark each yurt with a large X once searched, for effect. They didn't find Williams because Bashir had already half emptied his yurt by the time the Soviets arrived hiding him under a pile of rugs beside the yurt. After hearing the news of the unsuccessful search for the American the Soviet leader was very unhappy and told his men to gather everyone in the yurt settlement so he could address them. Once gathered he told them that if no one comes forward right now and tells him where the American is hiding there will be severe consequences each yurt owner will need to select a member of their family and have them wait outside their yurt and these selected individuals will be shot and the yurts burned to the ground until the whereabouts of the American are known. A collective gasp went up from the gathered crowd and a man at the front shouted at the Soviet leader that his men had already searched every yurt in the settlement so it should be obvious the person they were looking for was not here and there was nowhere to hide inside an empty yurt. The Soviet leader shouted back that he didn't care because he knew the American was here somewhere and said he didn't want to shoot people or burn yurts down but he had no choice. The gathering broke up with a lot of yelling and screaming and Bashir ran back to his yurt and after ensuring no one was watching began talking to the heap of rugs Williams was hiding under telling him as best he could that they were going to start shooting people and burning yurts down until he was given up. Williams said in a muffled voice that surely the Soviet leader was bluffing but if he wasn't before anyone got killed he would give himself up.

"I can already see them moving towards the first yurt" said Bashir "So he is not bluffing."

The Soviet leader upon arriving at the first yurt asked those gathered around who they had selected and hearing this Bashir told Williams it looked like the Soviet leader was going to go through with his threat and was raising his pistol to shoot an elderly man. Williams scrambled out from under the rugs and ran towards the Soviets waving his arms in the air shouting "I'm here don't shoot anyone."

Seeing Williams several Soviets raced towards him with their pistols drawn shouting what sounded like put your hands up. The Soviet leader holstered his pistol and shouted to his men to secure Williams and they grabbed him and pulled and pushed him towards the Soviet leader.

"Mr. Williams I knew you were here somewhere" the Soviet leader said in heavy accented English.

Williams looking sullen didn't say anything.

He was dragged into the Soviet leader's tent and shackled to one of the main support posts after this the Soviet leader told his men to pack up the camp. He told Williams he had done very well to get this far away from Sheberghan prison and would now be going to a prison in the Soviet Union.

"Do you know how my friend Peter Shelby another American at Sheberghan is doing?" asked Williams.

"Sorry I have no information about the goings on at Sheberghan prison all I know is that you escaped from there" replied the Soviet leader rather jubilantly still excited about having captured Williams.

"Well if you know about me you must know about him and given I've got this far why do you want to capture me why not let me continue my journey to China?"

"You think it's my idea to capture you, there are many more powerful people above me who want you captured and if I don't bring you back there will be severe consequences for me and my men."

At that moment one of the Soviet leader's men came into the tent and told him the men were ready to take his tent down and he responded to this by telling him to secure the prisoner first, Williams hearing this figured this might be an opportunity for him to try and escape. The officer left and returned with several other men who released Williams from the support post and once he was out of the tent ushered him towards an all-terrain vehicle and handcuffed him to one of its enclosed door handles after which Williams and several of the Soviets stood waiting in the rain while the Soviet leader's tent was taken down. The Soviet leader came over to the vehicles commenting jokingly to Williams "So you're still here. I figured you'd have escaped by now you must be losing your touch!"

"Very funny" replied Williams.

"You know I still can't figure out why you were taken to
Sheberghan?" muttered the Soviet leader.

It was raining heavily and night fall was approaching quickly and leaden grey clouds were hovering overhead. The Soviet leader told his men to get into their vehicles and personally undid William's handcuffs indicating he should sit in the front seat of the ATV which he was handcuffed to. With Williams shackled to the front seat and the Soviet leader in the back he could watch his every move. The lead vehicle moved off into the gathering dusk, rain pounding down onto the windshield of the ATV Williams was riding in. The Soviet leader could already envisage how muddy the road back to Kyzylrabot was going be but wanted to get home with his prized captive as quickly as possible the capture of Williams should get him bumped up a level which is what he thought he more than deserved.

The convoy hadn't gone far when it began to encounter deep puddles of muddy water and had to move very slowly through them. Once past these the convoy started to pick up speed until it reached a steep incline where the lead vehicle soon got stuck in the mud digging in deeper every time the engine was revved spinning the back wheels. The Soviet leader told everyone to get out of the ATV he was in including Williams who was released from his handcuffs the Soviet leader asking him to help. Williams along with the others tried to push the stuck vehicle out of the mud but it wasn't moving, mud was spraying everywhere and soon the men in the other ATV's came to try and help free the stuck vehicle. The Soviet leader was right behind Williams watching him like a hawk that is until he slipped down into the mud. This was William's chance. The Soviet leader was shouting for help to get up out of the mud and by the time he got up and out of it Williams was nowhere to be found. That was until the last vehicle in the convoy backed up turned around and drove off in the direction they had just come in. The Soviet leader covered in mud from head to toe ran down the slope yelling to his men to get into their vehicles and go after Williams. It was still raining hard as they turned their ATV's around and began to chase after him. Williams soon reached the big muddy puddles and slowed right down to slowly move through them like the Soviets had done. He couldn't see any headlights behind but knew the Soviets would be coming after him and sure enough as he continued to move slowly through the puddles headlights appeared behind him through the pouring rain. The Soviet vehicles hit the big puddles too fast and without exception all their ATV's stalled. They were only able to start one of them and the Soviet leader transferred into this one and as they set off was berating everyone in the vehicle. Williams could see headlights behind him that seemed to be gaining on him rapidly and it wasn't long until the ATV chasing him came up alongside and bumped him. As he accelerated away there was a metal on metal crunching sound and William's vehicle skidded off the side of the path but he somehow managed to move in front again. The Soviet leader's vehicle came alongside again and Williams heard automatic gunfire as he pulled away once more. He managed to get several car lengths ahead and the gunfire stopped and he couldn't see headlights behind him anymore as he sped on into the night. The Soviet leader was urging the driver to go faster as they chased after Williams through the pouring rain but the ATV kept encountering muddy puddles. Williams had already decided he wouldn't burden the people in the yurt settlement with his presence again and proceeded to drive right past it. Several men tending to their livestock beside the path were most surprised to see a Soviet ATV returning to the settlement and one of them caught a glimpse of Williams as he sped by. He shouted to the others that it was the American. The other men cheered and waved to Williams but he had already gone by and didn't see them. The herder who had seen Williams immediately directed some of his multi-colored, black, brown and white sheep onto the path in case he was being followed. Sure enough a few moments later another Soviet ATV came into view heading straight for the sheep. The herdsman turned to look at the vehicle as if he was surprised to see the Soviets and herded his sheep further along the road putting his hand up requesting them to wait. The Soviet leader jumped out and ran towards the herder waving his pistol and shouting obscenities indicating he wanted him to get the sheep out of the way. The few minutes it took to get the sheep off the path was all Williams needed. He abandoned the ATV, crossed a bridge over a raging stream and found a hiding place in dense bushes halfway up a hillock. Given the steady rain and darkness Williams figured it would be very hard to find him.

Several minutes later an ATV pulled up behind the one he had abandoned. Williams was surprised there was only one ATV because there were five altogether including the one he had abandoned. He knew that one of them was probably still stuck in the mud and there were two here so where were the other two? The Soviet leader and three of his men were standing talking beside the ATV Williams had abandoned. They wouldn't find the key for the ignition because he'd thrown it into the stream as he'd crossed the bridge. The Soviet leader seemed to be sending his men off in all directions, east, west, south and north, the Soviet leader going north further down the trail. Williams could see someone coming his way crossing the bridge over the stream shining a flashlight, he had an automatic weapon slung over his shoulder. Williams figured he was up high enough that the Soviet wouldn't find him but he seemed to be heading right towards where he was, climbing up through the bushes as if he knew exactly where he was hiding. He was almost on top of Williams when there was a shout, the Soviet turned and shouted back. The Soviet leader had returned and had shouted his name and he had shouted back something like "Nothing yet!"

Unfortunately for Williams he turned and continued up to where he was hiding and was about to trip over him when Williams surprised him by grabbing for his legs and tackling him. The Soviet lost his balance and fell into the bushes. Williams knew he needed to subdue him quickly before he could shout out. The Soviet had dropped his flashlight when he'd been tackled and Williams picked it up and began to pummel him with it blood spurting from the Soviets nose and forehead. Williams was now kneeling on top of him pinning him with his knees and already knew it was going to be a life and death struggle. The Soviet was struggling to get William's off him when there was another shout from the Soviet leader.

Williams put his hand over the Soviet's mouth and shouted as loudly as he could "Nyet Not Yet!" very quickly which he hoped would be sufficient for the Soviet leader to know everything was alright at least one of the words was Russian and it seemed to have worked. The bushes were quite high where they were scuffling so he doubted the Soviet leader could see what was going on. The Soviet battered and bleeding managed to push Williams off him and was scrambling to get up when Williams punched him in the face knocking him back down again. William's could see the Soviet's automatic weapon in the bushes not far from where they were fighting and was reaching for it when the Soviet kicked out at him causing him to lose his balance. Fortunately he fell towards the automatic weapon getting a grip on it as the Soviet jumped on his back. Williams swung around knocking him off and pointed the weapon at him knowing he couldn't use it because the other Soviets would come running however the Soviet reached out and knocked the weapon out of William's hands. Williams instinctively punched out catching the Soviet in the eye and picking up the weapon swivelled around and hit the Soviet squarely in the face with the butt end of the rifle. The Soviet had raised his hands to protect his face from the blow and was grimacing in pain bleeding from his nose and mouth and some of his fingers looked like they might have been broken. Williams got up and put his muddy boot on the Soviet's neck pinning him down. The Soviet wasn't trying to fight back anymore.

"So what am I going to do with you comrade?" asked Williams sarcastically.

"Don't kill me I will keep quiet I promise tie me up you have already broken my nose and badly hurt my fingers and I am in a lot of pain" pleaded the Soviet in reasonably good English.

"Tie you up with what?" laughed Williams.

"Use my socks I've tied people up with socks before." "What about for your mouth?"

"Use my shirt."

"Boy you are full of good ideas I could learn a lot from you."

"In the Soviet Union we don't have much so we have to make do with whatever we can find we don't have fancy things like you Americans."

"What like cord?"

"We have it but it isn't always available so we have to make do with whatever we can find."

Williams lifted his boot off the Soviets neck and told him to take his jacket, shirt and socks off. The Soviet was wearing long woollen socks which were wet and covered in mud. After wringing them out Williams used one of them to tie the Soviets hands behind his back and used the other to tie his feet together. The shirt was not ideal for a gag but after ripping the bottom of one of the Soviet's pant legs off and stuffing it in his mouth he used the shirt to keep the rag in place. The Soviet was lying on his side in the mud determined to stay alive as Williams looked up and could see that the two missing ATV's had arrived and were parked behind the other two. Several men were looking into the other two ATV's and a short time later the Soviet leader and the other Soviets appeared. Williams could hear the Soviet leader shouting at the newly arrived men, likely reprimanding them for only just getting there.

Addressing the newly arrived men he said "As we haven't found the American yet now you are here we'll start searching all over again."

One of the men who had already been searching said his friend Yuri was missing and the Soviet leader asked him if he knew where he'd been searching.

"Over on the other side of the stream" replied Yuri's friend.

The Soviet leader asked him and another man to come with him and the three of them crossed the bridge over the stream in the torrential rain. Unlike Yuri they moved along the bottom of the slope in both directions. Williams still couldn't figure out how the Soviet had come straight to where he'd been hiding. The Soviet was out of sight and seemed to be sleeping which was probably helping with his various aches and pains. The Soviet leader's men completely drenched by now figured they were looking for a needle in a haystack trying to find the American on a night like this. The Soviet leader eventually came to the same conclusion and called the search off for the night and the men made their way back to their vehicles where they would be spending the night.

Williams realized he needed to get as far away as he could under the cover of darkness and set off back in the direction of the yurt settlement. He walked briskly along beside the raging stream getting completely drenched. He had no idea what time it was but figured he still had a few hours left before dawn. He could see the yurt settlement up ahead over on the other side of the stream as he moved further up the valley. The rain was beginning to turn into wet snow as he was getting closer to the mountains and he couldn't stop shivering as he continued up the valley.

The Soviets resumed their search once the first shards of sunlight began to appear and in the daylight soon found Yuri who told them Williams had gone up the valley towards the yurt settlement during the night. They jumped in their ATV's and headed back towards where they had been camped near the yurt settlement the day before. They would be back there soon and the Soviet leader was not sure what he was going to do when he got there. He had a feeling Williams wouldn't be hiding out there again so wasn't going to waste time looking for him there. He would keep going up the valley even though it was still raining hard and the weather was still very bad.

Williams had found a cave-like overhang in the foot hills of the mountains and was trying to light a fire by rubbing sticks together over a pile of dry leaves. There were leaves and would-be kindling everywhere under the overhang so he was optimistic that if he could light a fire he would be able to get warm. There had been a lot of white smoke so far but no sparks as he continued to rub the sticks together over the dry leaves. After having no success with the leaves remembering having seen this method used with string-like packing materials he looked around and found some dry strands of grass which resembled the packing materials figuring these might be better than the powdery dry leaves. He rubbed the sticks together over the dry grass and within several minutes it had caught fire. He placed the burning grass on top of the dry leaves until they caught fire and carefully nurtured the small fire adding fragments of wood which slowly began to catch fire and burn. The heat from the fire began to feel really good as he continued to build it up until it began to blaze. Even though he felt it was quite drastic he removed his boots and all of his wet clothes figuring if he was going to avoid hyperthermia or pneumonia he really had no choice. Now naked as the day he was born he had stopped shivering and was beginning to feel warmer even though he could see snow falling beyond the overhang. He put his mud caked boots next to the fire and held some of his clothes over the fire on a stick his arm soon beginning to get tired so he looked around for something else to use. He found some sticks all about the same length and tied them together with a bunch of dry strands of grass. He placed the sticks beside the fire and hung his wet clothes over them. He had got lucky with the weather because as the white smoke drifted up from under the overhang it was barely noticeable as it mingled with the falling snow. While he was waiting for his clothes to dry he was wishing he had something to cook over the fire but hadn't found anything dead or alive. He thought about his next move and decided it needed to be back to the Bashir's at the yurt settlement to get his makeshift hiking equipment. He couldn't set off into some of the highest mountains in the world with no equipment at all. Several hours had passed by now and his clothes and boots were almost dry. Williams had spent the best part of the day there and knew he'd got lucky. An hour later his clothes and boots were dry. He was pretty sure Bashir would help him even though the Soviets were close-by so he set off hoping it would keep snowing hiding him until he got back to Bashir's.

With the snow still falling heavy at times the Soviets were sheltering inside their ATV's. All five ATV's were operational again after they had hot-wired the one Williams had stolen and freed the one that had been stuck in the mud. The Soviet leader had told his men to wait until the snow stopped before resuming the search. He said he knew the American was somewhere close by and suggested in the meantime they break out their rations. The doors to their ATV's were open and while they were eating the Soviet leader was telling them how he wanted the search to be conducted once it stopped snowing. He was wondering whether to set up tents again but decided to hold off on the decision until the weather showed signs of improving. It was still snowing lightly and beginning to get dark which were obviously not the best conditions for resuming the search but their chances of finding the American were lessening the longer they waited. The Soviet leader gathered his men around him and told them to spread out and start searching even though it would soon be dark. His men were tired and none of them held out much hope of finding the American. They also knew he was a very formidable foe and every one of them inwardly hoped they didn't encounter him. The opposite of this was the Soviet leader a ruthless killer in his own right who hoped he did meet up with Williams this time capturing him dead or alive. Some of the men hadn't been searching for very long when they came across an overhang and the remains of a fire which was still warm. The Soviet leader got most excited when he was informed about the fire knowing this was likely where the American had been hiding out during the snowstorm. The question now was where had he gone? The Soviet leader figured he had probably continued to make his way up the valley and instructed his men to start looking further east until the search had to be called off for another night.

When Williams reached Bashir's yurt he drew the curtain over the door back and found no one inside. He didn't want to enter on his own so he sat outside and waited. When Bashir eventually showed up he was very surprised to see Williams and invited him for tea and something to eat while he listened to how he had escaped from the Soviets. After telling Bashir about his escape and where he'd been hiding he asked him if he still had his skis and camping stuff and if he could stay overnight. Bashir said he did and that he could stay as long as he wanted.

Early the next morning two Soviet snipers arrived and after a lengthy discussion the Soviet leader gave up the idea of trying to capture the American and agreed to leave it to the snipers to kill him.

Bashir woke early the next morning to find Williams had gone. He got dressed quickly and went outside and could see Williams high up on a mountain pass and made an ancient hand sign to bring him luck a gesture Williams would never know about but would benefit from.

As Williams moved through the deepening snow he was thinking that this had to be the final leg of his journey. He was still wearing the boots he'd taken from one of the men who had tried to rape him, woollen gloves and a well-worn dirty white parka Bashir had given him. He had a tightly folded tent, telescopic tent poles, food supplies, water, ski shoes, skis and ski poles which Daoud and Azat had acquired for him. As far as he was concerned this was his only chance of freedom from sure death or imprisonment which he knew from his own experience was pretty much the same thing in this part of the world. He remembered Mohammad telling him that this area had once been coined "The Roof of the World" by a famous British explorer and looking around he could see why, he had never seen such amazing scenery and realized his only enemy now was going to be the elements. As he was approaching a snow covered glacier he was thinking about whether Sir Edmund Hilary was so different to him surely he was only flesh and blood and what about Marco Polo, surely he hadn't had a down filled Parka and ski's when he came thorough here so how bad could it be?

The Soviet snipers were dug in with their ungainly-looking Dragunov sniper rifles resting on tripod supports in the snow. They hoped to have the target within their scope's crosshairs soon and figured the American should be a sitting duck. Although not the best the Soviet Union had to offer they still had over twenty kills to each of their names. They were about half a mile away from where they anticipated the target would appear and based on statistics one of them had a fifty percent probability of hitting it and given there were two of them and they could get off multiple rounds their chances of hitting the target were much improved. They would really have liked to have been closer but this was impossible due to the flatness of the glacier. As Williams was slowly making his way across the snow covered glacier he was thinking how the mission was almost over and what a huge toll it had taken. He was half-dead.

Shelby was probably dead and Yusuf, his brother and the others were definitely dead. Yusuf's wife was a widower and a number of other Afghan families had lost their loved ones and providers. He couldn't stop thinking about Yusuf's wife and sister feeling responsible for what they were likely going through. He'd planned the last raid knowing it was going to be risky but had no idea how bad it would turn out. He didn't know if Yusuf 's wife wanted to leave Afghanistan but her sister Rashida had told him she did but like those he had left behind in Sheberghan prison there was no way he could help any of them and he'd been stupid to have thought he ever could. He didn't know what happened to a woman when she was widowed in Afghanistan but figured there must be a lot of them during the bloody Soviet occupation. He'd been making his way across the glacier for several hours now and so far hadn't seen any crevasses or gaps in the ice so decided to put his skis on and try skiing and although he found it to be very uneven and quite difficult he was moving a lot faster. He didn't have the same feel on skis as he did on foot and had to pay close attention to anything out of the ordinary as he crossed the expanse of ice and snow.

Suddenly gunshots rang out bullets whizzing over his head. He hit the ground lying as flat as he could in the snow as the gunshots continued to ring out. The bullets seemed to be coming from the north so it had to be the Soviets he'd been told the border guards were trigger happy. Lying face down in the cold snow his legs began to hurt him due the angle his skis were at but he was too frightened to move. It would be less than an hour until sunset so he figured he'd have to wait it out. The snipers assumed they had hit the target because they'd both had the American in their crosshairs and he'd dropped to the ground immediately and they didn't have anything to shoot at anymore because the target was no longer visible. The light was quickly fading and they began to worry they wouldn't be able to find their way back to their ATV once it got dark.

Williams wasn't sure if he was still being hunted or whether it was the border guards who had shot at him either way this was already making his journey more difficult fighting both the elements and the Soviets. He'd heard no gunfire for quite a while now and it was almost dark and he couldn't see anyone so he figured it must have been the border guards and they wouldn't be able to see him anymore. Figuring it would be too perilous to continue to ski across the glacier in the dark he packed his skis and poles away and set off on foot even though he'd been told it wasn't a good idea to cross a glacier at night. During the daylight hours he hadn't noticed any unusual formations so hoped it would continue to be that way. What he didn't know was that the Soviet snipers who had tried to kill him were already on their way back to the Soviet Union. They'd already decided to tell their superiors that without a doubt they had taken the target out cold and figured he should make camp for what remained of the night. He'd already decided on a system for keeping warm overnight. Up until midnight he planned to light a candle in his tent and sleep in his day time clothes and at midnight he was going to get into the sleeping clothes Bashir had given him and get in his sleeping bag blow out the candle and put a balaclava over his face and only sleep for five hours maximum. He'd been told if he slept any longer without heat his hands and feet would begin to hurt with the onset of frostbite even wearing socks and gloves so by five-thirty each morning he planned to be ready to resume his trek. He figured by now it must already be close to midnight if not past so he would have to forego the candle tonight at the end of his first eventful day in the mountains.

He awoke as planned at five thirty and didn't actually feel that cold. He ate a breakfast consisting of dry naan bread and soup from a thermos Bashir had left out for him and as the first shards of sunlight began to appear through the flap of his tent thought about how Bashir had risked his life to help him a complete stranger and an American. He quickly packed up his tent and set off a miniscule figure in a huge mountainous landscape. The weather was dry the only clouds in the sky were above the snow covered mountain peaks. He had completed the glacier crossing by the afternoon and spent the rest of day skirting the high mountains occasionally encountering snow drifts which were a challenge to get over. That night he followed his system and it worked well especially the candle experiment and felt he had made good progress on his second day in the mountains.

The next day higher up in the mountains off in the distance he could see the edge of a plateau which seemed to be at a much lower elevation and wandered if it could be China. The timing was about right he'd been told it would take about four days to get to the Chinese border depending on the weather conditions which had been excellent so far the sun whenever it appeared between the mountain peaks felt warm. As he was making his way along an icy ledge something caught his eye and he was surprised when it turned out to be a big cat. Bashir had warned him about the snow leopards. The big cat was basking in what was left of the afternoon sun nestled high up in the rocks above him. It was a light yellow colour with grey spots and was beginning to make its way down the mountain. As it was making its way down to where he was he unhooked one of the skis from his backpack to use as a weapon in case it got too close. Doing his best not to look up he had a feeling the leopard was right above him now and with one giant leap it jumped off the rocks blocking his way forward snarling at him its huge teeth showing. He thrust his ski at it and it retreated a few paces growling and showing its teeth and he was startled when another leopard jumped down and joined the other one growling and looking ready to pounce. Williams had been racking his brain for something to scare the first one his backpack and pulled out a map and a lighter and quickly set fire to the map hanging it over the end of the ski and thrusting it towards the leopards. It was scaring them and they backed off so he figured he'd need to make the most of the burning map before it burned out and quickly moved towards them thrusting it at them. The fire scared them and they jumped back up onto the rocks still snarling and growling. He continued to thrust the burning map at them as he moved beyond them and was thankful they didn't follow after him. The encounter was over. He continued on through the mountains without incident for the remainder of the day up until it was time to setup his tent for another night. He couldn't wait to crawl in and shut out the world still shaken up by the encounter with the snow leopards. It was the end of his third day in the mountains.

On his fourth day he was feeling quite fatigued and had nowhere near the energy he'd had when he'd left Bashir's several days earlier. He knew there was no turning back even though he still had no idea how far it was to China. He had been told on numerous occasions what would befall him once he set foot on Chinese soil which varied from being shot on sight to being captured and imprisoned for the rest of his life. He'd also been told the Afghan-Chinese border was closed and strictly off limits to civilians and the Chinese side was a patrolled military zone. For most of the day he'd been skiing across the plateau he'd seen off in the distance the day before and could see what looked like large tombstones which he hoped would turn out to be border markers. He figured he was so close to freedom now but also so close to the opposite of freedom if there was a word for this and if there wasn't he wondered why not. It certainly was the perfect time to cross the border late afternoon beginning to get dark and starting to snow. Moving past a People's Republic of China border marker he figured he had made it to China. He was somewhat disappointed that he wasn't being greeted by automatic gunfire or confronted by bayonet wielding border guards, instead it was just more of the same old boring snow and ice with no sign of man or beast but it already felt really good knowing he was no longer in Afghanistan. By now it was almost dark so he figured it was time to make camp for another night and followed the same routine which had worked so well so far. It was snowing hard as he settled in for another night.

Early the next morning when he peered out of the tent he found it had stopped snowing even though the sky was still a solid battleship grey. He set out skiing again until to his surprise he came to a snow covered track and after skiing along beside it for several hours was surprised when he heard a vehicle approaching from behind. As it got closer he could see it was a military truck and panicked skiing as far away from the track as he could as it passed by its exhaust fumes leaving a trail of black smoke behind. At that moment feeling totally exhausted he realized the chances of anyone showing any interest in him not to mention giving him a ride were probably nil and as he continued to ski on across the snow covered terrain he hoped he was still in China. As he skied on in what must be one of the remotest parts of the world he was thinking that the last few months in Afghanistan had without a doubt been the worst of his life but at least he was still alive.

He had to stop and while resting was racking his brain trying to remember where he had put the envelope Suzy had scribbled her phone number on and was about to move off when he thought he heard someone shout his name. He could see two figures skiing towards him and his first reaction was the Soviets had caught up to him. But as the skiers got closer he could see that one had an amazing resemblance to Shelby and the other had Afghan-Mongolian features.

"Pete is that you?" shouted Williams as the skiers approached.

"You bet your bottom dollar it is" Shelby shouted back as he skied up to Williams.

"Holy crap I thought for sure you were dead!" shouted
Williams.

"It's a long story but as you can see I'm very much alive" replied Shelby as he hugged Williams.

"Welcome to the People's Republic of China" quipped Williams jokingly, pulling free from Shelby's grip "How do you like it so far?"

Bashir came over and hugged Williams kissing him tears running down his face.

"I believe you know Bashir he's been my guide and has helped me find you" offered Shelby.

"You bet great to see you again Bashir and thanks for re-uniting me with my best buddy in the whole wide world. This is truly unbelievable, a miracle even" responded Williams.

"So where are you heading?" asked Shelby.

"As far away from Afghanistan as I can get" said Williams laughing "How about you are you coming with me?"

Before Shelby could answer Bashir said he had to get started back for home before the next storm came. Shelby and Williams thanked him one more time and watched him ski off back to Afghanistan. They then skied off in the opposite direction Williams asking Shelby how he managed to survive.

Shelby began "There was an escape from the prison and the next day the Soviets came to investigate and search for those who had escaped and because of the escape they finally seemed interested in us realizing we had been overlooked up until then. Well they must have had some kind of wonder drugs because within less than two weeks the swelling on my face had gone down although I still have a scar where Mohammad stitched me up and I began to breathe normally and was able to eat and drink again. They gave me their food so I wasn't eating left over scraps anymore and as soon as I was well enough to travel they took me to a Soviet base camp not far from the prison, a collection of warehouses in a large compound. They told me what had happened to you that you died in your cell and been cremated but I vaguely remembered you had visited me in the Infirmary so I put two and two together and figured it was you who had gone over the wall. It was only when I got to the yurt settlements in the Wakhan Corridor a few days ago that I knew for sure it was you who had escaped and you were still alive and once I found Bashir it was just a matter of time until I caught up with you."

"But what about the Soviets?" asked Williams.

"I was with them they were using me to get to you."

"So that's how they knew about me" said Williams "I couldn't figure out how they got onto me especially Soviets from the Soviet Union."

While they had been skiing the weather had been deteriorating and they were now moving through blizzard like conditions so Williams suggested they head for a stand of trees which should at least provide some shelter from the storm and once they were hunkered down Williams asked Shelby to tell him the rest of the story.

Shelby started again "It didn't take me long to realize why they had nursed me back to good health it was to interrogate me. I was left in a small dark cell and they didn't give me water on a regular basis and hardly any food. Then it began I was brought before a panel of senior Soviet officers who asked me all kinds of questions about what you and I had been doing in Afghanistan. Initially I told them a pack of lies that we were working for a German construction company designing a new irrigation system, something I had read in a novel. They kept asking me why we had been captured in the company of rebel fighters near the Termez garrison where there had been several raids. When I said I didn't know what they were talking about they began to rough me up. I brought up the Geneva Convention for the treatment of prisoners of war but they argued that based on my original story I was working in Afghanistan for a private company so how could I be a prisoner of war so getting nowhere with me they began to torture me constantly dipping my head in buckets of water until I couldn't breathe and often passed out which they did many times. They would also strangle me choking me until I couldn't breathe and it felt like I was about to die. These tortures were all terribly painful one as bad as the other and in the end I couldn't take it anymore and told them everything they wanted to know which was surprisingly only about half of what I knew. They asked me about all kinds of things. I told them about the raids and the only one they were interested in and angry about was the raid on the armory. I was severely beaten after telling them about this. They hung me upside down for several hours and beat my feet with a wooden paddle and I was in great pain for days after this. But at least I didn't get the famous electrodes on the testicles torture which I was thankful for. They kept asking me about you and I kept saying I was told you had died while I was in the Infirmary. They wanted to know where we were staying and with whom and I told them it was someone called Yusuf who had been murdered along with his brother and other members of his family the night we were captured near the garrison. In the end they realized I didn't have any significant information about the things they were most interested in like American funding, what was going on in Pakistan and weapons supply lines. One thing I must have told them during my torture sessions was that it was you who had escaped. I don't remember telling them this but I was told it was while I was coming out of an unconsciousness state unable to control my inner thoughts. This by the way seemed to be the only thing that excited them out of everything I had told them. I must have told them that you planned to escape to China through the Wakhan Corridor because a few days later I was bundled into an ATV and told I was going to the border with China.

"How can they get to your inner thoughts through torture and interrogation?" asked Williams.

"Oh I didn't tell you they also drugged me which could account for it."

"Well, there is obviously more to the story because I don't see any Soviets escorting you?"

"You noticed that, well that's perhaps the most bizarre part of the story. I am sure we must have travelled the same route as you reaching Feyzabad and then making our way through the lower Wakhan Corridor and when the trail ended at the last yurt settlement I was told that the Soviets I was with had got word that you had been killed by snipers two days before. Our arrival caused a great deal of consternation and before we knew it we were completely surrounded by angry well-armed Afghan-Mongolians on horseback.

"It seems fortunately for me we had arrived as the Afghan-Mongolians in the corridor were gathering to celebrate the end of growing season. It reminded me of our initial trip into Afghanistan when we kept being stopped and surrounded by the men along the road" continued Shelby "I found out later that the Afghan-Mongolian warlords knew about you which is why they showed so much hostility towards the newly arrived Soviets who were nowhere near as well-armed as them. The Soviet leader met with several of the warlords and it seemed an agreement was reached to allow the Soviets to leave unharmed if I was released because soon after I was shoved out of the ATV I had been riding in and the Soviets sped off in the direction they'd come in. This was obviously a minor victory over the Soviets and the warlords and their men celebrated for hours afterwards. After the celebrations finally died down when the people in the yurt settlements found out I was an American they came from far and wide to tell me they knew you. Everywhere I went anyone I met asked me if I was a friend of yours it seems everyone in the Wakhan Corridor seems to know you, you certainly leave an impression wherever you go. Eventually I met up with Bashir who acted like he was you're half-brother and he offered to lead me to you apparently feeling he had been snubbed when you left early one morning without saying goodbye. He kept telling me you would still be alive despite what my Soviet captors had been told about snipers killing you.

"So here you are we're together again and I must say I never thought I'd see you again but everything's better with two even when you're in outer-Mongolia or wherever we are" offered Williams reaching into his backpack and bringing out the metal flask Daoud had given him on the road from Feyzabad which he handed to Shelby.

"Russian vodka at least they're known favourably around the world for producing this stuff" laughed Williams.

Shelby took a swig of the strong tasting vodka and handed the bottle back to Williams who did the same.

"By the way" said Shelby "We found your campsites and only slept for a few hours each day so we'd be sure to catch up to you."

"Did you see the snow leopards?"

"No we mainly travelled at night guided by the moon and stars sounds kind of romantic doesn't it but it certainly wasn't?" laughed Shelby.

"Boy you had it easy I got shot at by Soviet snipers apparently, crossed a glacier at night and almost got eaten alive by snow leopards" laughed Williams "Anyway it seems to have stopped snowing so are you ready to see if we can find sanctuary in China?"